I0651225

Republican Congressional Committee

Campaign Documents

Republican Congressional Committee

Campaign Documents

ISBN/EAN: 9783337423292

Printed in Europe, USA, Canada, Australia, Japan

Cover: Foto ©Andreas Hilbeck / pixelio.de

More available books at **www.hansebooks.com**

Bonds or Greenbacks?

FROM THE REMARKS OF

Hon. ARTHUR P. GORMAN, of Maryland

Hon. WILLIAM LINDSAY, of Kentucky

Hon. AMOS J. CUMMINGS, of New York

From the Congressional Record.

In the SENATE OF THE UNITED STATES, May 24th and
May 27th, and the HOUSE OF REPRESENTATIVES,
May 3, 1898

BONDS OR GREENBACKS?

In the SENATE OF THE UNITED STATES, May 24th and May 27th, and the HOUSE OF REPRESENTATIVES, May 3, 1898.

———

The Senate having under consideration the bill (H. R. 10,100) to provide ways and means to meet war expenditures—

MR. GORMAN said:

It is said we propose to issue bonds. Mr. President, of course it is proposed to issue bonds. Why not issue bonds? What declaration has ever been made by any political party against issuing bonds in time of war? What war was ever conducted without issuing bonds, and issuing them in the very beginning of the conflict? Before the first gun was fired at Sumter in the war of the rebellion we began to issue bonds, and we also issued $150,000,000 of greenbacks as a war measure. What were the conditions? Gold and silver had disappeared; they could not be found or followed into their hiding places; there were no national banks, and the State banks had disappeared, or, at least, they were useless so far as the purposes of the Government were concerned.

An enlarged currency was necessary. The act of July 11, 1862, authorized the issue of $450,000,000 of greenbacks or legal-tender notes, and this was the only issue authorized. They were receivable at the Treasury for all dues and were then reissued time and again; but the total amount outstanding at any one time was not over $450,000,000. There were:

Old demand notes	$60,000,000
One and two year notes, bearing 5 per cent. interest	211,000,000
Compound-interest notes, bearing 6 per cent. interest	266,000,000

The total amount of notes issued by the Treasury from 1861 to 1869 was as follows:

Demand notes	$392,070
United States notes (greenbacks)	427,768,499
Fractional currency	26,057,469
Matured debt, interest ceased	1,373,920
Unpaid requisitions	660,960
Total	$456,252,858
While from 1861 to 1869 the debt bearing interest was	$2,351,699,479

(2)

BONDS IN TIME OF WAR.

Mr. President, it is said that the great cormorants of the moneyed institutions are now after these bonds; that they are the men who urge their issuance. Yes; but the man with money, whether he be a small or a large holder, can only get bonds by paying his money for them, loaning it to the Government on a security as good as gold or silver, and the bonds will be paid when they become due.

Why should Senators on this side of the Chamber, why should the distinguished Senator from Missouri [Mr. COCKRELL], denounce the issuance of bonds in time of war? Our party convention, which met at a time when every Democrat was incensed at the action of a man whom we had elected President, who had asked us to issue gold bonds so as to save $16,000,000, a proposition which was rejected, passed a resolution, not against bonds as bonds, but only against the issuance of bonds in time of peace.

The Senator from Arkansas [Mr. JONES], who had probably more to do with the framing of that declaration than anybody else—at least we hold him responsible, whether he was actually so or not—is too astute a politician to have put any other declaration in that platform. He would not have gone before the people of the country in that campaign with the candidate who was our nominee and the platform upon which he ran, a campaign which was a campaign of appeal to the masses of the people, with a declaration that the Government should not have the right in time of war to issue bonds to save the life of the nation.

I will refer to what we did on this side in 1862, 1864, and 1865, and will insert in the RECORD the list of the bonds that were issued.

UNITED STATES BONDS.

According to the statement of the public debt published October 31, 1865, the interest-bearing debt of the United States on that date was as follows:

Aggregate of debt bearing coin interest.............$1,161,137,691 80
Aggregate of debt bearing lawful-money interest... 1,190,561,787 46

Total interest-bearing debt...................$2,351,699,479 26

But in 1861, as Senators know—and I refer to it with great kindness—there were no great corporations south of the Potomac; there were no combinations which were robbing the people. The trusts and monopolies and money changers were not there.

THE ACT OF FEBRUARY 28, 1861, AUTHORIZED BONDS.

Mr. TILLMAN. And they are not there now.

Mr. GORMAN. And they are not there now, the Senator from South Carolina says. No. You were free from their control. You attempted to establish, and did establish, a government, and you conducted a great conflict such as the world has never seen conducted by a like number of people. But when you started your government the first financial act—the act of February 28, 1861—authorized bonds, coupon bonds, bearing 8 per cent.

interest, running for five and twenty years, and you continued to issue bonds and stock bearing interest up to nearly $800,000,000. Your unfunded debt amounted to more than double the bonds, or $1,600,000,000 of treasury notes and other obligations which did not bear interest—not legal tenders, a friend in my rear tells me. No; they were not legal tenders, but they were convertible into bonds, and they were received for taxes and a great many other things, but not in payment of the export duty on cotton.

GREAT MEN SUPPORTED BOTH GOVERNMENTS BY ISSUES OF BONDS.

The idea I wish to present is that it is only by example, and by history we can tell what is proper to be done. Here there were two great divisions of the American people; one representing exclusively agricultural interests, free from all of the great combinations which have been described here to-day, and the other, on this side of the Potomac, embracing within its confines practically all the great monopolies of which we hear so much; and yet those great men—for they were great men—supported both governments by issues of bonds. In so doing they followed only the teachings of history. When war begins no government is ever ready for it with ample supplies of money in its treasury, and with the exception of Germany, which was prepared for war, there is no other instance in the last one hundred years where any government has been able to successfully prosecute a war without making a loan on bonds in the very beginning.

If that be true, why should we hesitate here? Why should we hesitate to vote for the issuance of bonds running ten and twenty years at 3 per cent. interest? Every Senator is aware of the fact that if we fail to make provision for that sort of a bond at low interest, and the crisis comes, as come, in my judgment, it will, when within thirty days, before you can get your tax bill in operation, the President of the United States and his Secretary of the Treasury, following the example of their predecessors, and as I believe they will be in duty bound—although there is doubt, and great doubt, as to the right to issue bonds for ordinary purposes—will be compelled to issue bonds running a longer time and bearing a higher rate of interest than those proposed to be issued under the terms of this bill.

Why, then, are we opposed to bonds, Mr. President? In the Senate we have met that question quite recently. At the close of Mr. Harrison's administration, after the Presidential election of 1892 and before the inauguration of Mr. Cleveland, the condition of the Treasury was so threatening that bonds were asked for, and in this Chamber we placed upon an appropriation bill a provision authorizing the Secretary of the Treasury to issue 5 per cent. bonds on like terms with those described in this bill; and more Democrats voted for the proposition than against it. It was thrown out by the other House. It was thrown out, it was said, by secret instructions from the powers that were to be.

SALE OF BONDS UNDER THE ACT OF 1875.

Following within eighteen months after that influence and that action, came the transaction of the sale of the bonds authorized under the act of

1875, which every Democrat in the Senate, and which nearly all Democrats everywhere, denounced. What brought that condition about? A DEFICIENCY IN THE REVENUE, AND NOTHING ELSE. What will bring about the necessity for bonds now? A deficiency in the revenue. In my judgment—I only speak for myself—Senators will be estopped from protesting against bonds. The President may sell $300,000,000 of bonds under the authorization of the act of 1875, if, in his judgment, it be necessary to maintain the honor, the dignity, and the glory of his country, and to secure the success of our arms.

I think the amendment of the minority of the committee is wise. The bonds are limited in amount and to a certain purpose, to be issued only after certain things have occurred. I THINK, WITH ALL DUE DEFERENCE TO THE AUTHORS OF THAT PROVISION, EVEN THAT IS TOO RESTRICTED.

Mr. President, at this session of Congress the appropriations already made for all purposes of the Government, or which are pending and about to be made, including the war expenses and contracts authorized, including the sinking fund, amounted to $923,682,797; excluding the sinking fund, to $872,682,797; and more is to be appropriated before the Senate adjourns. Senators who have spoken seem to be fearful of providing too much money. In my humble judgment you have not provided enough, even with the provision of the Finance Committee for bonds and certificates. I was not anxious that we should enter upon this contest. I had hoped we might adjust the matter without a conflict of arms in a manner honorable to the American people. But that has passed and gone.

COST NO MAN CAN ESTIMATE.

We have entered upon a contest. When and where it will stop no man can tell. How much it is to cost no man can estimate. That it will cost during this year $100,000,000, $500,000,000 possibly, is, in my judgment, a moderate estimate. If it were to close and peace be declared within six months from this time, your expenditures would go on at a rate, compared with peace expenditures, that no man can measure to-day. The complications that may come from this war nobody knows. The cost of closing and adjusting all the questions that will arise can not be measured by tens of millions of dollars to-day, in my judgment. We have a fair Navy.

Who, after the occurrences of the last few months, expects this government to suspend building war ships? They will be multiplied until the number reaches that point where we will be supplied, in the judgment of the people, with sufficient war ships to defend us from any act of aggression. Who can tell how far we are to go in looking to the development of the trade and commerce which is being strived for by all the nations of the earth? I do not expect to see any action which will prevent us from getting our full share of that trade and providing all the facilities for our war ships and ships engaged in commerce.

Mr. President, there is only one other feature of the bill to which I desire to allude, and that is the provision reported by the majority of the committee and so strongly advocated by the distinguished Senator from Missouri [Mr. COCKRELL]—the issuance of $150,000,000 of greenbacks. I confess my amazement that that distinguished Senator and others should, in the year 1898, advocate and hold that the issuance of greenbacks, legal-tender notes of the Treasury, is now or ever was the Democratic doctrine or was ever maintained by either of the great parties, except for the great emergency of the war. I shall take the liberty of reading from one or two eminent Democrats who have spoken for the Democratic party in times past.

JUDGE THURMAN'S REPLY.

There was Judge Thurman. In 1874, on the floor of the Senate, when the question of issuing only a few millions more of greenbacks was under consideration, he made a speech. He had been charged with being in favor of inflation, the issuing of notes by the Government, because he had gone through the Ohio campaign of 1873 with his party, which there, under the control of Mr. Allen, advocated the greenback theory. Mr. Thurman's reply to this charge will be found in the CONGRESSIONAL RECORD for the session of 1874, page 2394, when he said:

"Never did any man hear me utter one word in favor of inflation. Not one word, sir. I have spoken against a contraction of the currency that would bring about too speedily a resumption of specie payments; but never have I spoken in favor of that inflation of the currency which I think I see full well means that there never shall be any resumption at all. That is the difference. It is one thing to contract the currency with a view to a resumption of specie payments; it is another thing neither to contract nor enlarge it. But let resumption come naturally and as soon as the business and production of the country will bring it about; but it is a very different thing to inflate the currency never in all time to redeem it at all, and that is precisely what this inflation means. It means demonetizing gold and silver in perpetuity and substituting a currency of irredeemable paper based wholly and entirely upon Government credit and depending upon the opinions and the interests of members of Congress and their hopes of popularity, whether the volume of it shall be large or whether it shall be small. That is what this inflation means. Sir, I have never said anything in favor of that. I am too old-fashioned a Democrat for that. I have heard and preached too many hard-money lessons to advocate such a theory as that, and although there are many friends who differ with me in opinion, and from whom it pains me to differ, I can not give up the convictions of a life-time, whether they be popular or unpopular, whether they please or whether they displease."

THE PRESIDENTIAL CONVENTION OF 1876.

Now, following that, which was in 1874, came the Presidential convention of 1876. In the greenback campaign which was made in Ohio the Democratic party had lost. The Democratic party had been for hard money, for gold and silver, the money of the Constitution, and it wanted to right itself and relieve itself from those in Ohio who were carrying it toward the Populistic idea. The Democrats wanted to recover it and bring the party back to its old moorings and its old doctrines, and they cast about the country for some man to lead them, and they found in Samuel J. Tilden, of New York, a man who could carry them, as they thought, to victory. They made a platform to suit his views upon the financial question, ignoring entirely the greenback theory and the Ohio idea, as it was called, and placed him upon a sound-money platform of gold and silver. They did it with the knowledge of the fact that Mr. Tilden in 1875, right after this discussion and after the veto by the President of the greenback bill, had delivered a message to the New York legislature in which he said:

LEGAL TENDERS DURING THE CIVIL WAR, GREATLY INCREASED INFLATION OF PRICES.

"There is no doubt that the issue of legal tenders during the civil war hastened and greatly increased that inflation of prices which naturally resulted from the increased consumption and the waste resulting from military operations, and from the diminished production occasioned by so large a withdrawal of workers from their ordinary industries. It is the nature of credit to be voluntary; it is founded on confidence. Credit on compulsion is a solecism. Therefore a forced loan of capital from all existing private creditors can not but be costly.

"It was made in this instance on a security which bore no interest, and interest on which could only be represented in discount from its par value. It gave to the lender an agreement to pay which, being instantly due on demand, started in its career a broken and dishonored promise. Every successive holder was left to conjecture when it would be redeemed by the issuer, how far it might be absorbed in the Treasury receipts, whether it could still be paid out to some private creditor, and at what loss it could be passed away in new purchases on a market advancing rapidly and irregularly. Everybody was advised that the Federal Government, unwisely distrusting the intelligence and patriotism of the people, shrank from exercising its borrowing power, supplemented by its taxing power, and instead of resorting at once to the whole capital of the country capable of being loaned, which forms a vast fund, perhaps thirty or forty times as large as the then existing currency, it chose to begin by debasing that comparatively insignificant part of circulating credits, creating fictitious prices for the commodities and services for which it was next to exchange its bonds, in an expenditure ten times as large as the whole amount of the legal tenders it ventured to put afloat.

"No man could know how often or how much of legal tenders might be issued under possible exigencies of the future. It could not be wholly forgotten that such issues, made by our ancestors to sustain the victorious war for national independence, were never redeemed, while the public loans made for the same purposes were all paid. It was remembered that history affords other warning examples to the same effect. These elements of distrust were needlessly invoked. But the system stopped short of the logical completeness of the expedients of the French convention in 1793. While it compelled the existing private creditor, or anybody who should grant a new credit, to accept payment in legal tenders, it did not assume to regulate the prices of commodities. The seller, therefore, gradually learned to represent the depreciation of the currency in the price of the article he exchanged for it. As compared with gold, the currency, during all the last year of the war, was depreciated to between 40 and 50 cents on the dollar, touching at its lowest point 35 cents on the dollar.

*   *   *   *   *   *   *   *

TESTIMONY OF THE GREATEST LEADER OF HIS PARTY.

"Governments in times of public danger can not be expected always to adhere to the maxims of economical science; the few who would firmly trust to the wisest policy will often be overborne by the advocates of popular expedients, dictated by the general alarm. If the Federal Government had paid out Treasury notes, not made a legal tender, in its own transactions whenever it was convenient, and redeemed them by the proceeds of loans and taxes on their presentation at a central point of commerce, and meanwhile had borrowed at the market rates for its bonds, secured by ample

8

sinking funds founded on taxation, and had supplemented such loans by all necessary taxes, the sacrifice would not have been half that required by the false system adopted, perhaps the cost of the war would not have been half what it became."

There, Senators, is the testimony of a man who was the greatest leader of his party in my time. It was his wisdom, his statesmanship, his courage, his control of men, his influence with capital that enabled us to have a reunited party in either Hall of Congress. Will you now, when his grave is still green, go back and repeat the folly of 1873, when there is no necessity whatever for such an experiment ?

"A GREAT WAR CANNOT BE CARRIED ON BY PIECES OF PAPER."

Mr. President, I dislike to go outside of my party for authorities against the issuing of greenbacks, but there is one, an honored member of this Chamber, one who now, as I understand, makes the majority of the committee who report in favor of the issuance of $150,000,000 of greenbacks, whom I will quote. I mean the Senator from Nevada [Mr. JONES]. He has a perfect right to change his opinion. We all do that, but he uttered truths upon this floor in 1874. No matter why he has changed his opinion since. No man has ever answered and no man, in my judgment, can answer the truths he then enunciated. I will let him speak for himself. In this debate, when it was proposed to increase the greenback circulation only $18,000,000, the Senator from Nevada, speaking of the action of Congress in 1862 and 1863, when they authorized the issue of greenbacks, legal-tender notes, said:

"Ignoring the history of other nations, taking no warning from the wrecks of financial systems strewn along their pathway, the first thing we did was to make irredeemable paper a legal tender, and thereby almost immediately advance the price of everything 100 per cent. Having thus made everything we were compelled to buy double its former price, we then entered upon the negotiation of loans and a rigorous system of taxation to raise money with which to buy. This we should have done in the start, and what we could have done. But we first thoroughly demoralized the whole country and all its industries, we plundered the creditors and allowed the debtors to discharge their obligations by paying from 30 to 50 per cent. less than they owed, and then we started to raise money for putting down the rebellion in the only way we should have done in the commencement. We resorted at the outset to measures condemned by financiers everywhere. To that which I would only have been willing to do at the last extremity. * * * A GREAT WAR CANNOT BE CARRIED ON BY PIECES OF PAPER PAYABLE AT CONVENIENCE AND BEARING NO INTEREST."

I commend that sentiment to every Senator on this floor. It is a truth that will last for all time.

"This paper currency, instead of adding strength to the imperiled country, was a source of weakness. Its issuance was an impeachment of the patriotism of the nation and an underrating of the resources of the country. It was a cheat upon the people in teaching them the pernicious idea that in carrying on a great civil war economy and industry were not necessary; that production and destruction were convertible terms, and that the activity of the printing press in the production of paper money would amply compensate for the activity of armies in the destruction of wealth."

SUSTENANCE OF THE GOVERNMENT WHEN FACING A FOREIGN FOE.

Said he, in reply to Mr. Morton, whether he regarded the greenback as a curse:

"I do, most undoubtedly. and I further believe that it is the duty of men to face that question."

Those declarations were true when he uttered them, and they are true to-day. In my judgment, the results of the legislation of 1862 to 1865 will follow this measure if you enact it. You may impair the credit of the Government by this act. No Senator desires to do that, I know, but I appeal to all to stand by the uniform action of governments heretofore and supply the money in the only way in which history shows it can be supplied without jeopardy.

As I said at the outset, I am aware of the fact that there are differences on the tax provisions of this bill. They are matters of individual opinion, of honest judgment. If I wanted to treat it alone from a political standpoint and gain advantage for my party, I would support the measure as I have indicated that I will support it.

I believe that if any advantage politically could come, it would come because there had been on my part a perfect sustenance of the Government when it was facing a foreign foe. The benefit would come because I have adhered to the doctrines of the party to which I belong, it would come because I have considered nothing but gold and silver the money of the Constitution. It would come because I have followed every great leader from Jackson down to Buchanan in maintaining the integrity of the Government and of its currency, so that it could be used to pay our soldiers at home and the sailors and soldiers who are now fighting and bleeding and dying for us in a foreign land.

DEMOCRATIC IDEA ON GREENBACKS IN JANUARY, 1895.

[From the speech of Senator Wm. Lindsay, of Kentucky, May 24, 1898.]

Mr. RAWLINS. I do not understand, or if I do I hope the Senator will make it clear, that the Senator contends that we are here in our legislative policy to conform to the declaration of a political platform, especially of the Republican party, which has not been embodied into law.

Mr. LINDSAY. I do say that if we do not legislate in view of conditions which we know to exist, then we do not legislate wisely or intelligently. That is my answer to the question.

But my friend need not be uneasy about the redemption of these greenbacks in gold. The amendments reported by the majority of the Committee on Finance do not provide for the repeal of the act of 1875. They leave that act in full force, and while the majority of the committee object to issuing bonds to raise money to pay the expenses of the war, preferring to issue greenbacks payable on demand, and which this Administration is pledged to pay in gold, they leave the act of 1875 in full force, so that when a raid may be made upon the Treasury, if the raid shall be made, with the additional $150,000,000 of greenbacks, this Administration can keep its pledge, as the last Administration maintained the gold standard, by selling bonds more objectionable in their form and conditions than the bonds provided to be sold under the bill as it came from the House, and especially under the report of the minority of the Finance Committee.

So we are in this attitude: It is a question whether we shall sell bonds to raise money to pay the expense of the war or whether we shall increase the volume of greenbacks and force the Government to sell bonds to put gold in the Treasury to keep the greenbacks at par with gold, when the gold speculators choose to make a raid upon the Treasury, after we have increased their facilities 25 per cent. by the bill you propose to enact into law.

NOT A QUESTION OF BONDS.

Mr. SPOONER. That is the object of it.

Mr. LINDSAY. It is not a question of bonds. In either end of the line we have bonds. It is a question whether we will sell bonds as provided for by the minority report of the Finance Committee or whether we will sell bonds under the act of 1875, and everybody knows this to be the case. There will probably be no raid upon the Treasury, I hear it intimated. When did we get this sudden confidence in the moderation of the gold speculators and the Treasury raiders? What has happened in the last two years to make us believe that when those people can make money by exporting gold they will not raid the Treasury with the greenbacks now outstanding, and raid it the more successfully with the greenbacks which this bill provides shall be put into circulation?

My friend from Texas [Mr. CHILTON] two years ago, in discussing this question, did not give his unqualified approval to legal-tender money. Stating his objections, or stating points that did not meet his approbation, he said:

"One of these is found in that part of section 4 which compels the reissue of greenbacks whenever redemption takes place. For myself I do not believe we shall achieve the restoration of orderly finance until the present system of reissuing demand notes of the Government is abandoned; and whenever a fair and conciliatory plan looking to that end is presented to the Senate, I expect to vote for it."

With that sentiment I am in hearty accord.

The point I make is this: We can not have at this time the free and unlimited coinage of silver. We can not and we do not propose to put silver dollars in the reserve fund to redeem greenbacks. Now, then, if it would be bad policy, after we had the right to redeem the legal-tender notes with both gold and silver, to reissue them, I submit, is it not worse policy to reissue them and keep them outstanding as demands against the Treasury when we have only one kind of coin in which we can redeem them? * * *

Mr. BACON. I fully agree with the Senator. If we could have all coined money, of course I should be opposed to any paper money; but as the barrier has been put up and you say we shall not have coined money, but that the great majority of our currency shall be paper, then the best obligation is the obligation of the Government.

GREENBACKS FOR THE PURPOSE OF TAKING THE GOLD OUT OF THE TREASURY.

Mr. LINDSAY. Now, let us see about that best obligation. Two years ago this matter was under discussion. I believe my friend here [Mr. ALLEN] was responsible for it. A distinguished member of the Finance Committee, the Senator from Arkansas [Mr. JONES], had occasion to comment upon this kind of money. I think my friend from Nebraska [Mr. ALLEN] had indulged in some statement to the effect that the greenbacks were ideal money, and the best we ever had.

Mr. ALLEN. I will say it now.

Mr. LINDSAY. The Senator from Arkansas said then:

"The truth is that the silver certificates are to-day performing the office of the paper money of this country. The greenbacks are not performing it. On the contrary, they are held by the banks for the purpose of taking the gold out of the Treasury whenever they want it, whenever they choose to increase their holdings. In the last sixty days—

I think this was January, 1895—

as I have just stated, there has been more than $50,000,000 in gold so drawn out of the Treasury, and of that $50,000,000 only $15,000,000 was drawn out for export. The other $35,000,000 was drawn out to be hoarded, to be held in banks; and this will continue—

Now, how long?—

and this will continue as long as we allow this convenient means of depleting the Treasury to remain in their hands—

Now, we have permitted it to remain in their hands until to-day, and the proposition now is to increase their facilities 25 per cent. over the facilities they held at the time these statements were made—

"Whenever they choose to force a bond sale they can do it by drawing out the gold to the limit which the President considers dangerous, and after the bonds are bought the gold paid for them can be immediately drawn out of the Treasury to be hoarded in the banks, as stated by the President, and we are no nearer relief after it has been repeated a dozen times, and after $100,000,000 or $200,000,000 or $300,000,000 of bonds have been issued than we were when we began."

That was the Democratic idea of greenbacks in January, 1895; that they did not answer the purposes of money; that they were held by the banks and by gold speculators, and that the banks and speculators raided the Treasury with them whenever they could make profit by raiding the Treasury, and thereby compelled the sale of bonds under the act of 1875. This bill proposes to give them $150,000,000 of demand notes in addition to what they held in 1895; it stands by the gold standard, as this Administration is pledged to stand; it leaves the act of 1875 in force, so that the excellent gentlemen who make money by raiding the Treasury can raid it 25 per cent more successfully than they could when the Senator from Arkansas exposed conditions which no man then disputed and no man can now dispute.

But we do know this much: If you put these greenbacks out, they will be redeemed in gold, and you do know when they do redeem them they will again issue them, and again redeem them in gold; and you do know that if it is necessary to get the gold, they will sell bonds again under the act of 1875 to get it.

A PROPOSITION BY THE SENATOR FROM KANSAS.

In 1895 a bill came over from the Republican House of Representatives proposing to sell $200,000,000 of bonds, very much like the $300,000,000 of bonds which are proposed to be sold by the minority amendment of the Finance Committee. The bill went to the Finance Committee, and that committee reported back a substitute in the nature of a bill for the free and unlimited coinage of silver. When that substitute came up for discussion, a good deal was said by the Senator from Nevada, doubtless, but I do not remember what it was. The argument was made that if we should go to free silver, then gold and silver would come to a parity. My opinion was that if that was a well-founded belief—and I had no right to doubt that my silver friends thought it was—and we were going to make an experiment, there could be but one of two results. Either gold and silver would go to a parity, or else this country would go to a silver basis. Therefore I was of the opinion that in either alternative there was no propriety in selling bonds to keep up a redemption fund.

A proposition was made by the then Senator from Kansas [Mr. Peffer] looking to that view, which was rejected. Then my distinguished friend from Nebraska [Mr. ALLEN], who is consistent always, whether right or wrong—he claims he is sometimes right—offered this amendment to that substitute:

"*Provided*, That after the passage of this act the Secretary of the Treasury shall be deprived of the power to issue bonds or other interest-bearing obligations of the Government unless Congress shall first declare the necessity therefor, any act of Congress now in force to the contrary notwithstanding."

So that with this amendment the substitute would have provided for the free and unlimited coinage of silver at the ratio of 16 to 1, with the provision that the Secretary of the Treasury should have no power to sell bonds except by express act of Congress, and then only according to that act. If there was a deep-seated, undying hostility to the sale of bonds, an opposition holding that bonds should not even be sold in time of war, it seems to me that was the time for the opponents of such a policy to manifest their opposition.

DEMOCRATS VOTED IN THE NEGATIVE.

The yeas and nays were called on the proposed amendment, and it received 21 votes. It was defeated by a vote of 54. Now, let us see who voted for it. The following Democrats voted for the amendment: BACON, BERRY, Blanchard, Call, Hill, Irby, LINDSAY, MILLS, and ROACH. Those were all the antibond-selling Democrats who were then on this side of this Chamber.

This substitute was defeated, and I find among those who did not then regard the sale of bonds as an unpardonable sin, even in time of peace, and who were willing to sell bonds, or at least not willing to take away from the Secretary of the Treasury the right to sell bonds to buy gold to redeem greenbacks, for that was the only statute that was then in force, the following Democrats voted in the negative: BATE, CHILTON, COCKRELL, DANIEL, FAULKNER, George, Gibson, GORMAN, GRAY, Harris, JONES of Arkansas, MARTIN, MITCHELL of Wisconsin, MORGAN, MURPHY, Palmer, PASCO, Pugh, TILLMAN, VEST, Vilas, Voorhees, Walthall, and WHITE.

In 1895 three-fourths of the Democrats were opposed to repealing the act of 1875 and taking away from the President the right to sell bonds to buy coin to redeem greenbacks.

Mr. TILLMAN. If I understand the Senator, he contends that the issue of greenbacks which we favor would entail an obligation, or at least afford an opportunity to the Administration—

Mr. LINDSAY. That is better.

Mr. TILLMAN. To sell bonds for gold?

Mr. LINDSAY. Yes.

BONDS SOLD FOR MONEY AS GOOD AS GOLD.

Mr. TILLMAN. His substitute, or that which he proposes to vote for as a substitute, is to allow the Administration to issue bonds to carry on the war. What will it sell those bonds for when it sells them? Will it demand gold for them?

Mr. LINDSAY. The bonds will be sold for money as good as gold, exchangeable for gold, and that money will be used to pay the young men we are send' ig to Cuba to face Spanish bullets and the yellow fever.

REPRESENTATIVE AMOS J. CUMMINGS ON THE WAR REVENUE BILL.

(From the Congressional Record of May 3, 1898.)

Mr. CUMMINGS. Mr. Speaker, the gentleman from Washington for some inscrutable reason has seen fit to embalm me in the honey of his intellectuality. [Laughter.] He asks above which party does patriotism rise in the House. It rises, Mr. Speaker, above both parties. As a war Democrat, I enlisted in the war for the Union, not because it was Democratic policy, not because it was Republican policy, but because the country was in danger, and I was due. [Great applause.]

I am due to-day, and I have made it known by my vote. I do not talk of the "meritoriousness" or "meretriciousness" of my action. The words are not synonymous. They are in no way allied to each other. And although I have not had a college education, as the gentleman has had, I do know enough to know not to use such words in the same sense. [Laughter.] I admire the gentleman from Washington. His raiment is exquisite [great laughter]; his hirsute adornments are magnificent [renewed laughter]; even the spats on his shoes are effulgent. [Great laughter.] They all bear a due relation to the brilliancy of his intellect [renewed laughter], and his intellectuality is beyond comparison.

BONDS TO RUN THE GOVERNMENT IN TIME OF WAR.

I say that the true spirit of Democracy is patriotism, and a Democrat who sneers at patriotism does not deserve the name of Democrat. The gentleman voted, without talking, for the $50,000,000 appropriation. Why did he not think of "contractors" then? Was not the time to speak beforehand, and not afterwards? Why is it that he is already accusing men in high standing of corruption when the war has hardly begun?

Mr. LEWIS of Washington. But they have. [Laughter and applause.]

Mr. CUMMINGS. Make your statements clear, produce your proof, and then slander your Government if you must. Do not do it under suspicion. [Great applause.]

Now, Mr. Speaker, I did believe, when I voted for the bill proposing to raise revenue to carry on this war, and the Democratic side of the House almost unanimously voted for war, that I was doing fully as patriotic a thing as the gentleman did when he voted for the $50,000,000, to be placed at the disposal of the President without conditions. I BELIEVED THAT IF A DEMOCRATIC ADMINISTRATION WAS FORCED TO SELL $300,-000,000 IN BONDS TO RUN THE GOVERNMENT IN TIME OF PEACE, THAT A REPUBLICAN ADMINISTRATION MIGHT BE ALLOWED TO SELL BONDS ENOUGH TO RUN THE GOVERNMENT IN TIME OF WAR. [Great applause on the Republican side.]

ACTION BY A PRESIDENT INDEBTED TO THE SOUTH FOR HIS NOMINATION.

This action was taken by a President who was indebted to the South for his nomination. You who came from the South, went into the Democratic national convention over five years ago, and rammed Grover Cleveland down the throats of the New York Democracy, with its whole delegation strenuously protesting against it. You are responsible for him, not we. [Applause.]

Mr. GAINES. Do you say that we are responsible for Grover Cleveland?

Mr. CUMMINGS. I say so, knowing it to be so.

Mr. JONES of Washington. I want to ask the gentleman——

Mr. GAINES. There have been a great many sins charged against the South, but I have never before heard it said that Grover Cleveland came from the South.

Mr. CUMMINGS. It is true. I challenge the record. He was nominated and elected by the votes of the South, with his gold letter staring you in the face. You forced him down our throats against our unanimous protest. Deny it, if you dare. [Loud applause.]

A POPULAR LOAN WILL CEMENT THE PATRIOTISM OF THE PEOPLE.

I did believe that if it was necessary to sell bonds in time of war, we should sell them in sums of $25 and $50 to the mechanics and farmers and the honest producing people of the United States [applause], and not, as was done under the Cleveland Administration, sell them at private sale to a syndicate that within two months netted $8,000,000 for simply turning them over to outside parties. [Loud applause.]

There was no war then, and the safety of the nation was not imperiled. I believe, if we must have a loan, in a popular loan. I advocated a popular loan when the Cleveland Administration was planting the second issue among the syndicates. A popular loan will cement the patriotism of the people of the United States, and the people will never overflow with gall, as did the gentleman this afternoon, in aid of the enemy. I am on record as voting not only for the war, but as voting for supplies for the war, and with that record I am content, politics or no politics. [Applause.]

Mr. Speaker, I regret that I have not 1,000,000 six-syllable adjectives to shower on the House. Adjectives are adjectives, and votes are votes. I confine my speech to plain Anglo-Saxon. I am an Anglo-Saxon; I am an American; I am a Democrat. Patriotism itself is Democracy. [Loud applause.]

Mr. CLARK of Missouri. There is not a man on the floor of the House for whom I have a more tender personal affection than I have for the gentleman from New York, Mr. AMOS J. CUMMINGS——

Mr. CUMMINGS. And the feeling is reciprocated.

Mr. CLARK of Missouri (continuing). And he knows it, and I know that it is reciprocated. But I say, in perfect respect for him and in the presence of all of these witnesses, that he has made the most outrageous speech on the floor of the House to-day that ever, in my judgment, was delivered in this body. [Laughter and applause.]

I do not care anything about his assault on the gentleman from Washington [Mr. LEWIS]. That is not "my pie." [Laughter.] I have no hand in it. [Laughter.] But when he commits the "unpardonable sin" of putting into this discussion the statement that a Democratic Administration issued $300,000,000 of bonds in a time of peace I deny his right to be the spokesman for my party, at least on that subject.

MISSOURI VOTED TO NOMINATE GROVER CLEVELAND.

Mr. CUMMINGS. Will the gentleman allow me an interruption?

Mr. CLARK of Missouri. Certainly.

Mr. CUMMINGS. I will state for the gentleman's benefit that the delegation from Missouri voted unanimously to nominate Grover Cleveland in Chicago, although they had no instructions. [Laughter and applause.]

WOULD READ OUT OF THE DEMOCRATIC PARTY EVERY MAN · WHO VOTED FOR THE BILL.

Mr. CLARK of Missouri (continuing). If it were not for my personal affection for the gentleman from New York, I WOULD INAUGURATE A MOVEMENT AMONG THE DEMOCRATS IN THIS AND THE OTHER END OF THE CAPITOL TO READ OUT OF THE DEMOCRATIC PARTY BY NAME EVERY MAN ON THIS FLOOR WHO VOTED FOR THE BOND BILL THE OTHER DAY. [APPLAUSE ON THE DEMOCRATIC SIDE.]

THE VOTE.

(From the Congressional Record, April 29, No. 104, Vol. 31.)

[Republicans in Roman, Democrats in *Italics*, Populists in SMALL CAPS, Fusionists in *Italic CAPS*, Silverites in CAPS.—From the Official List of Members, December 6, 1897.]

YEAS—181.—Acheson, Adams, Aldrich, Alexander, Arnold, Babcock, Baker, Md. Barham, Barney, Barrows, Bartholdt, Beach, Belden, Belford, Belknap, Bennett, Bingham, Bishop, Booze, Boutell, Ill.; Boutelle, Me., Brewster, Broderick, Bromwell, Brown, Brownlow, Brumm, Bull, Burleigh, Burton, Butler, Cannon, Capron, Chickering, Clark, Iowa, Connell, Cooper, Wis. Corliss, Cousins, Crump, Crumpacker, *Cummings*, Curtis, Iowa, Curtis, Kans. Dalzell, Danford, Davidson, Wis. Davison, Ky. Dayton, Dingley, Dolliver, Dorr, Dovener, *Driggs*, Eddy, Ellis, Evans, Faris, Fenton, Fischer, *Fitzgerald*, Fletcher, Foote, Foss, Fowler, N. J., Gardner, Gibson, Gillet, N. Y., Graff, Griffin, Grosvenor, Grout, Grow, Hager, Hamilton, Harmer, Hawley, Heatwole, Hemenway, Henderson, Henry, Conn., Henry, Ind., Hepburn, Hicks, Hilborn, Hill, Hitt, Hooker, Hopkins, Howe, Howell, Hull, Jenkins, Johnson, Ind., Johnson, N. Dak., Joy, Kerr, Ketcham, Kirkpatrick, Knox, Kulp, Lacey, Landis, Lawrence, Littauer, Loud, Loudenslager, Lovering, Low, Lybrand, *McAleer*, McCall, McCleary, *McClellan*, McDonald, McEwan, McIntire, Mahon, Marsh, Mercer, Mesick, Miller, Mills, Minor, Mitchell, Moody, Morris, Mudd, Northway, Olmsted, Otjen, Overstreet, Parker, N. J., Payne, Pearce, Mo., Pitney, Powers, Pugh, Ray, Reeves, Robbins, Royse, Russell, Snuerhering, Shannon, Shattuc, Sherman, Showalter, Smith, Ill., Smith, S. W., Smith, Wm. Alden, Southard, Southwick, Spalding, Sperry, Sprague, Steele, Stevens, Minn., Stewart, N. J., Stewart, Wis., Stone, C. W., Stone, W. A., Strode, Nebr., Sturtevant, Sulloway, Tawney, Taylor, Ohio, Tongue, Updegraff, Van Voorhis, Wadsworth, Walker, Mass., Walker, Va.. Wanger, Ward, Weaver, *Wheeler*, Ala., White, Ill., Williams, Pa., Wise, Young.

NAYS—131.—*Adamson, Bailey, BAKER, Ill., Ball, Bankhead, BARLOW, Bartlett, BELL, Benner, Pa., Benton, Berry, Bland, Bodine, BOTKIN, Bradley, Brantley, Brenner, Ohio, Brewer, Broussard, Brucker, Brundidge, Burke, Carmack, CASTLE, Clardy, Clark, Mo., Clayton, Cochran, Mo., Cooney, Cooper, Tex., Cowherd, Cox, Davey, Davis, De Armond, De Graffenreid, De Vries, Dinsmore, Dockery, Elliott, Fitzpatrick, Fleming, FOWLER, N. C., Fox, Gaines, GREENE, Griffith, Griggs, GUNN, Handy, HARTMAN, Hay, Henry, Miss., Henry, Tex., HOWARD, Ala., Howard, Ga., Hunter, Jones, Va., JONES, Wash., KELLEY, King, Kitchin, Kleberg, KNOWLES, Lamb, Lanham, Latimer, Lentz, Lester, Lewis, Ga., LEWIS, Wash., Linney, Little, Livingston, Lloyd, Love, McCORMICK, McCulloch, McDowell, McMillin, McRae, Maddox, Maguire, MARTIN, MAXWELL, Meyer, La., Miers, Ind., Moon, Norton, Ohio, Norton, S. C., Ogden, Osborne, Otey, PETERS, Pierce, Tenn.; Rhea, Richardson, RIDGELY, Rixey, Robb, Robertson, La., Robinson, Ind., Sayers, Settle, SHAFROTH, SHUFORD, SIMPSON, Sims, SKINNER, Slayden, Smith, Ky., Sparkman, Stallings, STARK, Stephens, Tex, Stokes, STROWD, N. C., Sullivan, Sulzer, SUTHERLAND, Swanson, Talbert, Taylor, Ala., Thorp, Underwood, Vandiver, Vehslage, VINCENT, Wheeler, Ky., Wilson, Zenor.*

HAWAII

"There is such a thing as an American Spirit."

Hon. JOHN T. MORGAN, of Alabama

Hon. CHAS. H. GROSVENOR, of Ohio

Capt. MAHAN, U. S. Navy

General SCHOFIELD, U. S. A., Retired

Admiral DUPONT

Prominent Labor Leaders

From the Congressional Record

HAWAII

"I WILL NOT BE A PARTY TO ANY MISERABLE POLITICAL TRICK AND INTRIGUE LIKE THAT."

[From the Speech of Senator Morgan, (Dem.), in the Senate of the United States, June 25, 189 .]

Mr. MORGAN. I should like to know whether these fine, silken, glossy arguments about the Constitution of the United States and about the right of the President of the United States to coal his ships and stop and refresh his troops in Hawaii and in Cuba are to stand for a moment in the presence of the events that are encumbering this people and causing them to lay their lives down at our command, and whether we can afford to stand here and quibble about little points like this, and obstruct the war, prevent it, and put to peril the troops that we have sent out upon the high seas. I should like to know it. WE HAVE GOT TO FACE IT, AND I AM DELIGHTED TO FIND THERE IS A MAJORITY HERE WILLING TO DO IT. AND I AM DELIGHTED TO ACT WITH THEM, THOUGH THEY ARE NOT MY FRIENDS POLITICALLY. I WILL STAND BY THEM THROUGH THICK AND THIN FOR MY COUNTRY AND ITS FLAG.

Mr. President, we shall presently be having wounded men and men sick with all manner of tropical diseases coming back from the Philippines. Are they there unlawfully? Are they there without our command? Are they there in some unholy exploit from which we are not willing to relieve them, or have they, while they are there, and those who go to re-enforce them, been marking upon the records of history the highest tribute to American power and American character that has ever been drawn by the hand of man with the sword? These men will be coming back presently, many of them, and Senators are here on this floor filibustering to prevent those men from having a friendly welcome and a landing under their own flag and their own country at Hawaii as they come back, saying, "We will make you sail across the Pacific or else die while you are trying." That is the situation we are in.

"I WILL NOT BE A PARTY TO ANY MISERABLE POLITICAL TRICK AND INTRIGUE."

No, sir; I repudiate it from my soul. I repudiate it; I will have none of it; I WILL NOT BE A PARTY TO ANY MISERABLE POLITICAL TRICK AND INTRIGUE LIKE THAT. THERE ARE MEN ON THIS FLOOR, PLENTY OF THEM AND THEY HAVE ALREADY STARTED THE MOVEMENT TO DEFER THE QUESTION OF THE ANNEXATION OF HAWAII UNTIL NEXT WINTER. When the Senate of the United States makes that vote, what do we do with the President of the United States but to express our disapprobation that he in the meantime should permit one of his soldiers to land upon those islands for refreshment?

Mr. ALLEN. I should like to ask the Senator a question. He has spoken about filibustering, and I regret the disposition on the other side to do that.

Mr. MORGAN. THE FACETIOUS REMARK OF THE SENATOR FROM NEBRASKA CHARGING THE OTHER SIDE WITH FILIBUSTERING DOES NOT DO JUSTICE TO THE RECORD. IT DOES NOT DO JUSTICE TO THE TRUTH. IT DOES NOT DO JUSTICE TO THE SOLEMNITY OF THIS OCCASION. THE SENATOR FROM NEBRASKA HAS HIMSELF SET UP A REGULAR FILIBUSTER AS WE CALL IT HERE—I DO NOT KNOW ANY BETTER NAME FOR IT—AND HE HAS BEEN CONTINUING IT FOR THE LAST HOUR.

"FILIBUSTERING FOR THE PURPOSE OF PREVENTING A MAJORITY OF THIS BODY FROM VOTING."

Mr. ALLEN. The accusation is very serious, and I hope the Senator will permit me to say a word. I do not yet know whether I am going to vote with the Senator from Alabama or not. I do not know what policy ought to be pursued respecting these islands. It is a grave question. If the Senator will permit me to occupy his time just a moment, here it is 5 o'clock Saturday night, and we are to meet at 11 o'clock Monday morning. Now, because I protest against going on with this debate to-night, when we can accomplish nothing, does the Senator feel that I ought to be characterized as a filibuster? I leave that to his sense of propriety.

Mr. MORGAN. I have not characterized the Senator as a filibuster. I merely characterized what has been done here as falling within that category, the disagreeable things that I call FILIBUSTERING, FOR THE PURPOSE OF PREVENTING A MAJORITY OF THIS BODY FROM VOTING.

NOW, SIR, PERSONAL CONVENIENCE IS SPOKEN OF, AN AFTERNOON OF SATURDAY; "IT IS HOT;" "SENATORS ARE FATIGUED." DO YOU SUPPOSE THAT GENERAL SHAFTER'S TROOPS, WHO EXPECT TO FIGHT YOUR BATTLE TO-MORROW, SUNDAY, AS IT IS OF GREAT MAGNITUDE, ARE SAYING TO THEIR COMMANDING OFFICERS THIS AFTERNOON, "IT IS PERSONALLY INCONVENIENT FOR US TO MOVE TO-MORROW OR THIS EVENING; WE PREFER TO CONSULT OUR EASE; WE DO NOT WANT TO GO INTO THE FIGHT TO-NIGHT?"

"POLITICAL INTRIGUES FOR NEXT NOVEMBER ELECTIONS."

Mr. President, who are we representing here? MEN WHO ARE SHEDDING THEIR BLOOD FOR US UPON THE FIELD OF BATTLE, AND WE ARE TALKING ABOUT PERSONAL INCONVENIENCE! We are spoiled to death, Mr. President, by our prosperity. If this Senate had to march out and shoulder arms for the defense of this capital, and stand guard to-night and for the next week, it would do us all good. WE WOULD THEN LEARN WHAT IT WAS TO STAND FOR OUR COUNTRY, NOT TO SLEEP ON OUR POSTS, AND HAVE OUR LITTLE POLITICAL INTRIGUES FOR THE NEXT NOVEMBER ELECTIONS AND TALK ABOUT PERSONAL INCONVENIENCE.

4

Sir, when the pending joint resolution has been debated to the full extent of the wishes of the gentlemen who oppose it, it ought to be allowed to be voted upon. That is all of it. THERE OUGHT NOT TO BE AN INTERPOSITION HERE OF TACTICS OF THE SORT EXHIBITED THIS EVENING FOR THE PURPOSE OF THROWING ENORMOUS BURDENS UPON THE PRESIDENT OF THE UNITED STATES. WHY, SIR, IF THESE MEN FORCE THE PRESIDENT OF THE UNITED STATES TO RAISE OUR FLAG IN HAWAII AND TO TAKE CARE OF IT THERE IN ORDER TO SHELTER OUR WOUNDED AND SICK PEOPLE WHO ARE COMING BACK FROM MANILA, AND THE COAL, AND THE SUPPLIES, AND THE WATER NECESSARY FOR THE MAINTENANCE OF THE CREWS ON OUR SHIPS, THE VERY MEN WHO FORCE HIM INTO THAT CATEGORY WILL BE FOUND HERE RISING ON THEIR FEET AND MOVING TO IMPEACH HIM BECAUSE HE VIOLATED SOME POSSIBLE SHADOW OF THEIR INTERPRETATION OF THE CONSTITUTION OF THE UNITED STATES.

"THERE IS SUCH A THING AS AN AMERICAN SPIRIT."

I AM GLAD, SIR, THAT I HAVE GOT THE OPPORTUNITY JUST AT THIS MOMENT TO ANTICIPATE THAT MISERABLE SCHEME AND LAY IT BARE TO THE BONE. You will not be heard, gentlemen, hereafter to accuse the President of the United States of violating the constitutional rights and powers of the Chief Executive when he and his friends and his countrymen, whether of his political party or not, turn to you and say: "YOU FORCED HIM TO THAT SITUATION BY CONDUCT ON YOUR PART THAT MADE IT ABSOLUTELY INDISPENSABLE IN THE NAME OF CHRISTIANITY AND HUMANITY THAT HE SHOULD DO SUCH A THING."

When you return to your constituents, gentlemen, and meet the fathers of the sons who have gone to Manila, and tell them that you obstructed by filibustering tactics the passage of a law that would make it legal for them to stop in Hawaii on their return with their wounds or their sickness and find shelter in the bosom of that hospitable and splendid people, that father will spurn you as not being his representative or the representative of the true American spirit.

There is such a thing, thank God, as an American spirit. It is hovering over the Senate now. It keeps Senators in their seats who have strong reasons for being absent. IT HAS NOT BEEN STRONG ENOUGH TO INVITE ALL THE ABSENTEES TO BE HERE; BUT THEIR NAMES OUGHT TO BE PUT ON RECORD TO SEE WHO IT IS WHO IS NOT WILLING TO STAY HERE AND SERVE HIS COUNTRY WHILE THE MEN IN MANILA AND THE MEN IN SANTIAGO DE CUBA ARE FIGHTING UNDER OUR FLAG FOR THEIR COUNTRY. THEY OUGHT TO BE PUT ON THE RECORD TO SHOW WHO THEY ARE AND WHY THEY ARE NOT PRESENT HERE PERFORMING THIS BEAUTIFUL, SPLENDID, EASY, NICE, COMFORTABLE, AND DISTINGUISHED DUTY OF VOTING TO THE PEOPLE WHO ARE IN THE ARMY THE ALLOWANCE OF A HOSPITABLE RECEPTION IN THE ISLAND OF HAWAII.

"A FITTING RESPONSE TO THAT SPLENDID SPIRIT OF OUR FATHERS."

There is such a thing, Mr. President, as an American spirit, and I rejoice in it. It is my privilege to do so, and I will not be found doing anything at all that in the slightest degree obstructs the full flow of that glorious and magnificent spirit which already has won for us a fame that time itself will honor the longer time shall last. For deeds have been performed even during the brief period of this war which show two things: First, that the United States is capable of waging war with all the resources and all of her men for the sake of humanity, Christianity, and liberty. That response coming back from the people of the United States at the close of the nineteenth century is a proper and fitting response to that splendid spirit of our fathers who planted this magnificent Republic upon this wonderful country of ours. There is such a spirit here.

Not only, Mr. President, are they fighting in a cause in which they have no motive but justice, liberty, humanity, and Christianity, but, sir, they are fighting with intrepidity and honor, with marked skill, ability, valor which have not been excelled in any history that has ever been written by the pen of man. No nation stands higher to-day than the United States on the rolls of glorious warfare and magnanimous conduct.

"POWERFUL IN THE MOTIVES OF WAR."

The very example we have set before the world in the last two months will warn the nations of this earth that while we are a peace-loving people and are disposed to do all that can be done to keep on good terms with humanity and all the nations of the world, there is not that nation which exists, though it may be the most powerful monarchy that was ever knit together by the hands of oppression and craft, that does not feel to-day that the people of the United States and their Government are more powerful than any other nation that exists on the earth—not powerful only in war, but powerful in the motives of war. That we have already achieved.

I CAN NOT RECONCILE IT TO MYSELF THAT THIS GREAT AND AUGUST BODY, OF WHICH I HAVE HAD THE HONOR OF BEING A MEMBER NOW FOR TWENTY-ONE YEARS, COULD SET ITSELF IN THE ATTITUDE WE OCCUPY THIS EVENING OF ANTAGONISM TO THE ADMINISTRATION THAT IS CONDUCTING THIS WAR, AND DOING IT SO WELL AND WITH SUCH HIGH PURPOSES AND MOTIVES; THAT WE SHOULD BE HERE LAYING PIPE FOR THE PURPOSE OF CONTROLLING ELECTIONS IN NOVEMBER, AND THAT THAT SHOULD BE THE MOTIVE OF OUR CONDUCT. IF THAT IS NOT THE MOTIVE, LET THE JOINT RESOLUTION COME TO A VOTE WHEN THE DEBATE IS EXHAUSTED.

Mr. PRESIDENT, I HOPE WE WILL NOT HAVE ANY MORE OF THIS PROCEDURE ON THIS CASE, TO SAY THE LEAST OF IT.

Annexation from the Standpoint of American Interest.

(From the Congressional Record, No. 139, Vol. 31.)

Mr. GROSVENOR said:

Mr. Speaker, I had been at great pains, with a great deal of very valuable help, to try to answer, in a modest way, the very able argument made against this proposition by the distinguished and eloquent gentleman from Indiana (Mr. Johnson). I have taken up the able suggestions of that gentleman to the number of about sixty-five paragraphs, and have tried in a very concise sort of primer-like way to answer each one of his suggestions.

Point 1.—The Hawaiian nation has everything to gain and nothing to lose by annexation. Annexation should be discussed, considered, and decided solely from the standpoint of American interest, and with the single purpose of promoting the happiness and welfare of those who dwell under the shadow of the American flag.

Reply.—He first admits that annexation will be beneficial to Hawaii. He then says it should be considered solely from the American standpoint, and then purposes to go behind the record and oppose annexation on the grounds:

That the Hawaiian people are opposed to it.

That the Hawaiian Government is misrepresenting the Hawaiian people.

That a petition from Hawaiians has been filed against it.

That supporters of annexation do not submit the proposition to popular vote.

REPUBLIC OF HAWAII A DE FACTO GOVERNMENT.

This country and the world has recognized the Republic of Hawaii as a de facto and de jure government.

It has maintained itself for five years, since January 17, 1893.

It has lawfully and peaceably adopted a constitution directing its executive to negotiate a treaty of annexation with the United States. (Art. 32, constitution Republic of Hawaii.)

It has not withheld the franchise from any citizen, native or foreign born, the sole change made by the Republic in the qualification of voters being that the oath of allegiance shall be to the Republic instead of the monarchy.

Under this constitution a Senate and House of Representatives was elected in 1894, both of which, at both the special session of 1894 and the regular session of 1896, passed unanimous resolutions in favor of annexation.

All elections in Hawaii are under the Australian ballot system and are absolutely secret.

No charge has been made by even the Royalists that the elections are not fairly conducted and a free expression of the wishes of the voters. A majority of those who have taken the oath of allegiance to the Republic of Hawaii, and who are now voters, are native Hawaiians. A majority of the members of the first House of Representatives, including the speaker, were full-blooded native Hawaiians.

The second general election under the Republic in September, 1897, resulted in the return of a Legislature again unanimously pledged to annexation.

The Hawaiian Government has negotiated a treaty of annexation in accordance with the terms of the constitution, in accordance with the verdict of two general elections, in accordance with the unanimous vote of both houses of the Legislature at two sessions of the same, and the treaty has been ratified by the Hawaiian Senate.

Point 2.—The masses of Americans are indifferent. "The very few of our countrymen who have given any attention to the subject are inclined to favor annexation." "The superficial and unreflecting" are appealed to by national vanity and find the project hard to resist.

The proper method of disabusing the public is to break down the doors of the Senate and let the people see "the danger that lurks in the proposition."

Reply.—He admits that those who have studied the subject favor annexation.

The following is a list of a few of the "superficial and unreflecting" who have favored annexation, in addition to a majority of the present Senate, who are admitted by Johnson to support it:

A FEW OF THE "UNREFLECTING" FAVORING ANNEXATION.

President Franklin Pierce (Annexation Handbook, page 42), President Andrew Johnson (Annexation Handbook, page 43), President U. S. Grant (Annexation Handbook, page 43), President Benjamin Harrison (Annexation Handbook, page 44), President William McKinley (Annexation Handbook, page 45.)

Secretary of State William L. Marcy (Annexation Handbook, page 51), Secretary of State William H. Seward (Annexation Handbook, page 51), Secretary of State Hamilton Fish (Annexation Handbook, page 51), Secretary of State James G. Blaine (Annexation Handbook, page 52), Secretary of State Thomas F. Bayard (Annexation Handbook, page 53), Secretary of State John W. Foster (Annexation Handbook, page 54), Secretary of State John Sherman (Annexation Handbook, page 54).

Ministers to Hawaii Luther Severance (Annexation Handbook, page 58), David L. Gregg (Annexation Handbook, page 59), Edward McCook (Annexation Handbook, page 60), Henry A. Pierce (Annexation Handbook, page 61), John L. Stevens (Annexation Handbook, page 62), Harold M. Sewall.

Gen. J. M. Schofield, Gen. B. S. Alexander, Admiral Dupont, Admiral George Brown, Admiral Belknap, Captain Mahan, Admiral Porter, ex-Senator Dolph, of Oregon; ex-Senator Ingalls, of Kansas; ex-Senator Butler, of South Carolina; Dean Wayland, of Yale Law School; ex-Secretary of the Navy Benjamin F. Tracy, Civil Service Commissioner Proctor, ex-Governor Stone, of Missouri; ex-Governor Johnson, of Missouri; ex-Secretary of the Interior Noble.

FRAUDS IN ANTI-ANNEXATION PETITION.

Point 3.—Two-thirds of the native Hawaiians have signed a petition protesting against annexation.

Reply.—Four thousand nine hundred and thirty-eight, or 23 per cent, of the signers of the petition are minors.

The petition states that the minors are between the ages of 14 and 20.

It shows upon its face that there are 677 of the petitioners under 14 years of age, of whom no less than 13 are only 2 years of age.

The ages of 278 of the minors under 14 years of age have been fraudulently raised to over 14 years of age in order to try and make it appear that they are of more responsible age, and to conform to the certificate in the petition that they are over 14 years of age.

The petition shows on its face that the signatures of over 1,400 of the adult signers are not original, but are forgeries.

In one case a whole page of the male signatures and one page of the female signatures are all in one handwriting.

In one case 126 signatures and in another 178 are all in the same handwriting.

The ages of the petitioners are unreliable, many of them being filled in at a different time from the signatures and giving round numbers instead of exact figures.

Each and every page containing the fraudulent insertions, as above stated, is certified to as being genuine by the officers getting the petition up, showing entire lack of good faith on their part.

METHOD OF ACQUIRING TERRITORY BY TREATY

Point 4.—The supporters of annexation are unwilling to submit the question of annexation to the ballot of the people of Hawaii.

Reply.—In the first place, why should the question of annexation be submitted to popular vote in Hawaii any more than in the United States? The people of the United States assume obligations and responsibilities by virtue of annexation as well as do the people of Hawaii. Why should not the question, therefore, be submitted to a popular vote in the United States?

The reply to this is that the Constitution of the United States does not provide that annexations of territory shall be submitted to popular vote. Neither does the constitution of Hawaii.

The Constitution and precedents have established the proposition that the legal method of acquiring territory is by treaty, which shall be ratified by the Senate; or by joint resolution or bill, approved by a majority of both Houses.

For United States Supreme Court decisions affirming the constitutional power of annexation, see Thurston's Handbook on Annexation, page 24.

In none of the annexations which have been made by the United States, with the exception of Texas, has either a direct or indirect popular vote been taken in the United States or in the country annexed. In the case of Texas, an indirect vote was taken by the adoption of a State constitution by the people of Texas after the Texas Legislature had ratified the joint resolution passed by the Congress of the United States.

ACT AUTHORIZING THE KING TO NEGOTIATE A TREATY.

The constitution of the Republic of Hawaii, under which two Legislatures have been elected, contains a specific clause authorizing and directing the president to negotiate a treaty of annexation with the United States, subject to the ratification of the Hawaiian Senate. (Art. 32, Constn. Rep. Hawaii.)

It is claimed that this is a new authority which has been usurped by a revolutionary government, and that the Government has not the power to negotiate such a treaty except upon popular vote.

The reply to this is that from ancient times the power to negotiate all treaties, annexation or otherwise, has been exclusively in the executive of Hawaii, as is evidenced by precedents in the past.

In 1851, in view of aggressions then being committed by the French, Kamehameha III, without even consulting the Legislature, executed a provisional cession of Hawaii to the United States.

In 1852 the Hawaiian Legislature passed a specific act authorizing the King to negotiate at any time a treaty of annexation.

This act has never been repealed and still remains a part of the law of Hawaii.

KING KAMEHAMEHA ANNEXATION TREATY OF 1854

In 1854 King Kamehameha III negotiated a formal treaty of annexation with the United States, with provision for popular vote.

Not only has the present treaty been negotiated in accordance with the general powers of the Executive of Hawaii, the statute of 1852 above referred to, and the specific authority of the constitution of the Republic, but the Legislature of Hawaii in both Houses has voluntarily at two successive sessions unanimously passed resolutions ratifying and approving of the annexation proposition, and a new Legislature has just been elected which is committed to annexation.

For the United States to now refuse to annex Hawaii unless a popular vote were first taken, would be to take, not only an entirely new position for which there is no precedent, but to go behind the Hawaiian records and require something to be done which neither the laws of the United States nor Hawaii have ever required to be done in the past and do not require to be done now.

Again, the proposition is not that the vote should be submitted to the lawful voters of Hawaii, but to "all the people of Hawaii."

In the first place, nearly one-half of the people of Hawaii are Chinese and Japanese, who have no right to vote now, and never had the right to vote there, and who by the constitution of Hawaii are not eligible to exercise the franchise.

If it is claimed that what is meant by the "people of Hawaii" are those who could vote under the Monarchy, the reply is that, under the constitution of the Republic of Hawaii, all who were voters under the Monarchy can become voters under the Republic by simply taking the oath of allegiance to the Republic, and no one is eligible to become a voter under the Republic unless he takes such an oath.

All those who are not now voters are therefore nonvoters, simply by reason of their unwillingness to accept the Republic and their adhesion to the cause of monarchy.

Point 5.—The monarchy was overthrown by American citizens. Although he argued the other way before, "the color is given to the accusation by the pertinacity and determination with which this treaty is now being pressed."

Reply.—For reply to the charge that the monarchy was overthrown by United States officials, see Thurston's Handbook, page 38, reply to eighteenth objection.

There is no more pertinacity and determination being displayed now than there was in 1893 and 1894, when Mr. JOHNSON very ably refuted this charge. (See Morgan Report, volume 1, page 7; Senate Report No. 227, Fifty-third Congress, second session.)

Point 6.—The people of Hawaii are not sufficiently intelligent to be incorporated into our domain.

Intelligence is the exception there; ignorance is the general rule.

Even if Americans "pour into and take possession of the islands, the ignorance will remain."

EIGHTY-FOUR PER CENT. OF HAWAIIANS ABLE TO READ AND WRITE.

Reply.—The last Hawaiian census, taken in September, 1896, gives the percentage of those able to read and write, as follows:

(The age from which illiteracy is reckoned in Hawaii is 6 years instead of 10 years, as it is in this country. If 10 years were made the basis, as in this country, the percentage of those able to read and write would be much higher.)

Hawaiians, pure blooded, per cent able to read and write, 83.97; part Hawaiians, mixed blood, per cent able to read and write, 91.21; the two making an average of 85.28 per cent.

The statistics show that 26 per cent of the pure-blooded and 69 per cent of the part Hawaiians are able to read and write in English.

The statistics also show that of the 14,000 children between 6 and 15 years of age, 81 per cent are attending school, in addition to which there are several thousand under 6 years of age attending kindergarten schools, and over 2,000 who are over 15 years of age attending school.

Free public schools, all taught in English, are maintained throughout the country at Government expense, while there is a compulsory-education law under which all children are obliged to attend school between the years of 6 and 15.

The Census, page 100, says:

"The system of enforcing the law for bringing children into school is peculiarly efficient in these islands. Very few children escape being obliged to attend school. * * * There are very few countries, however, where education is so universal. * * * Those who are illiterate come to us from abroad."

With regard to the Portuguese and their alleged undesirability, the charge is without foundation. Like the poor peasant population of other countries which comes to the United States, the majority of them are unable to read or write, the percentage in Hawaii who are able to read and write being 28.

But they are industrious, economical, and moral, constituting to-day the best laboring population of Hawaii.

Neither the Chinese nor Japanese are eligible to citizenship in Hawaii. They are aliens there as in the United States, and annexation will not change that status. They have no control in the Government now and they will not after annexation.

ADMISSION TO STATEHOOD.

A fair general estimate may be made that within five years after any given lot of Japanese arrive in Hawaii, one-third of them will have returned to Japan, and thereafter not less than 10 to 15 per cent will return each year.

Point 7.—The supporters of annexation say that annexation does not necessarily imply that it is to become a State.

"For this very reason I antagonize it with all the more resolution."

No territory should be annexed unless "in due course of events it will become entitled to membership in the Federal Union."

Reply.—There is no reason, precedent, common sense, or law requiring the admission of any given territory to statehood until it and its inhabitants are fitted therefor.

Louisiana was annexed in 1803, and the northwest portion thereof was only admitted to statehood in 1890.

New Mexico and Arizona were annexed in 1849. They have not yet been admitted to statehood.

Alaska was annexed in 1867, and has not yet even been provided with a Territorial government.

If it is not inconsistent with law and American institutions to acquire territory and withhold statehood for thirty, fifty, and ninety years, why can not the same or any other territory be held for a hundred or any other period of years, until it is fitted for statehood?

If that time never comes, well and good. When it does come, if ever it does, is time to change its status, and neither in the making or changing of that status is there any violation of the principles of American institutions.

The treaty leaves the form of the government of Hawaii absolutely in the hands of Congress, providing that until changed by Congress the local laws not inconsistent with the United States Constitution shall continue in force.

HAWAII HAS A FULLY ORGANIZED GOVERNMENT.

Hawaii already possesses so fully organized a government that only a few general adaptive statutes will have to be enacted by Congress in order to create a fully equipped American Territorial government.

Point 8.—In paragraphs 22 and 23 he dwells on the "sordid policy," "unbefitting the genius of a great and free people," to have territory under a government other than statehood, and enters a "solemn protest against the consummation of this colossal blunder."

Reply.—There is no connection between territory being held as a Territory and a "sordid policy."

The Territories of the United States have practically self-government in all local affairs. Their sole limitation is in participation in the Federal Government.

The limitations connected therewith are precisely the same as in the great self-governing colonial governments of Canada and Australia. In both cases local affairs are controlled by the local people, and in each case there is no participation in the Federal Government.

No one certainly will claim that the Canadian and Australian governments are the victims of a "sordid policy."

This talk is buncombe.

Point 9.—We do not need this territory in which to expand our population. * * *

We shall not require an overflow for a century.

We have a vast empire sparsely settled.

Our 70,000,000 of people can be put into Texas alone without interfering with their freedom of action.

There is nothing in the national growth, either present or prospective, which requires annexation.

THE PRIME VALUE OF HAWAII.

Reply.—The same argument would have excluded Louisiana, Florida, Texas, and California.

All the population of the United States could to-day be accommodated east of the Mississippi, but it does not rationally follow that if the United States had remained east of the Mississippi only it would not have been beneficial to them to secure territory west of the Mississippi.

The physical possibility of squeezing a given population into a given territory is not the criterion by which the benefit of acquiring additional territory should be judged.

It may be physically possible for all the people now in the United States, or who may live there for a hundred years to come, to exist within the present limits of the country; but conditions have demonstrated that already the need of foreign markets for United States products is pressing.

The prime value of Hawaii to the United States is not by reason of the trade or area of Hawaii alone, but the vastly greater trade of the Pacific with which it is so intimately connected and which it to so great a degree controls.

Point 10.—"The acquisition of Hawaii means the strengthening, not of the centripetal, but of the centrifugal, force in this nation."

He favors "centralized and unified power," and opposes "the acquisition of insular territorial possessions, pursued in flagrant violation either of lines of latitude or longitude."

"Every island and every ignorant alien taken into the Union makes for dismemberment and disintegration."

OBJECT OF ACQUIRING HAWAII.

Reply.—The objection that the acquiring of colonies and outlying territory tends to weaken the central government is directly contrary to the argument usually made in this connection, which is that the control by the central government of provinces which are not fully self-governing produces an undue centralization of power in the "central government."

So far from the acquisition of Hawaii being "pursued in flagrant violation either of lines of latitude or longitude, " Hawaii is well within them.

Hawaii lies on almost the same line of latitude that Key West does, and lies 500 miles within the line of longitude bounding the western limit of the mainland of Alaska and more than a thousand miles within the line of longitude bounding the Aleutian and Midway islands, both of which belong to the United States.

So far as the inclusion of Hawaii within the boundaries of the Union tending to "disintegrate and dismember," the main object of acquiring Hawaii is to defend that which the United States already owns on the Pacific coast, and to protect its commerce upon the Pacific, which is rapidly growing to be the greatest in the world.

The local government of Hawaii will settle all local problems, of which there will be many, without involving the National Government or the people of other localities in the United States, any more than does the settlement of a county-seat fight or a local-option election in Arizona.

Point 11.—It is a departure from the traditions of the country, a foolish experiment, to annex territory not contiguous. The one experiment, Alaska, is still an experiment.

Reply.—There is no departure from the traditions of the country.

The country has already made numerous annexations of insular territory.

MIDWAY ISLAND.

This island was annexed in 1868 by order of the executive department of the United States. The action taken thereunder is fully described in Senate Executive Document No. 79, Fortieth Congress, second session. An appropriation of $50,000 was made by the third session of the Fortieth Congress by act approved March 1, 1869.

This is contained in United States Statutes at Large, volume 15, chapter 48, page 279. It is also referred to in the Report of the Secretary of the Navy for 1870, on page 8, and Report of the Secretary of the Navy for 1871, pages 6, 7, and 8.

The object of the annexation was to create a naval station there. Midway Island is the westernmost of the Hawaiian group.

OTHER ISLAND ANNEXATIONS.

The United States owns the Aleutian Islands, extending a thousand miles west of Hawaii, which it acquired in conjunction with Alaska. It also owns fifty-seven other islands and groups of islands in the Pacific and thirteen in the Caribbean Sea, which have been taken possession of by American citizens under act of Congress dated August 15, 1856, which provides for the registration and protection of islands so annexed. The principal object of such annexations was to secure the guano located on such islands, but it only makes the precedent so much the stronger in that it indicates that so small a matter as the securing of a limited amount of fertilizer is sufficient reason for insular annexation.

The traditions of the country are to annex whatever territory or country is needed.

The fact that the greater portion of the territory annexed was not insular is no precedent or tradition against insular annexations when such annexations would be valuable to the country.

In other words the question of whether the territory proposed to be annexed is insular or continental is not and should not be the criterion, but the deciding line is whether or not its annexation would be valuable to the United States.

The names, location, and date of acquisition of the islands which have become United States territory under the above-mentioned act of 1856 are as follows:

Date of acquisition.	Name.	Date of acquisition.	Name.
October 28, 1856......	Bakers.	February 8, 1860....	Liderous.
	Jarvis.		Low Islands.
August 31, 1856	Navassa.		Mackin.
December 3, 18.4.....	Howlands.		Mary Letitias.
September 6, 1859....	Johnsons.		Marys.
December 27, 1859...	Barren or Starve.		Mathews.
	Enderbury.		Nassan.
	McKean.		Oniros.
	Phœnix.		Palmyros.
December 29, 1859...	Christmas.		Pescado.
	Haldens.		Phœnix.
February 8, 1860....	America.		Prospect.
	Annes.		Rioreens.
	Barbera.		Rogewiens.
	Baumans.		Samarang.
	Birnics.		Sarah Anne.
	Caroline.		Sidneys,
	Clarence.		Starbuck of Hero.
	Dangerous.		Steavers.
	Danger's Rock.		Walkers.
	Davids.		Washington of Ushaga.
	Duke of York.	December 30, 1862..	Great and Little Swan in the
	Enderbury.		Caribbean Sea.
	Farmers.	August 12, 1869......	Islands in the Caribbean Sea
	Favorite.		not named in latitude 4° 40′,
			longitude 160° 07′.
	Flint.	November 22, 1869..	Pedro Keys.
	Flints.		Quito Sereno.
	Frances.		Petrel Roncador.
	Frienhaven.	September 8, 1879..	Serranilla Keys.
	Gardners.		Morant Keys.
	Gallego.	September 13, 1880..	De Aves.
	Ganges.		Serranilla Keys.
	Gronique.		Western Triangles.
	Humphreys.	October 18, 1880......	Islands of Arenas.
	Kemns.	June 21, 1891.........	Alacrans Islands.

See records of the State and Treasury Departments.

In the Pacific... 57
In the Caribbean Sea.. 13

Total... 70

AGGRESSIONS OF THE FRENCH.

Point 12.—Hawaii was offered to the United States in 1853 and declined by President Pierce and Secretary of State Webster.

Reply.—Mr. Johnson is incorrect in saying that Hawaii was offered to the United States and declined.

The transaction which he refers to was the document which was dated March 10, 1851, to be found in volume 2, page 896, of the Morgan report to the Senate of 1894, being Senate Executive Document No. 45, Fifty-second Congress, second session.

The document mentioned simply states that by reason of the aggressions of the French, the King of Hawaii placed the country under the protection and safeguard of the United States of America until some arrangements could be made to "place our said relations with France upon a footing compatible with my rights as an independent sovereign under the laws of nations, and compatible with my treaty engagements with other foreign nations," with the proviso that if such arrangements be impracticable the protection of the United States should be perpetual.

This document was delivered to the American minister in Hawaii, but the French learning thereof and ceasing their aggressions, no action was taken thereon by the United States.

Point 13.—The "possession of Hawaii means that they will become a source of irritation for all time to come between ourselves and foreign nations."

"Insular territorial possessions are a prolific source of contention."

Annexation will devolve upon the United States "the responsibility for their management and control."

"Vexed and annoying questions" will "arise with powerful maritime nations" concerning the "occupation by them of Hawaiian waters and harbors, the use of the islands for coaling stations, and the hundreds of controversies which are liable to arise with respect to this territory."

UNITED STATES WILL NOT ALLOW ANY OTHER COUNTRY TO CONTROL HAWAII.

Reply.—The possession of Hawaii is far less liable to prove a source of "irritation with foreign nations" than is Hawaii's continued independence and the declaration of the United States which has been constantly reiterated that the United States will not allow any other country to control Hawaii.

So far as interference in Hawaii by other countries is concerned, this country is already committed to the full responsibility which ownership would devolve upon it, without any of the control of ownership.

Annexation will give the United States the control as well as the responsibility, while under the present status it has all the responsibility with no control to keep the islands from getting into difficulties with foreign governments.

"Vexed and annoying questions will arise with foreign governments concerning the occupation of Hawaiian waters and harbors."

These are the very questions which will arise in case annexation does not take place, but which can not arise in case of annexation any more than they arise concerning the waters of California and Florida.

What controversies will arise concerning Hawaii that do not arise in any other territory which the United States has annexed?

Point 14.—"This nation is practically invulnerable to successful attack from a foreign foe. The ocean forms an impassable barrier to dangerous aggression."

"We have a splendid navy and excellent coast defenses."

"Annexation will destroy our contiguity, take away our base of supplies, surrender the natural advantages of defense, and furnish a bone of contention to fight over and defend in time of peace."

Reply.—The statement that the nation is now practically invulnerable, and that "the ocean forms an impassable barrier" to dangerous aggression, is considered by the military and naval authorities, and replied to in their statements contained in the pamphlet herewith.

They unite in the opinion that with the control of Hawaii the Pacific coast would be impregnable, but without its control it will be liable to attack.

Moreover, the proposition that the United States is safe by remaining on the continent does not cover the safety of its foreign commerce, which is now so large and rapidly growing.

So far from the acquisition of Hawaii "taking away the bases of supplies," it secures to the United States the base of supplies which controls a larger area of the earth's surface than any other one spot and prevents any foreign nation from securing a base of supplies from which the commerce and the coast of the United States on the Pacific can be interfered with.

Point 15.—In case of annexation we must fortify Hawaii. We must increase our Navy to defend and communicate with them. This will enormously increase appropriations.

CONTROL A MEASURE OF ECONOMY.

Reply.—It will be necessary to maintain a navy in connection with American interests in the Pacific, but it will require a larger navy and expenditures to protect the Pacific coast without than with Hawaii.

The control of Hawaii, so far from being a source of expense, will be a measure of economy, in that by fortifying one point in Hawaii, the battle ships of all nations can be prevented from getting to the Pacific coast, because they can not carry coal enough to cross the Pacific without recoaling at Hawaii.

Therefore the one fortification at Hawaii will answer the same object that would the fortification of all the principal points on the Pacific coast.

Point 16.—Annexation will form a bad precedent and will be followed by the annexation of Cuba and Samoa.

This "will be fortified by artful sophistries of men who will pander to the national vanity and cupidity."

Annexation is, as a rule, a source of weakness.

Reply.—So far as precedent is concerned, the United States does not stand in need of any precedent in the way of annexing territory.

It has annexed territory all the way from the Tropics to the Arctic, on the Atlantic, the Gulf, the Pacific, and the islands of the Pacific, and in the Caribbean Sea.

So far as precedents are concerned, there are precedents enough on hand to form a basis of justification for annexing anything in the Western Hemisphere.

So far as the annexation of Hawaii is concerned, there is no parallel between it and the islands on the Atlantic side, for the reason that Hawaii stands alone as a base of supplies within the practical steaming distance of the Pacific coast.

The securing of this one point removes practically all possible bases of trans-Pacific attack.

On the other hand, there are so many islands on the Atlantic side, any one of which can be made a base of attack, that in order to secure immunity from attack on that side all the islands must be annexed, a practical impossibility.

The status of Hawaii, therefore, is unique and entirely different from Cuba or any other Atlantic island.

Point 17.—The United States should heed the advice of Washington and "avoid all entangling alliances," and turn its attention to the development of its own resources.

"We shall be wise if we devote ourselves to internal development and growth."

ANNEXATION IN CONFORMITY TO THE ADVICE OF WASHINGTON.

Reply.—The annexation of Hawaii is in direct conformity with the advice of Washington to "avoid entangling alliances."

The opponents of annexation have advocated in the past, and advocate now, that the United States should enter into a joint agreement with European nations concerning Hawaii, thereby directly entering an "entangling alliance."

By absorbing Hawaii the United States will remove the possibility of "entangling alliances" and will effectually eliminate Hawaii from international disagreements.

As long as Hawaii remains independent, without the power to maintain its independence, it will be a source of international irritation and be a menace to the peace of the Pacific.

The necessary incidentals to the development of internal resources are the development of foreign commerce, and Hawaii is indirectly incidental to the control of that commerce in that all the commerce to and from the Pacific and trans-Pacific nations must pass its door.

Point 18.—The United States is all powerful. All people realize our great strength and therefore seek no difficulty with us.

Reply.—Whether or not the strength of the United States is sufficient to prevent foreign aggressions is unnecessary to discuss in view of current events.

The reiterated sentiments of Washington, Jackson, and others, "that preparedness for war is the most certain method of maintaining peace," applies as well to Hawaii as it does to Spain.

The incidents of the day demonstrates more than argument the necessity of a navy, and if the United States is to have any navy on the Pacific it must, in order to maintain its control of the Pacific, have a coaling station at Hawaii, and it can not have that coaling station in time of war unless it owns the country. * * *

ORGANIZED LABOR IN FAVOR OF ACQUISITION.

Now, the gentleman spoke of the opposition of organized labor to the passage of the bill. There has been published in a morning paper a declaration of a certain gentleman who says that he is opposed to the admission or the acquisition of these islands because he has some fears—born, in my judgment, of a lack of intelligence and a lack of experience in the United States, and a lack of knowledge of its institutions; born of the fact that he was not born under them. I hold in my hand and will publish a letter from representatives of the Brotherhood of Locomotive Engineers, the Brotherhood of Locomotive Firemen, the Order of Railway Conductors, the Brotherhood of Railway Trainmen, the Order of Railway Telegraphers, and a telegram just received from Montreal from Mr. Sargent, the head of the Brotherhood of Locomotive Firemen and Locomotive Engineers, and also a letter from a distinguished gentleman representing the Order of Knights of Labor, and I will summarize what they state.

They state, first, that there never was any action by the organized labor of this country against the acquisition of these islands, and they state, in the next place, that so far as their knowledge goes they are all of them in favor of this acquisition. I can not conceive how it is possible that the workingmen, the laboring men of America, can be opposed to the opening up of the magnificent opportunities that seem to me to be presented by the acquisition of these islands.

18

MR. GOMPERS STANDS ALMOST ALONE.

WASHINGTON, D. C., *June 13, 1898.*

DEAR SIR: In reply to your inquiry of even date as to the feeling of "organized labor" on the question of the annexation of Hawaii, I beg leave to state that my individual opinion, based on thirty-three years experience as wage-earner and twenty years among organized men, constrains me to take issue with Mr. Gompers, who was quoted as opposed to annexation by Hon. CHAMP CLARK, of Missouri, in his speech in the House of Representatives on Saturday last.

In this opinion Mr. Gompers should have been quoted as an individual and not as a representative of organized labor, and no man has authority to say that organized labor is for or against annexation, for the question has never been placed before organized labor.

Mr. Gompers himself, I am reliably informed, is a man of limited experience as a wage-earner, and does not correctly gauge the patriotic feeling among American workingmen, who desire to uphold in time of war the Administration, regardless of their own political opinions, and he seems to ignore their oft-expressed desire to "extend commerce and multiply the opportunities to labor." My belief is that Mr. Gompers, on this question, stands almost alone, as I am informed he did at the last convention of his own organization on the anti-Cuban war resolution.

I have the honor to be, very respectfully,

A. M. LAWSON,
Master Workman District Assembly 66, Washington, D. C.

Hon. CHARLES H. GROSVENOR,
House of Representatives.

———

THE HOTEL RALEIGH, *Washington, D. C., June 13, 1898.*

As to the annexation of Hawaii, which in no sense is a party issue, while it is true that we have not in any council or convention taken any position on the matter, it is also true that the sentiment of the great mass of the membership favor the proposition, as do many of their chief executive officers, as shown by the inclosed telegrams. This expression has become more pronounced as the apparent necessity grows since the brilliant victory of Manilla. Such feelings are inspired by the same motives which prompted so many of our members to enter the volunteer service.

It is not at all probable that in the event of annexation the condition of labor in Hawaii would or could be transplanted to this country, no more than the quasi serfdom of Mexico would find lodgment under our Constitution, but, on the contrary, I submit there is every reason to believe that the advanced intelligence, conservatism, and patriotism of the organized American workman would meet such conditions and vastly improve them. There are so many illustrations that it would be idle to enumerate them.

Yours truly,

W. F. HYNES,
Representing Brotherhood Locomotive Engineers, Brotherhood Locomotive Firemen, Order of Railway Conductors, Brotherhood of Trainmen, Order of Railway Telegraphers.

Hon. CHARLES H. GROSVENOR,
House of Representatives, Washington, D. C.

MONTREAL, QUEBEC, *June 14, 1898.*

W. F. HYNES, *Raleigh Hotel, Washington, D. C.:*

As an American citizen, I am heartily in favor of the annexation of Hawaii.

F. P. SARGENT,
Chief of Brotherhood of Locomotive Firemen.

———

PEORIA, ILL., *June 14, 1898.*

W. F. HYNES, *care C. Grosvenor:*

Answering your telegram, in my opinion the United States should annex the Hawaiian Islands. The necessity of our control over the islands in time of war is now apparent to everyone. Commercially, too, they are of great importance to us.

P. H. MORRISSEY,
Grand Master Brotherhood Railroad Trainmen.

———

CEDAR RAPIDS, IOWA, *June 14, 1898.*

W. F. HYNES, *The Raleigh, Washington, D. C.:*

In the position which it seems the United States must hereafter occupy I deem Hawaii a very valuable, if not indispensable, acquisition.

E. E. CLARK,
Chief Order of Railway Conductors.

———

CAPTAIN MAHAN ON THE NECESSITY OF ANNEXATION.

From the speech of Hon. Robert Hitt, of Illinois (Congressional Record 142, vol. 31, p. 6766).

Captain Mahan, the most distinguished writer and authority of our time on the history of sea power, says:

"It is obvious that if we do not hold the islands ourselves, we can not expect the neutrals in the war to prevent the other belligerent from occupying them; nor can the inhabitants themselves prevent such occupation. The commercial value is not great enough to provoke neutral interposition. In short, in war we should need a larger Navy to defend the Pacific coast, because we should have not only to defend our own coast, but to prevent, by naval force, an enemy from occupying the islands; whereas, if we preoccupied them, fortifications could preserve them to us.

"In my opinion it is not practicable for any trans-Pacific country to invade our Pacific coast without occupying Hawaii as a base."

GENERAL SCHOFIELD ON ANNEXATION.

General Schofield, who spent three months on the islands and made a careful survey of Pearl River Harbor, stated to our committee:

"At this moment the Government is fitting out quite a large fleet of steamers at San Francisco to carry large detachments of troops and military supplies of all kinds to the Philippine Islands. Honolulu is almost in the direct route. That fleet, of course, will want very much to recoal at Honolulu, thus saving that amount of freight and tonnage for essential stores to be carried with it. Otherwise they would have to carry coal enough to carry them all the way from San Francisco to Manila, and that would occupy a large amount of the carrying capacity of the fleet, and if they recoil at Honolulu all that will be saved. More than that, a fleet is liable at any time to meet with stress of weather, or perhaps a heavy storm, and there might be an accident to the machinery which will make it necessary to put into the nearest port possible for repairs and additional supplies. By the time it reaches there its coal supply may be well-nigh exhausted; it then has to replenish its coal supply to carry it to whatever port it could reach. * * * * * * * Now, let us suppose, on the other hand, that the Spanish navy in the Pacific as well as in the Atlantic, or both, were a little stronger than ours instead of being somewhat weaker. The first thing they would do would be to go and take possession of the Sandwich Islands and make them the base of naval operations against the Pacific coast.

"You have only to consider the state of mind which exists all along the Atlantic coast under the erroneous apprehension that the Spanish fleet might possibly assail our coast to see what would be the case if the Spanish fleet were a good deal stronger than ours and took possession of Honolulu and made it a base of operations in attacking the points on the Pacific coast. We would be absolutely powerless, because we would have no fleet there to dispute the possession of the Sandwich Islands, whereas, if we held that place and fortified it so that a foreign navy could not take it, it could not operate against the Pacific coast at all, for it could not bring coal enough across the Pacific Ocean to sustain an attack on the Pacific coast. Then the Sandwich Islands would be a base for naval operations just as Puerto Rico is against the Atlantic coast. If Spain is strong enough to hold Puerto Rico, so that a squadron can replenish with supplies—coal, ammunition, and provisions—there, the whole Spanish fleet can raid our Atlantic coast at will.

"It happens that in this war we have picked out the only nation in the world that is a little weaker than ourselves. The Spanish fleet on the Asiatic station was the only one of all the fleets we could have overcome as we did. Of course that can not again happen, for we will not be able to pick up so weak an enemy next time. We are liable at any time to get into a war with a nation which has a more powerful fleet than ours, and it is of vital importance, therefore, if we can, to hold the point from which they can conduct operations against our Pacific coast. Especially is that true until the Nicaragua Canal is finished, because we can not send a fleet from the Atlantic to the Pacific. We can not send them around Cape Horn and repel an attack there. If we had the canal finished, we would be much better off in that respect; but even then we would want the possession of a base very much."

Admiral Walker, who has had long experience in the waters of the Hawaiian Islands, emphatically confirmed the views of General Schofield, especially that it would cost far less to protect the Pacific coast with the Hawaiian Islands than without them; that it would be taking a point of vantage instead of giving it to your enemy.

VIEWS OF ADMIRAL DUPONT IN 1851.

Admiral Dupont, in a report made as long ago as 1851, expressed his view in these words:

"It is impossible to estimate too highly the value and importance of the Sandwich Islands, whether in a commercial or military point of view. Should circumstances ever place them in our hands, they would prove the most important acquisition we could make in the whole Pacific Ocean—an acquisition intimately connected with our commercial and naval supremacy in those seas."

THE DINGLEY BILL

FROM THE SPEECH OF

Hon. JESSE OVERSTREET

Of INDIANA

Friday, April 29, 1898

❦ ❦ ❦

WAR EXPENDITURES

FROM THE REMARKS OF

Hon. JOSEPH CANNON

Of ILLINOIS

IN THE HOUSE OF REPRESENTATIVES

JULY 8, 1898

THE DINGLEY BILL

FROM THE SPEECH OF

Hon. JESSE OVERSTREET

Of Indiana

In the House of Representatives, Friday, April 29, 1898

The House being in Committee of the Whole House on the state of the Union, and having under consideration the bill (H. R. 10100) to provide ways and means to meet war expenditures—

Mr. OVERSTREET said:

In saying that war at its best is deplorable I call attention to the interrupted progress of our prosperity, which, beginning with the passage of the wise measure for the protection of our industries at the special session of this Congress, showed a steady upward tendency to the middle of March, and then, in consequence of the rapidly hastening crisis that culminated in hostilities with Spain on April 21, began to fluctuate and to show a reverse tendency. The predicted surplus made its appearance in January, 1898; it was $2,000,000 in February. Deducting the war expenses from the revenues for March, the surplus in the Treasury, comparing receipts with expenditures, was for that month nearly equal to the surplus for February, so that it is mathematically demonstrable that but for the heavy expenditures made necessary by the preparations for war, coupled with the business disturbance incident to the actual prosecution of the war, the normal receipts from the Dingley bill would have provided ample revenue to run the Government in times of peace. This I shall show in greater detail when I come to it.

BONDS TO PROSECUTE THE WAR.

I regret that gentlemen on this floor have seen fit to inject partisan questions into this debate. I regret that the question of the proposed issue of Government obligations—bonds not issued in times of peace to replenish an impoverished Treasury, as under the late Democratic Administration, but proposed to be issued to enable us to prosecute the war with vigor; to feed, clothe, and equip our soldiers—I say I regret that this measure should, for purely partisan advantage, be made to stand for renewed agitation of the silver question, the problem of paying these bonds in silver, in gold, or in "coin."

I can not let this opportunity pass without replying, to the extent of my humble ability, to some of the criticisms made in this debate on Republican policies, and to review as succintly as possible the statistics and sources of information which shed light upon the issues raised here.

REVENUE RECEIPTS UNDER THE DINGLEY ACT COMPARED WITH THE WILSON TARIFF.

Lack of revenue compelled the Cleveland Administration to encumber the taxpayers with an additional burden of $262,330,692 by the issue of bonds in time of peace to provide means to run the Government.

Under the operations of the McKinley act there was no lack of funds in the Treasury, nor has the Government been embarrassed for funds at any time under Republican tariff policy. This embarrassment began with the enactment of Democratic tariff legislation—the passage of the Wilson bill. Revenues began to fall off soon after the triumph of the Democratic party at the polls in 1893, when it became known that the new House would lower the duties on imports, and importers began to hold back in anticipation of a reduced tariff. For the first three years of the McKinley act the receipts from customs were:

Twelve months ending September 30, 1891	$196,794,357 89
Twelve months ending September 30, 1892	185,838,859 19
Twelve months ending September 30, 1893	189,182,905 45
Total	$571,816,122 54

The election took place in November, 1892, and with the triumph of the Democratic party the revenue from imports fell off $76,591,965.69, amounting to only $112,590,939.77 for the eleven months ended August 31, 1894. For July and August, under the McKinley bill, customs receipts were abnormally small for the reason stated, amounting to only $8,427,338.46 for the first and $11,804,911.21 for the latter month, against average monthly receipts of $15,765,242.12 for the twelve months of the year preceding.

DEFICIENCY UNDER THE WILSON ACT.

The Wilson Act took effect on the 28th day of August, 1894, and was repealed July 24, 1897, by the Dingley tariff. Receipts from customs for the three years were as follows:

Twelve months ending August 31, 1895	$161,201,169 35
Twelve months ending August 31, 1896	154,218,813 94
Eleven months ending July 31, 1897	168,888,654 11
Total	$484,308,637 40
McKinley Act, three years	571,816,122 54
Wilson Act, three years	484,308,637 40
Increase over Wilson Tariff	$87,507,485 14

The four-years record of the deficiency under the Wilson act is as follows for each fiscal year ended June 30—

1894	$69,803,260
1895	42,805,223
1896	25,203,246
1897	18,052,454
Total deficiency	$155,864,183

For reasons the reverse of those which caused imports to be abnormally small during the closing period of the McKinley Act, there was an abnormally large increase in customs receipts under the Wilson Act for the closing months of its existence.

Importers rushed in wool, sugar, and other imports in large quantities to avoid the payment of the higher rates under the Dingley Act, and receipts from customs for March, 1897, rose to $22,833,856.46; for April, $24,454,351.74; for May, $16,885,011.55; for June, $21,560,152.36, and for July, $16,966,801.65. As a result, when the Dingley Act took effect, July 24, 1897, receipts from this source dropped to $6,987,702, because the immediate demand had been supplied by excessive importations under the lower rates of the Wilson tariff.

RECEIPTS FOR FEBRUARY EXCEEDED DISBURSEMENTS.

This was foreseen by the Republican leaders, and in all the debates on the Dingley bill in Congress this temporary dropping off of revenue was taken account of and coupled with the general prediction that as soon as the effect of these anticipatory importations had been overcome the operation of the new tariff act would provide revenues sufficient to run the Government without further bond sales. Within seven months from the passage of the bill this prediction has been verified, and the receipts for February, 1898, for the first time since the election of 1894, exceeded the monthly disbursements of the Treasury.

The following table will show the customs receipts for the first six months under the Wilson and Dingley acts:

Month.	1894-95 (Wilson tariff).	1897-98 (Dingley tariff)
September	$15,564,990 56	$7,943,100 28
October	11,962,118 17	9,713,494 62
November	10,260,692 56	9,830,025 00
December	11,203,049 40	11,660,788 74
January	17,361,916 25	14,269,492 08
February	13,334,691 99	15,040,680 74
Total	$69,687,448 93	$68,457,581 46

It will be noticed that while the receipts under the Wilson Act for February were more than two millions less than for September, the receipts under the Dingley Act were seven millions larger for the same periods, and while there was almost a continuous falling off for October, November, and December under the former, there was a steady increase under the Dingley tariff. In January, 1895, customs revenues showed a spasmodic increase of six millions, only to drop back four millions in February. The seventeen-million mark for January was never again reached under the Wilson tariff, except during the five months preceding its repeal; and, taking this out of consideration, it will be seen that the receipts for February, 1898, under the Dingley Act were not eclipsed during the first six months of the Wilson bill, save by a small sum for September, owing to the increased importations from the repeal of the higher duties under the McKinley Act.

Deducting the receipts for January from both, it will be found that the receipts under the Dingley Act for five months exceeded those of the

Wilson bill for the same period $1,862,556.69, while the receipts for February under the Dingley Act were but $2,321,235.51 lower than the highest receipts under its predecessor, the record of January, 1895, except the five months marking the debate of the repeal of the Wilson tariff in Congress.

TABLE SHOWING CUSTOMS RECEIPTS UNDER DINGLEY LAW, BY DAYS AND MONTHS.

Date.	Average daily receipts.	Total receipts for month.
August, 1897	$225,409	$6,987,702
September, 1897	264,770	7,943,100
October, 1897	313,338	9,713,494
November, 1897	327,667	9,830,025
December, 1897	376,154	11,660,788
January, 1898	460,306	14,269,492
February, 1898	537,167	15,040,680

BALANCE IN FAVOR OF THE DINGLEY LAW.

As a guide, indicating what a tariff bill is required to produce in order to yield sufficient revenues, it may be stated that for the first three years of the McKinley Act the average monthly revenues from imports amounted to $15,883,781. This left a surplus. The Wilson bill, for the entire thirty-five months of its operation, yielded only $13,837,389 per month, and this includes the abnormal record of the five months closing its history, during which the importations were vastly in excess of any other months, for reasons explained. Consequently the revenues derived from imports under the Dingley Act for the month of February this year were sufficient to equalize the expenditures, while as a revenue getter, when we include the receipts from internal revenue as well as customs, the Dingley Act comes fully up to the expectations of its friends.

Compared with the Wilson Act the Dingley law has yielded revenues from all sources as follows:

	Wilson law.	Dingley law.
First month	$22,621,228	$19,023,614
Second month	19,139,240	21,933,098
Third month	19,411,403	24,391,415
Fourth month	21,866,136	25,168,987
Fifth month	27,804,399	27,931,494
Sixth month	22,888,057	28,795,227
Seventh month	25,470,575	28,572,358
Total	$159,201,038	$175,816,193

Balance in favor of Dingley law, $16,617,743.

The Wilson bill was in operation nine months before it showed surplus revenue. The amount, then, was only $3,932,445, while the Dingley Act yielded a surplus of $1,973,102.47 at the end of the sixth month of its existence and in spite of the fact that it bore the burden of vast anticipatory importations rushed through our custom-houses during March, April, May, June, and July, 1897, to take advantage of the lower rates and defective appraisement under the Wilson bill,

DOMESTIC EXPORTS FOR CALENDAR YEARS 1896 AND 1897.

President McKinley was installed but ten months at the close of the calendar year 1897, and the Dingley act was operative less than six months, yet, under the stimulus of Republican success and the wise legislation of the extra session of Congress, the domestic exports for 1897 rose to the unprecedented figure of $1,079,863,018, or a grand total, including exports of foreign merchandise, of $1,099,743,554, while the excess of exports over imports was $357,112,204, and the total value of exports in 1897 exceeded those of 1896 in the sum of $93,906,313, the exports of 1896 being themselves phenomenally large, owing, unquestionably, to the impetus given to the business enterprise of the country by the result of the election and the exceptional demand for our breadstuffs abroad. These figures are taken from the Monthly Summary for December, 1897 (page 828), prepared by the Bureau of Statistics, under the direction of Mr. Worthington C. Ford, a hold-over from the Cleveland Administration.

For the seven months ended January, 1898, our exports of merchandise amounted to $718,435,950, an increase of $63,258,823 over the same period of 1897, while we imported $340,620,389, or $22,657,628 less than for the same period of 1897, the exports for the seven months exceeding the exports for the seven months of the preceding year by $85,916,451.

Exports and imports for the single month of January, 1898, compared with January, 1897, were as follows:

EXPORTS.

January, 1898..	$108,489,455
January, 1897..	93,951,883
Increase, 1898..	$14,537,572

IMPORTS.

January, 1897..	$51,354,018
January, 1898...	50,802,909
Decrease in imports..	$551,109
Excess of exports over imports, January, 1898..	$57,686,546

GOLD EXPORTS.

At the same time our exports of gold coin and bullion for the seven months ended January, 1898, decreased $3,678,195, while the imports, amounting to $30,885,138, show a strong reverse tendency from the outflow of gold for several years under Cleveland.

FARM PRODUCTS AND IMPLEMENTS.

For the calendar year 1897, under a Republican Administration, the value of our exports of agricultural implements exceeded that of 1896 by $659,078, while our farmers sent abroad 52,697 head of cattle more than in 1896, at a gain of $2,803,120; of horses, 17,010 more than in 1896, at a gain of $2,016,128; of mules, 1,219 head more than in 1896, at a gain of $156,798; of other animals and fowls to the value of $137,870 more than in 1896, or, taking the lump sum of all, $5,113,916 more than in 1896, realized from the export of cattle, horses, mules, and other animals and fowls, exclusive of hogs and sheep. These are the official figures:

EXPORTS OF DOMESTIC ANIMALS.

	1896.		1897.	
	Head.	Value.	Head.	Value.
Cattle	394,772	$36,576,412	447,469	$39,379,532
Horses	28,632	3,601,137	45,642	5,617,265
Mules	6,534	475,106	7,753	631,904
All other,* and fowls		49,840		187,710
Total	429,938	$40,702,495	500,864	$45,816,411

* Exclusive of sheep and hogs.

	Animals.	Value.
1897 (Republican)	500,864	$45,816,411
1896 (Democratic)	429,938	40,702,495
Increase	70,926	$5,113,916

Other exports for the twelve months ending December 31 were:

	1896.	1897.
Wheat	$59,263,352	$99,625,440
Wheat flour	56,886,013	58,182,188
Corn	44,127,276	59,662,518
Barley	6,594,193	6,835,174
Bread and biscuits *	663,508	728,682
Buckwheat	229,544	737,325

* Not enumerated prior to July, 1896.

Total breadstuffs, 1897	$252,536,188
Total breadstuffs, 1896	182,806,242
Increase, 1897 over 1896	$69,729,946

Here is an excess in wheat exports for the calendar year 1897 over 1896 of $40,362,088; of corn $15,535,242, and of total bread-stuffs, as shown, $69,729,946—surely a pretty fair showing for the first year of the Republican Administration.

BRYAN'S OWN ORGAN ADMITS THE REVIVAL OF BUSINESS.

Even Mr. Bryan's personal organ, the Omaha World-Herald, of which he was editor, and in which he is said to be still a stockholder, admits that good times were returning, for it said editorially not long ago:

"**Every** Democratic newspaper in the land admits that business is improving, and rejoices that it is so. Only organs that support Republican administrations rejoice when American business is prostrate. This statement is backed up by the proof. If the Star doubts it, let it search the editorial pages of its Republican contemporaries, beginning about January 1, 1893, and ending promptly on November 4, 1896."

And following I present a compilation from the market quotations in the Omaha World-Herald, showing the price of farm products July 10, 1896 (the date of Mr. Bryan's nomination), and their price one year after McKinley's inauguration, March 10, 1898:

	July 10, 1896.	March 10, 1898.
Bar silver (New York)	$0 68⅞	$0 54¼
Beef steers	4 15	4 90
Cows	3 00	3 90
Heifers	3 00	4 10
Calves	5 00	6 00
Bulls	2 00	3 75
Stags	2 90	4 00
Stockers and feeders	3 55	5 30
Hogs	3 15	3 85
Stock sheep	3 25	3 90
Veal	06½	03
Extra short clears, dry salt	04½	06¾
Regular short clears, dry salt	04⅞	06¾
Bellies	04¾	07⅞
Lard, Calumet	04¾	05¾
Cheese, young American	09½	11½
Native steers	06¼	07
Pork loins	05½	06½
Shoulders	04½	05¼
Green hides, No. 1	04	07½
Green hides, No. 2	03	06½
Dry hides	09	14
Sheep pelts, green	40	75
Tallow	02½	02¾
Wool, unwashed, heavy	07	15
Wool, unwashed, light	09	18
Wool, washed, medium	18	23
Wool, tub washed	18	30
Wheat, western Nebraska and Dakota	63	82

	July 10, 1896.	March 10, 1898.
Wheat, No. 3, by carload (new)...	50	80
Rye	30	40
Flaxseed...	74	1 10
Flour, best patent...per 100 pounds...	1 85	2 70
Flour, second best patent...do......... ..	1 70	2 80
Corn (car)...	18	25
Oats (car)...	15	25
Bran...per ton..	8 00	11 50
Middlings..do.........	9 00	12 50
Chop ....do.	9 00	10 50
Linseed meal	17 00	28 00
CHICAGO MARKETS.		
No. 2 red wheat...	56½	1 08
No. 2 cash corn..	26½	29½
No. 2 white oats...	18	30

IMPROVEMENTS IN AGRICULTURAL PRODUCTS.

In order to show more conclusively still than by the evidence of Mr. Bryan's own paper that prosperity has affected our farmers, I ask leave to incorporate in these remarks an interview with Statistician John Hyde, of the Agricultural Department, relative to the improvement during the last twelve months in all lines of agriculture, which I clip from the Kansas City Journal of March 16, 1898:

"A careful estimate," said Mr. Hyde, in speaking of the general result of his investigations, "shows that in 1897 the farmers received for their wheat and other cereals $130,000,000 in excess of such receipts for 1896, and at least $80,000,000 more than in any year since 1892. The hay crop, although the largest, with one exception, ever raised in this country, commanded an increased price per ton; wool is much higher than at any time since 1893, and cotton is the only important product in which there is not substantial improvement over the conditions of a year ago."

"And have farm animals kept pace in the general rise?" asked the Journal correspondent.

"The figures relating to farm animals show still more clearly the improved conditions of the farmer. During 1897 the farm horses of the country increased in value over $25,000,000, the mules over $6,000,000, milch cows over $65,000,000, other cattle over $104,000,000, sheep over $25,000,000, and swine over $8,000,000—making a total increase of farm stock during the year of more than $236,000,000."

IMPROVEMENT IS GENERAL.

"Do you find this condition confined to any particular section or class of States?"

"Not to any. On the contrary, my reports from all over the country show the remarkable increase to be well distributed. There is not a single State or Territory in the Union that does not report an increase in the average farm price per head of cattle and sheep, and in most cases such increase includes all farm animals.

"In Georgia the total value of farm animals increased during 1897 $3,000,000; in Pennsylvania nearly $7,000,000; in Ohio, over $10,000,000; in Kansas, over $20,000,000, and in Nebraska, over $22,000,000, the increase in Kansas and Nebraska being in the single year 24 and 41 per cent., respectively. Combining the products of the soil and the values of the various farm animals, there is no doubt that the farmers of the country produced $500,000,000 more in value in 1897 than in the preceding year. This is considered a conservative estimate and well within the actual facts.

"The Department figures on the acreage and crops of various products of the soil show corn far in the lead with over 80,000,000 acres and a total yield of 1,902,967,000 bushels. Wheat comes next with 39,000,000 acres and 530,150,000 bushels. Oats has 25,730,000 acres and a yield of almost 700,000,-000 bushels. Rye has 1,703,000 acres and 27,363,000 bushels; barley, 2,719,116 acres and 66,600,000 bushels; potatoes, 2,534,577 acres and 164,000,000 bushels. Hay takes an important place, with over 42,000,000 acres and a yield of 60,664,270 tons, being in value the third product, corn and wheat taking the first and second places, respectively.

NUMBERS AND VALUES.

"The following table gives the totals of the Department's estimates of the number and value of the live stock in the country and the average price per head:

/	Number.	Average price per head.	Total valuation.
Horses	13,960,911	$34 26	$476,362,407
Mules	2,256,668	43 66	99,032,062
Milch cows	15,840,886	27 45	434,813 828
Oxen, etc.	29,264,197	20 92	616,296,634
Swine	39,769,893	4 39	174,351,409
Sheep	37,656,960	2 46	92,721,133

"A great variation is shown in the figures by different States, both as to the number, of course, as well as the average value per head. Massachusetts, for instance, has 63,162 horses, with a total valuation of $4,001,549, whereas Vermont has 95,469, with a total valuation of only $3,781,069. The average price per head in Massachusetts is thus $63.35, against $44.14 per head in Vermont.

"In Rhode Island the average is $76, the highest of any State. Illinois has the greatest total value, $37,512,129, although her average valuation per head is only $36.05. She has 1,040,767 horses. Texas, with 1,148,500, has the greatest number of horses, but as their average value is only $17.30, her total valuation is comparatively small, being $19,866,178.

"The figures on the number and prices of mules show the favor these animals find in the South. Georgia, for instance, has but 111,380 horses, valued at $5,077,000, against New York's 608,916 horses, valued at $33,000,000, but she has 163,202 mules, valued at $10,691,000, against 4,511 mules for New York, valued at $262,745. Wisconsin has less than 5,000 mules, but South Carolina has 98,340, valued at $61 each, and representing $6,024,000. Texas has the greatest number, 265,349, valued at $8,214,000.

NEW YORK LEADS IN MILCH COWS.

"In milch cows New York takes the lead, having 1,402,164, valued at $44,-869,248, with an average of $32. Pennsylvania has 928,905, with an average value of $29.60; total, $27,495,000. Massachusetts has 174,554, with an average value of $32.80. Rhode Island again averages the highest, with $34, although she has but 25,258 milch cows.

"In oxen and cattle other than milch cows Texas takes the lead both as to number and aggregate value. She has 4,823,295, at an average value of $15.27, and a total value of $73,639,656. Rhode Island again has the highest average value, $30.18, and has 10,676 of such animals. Massachusetts has 74,134, at an average value of $25.82. Pennsylvania has 550,981, with an average value of $23.64. Kansas and Iowa have each above 2,000,000 such animals, and Illinois, Missouri, Nebraska, and Montana above 1,000,000 each.

"In sheep there is even more variation in the prices than in other articles. The far Western States have the advantage in numbers, but the Eastern and Middle States in average values. Montana has the largest number; New York has the highest value per head. New York has 825,446, worth $3,332,739, the average value being $4.04. Montana has 3,247,641, with a total value of $7,604,081, and an average value of $2.40. Ohio, however, has a combination of numbers and values which carries her total valuation to $8,274,-777. Her sheep are worth each an average of $3.42, and she has 2,316,346 of them. The Oregon sheep are worth only $1.86 per head, while those of Alabama are still lower, being $1.20 each.

"In hogs the variation in prices is also very great, ranging from $2.13 for the average Florida razorback to $9.83 for the Connecticut porker. Iowa takes the lead both as to number and total valuation, having 3,625,831 animals, valued at $21,704,225, with an average value of $5.99 per hog. Pennsylvania has 1,033,001, averaging $6.78 each. Nevada has the lowest total, having only 11,000 hogs, averaging $3.94 in value each.

EXPORTS UNDER REPUBLICAN AND DEMOCRATIC ADMINISTRATIONS.

Mr. Chairman, the movements of domestic exports show a peculiar sensibility to the influence of parties. From 1881 to 1897, a period of sixteen years, embracing two Democratic and two Republican Administrations, the exports of domestic merchandise show a steady rise under Republican power and a steady decline under Democratic. The Garfield-Arthur Administration was in power from 1881 to 1884, inclusive. The exports ranged as follows:

1881	$814,162,951
1882	749,911,309
1883	777,523,718
1884	733,768,764
Total	$3,075,366,742

Cleveland was elected in 1884, and during the four years of his administration we exported:

1885	$675,593,506
1886	699,515,430
1887	703,319,692
1888	679,597,477
Total	$2,756,026,105

In other words, comparing the footing for these two periods, the election of a Democratic Administration cost the producers of this country in four years $319,340,637.

Cleveland was succeeded by a Republican Administration, that of President Harrison, and for the four years ensuing the exports again rose.

1889	$814,154,864
1890	845,990,003
1891	957,333,551
1892	923,237,315
Total	$3,540,725,333
Under Cleveland's first Administration	2,756,026,105
Increase under Harrison	$784,699,228

Cleveland succeeded Harrison, and again, under a Democratic Administration, the demand for our home products fell off:

1893	$854,729,454
1894	807,312,116
1895	807,742,415
1896	986,830,080
Total	$3,456,614,065

Here is a loss in four years to our producers of $84,111,268. In other words, the two Democratic Administrations since 1885 have cost American producers in loss of exports a total of $403,451,905.

AMERICAN TIN PLATE FOR EUROPE.

The evidence of a general revival of business among our manufacturers is overwhelming. I read the following Associated Press telegram to show what protection has been doing for the tin-plate industry:

ELWOOD, IND., *August 11, 1897.*

"The first tin plate manufactured in America to be sent to Europe is, according to local manufacturers, that started to-day by the American Tin Plate Company, of Elwood, on its way to Italy.

"It was a carload, consisting of 500 boxes of the most expensive tin plate made here, and it is said that this will be followed by other shipments, because of a growing demand abroad for American tin plate. The company will to-morrow make a similar shipment to England."

After the passage of the McKinley law, which created this industry, Democratic stump orators all over the United States declared it to be a physical impossibility to compete with the tin-plate manufacturers of Wales, and denounced Major McKinley and the Republican party for attempting to develop this industry at home.

TIN PLATE—DECLINE IN IMPORTS SINCE THE McKINLEY ACT.

The imports of tin plate reached their high-water mark in 1891, when the McKinley bill took effect and practically turned the industry of tin-plate making over to the American manufacturer. From the date of the enactment of this measure the importations steadily decreased in proportion as the American manufacturers were able to supply the demand. This decrease of imports is shown in the following table compiled by the Bureau of Statistics of the Treasury Department:

Year.	Quantity.	Value.
	Pounds.	
1891	1,036,489,074	$35,746,920
1892	422,176,202	12,315,562
1893	628,425,902	17,565,640
1894	454,160,826	11,969,518
1895	508,038,938	12,144,080
1896	385,138,983	8,950,656
1897	230,073,683	5,344,638

The amount of manufactures of domestic tin exported in 1897 was valued at $284,020 as compared with $268,581 for 1896, an increase of $15,439.

SOUTHERN COTTON INDUSTRY GROWING AT THE EXPENSE OF NEW ENGLAND MILLS.

A great deal was said in recent debates about the strike of the cotton-mill operatives in New England.

The condition of the New England cotton-spinning industry during the early part of the year was due to perfectly natural causes, and can not be distorted into evidence of a failure of prosperity. Strikes are in themselves no proof of hard times.

The great Homestead strike occurred in the most prosperous year in the history of the United States. The New England strike was chiefly due to a reduction of wages made necessary by the competition of the Southern cotton mills. There are laws in New England restricting the hours of labor, regulating child labor in factories, supervising the health and educational condition of the working classes, and lastly, wages are better than in the South.

These things militated against New England spinners. The rapid growth of this industry in the South is shown by the valuable table compiled by Mr. Alfred B. Shepperson, of New York, and embodied in the Statistical Abstract for 1897, showing the amount of cotton taken for home consumption from 1848 to 1897. Only the last ten years are here shown; the figures stand for thousands of bales:

Year.	Taken for Home Consumption.		
	By Northern Mills.	By Southern Mills.	Total.
1887..	1,687	401	2,088
1888..	1,805	456	2,261
1889..	1,790	480	2,270
1890..	1,780	545	2,325
1891..	2,027	613	2,640
1892..	2,172	684	2,856
1893..	1,652	723	2,375
1894..	1,580	711	2,291
1895..	2,019	852	2,871
1896..	1,605	900	2,505
1897..	1,793	999	2,792

It will be observed that in 1893 and 1896 the total output of the Northern mills was less than that of 1887, while the increase for 1897 over that of 1887 was but 106,000 bales, whereas the Southern mills show a steady increase every year, and the output in 1897 was 589,000 bales greater than that of ten years before. Nearly all the Southern cotton mills were started by New England capital, and the successful way in which this new industry is competing with the old mills of New England, many of them with superannuated manufacturing machinery, only goes to show what well-directed efforts may do for the manufacturing interests of the South.

RAILROAD FREIGHT RATES—THEIR RELATION TO THE COST OF FARM PRODUCTS.

No careful student of economic conditions can afford to ignore the relation of railroad freight rates to the market price of farm products and merchandise. According to the tables prepared by Mr. John P. Meany, editor of Poor's Railroad Manual, there has been a very material reduction in rates since "the good old bimetallic times." In those times it cost the farmer nearly three times as much to ship a ton of his products to market as it does now. I call attention to the following table of average receipts per ton per mile of leading railroads for the years 1870, 1880, and 1896:

	1870.	1880.	1896.
	Cents.	Cents.	Cents.
Lines east of Chicago..	1.61	0.87	0.60
West and Northwest lines..	2.61	1.44	.98
Southwestern lines...	2.95	1.65	.99
Southern lines..	2.39	1.16	.68
Transcontinental lines..	4.50	2.21	1.07
Average...	1.99	1.17	.78

In 1872, one year before the demonetization of silver, it cost an average of 33.5 cents to ship a bushel of wheat from Chicago to New York. In 1876 the average rate was 16.5 cents, and in 1897 it was only 12.32 cents. It cost an average of $1.3512 in 1868 to ship a barrel of flour from Chicago to New York. In 1874 the cost was reduced to 95.45 cents, and in 1897 it cost but 41.07 cents, or 94.05 cents less than during "the good old bimetallic times." In 1876 the rate on a bushel of wheat from St. Louis to New York by rail was 39.5 cents. In 1897 it was but 23.64 cents. To ship a bushel of wheat from St. Louis to Liverpool in 1883 cost 22.66 cents, and in 1897 the cost was but 12.89 cents.

APPROPRIATIONS FOR THE WAR WITH SPAIN.

Mr. CANNON said: The sum of $892,527,991.16 has been appropriated at this session of Congress. This includes $117,836,220 of permanent appropriations to meet sinking-fund requirements of and interest on the public debt, and for other objects, and $361,788,095.11 to meet expenditures of the war with Spain.

Deducting the last two from the sum first mentioned, there remains $412,903,676.05, representing the appropriations made at the present session to meet all ordinary expenses of the Government; which sum is only $4,246,816.75 more than was appropriated at the last session of the last Congress for the same purposes (including the appropriations made during the recent extra session), which apparent excess is almost doubly offset by the increased appropriation of $8,070,872.46 for the payment of pensions on account of the fiscal year 1898, provided for in a deficiency act at this session.

No river and harbor bill has been passed at this session; but the sundry civil act carries $14,031,613.56 to meet contracts authorized by previous Congresses for river and harbor works.

No laws authorizing the construction of public buildings in any of the cities throughout the country have been enacted, and otherwise the legislation authorizing expenditures and appropriations has been confined to the actual necessities of the Government, and to meet all demands incident to the existing war.

The following tables show, by acts, the appropriations made for war expenditures, and also the history of the appropriation bills for the session.

In addition to the appropriations made specifically for expenses of the conduct of the war since its inception and for the first six months of the fiscal year beginning July 1, 1898, contracts have been authorized on the naval appropriation act for new war vessels and for their armament, for which Congress will be called upon in the future to appropriate to an amount estimated at $19,216,156.

APPROPRIATIONS TO MEET EXPENSES INCIDENT TO THE WAR.

For the National defense, Act March 9, 1898	$50,117,000 00
Army and Navy deficiencies, Act May 4, 1898	34,625,725 71
Naval appropriation act, May 4, 1898—amount of increase over preceding naval appropriation act	23,095,549 49
Fortification appropriation act, May 7, 1898—amount of increase over act as passed by House	5,232,582 00
Naval auxiliary act, May 26, 1898	3,000,000 00
Additional clerical force, War Department, Auditors' Offices, etc., Act May 31, 1898	227,976 45
Life-saving Service, Act June 7, 1898	70,000 00
Army and Navy deficiencies, Act June 8, 1898	18,015,000 00
Appropriations in act to provide ways and means to meet war expenditures, June 13, 1898	600,000 00
Army, Navy, and other war expenses for six months, beginning July 1, 1898, in general deficiency act	226,694,261 46
Expenses of bringing home remains of soldiers	200,000 00
Total	$361,788,095 11

The tables referred to are as follows:

TITLE.	Law, 1898–99.		Law, 1897–98.
	Date.	Amount.	Amount
Agriculture	March 22...	$3,509,202 00	$3,182,902 00
Army	March 15...	23,192,692 00	23,129,344 30
Diplomatic and consular	March 9...	1,752,208 76	1,695,308 76
District of Columbia	June 30...	6,425,880 07	6,186,991 06
Fortification	May 7...	9,377,494 00	9,517,141 00
Indian	July 1...	7,660,814 90	7,674,120 89
Legislative, etc	March 15...	21,625,846 65	21,690,766 90
Military Academy	March 5...	458,639 23	479,572 83
Navy	May 4...	56,098,783 68	33,003,234 19
Pension	March 14...	141,233,830 00	141,263,880 00

Democratic Opposition to War Measures.

" Since the outbreak of the Spanish War they have committed—

That is, the Democrats in the House—

about every error possible. Giving a grudging sup= port to the various imperative measures which fol- lowed the original appropriation of $50,000,000 for the national defense, they lined themselves up almost solidly against the War-Revenue Bill, and capped the climax last Wednesday by casting the bulk of their vote in opposition to the annexation of Hawaii, a consummation devoutly desired by a two-thirds majority in both Houses of Congress and four-fifths of the American people without regard to party.

"The result is plain. What was intended to be, and what was originally a purely American war has degenerated in the eyes of the country into a Republican war with all that that implies.

"The Republican President stands before the world to-day as one pursuing a patriotic policy in the teeth of unreasoning Democratic opposition. When victory comes to him and Spain is humbled in the dust; when America's possessions are enriched by the addition of Hawaii, the Philippines, Puerto Rico, and perhaps the Canaries, Mr. McKinley can rise and truthfully say :

"'This is my work—mine and the Republican party's. As we saved the Union in 1861, so now do we glorify it with victory. Ours the triumph, ours the spoils, including a majority in the new House of Representatives !'"

"And the people, on the 8th of November, will cry 'Amen.'"—*An editorial published in a leading Democratic newspaper of the City of Washington, the Times, dated the 22d day of June, 1898.*

Congressional Record, p. 7281, June 29, 1898.

DEMOCRATIC OPPOSITION TO WAR MEASURES.

MR. HAY (Dem. of Virginia). IT DOES SEEM TO ME TO BE A CU-RIOUS FACT THAT NO BILL CAN BE REPORTED HERE WHICH LOOKS TO THE REAL DEFENSE OF THE COUNTRY AND TO THE REAL PUR-POSE OF DEFEATING THE FOE WITH WHOM WE ARE CONTENDING, WITHOUT ADVERSE CRITICISM BEING MADE, AND, IN MY HUMBLE JUDGMENT, THAT SORT OF CRITICISM WHICH OUGHT TO HAVE NO WEIGHT WITH THE MEMBERS OF THE HOUSE.

[Record, p. 5611, May 18, 1898.]

MR. BAILEY (Dem., of Texas). I simply desire to call the attention of the House to the fact that on several occasions within the last thirty days this House has been called upon to vote appropriations and permissions to meet extraordinary cases, and yet this House is not in the possession of any fact which warrants it in supposing that the executive department believes that any extraordinary emergency is upon the country.

ONLY A SHORT TIME AGO WE WERE COMPELLED TO VOTE TO PLACE $50,000,000 UNDER THE ABSOLUTE DIRECTION OF THE PRESI-DENT OF THE UNITED STATES. The situation at that time appeared so critical that no gentleman on this side was willing to resist that; and we all voted for it.

[Record, p. 3897, April 4, 1898.]

MR. RIDGLEY, OF KANSAS, (POPULIST), OBJECTS.

NAVAL BATTALION, DISTRICT OF COLUMBIA.

MR. HILBORN. Mr. Speaker, I ask unanimous consent to take from the table Senate bill No. 1316, to provide for organizing a naval battalion in the District of Columbia, and ask for its immediate consideration.

* * * * *

THE SPEAKER. Is there objection to the present consideration of the bill?

MR. BAILEY. Mr. Speaker, reserving the right to object, I would like an explanation of this bill. But in the first place I should like to ask the gentleman from California this question: Does this bill propose to perma-nently increase the naval force of the United States?

MR. HILBORN. As the bill is reported it does to the extent of these three companies forming this battalion of naval militia in the District. It will increase the general militia force of the District, of course, to that ex-tent.

* * * * *

MR. RIDGELY. I object, Mr. Speaker.

THE SPEAKER. Objection is made by the gentleman from Kansas.

[Record, pp. 4134, 4135, April 12, 1898.]

CUBA.

MR. ADAMS. Mr. Speaker, I am instructed by the Committee on Foreign Affairs to present the following resolution, and to ask unanimous consent for its immediate consideration.

THE SPEAKER. The gentleman from Pennsylvania, on behalf of the Committee on Foreign Affairs, asks unanimous consent for the present consideration of the following resolution.

The Clerk read as follows:

The Committee on Foreign Affairs, to whom were referred House joint resolutions Nos. 54, 58, 86, 94, 173, 186, 193, 200, 201, 204, 205, 206, 207, 208, 209, 210, 211 212, 217, 219, 220, 224, and 231, and House resolutions Nos. 256 and 279 and House concurrent resolutions Nos. 5 and 28, and Senate joint resolution No. 26, having fully considered the same and the numerous petitions relating to the subject, report the following joint resolution as a substitute for the said several resolutions and recommend its adoption. The committee refer to the facts set forth in the message of the President to Congress, dated April 11, 1898, to the consular reports accompanying it and to the reports of the naval court of inquiry upon the destruction of the U. S. battleship "Maine," in Havana harbor, February 15, 1898, in support of the joint resolution herewith reported.

ROBT. ADAMS, JR.,
Chairman, pro tempore.

Whereas, the Government of Spain, for three years past has been waging war on the Island of Cuba against a revolution by the inhabitants thereof, without making any substantial progress toward the suppression of said revolution, and has conducted the warfare in a manner contrary to the laws of nations, by methods inhuman and uncivilized, causing the death by starvation of more than 200,000 innocent noncombatants, the victims being for the most part helpless women and children, inflicting intolerable injury to the commercial interests of the United States, involving the destruction of the lives and property of many of our citizens, entailing the expenditure of millions of money in patrolling our coasts and policing the high seas in order to maintain our neutrality; and

Whereas, this long series of losses, injuries, and burdens for which Spain is responsible has culminated in the destruction of the United States battleship "Maine" in the harbor of Havana and in the death of 260 of our seamen:

Resolved by the Senate and House of Representatives of the United States of America in Congress assembled, That the President is hereby authorized and directed to intervene at once to stop the war in Cuba, to the end and with the purpose of securing permanent peace and order there and establishing by the free action of the people thereof a stable and independent government of their own in the Island of Cuba. And the President is hereby authorized and empowered to use the land and naval forces of the United States to execute the purpose of this resolution.

[Loud applause.]

THE SPEAKER. Is there objection?

MR. BAILEY. Reserving the right to object, I will ask that the views of the minority go with this report.

MR. BERRY. Pending the motion—

MR. ADAMS. I yield to the gentleman from Kentucky (Mr. Berry) for the purpose of offering the minority resolution and report, reserving my parliamentary rights.

THE SPEAKER. The Chair understands there is no objection to consideration.

MR. BAILEY. I reserve the right to object, because whether we shall object or not will depend in some measure upon whether a fair understanding about the debate can be arrived at. Before we proceed to that, I desire both propositions to be before the House.

MR. QUIGG. I ask for the regular order.

MR. BAILEY. Which is an objection.

THE SPEAKER. The gentleman objects.

MR. BAILEY. The gentleman from New York (Mr. Quigg) objected.

THE SPEAKER. The gentleman from Texas objects.

MR. BAILEY. "The gentleman from Texas" did not object. "The gentleman from Texas" reserved his right to object.

THE SPEAKER. Is there objection?

MR. BAILEY. "The gentleman from Texas" reserves his right to object.

THE SPEAKER. Is there objection to the request of the gentleman from Pennsylvania?

MR. BAILEY. I ask permission that the gentleman from Kentucky—

THE SPEAKER. The Chair will announce whether there is objection or not.

MR. BAILEY. The Chair is determined to try to force the minority— (Cries of "Regular order!")

THE SPEAKER. Is there objection?

MR. BAILEY. I object.

THE SPEAKER. Objection is made by the gentleman from Texas.

[Record, pp. 4187, 4188, April 13, 1898.]

MR. BAILEY (DEM.), OF TEXAS, AGAINST PROMOTION.

INCREASE OF NUMBER OF REAR-ADMIRALS.

Mr. BOUTELLE of Maine. Mr. Speaker, by instruction of the Naval Committee, I offer the resolution which I send to the Clerk's desk. I will briefly say that under the Revised Statutes of the United States in time of war a promotion to the grade of rear-admiral is made only for distinguished gallantry in conflict with the enemy, upon resolutions granting the thanks of Congress, upon recommendation of the President of the United States. In accordance with that statute, the Committee on Naval Affairs have instructed me to introduce a bill in this body for immediate consideration, and I may state that a similar bill has been or will be introduced in another body, in order to enable the Executive of the United States to carry out without delay the wishes of the American people that the highest honor possible under our laws may be paid to that distinguished naval officer who has illustrated the heroism and glory of the American Navy by adding another brilliant page to its history. I ask immediate consideration of the bill for the addition of another rear-admiral, for purposes understood by the House.

The Clerk read the bill, as follows

A bill (H. R. 10251) fixing the number of rear-admirals in the United States Navy.

Be it enacted by the Senate and House of Representatives of the United States of America in Congress assembled, That the number of rear-admirals in the United States Navy now allowed by law be, and is hereby, increased from six to seven, and this act shall be construed and taken as validating and making in force and effect any promotion to said rank of rear-admiral in the United States Navy made heretofore or hereafter and during the existing war and based upon the thanks of Congress.

Mr. BAILEY. Mr. Speaker, before unanimous consent is given I would like to ask the gentleman from Maine if under the existing law Commodore Dewey would not be entitled to promotion by virtue of the fact that the Congress has thanked him by name?

Mr. BOUTELLE of Maine. Under the statute he would not. There is no rear-admiralship to which he could be promoted, and the statute provides that during the time of war promotion to the grade of admiral can only be made under conditions like those of the present. To enable this promotion to be made this bill creates an additional position of rear-admiral, to which this officer, in the discretion of the Executive, may be appointed. I will state further to the gentleman that this action of mine and the Committee on Naval Affairs is based on consultation with the executive department, with the Senate, and ourselves, and is absolutely essential to carry out the purpose which I infer is in the heart of every member of the House, to enable the President to confer upon Commodore George Dewey the well-earned title of rear-admiral in the United States Navy.

Mr. BAILEY. Mr. Speaker, I desire to say that no title and no office that the Congress can confer upon Commodore Dewey will increase the respect in which the American people hold him. I am sure that he would rather enjoy the satisfaction that comes from this well-earned victory than to take any additional honor and emolument which Congress could confer upon him. I DO NOT INTEND IN THIS CASE TO MAKE AN OBJECTION, FOR IT IS A PECULIARLY MERITORIOUS ONE; BUT I THINK WE MIGHT AS WELL UNDERSTAND NOW THAT THE SPIRIT OF PATRIOTISM SO HIGHLY COMMENDABLE IS NOT TO BE MADE A PRETEXT FOR CREATING A LARGE NUMBER OF IMPORTANT AND HIGHLY SALARIED OFFICES. THIS PARTICULAR CASE I SHALL NOT OBJECT TO; BUT IT MUST BE A VERY EXCEPTIONAL CASE IF I CONSENT TO THE CREATION OF ANY NEW AND PERMANENT OFFICE DURING THIS WAR.

Mr. BOUTELLE of Maine. I desire to say that this is a case without exception, and I deem it without a parallel, without a precedent in the history of any war.

The bill was ordered to be engrossed and read a third time; and being engrossed, it was read the third time, and passed.

MR. McMILLIN (DEM.), OF TENNESSEE, OBJECTS.

NAVAL HOSPITAL CORPS.

MR. BOUTELLE of Maine. Mr. Speaker, I move that the House resolve itself into Committee of the Whole House on the state of the Union for the consideration of the bill I send to the desk.

* * * * *

THE SPEAKER. The Clerk will report the bill called up by the gentleman from Maine (Mr. Boutelle).

The Clerk read as follows:

A bill (H. R. 10220) to organize a hospital corps of the Navy of the United States, to define its duties and regulate its pay.

Be it enacted, etc., That a hospital corps of the United States Navy is hereby established, and shall consist of pharmacists, hospital stewards, hospital apprentices (first class), and hospital apprentices; and for this purpose the Secretary of the Navy is empowered to appoint twenty-five pharmacists with the rank, pay, and privileges of warrant officers and to enlist, or cause to be enlisted, as many hospital stewards, hospital apprentices (first class), and hospital apprentices as in his judgment may be necessary, and to limit or fix the number, and to make such regulations as may be required for their enlistment and government. Enlisted men in the Navy or the Marine Corps shall be eligible for transfer to the hospital corps, and vacancies occurring in the grade of pharmacist shall be filled by the Secretary of the Navy by selection from those holding the rate of hospital steward.

Sec. 2. That all necessary ambulance and hospital service at naval hospitals, naval stations, navy-yards, and marine barracks, and on the vessels of the Navy, Coast Survey, and Fish Commission, shall be performed by the members of said corps, and the corps shall be permanently attached to the Medical Department of the Navy, and shall be included in the effective strength of the Navy and be counted as part of the enlisted force provided by law, and shall be subject to the laws and regulations for the government of the Navy.

Sec. 3. That the pay of hospital stewards shall be $60 a month, the pay of hospital apprentices (first class) $24 a month, and the pay of hospital apprentices $18 a month, with the increase on account of length of service as is now or may hereafter be allowed by law to other enlisted men in the Navy.

Sec. 4. That all benefits derived from existing laws, or that may hereafter be allowed by law, to other warrant officers or enlisted men in the Navy shall be allowed in the same manner to the warrant officers or enlisted men in the hospital corps of the Navy.

Sec. 5. That all acts and parts of acts, so far as they conflict with the provisions of this act, are hereby repealed.

THE SPEAKER. Is there objection to the consideration of the bill under the motion proposed by the gentleman from Maine?

MR. BAILEY. Mr. Speaker, reserving the right to object, I would like to have some explanation of this measure.

THE SPEAKER. The gentleman from Maine desires to move that the House consider the bill in the House as in Committee of the Whole.

MR. BAILEY. Which motion would not be in order.

THE SPEAKER. It would not be in order, of course, without consent.

* * * * *

MR. McMILLIN. Mr. Speaker, until I can get the information which the report fails to give us I object.

MR. BOUTELLE of Maine. **The gentleman** from Tennessee objects?
THE SPEAKER. The gentleman objects.

[Record, pp. 5440, 5443, May 12, 1898.]

MR. UNDERWOOD (DEM.), OF ALA., OBJECTS.

HOSPITAL CORPS OF UNITED STATES NAVY.

Mr. BOUTELLE of Maine. Mr. Speaker, I desire to call up the bill
(H. R. 10220) to organize a hospital corps of the Navy of the United States,
to define its duties, and regulate its pay.

The bill was read, as follows:

Be it enacted, etc., That a hospital corps of the United States Navy
is hereby established, and shall consist of pharmacists, hospital stewards,
hospital apprentices (first class), and hospital apprentices; and for this
purpose the Secretary of the Navy is empowered to appoint twenty-five
pharmacists with the rank, pay, and privileges of warrant officers, and
to enlist, or cause to be enlisted, as many hospital stewards, hospital
apprentices (first class), and hospital apprentices as in his judgment may
be necessary, and to limit or fix the number, and to make such regulations
as may be required for their enlistment and government. Enlisted men
in the Navy or the Marine Corps shall be eligible for transfer to the
hospital corps, and vacancies occurring in the grade of pharmacist shall
be filled by the Secretary of the Navy by selection from those holding
the rate of hospital steward.

Sec. 2. That all necessary hospital and ambulance service at naval
hospitals, naval stations, navy-yards, and marine barracks, and on vessels
of the Navy, Coast Survey, and Fish Commission, shall be performed by
the members of said corps, and the corps shall be permanently attached
to the Medical Department of the Navy, and shall be included in the
effective strength of the Navy and be counted as a part of the enlisted
force provided by law, and shall be subject to the laws and regulations
for the government of the Navy.

Sec. 3. That the pay of hospital stewards shall be $60 a month, the
pay of hospital apprentices (first class) $24 a month, and the pay of
hospital apprentices $18 a month, with the increase on account of length
of service as is now or may hereafter be allowed by law to other enlisted
men in the Navy.

Sec. 4. That all benefits derived from existing laws, or that may hereafter be allowed by law, to other warrant officers or enlisted men in the
Navy shall be allowed in the same manner to the warrant officers or enlisted men in the hospital corps of the Navy.

Sec. 5. That all acts and parts of acts, so far as they conflict with the
provisions of this act, are hereby repealed.

* * * * *

Mr. UNDERWOOD. Does not this bill increase the pay of the officers?

Mr. BOUTELLE of Maine. It makes a slight increase in the pay, the
aggregate amount being something like $11,000 a year.

Mr. UNDERWOOD. Why should the pay of these officers be increased
at this time?

Mr. BOUTELLE of Maine. Because it is desirable to get a superior
class of men. The original bill provided that the pay of the hospital
apprentices should be $24 a month of the first class and $18 a month
for the second class, but the Surgeon-General has called my attention since

to the slowness of the enlistment and the desirability of increasing this wage .rate sufficiently to enable them to get more quickly the men they desire.

Mr. UNDERWOOD. I do not think we ought at this time to increase the wages of these officers.

Mr. BOUTELLE of Maine. Perhaps the gentleman does not fully understand that the wages that are paid to the petty officers of the Navy have always been determined by the Department.

Mr. UNDERWOOD. But you are determining by this bill to increase it from what it is now.

Mr. BOUTELLE of Maine. This limits the amount to that rating, whereas the Department may make a rate of pay much exceeding this if they find the exigencies of the service require it, unless the limitation is put in here.

Mr. UNDERWOOD. In view of the fact that the country is being taxed by unusual and extraordinary expenses, I do not think we ought to increase the pay of these officers at this time.

MR. BOUTELLE of Maine. Well, it is the privilege of any member to take exception to any part of this bill or to place his own judgment about a matter of that kind against the judgment of officers who are carrying on the war now in progress. For myself, I feel under obligations to pay the very greatest deference to

* * * * *

Mr. UNDERWOOD. I will say to the gentleman again that if he will limit his bill to the present war, I will not object to it.

Mr. GAINES. There ought to be a larger increase in the wounded in this war before there is an increase in wages.

Mr. BOUTELLE of Maine. Then the gentleman wants to see more wounded men?

Mr. UNDERWOOD. I demand the regular order, Mr. Speaker.

Mr. BOUTELLE of Maine. Does the gentleman object to the consideration of this bill? Mr. Speaker, I desire the question put to the House.

The SPEAKER. The gentleman from Alabama demands the regular order, which is equivalent to an objection.

[Record, pp. 5767, 5768, May 24, 1898.]

MR. UNDERWOOD (DEM.), OF ALA., OBJECTS.

POST QUARTERMASTER-SERGEANTS OF THE UNITED STATES ARMY.

Mr. HULL. Mr. Speaker, I ask unanimous consent for the immediate consideration of the bill (H. R. 10051), to increase the number of post quartermaster-sergeants of the United States Army.

The Clerk read the bill, as follows:

Be it enacted, etc., That the number of post quartermaster-sergeants of the Army be increased by the addition of twenty-five post quartermaster-sergeants, to be appointed by the Secretary of War in the manner now provided for by law.

The SPEAKER. Is there objection to the present consideration of the bill which has been reported?

Mr. SIMPSON. Reserving the right to object, I hope we shall have some explanation of it.

MR. McMILLIN. I ask that the report be read.

Mr. HULL. I ask that the report be read, which will fully set it out.

The report (by Mr. Hull) was read, as follows:

* * * *, *

The SPEAKER. Is there objection to the present consideration of the bill?

Mr. UNDERWOOD. Mr. Speaker, in consideration of the importance of these bills, and that I do not think they are of such urgent nature as to need to be considered at once, believing that they ought to be considered in the regular way and not by unanimous consent when there is evidently no quorum of the House present, I shall be compelled to demand the regular order.

The SPEAKER. The gentleman demands the regular order.

[Record, pp. 6036. 6037, June 1, 1895.]

MR. UNDERWOOD (DEM.), OF ALA., OBJECTS.

MR. HULL. Mr. Speaker, I ask unanimous consent that Saturday next be set apart for the consideration of bills from the Committee on Military Affairs which have received the unanimous support of the committee. There are four or five bills that ought to be considered at an early day. One pertains to the Inspector-General's Department, one to the Ordnance Department, one to the Engineer's Department, and another bill that will fix the status of the chaplains of the volunteer regiments. These bills ought to be considered and passed this week.

THE SPEAKER pro tempore. The Chair would suggest to the gentleman that there is already a special order for Saturday.

* * * * *

MR. HULL. Well, I will make the request for next Tuesday.

MR. UNDERWOOD. Mr. Speaker, I am unwilling to give unanimous consent for the consideration of bills that I do not know what they are about, and unless the gentleman states what they are, and gives the House an opportunity to know what they are before unanimous consent is given, I shall object.

MR. HULL. I have stated what the bills relate to.

MR. SULZER. These bills are all unanimous reports of the committee.

MR. GAINES. Mr. Speaker, I think it is no more than right and just to the House that these bills should be printed before unanimous consent is asked for consideration.

MR. HULL. They are already printed. Mr. Speaker, I ask unanimous consent that next Tuesday be assigned for the consideration of these bills unanimously reported by the Committee on Military Affairs.

MR. UNDERWOOD. I object.

[Record, p. 6726, June 16, 1895.]

MR. BARTLETT (DEM.), OF GEORGIA, OBJECTS.

Mr. HULL. Mr. Speaker, I want again to ask unanimous consent that next Tuesday be set apart for the consideration of the following bills, reported unanimously by the Committee on Military Affairs—

* * * * *

Mr. McMILLIN. Is that the same request that was made this morning?

Mr. HULL. Yes, sir.

Mr. McMILLIN. While I did not object this morning, I did state that I thought when this request was made for unanimous consent for the consideration of bills, that we ought to be put in possession of the bill before consent is given, so that we should determine whether we should legislate or not by consent. I would suggest to the gentleman that I do not want to stand in the way of any proper bill, but I do not like, where large increases are to be made, for measures to come up in that way.

Mr. HULL. What was the gentleman's question?

Mr. GAINES. When did the committee agree to these bills?

Mr. HULL. The committee agreed on this bill for the Inspector-General's Department several days ago.

Mr. BARTLETT. I call for the regular order, Mr. Speaker.

Mr. HULL. I hope the gentleman will let us fix a day for the consideration of these bills; and I want to read the numbers of them, so that members may know what they are.

Mr. GAINES. The reason why I asked the question was because my colleague (Mr. Cox) has been absent for ten days, so that if any bills have been reported since that time, they have not been reported unanimously.

Mr. HULL. Some of these bills were agreed to since he left and others before he left.

Mr. BARTLETT. I call for the regular order.

[Record, pp. 6740, 6741, June 16, 1898.]

MR. BARTLETT (DEM.), OF GEORGIA, OBJECTS.

Mr. HULL. I ask unanimous consent that Thursday, the 23d instant, be set apart for the consideration of bills reported from the Committee on Military Affairs, and that only bills shall be considered which the committee by a vote have instructed the chairman to call up for consideration.

The SPEAKER pro tempore. The gentleman from Iowa asks unanimous consent for the present consideration of a resolution which will be reported by the Clerk.

Mr. BARTLETT. Reserving the right to object—I did not hear the resolution. Let it be read.

The SPEAKER pro tempore. Certainly.

The Clerk read as follows:

Resolved, That Thursday, the 23d instant, be set apart for the consideration of bills reported from the Committee on Military Affairs, and that only bills shall be considered which the committee by a vote have instructed the chairman to call up for consideration.

* * * * *

Mr. BARTLETT. If it is to be granted by unanimous consent, I object.

[Record, p. 6923, June 20, 1898.]

MR. BAIRD (DEM.), OF LOUISIANA, OBJECTS.

BUSINESS OF THE COMMITTEE ON MILITARY AFFAIRS.

Mr. HULL.   Mr. Speaker, I wish to ask unanimous consent again to fix next Tuesday for the consideration of bills reported from the Committee on Military Affairs, and I will be very glad to read the numbers of the bills and have them placed in the Record, so that all members may know what they are and what the committee proposes to call up at that time. They are reported from the Committee on Military Affairs and are mainly for the better administration of the Army during present conditions; they are recommended by the Secretary of War and are necessary for the successful prosecution of the business of the war.   Their passage is imperatively demanded in the interest of both efficiency and economy.

Mr. BAIRD objected.

[Record, p. 7032, June 23, 1898.]

"IT IS SIMPLY ANOTHER STEP IN THE SCHEME OF CENTRALIZATION, WHICH THIS EMERGENCY IS BEING USED TO PROMOTE."— *Mr. Maguire (Dem.), of California.*

MR. CANNON.   Mr. Speaker, I desire to report from the Committee on Appropriations, with favorable recommendation, and ask that it be considered at this time— which will take but a minute or two, I presume—a matter which I send to the desk.   I refer to Senate joint resolution No. 129.

THE SPEAKER.   The joint resolution will be read.

The joint resolution was read, as follows:

Joint resolution (S. 129) relative to suspension of part of section 355 of Revised Statutes, relative to erection of forts, fortifications, etc.

Resolved by the Senate and House of Representatives of the United States of America in Congress assembled, That in case of emergency, when, in the opinion of the President, the immediate erection of any temporary fort or fortification is deemed important and urgent, such temporary fort or fortification may be constructed upon the written consent of the owner of the land upon which such work is to be placed; and the requirements of section 355 of the Revised Statutes shall not be applicable in such cases.

MR. BAILEY.   Mr. Speaker, is this presented as a matter of privilege?

THE SPEAKER.   It is presented, as the Chair understands, for the unanimous consent of the House.

MR. BAILEY.   WELL, MR. SPEAKER, BEFORE ANY OTHER PREPARATIONS FOR WAR ARE MADE, I WANT TO KNOW WHETHER WE ARE GOING TO HAVE WAR.   I OBJECT TO THE IMMEDIATE CONSIDERATION OF THE RESOLUTION.

THE SPEAKER.   Objection is made to the consideration of the resolution at this time.

MR. CANNON.   Then let the bill take its place on the Calendar.   Or I move, if I may be recognized for that purpose, to suspend the rules and pass the bill.

THE SPEAKER.   The gentleman from Illinois moves to suspend the rules and pass the resolution, which will be again reported.

The resolution was again reported

MR. BAILEY.   I demand a second.

MR. McMILLIN. Let us have the resolution read again. There was so much confusion that it was impossible to hear it, and I ask that there be order while it is being read.

The resolution in the absence of objection was again reported.

MR. CANNON. Will the gentleman from Texas agree that a second may be considered as ordered?

MR. BAILEY. I have no objection to that.

THE SPEAKER. In the absence of objection, a second will be considered as ordered.

There was no objection.

MR. CANNON. Now, Mr. Speaker, I do not desire to do anything in the way of the discussion of this matter except to have the following letter read from the Chief of Engineers, and will then call attention to the section of the statute which is proposed to be suspended.

The Clerk read as follows:

> Office of the Chief of Engineers,
> United States Army,
> Washington, D. C., March 26, 1898.

Mr. Secretary: Section 355, Revised Statutes, prohibits the expenditure of any public money for forts, fortifications, etc., upon any site or land purchased by the United States until the written opinion of the Attorney-General shall be had in favor of validity of title and consent of legislature of State in which land may be to such purchase has been given.

I have the honor to suggest, in view of the present emergency, that Congress be requested to temporarily suspend this act during time of war, as there are important points on our seacoast where it will be absolutely necessary to erect temporary works immediately in case war should be declared and funds are available.

Very respectfully, your obedient servant,

> JOHN M. WILSON,
> Brigadier-General, Chief of Engineers, U. S. A.

Hon R. A. Alger, Secretary of War.

Approved.

> R. A. ALGER, Secretary of War.

March 31, 1898.

MR. CANNON. The Senate passed the resolution which was read a few minutes ago. I ask the Clerk to read that resolution again.

The resolution was again read.

MR. CANNON. Mr. Speaker—

MR. McMILLIN. Mr. Speaker, before the gentleman begins, I will call his attention to the fact that the resolution does not make any limitation upon the time within which it shall operate. It strikes me that if this is an emergency resolution, it ought not to be perpetual in its operation.

MR. CANNON. It has the emergency clause in it—in cases of emergency.

Mr. McMILLIN. But you leave it entirely to the discretion of the Executive to determine when an emergency exists.

Mr. CANNON. In the discretion of the President; that a temporary fort or fortification may be built if in the judgment of the President an emergency exists. Now, this is an amendment of the law covering such cases, and the law ought to be that permanently. It ought always to have been that.

This matter was very fully considered and inquiry was made by the sub-committee of which the gentleman from Texas (Mr. Sayers) is a member, and after consideration we believed it our duty to report this bill with a favorable recommendation.

Mr. MAGUIRE. When do you understand that operations could be commenced under this resolution, if it should pass?

Mr. CANNON. Oh, at once; wherever it is necessary.

Mr. MAGUIRE. Then, if operations may commence in time of perfect peace, when will they cease, under the language of the law?

Mr. CANNON. If this law is passed, it will go into effect as permanent law.

Mr. MAGUIRE. That is what I thought.

Mr. CANNON. Modifying section 355 of the Revised Statutes so that in cases of emergency the President shall have discretion to erect temporary forts and fortifications without awaiting the cession of jurisdiction by the legislature or the acquirement of title, only requiring that in such cases of emergency, for the erection of such temporary fortifications or forts, he shall have the written assent of the owner of the land.

Mr. MAGUIRE. But the President is permanently empowered, so long as this law stands, to be the judge of what constitutes an emergency requiring such action.

Mr. CANNON. Precisely, as the law, in the opinion of your committee, ought to be.

Mr. LENTZ. I desire to offer an amendment that will cover that ground.

Mr. CANNON. There is no amendment. The motion is to suspend the rules and pass the bill.

* * * * *

Mr. CANNON. No; I can not do that under the motion. (Cries of "Vote." "Vote!")

Mr. BAILEY. Mr. Speaker, I simply desire to call the attention of the House to the fact that on several occasions within the last thirty days this House has been called upon to vote appropriations and permissions to meet extraordinary cases, and yet this House is not in the possession of any facts which warrants it in supposing that the executive department believes that any extraordinary emergency is upon the country.

Only a short time ago we were compelled to vote to place $50,000,000 under the absolute discretion of the President of the United States. The situation at that time appeared so critical that no gentleman on this side was willing to resist that; and we all voted for it.

Mr. ARNOLD. Mr. Speaker, a point of order.

The SPEAKER. The gentleman will state it.

Mr. ARNOLD. Is this motion debatable?

The SPEAKER. Quite so.

Mr. BAILEY. It is, for twenty minutes on a side. I voted for that measure because I believed then that we were on the perilous edge of war. Nothing less than that could have justified it. I will go further. I do not hesitate to declare that if a Democratic President had asked a Democrat House for the absolute control of $50,000,000 I would have denied it. I would have said to him, "Send in your estimates and let Congress judge whether that money of the people ought to be expended or not." Those in power did not see fit to require such a course, and believing that a war was imminent the minority did not hesitate to vote for a proposition which, if our position with the majority had been reversed, we would never have asked them to support.

It is many days since we appropriated that $50,000,000, and much of it has been spent, yet the House has no knowledge of the manner in which it has been spent.

Again to-day we are asked to meet an emergency. What are the circumstances? Last Wednesday, when this House was called upon to meet a vital question, and to take decisive action upon it, the majority refused to meet it, and refused to take that action.

They declared that the question was soon to be settled. Everywhere they asserted that to-day the President of the United States would be ready to inform Congress of the state of his negotiations with Spain. The House was adjourned from Friday until to-day to give the President time and opportunity to prepare his message. The hour that such messages usually reach this House has passed, and every well-informed man on both sides of the House knows no message will come from the President to-day. Now, Mr. Speaker, it seems to me important that the country shall understand what Congress is doing and intends to do.

It seems to me equally important that this House shall know what the executive department is doing and intends to do. We ought not to be asked day after day and week after week to provide for an emergency which gentlemen on that side believe has either passed or never existed. I am ready, and every gentleman on this side of the Chamber is ready, to sustain the Administration in every proper measure to prepare for war. We are ready and eager to vote for every measure which may be necessary to conduct that war to a glorious and successful termination. (Loud applause on the floor and in the galleries.)

The SPEAKER. One moment. The gentleman will suspend. The Chair desires to say that the gallery must preserve order. It is not suitable that there should be expressions of either approval or disapproval. People who are occupying the gallery are occupying it as spectators.

Mr. BAILEY. Mr. Speaker, these galleries are but the American people in miniature; and if this Congress could face the people they would hear a condemnation infinitely more overwhelming than that which comes from the galleries of this House. (Applause on the Democratic side and further manifestations of applause in the gallery.)

The SPEAKER. The Chair will be obliged, if there is applause in the gallery, to clear the gallery of the House.

Mr. STEELE. I think that is hardly fair, in view of the fact that the gentleman is talking to the galleries. (Laughter and applause on the Republican side.)

The SPEAKER. The Chair cannot interfere with members.

Mr. BAILEY. I might as well speak to the galleries, for when I speak to that side of the House I appeal to deaf ears and hardened consciences. (Applause on the Democratic side.) I am not seeking to excite or exaggerate. I am refraining from it; but I am simply stating to the majority of this House that they have trifled with the minority and the country too long.

I say now, and after I have said that I reserve the remainder of my time, that if the President wants one day, or two days, or three days to prepare a message that will be approved by the American people we will be silent until he sends it here, but if the President of the United States wants two days, or if he wants two hours, to continue negotiations with the butchers of Spain, we are not ready to give him a minute longer for that purpose. (Loud applause.)

Mr. CANNON. I believe I have the right to close, and as I want not more than two or three minutes, I will ask the gentleman to consume some more of his time.

Mr. BAILEY. I yield three minutes to the gentleman from California (Mr. Maguire).

Mr. MAGUIRE. Mr. Speaker, in reply to my question, a few moments ago, the gentleman from Illinois (Mr. Cannon) stated that the pending measure is not intended to meet a present emergency and that its effect is not confined to times of actual war. It makes a permanent change in the law, giving unusual power to the President of the United States to put the country on a war footing at his discretion. It seems to me that we have gone far enough in that direction. We have gone far enough toward abdicating of the constitutional power of Congress to declare war, to provide for the common defense, and to regulate the land and naval forces of the United States.

I am willing to vote for a resolution putting such power in the hands of the Chief Executive temporarily in time of war; but I insist that such extraordinary power should be confined to times of actual war. My understanding of the existing law is that the President now has this very power in times of war, so that the purpose of the resolution is taking advantage of the present war scare to clothe him with this important power in times of peace. To this I am opposed. It is simply another step in the scheme of centralization which this emergency is being used to promote. A few days ago we appropriated $50,000,000 of public money to be expended by the President independently of Congress and without requiring any specific statement of even the emergency which it was intended to meet.

*   *   *   *   *

Mr. HOPKINS. Now, does the gentleman believe that the Chief Executive should point out in advance what he is going to do before any hostilities commence, or is it not better to make preparations for these fortifications without doing it with brass bands?

Mr. MAGUIRE. In times of war we should not be required to point out in advance what he is going to do, but in times of peace—and we are assured by our Chief Executive that these are times of peace—he should not be made a dictator and should not be given absolute power, independently of Congress, to do that which the Constitution of the United States expressly commits to Congress. All provisions for the national defense to be made in times of peace should be made upon recommendations of the Chief Executive by specific appropriations voted by Congress for definite purposes. That is what I contend for. If this legislation is necessary to meet the exigencies of presently imminent war, let it be so frankly stated, and let the legislation be limited to the occasion.

[Record, p. 3900.]

*　　*　　*　　*　　*

Mr. CANNON. It is reported from the committee. Now, I want to make just two observations; then I will yield to one or two gentlemen, and then ask a vote.

Mr. Speaker, there is a time for speech and a time for silence. There is a time for action. What is this resolution?

To permanently change the law as it ought to have always been, and give to the President in times of emergency, at his discretion, power, under the written consent of the owner of the land, without waiting for a cession of jurisdiction on the part of the legislature, or waiting for a perfect abstract of title, to build temporary forts or fortifications. What for? Take the harbor of New York, or a harbor of our Southern ports, anywhere on our 10,000 miles of seacoast, that the President may make a temporary fortification, and that moneys that may be available for the public defense may be so used. That is all there is in the resolution. It is proposed permanently, forever and a day, to make it a permanent law, unless this or some other Congress shall change the law or repeal it.

Mr. BAILEY. Will the gentleman say to the House just what is intended and whether this proposition is designed to meet a present emergency?

Mr. CANNON. The "gentleman from Illinois" will give the ground for the opinion he entertains.

A MEMBER. That is an excellent answer.

Mr. CANNON. And I will not have to get away, in giving that answer, from what is the fact.

Mr. UNDERWOOD. Will the gentleman from Illinois, before he leaves this question, state the substance of the proposition which he now submits to the House?

Mr. Cannon. I have done so twice but I will do so again for the information of the House.

Unless, Mr. Speaker, the statute is changed there can be no fortification erected on points of land necessary for the public defense now owned by private persons until the Government obtains a perfect title, and until the legislature of the State having jurisdiction shall have been assembled and has taken action in the premises.

Now, we know that this will take from six months to twelve months, or even five years. There is no knowing how long it may take.

Mr. UNDERWOOD. Does the gentleman from Illinois mean to say that they can not, in time of war, take such steps as are contemplated in this resolution? This, as I understand, is a war measure.

Mr. CANNON. It can not be done in time to meet hostilities which may be forced upon us at any moment; and I think with all due respect to the gentleman from Texas, who seems to be departing from his usual good judgment for the purpose of posturing, and taking a position on this question, it seems to me that he could well have agreed at this time to meet an occasion which might arise, before we are actually called on to take steps which may be necessary under the conditions which confront us.

I am talking business now, and the gentleman from Texas is simply posturing before the galleries and the country. I want action to properly defend the country in case of war.

Mr. UNDERWOOD. I would like to ask the gentleman from Illinois if the conference committee on the fortification apppropriation bill is not resisting the increase made by the Senate on that bill for the construction of new fortifications even at this very time?

Mr. CANNON. Oh, Mr. Speaker, the gentleman is trying to fight a man of straw. The President of the United States has authorized to be spent seven and a half millions to perfect the fortifications, under the emergency appropriation heretofore made, and can expend $20,000,000 more if necessary. The gentleman, like a cuttlefish, is trying to muddy the water so as to obscure the real issue.

[Record, p. 3596 to 3900, April 4, 1898.]

INTERVENTION IN CUBAN AFFAIRS.

SENATE, TUESDAY, APRIL 19, 1898.

MR. DAVIS (at 1 o'clock and 15 minutes a. m., Tuesday, April 19, 1898). Mr. President, on behalf of the committee of conference I submit a conference report.

The report was read, as follows:

The committee of conference on the disagreeing votes of the two Houses on the amendments of the House of Representatives to the amendment of the Senate to the joint resolution (H. Res. 233) authorizing and directing the President of the United States to intervene to stop the war in Cuba, and for the purpose of establishing a stable and independent government of the people therein, having met, after full and free conference have agreed to recommend, and do recommend, to their respective Houses as follows:

That the House recede from its amendment numbered 1, in line 1, striking out the words "are, and."

That the Senate recede from its disagreement to the amendment of the House numbered 2, in line 2, to strike out all after the word "independent" to and including the word "Island," in line 4; and agree to the same.

That the Senate recede from its disagreement to the amendment of the House to the title of the resolution omitting in line 2 thereof the words "and Republic;" and agree to the same.

C. K. DAVIS,
J. B. FORAKER,
Managers on the part of the Senate.
ROBERT ADAMS, Jr.,
JOEL P. HEATWOLE,
Managers on the part of the House.

MR. COCKRELL. I move to disagree with the conference report. * * *

The VICE-PRESIDENT. The question is, Shall the report be agreed to? on which the yeas and nays have been ordered. The Secretary will call the roll.

The Secretary proceeded to call the roll.

The result was announced—yeas 42, nays 35; as follows:

YEAS—42.

Aldrich, Allison, Baker, Burrows, Carter, Chandler, Clark, Cullom, Davis, Deboe, Elkins, Fairbanks, Faulkner, Foraker, Frye, Gallinger, Gear, Gray, Hale, Hanna, Hansbrough, Hawley, Kyle, Lodge, McBride, McMillan, Mason, Morgan, Morrill, Nelson, Penrose, Perkins, Platt, Conn., Pritchard, Proctor, Quay, Sewell, Shoup, Spooner, Warren, Wilson, Wolcott.

NAYS—35.

Allen, Bacon, Bate, Berry, Butler, Caffery, Cannon, Chilton, Clay, Cockrell, Daniel, Harris, Heitfeld, Jones, Ark., Jones, Nev., Kenney, Lindsay, McEnery, McLaurin, Mallory, Mantle, Martin, Mitchell Money, Pasco, Pettigrew, Pettus, Rawlins Roach, Stewart, Teller, Turley, Turner, Turpie, White.

NOT VOTING—12.

Gorman, Hoar, Mills, Murphy, Platt, N. Y., Smith, Thurston, Tillman, Vest, Walthall, Wellington, Wetmore.

So the report was agreed to.

* * * * *

Mr. COCKRELL. I have never believed a word of the rumors that were circulated all around here that if we passed the joint resolution with the clause in it recognizing the independence of the Republic of Cuba, President William McKinley would veto it. I think it was done by his indiscreet friends for the purpose of whipping in those who were not disposed to follow their recommendations and their policies, not those of the President.

But now let us come back to the policy of the President and see what it was.

THIRTY-FIVE DEMOCRATS VOTING "NAY."

Mr. HALE. Will the Senator allow me?

The PRESIDING OFFICER. Does the Senator from Missouri yield?

Mr. COCKRELL. Certainly; as a matter of course.

Mr. HALE. I do not want to prolong the discussion, but before the Senator sits down I should like to have him answer this question: Why, on the proposition which passed the Senate, the first of which resolved that the people of the Island of Cuba are, and of right ought to be, free and independent; on the second, which demands the withdrawal of the Spanish forces and the abandonment of Cuba; on the third, which authorizes the President to use the Army and Navy to that end, and on the fourth, which repudiates the theory of annexation—why was it that on the roll call on those resolutions, covering such broad grounds of immediate action toward the independence of Cuba, thirty-five Democrats were found almost in solid rank voting "nay?" I wish the Senator would explain that. I can understand that the Senator is sensitive and that his associates are sensitive overnight.

Mr. COCKRELL. Not a bit of it. I never rejoiced more in my life over any vote I ever cast than the vote I cast last night. I am glad of it, and it will stand as a monument of my devotion to the interests of a struggling people for a free and independent government in answer to their appeals to the oldest Republic in the world, which appeal I am sorry has been unheeded.

Mr. HALE. I want the Senator before he sits down to explain the reasons, why, when it was apparent that that was all that could be done, and also in the view that afterwards his associates in another body took the ground of voting for these resolutions, and did it—

Mr. COCKRELL. The questions were entirely different.

Mr. HALE. Why did the thirty-five Democrats who voted against these resolutions and would not put themselves on record in favor of them take that attitude and seek to prevent any action ?

Mr. TILLMAN. Mr. President—

Mr. COCKRELL. Wait a minute. I will answer the Senator from Maine myself.

SENATORS CLAMORING FOR WAR VOTING "NO."

Mr. HALE. I did, in a speech made on Saturday last, which has been alluded to and which has aroused some trouble, make a little forecast, and that was that I PREDICTED THAT THE SENATORS WHO HAD BEEN CLAMORING FOR WAR, CLAMORING FOR ACTION, WHO WERE DENOUNCING THE PRESIDENT, AND IN SOME CASES—not the Senator from Missouri himself—ABUSING THE PRESIDENT, ERE LONG WOULD BE FOUND VOTING "NO" AND OBSTRUCTING THE MOVEMENT.

I did not expect a realization to come so soon as Monday night. I did not expect, when we had come to resolutions that covered every ground but one, that meant immediate intervention and freedom for Cuba and the interposition of the armies and navies of the United States—I DID NOT QUITE THINK THAT SO SOON AS MONDAY NIGHT WE WOULD FIND ALMOST THE SOLID DEMOCRATIC PARTY VOTING "NO." IT CAME SOONER THAN I EXPECTED, AND I WAS A BETTER PROPHET THAN I SUPPOSED MYSELF TO BE.

Mr. TILLMAN. Will the Senator allow me?

Mr. COCKRELL. I will yield to the Senator from South Carolina for just a minute.

Mr. TILLMAN. I want to ask the Senator from Maine a question. Does he claim any part or parcel in the paternity of the resolutions which were passed last night?

Mr. HALE. I certainly helped to pass them.

Mr. TILLMAN. After you had fought them for four days.

Mr. HALE. After I had fought for the freedom of Cuba without the scheme of recognition being added to the resolutions,

Mr. COCKRELL. If the Senator wants to ask me a question, I will answer, but I am not going to have other Senators interject their speeches into mine. There is plenty of time, and we have nothing else to do but to talk about this question. Remember, I never occupied a minute of the time of the body on this question when it was important to have prompt action; but it has now passed, and we can talk as much and as long as we please.

Mr. HALE. If the Senator does not yield, I will not insist on putting questions to him.

Mr. COCKRELL. I am always glad for a question, but not for a speech.

Mr. SPOONER. I want to appeal to my friend from Maine (Mr. Hale) that he should not interject any remarks of his into any political speech of the Senator from Missouri. It is not fair.

Mr. HALE. I think there is something in that. I was going to answer the Senator from South Carolina (Mr. Tillman), but if the Senator from Missouri (Mr. Cockrell) desires to go on, as the Senator from Wisconsin (Mr. Spooner) has suggested, and complete his exculpatory speech, his political speech, I shall not intervene.

Mr. COCKRELL. I do not care a continental cent whether you call it a political speech or not. I am not hidebound.

Mr. HALE. I think the Senator from Wisconsin is probably correct.

Mr. COCKRELL. I want you to understand distinctly that I am a Democrat; that I believe in the cardinal, imperishable, and monumental principles of that oldest, grandest, and noblest of all political organizations that has ever existed on American soil—the Democratic party.

Mr. HALE. I thought so.

* * * * *

[Record, pp. 4461 and 4488.]

TARIFF, MONEY

AND

History of Financial Legislation in the United States

SPEECH OF

HON. J. W. BABCOCK

of Wisconsin

IN THE HOUSE OF REPRESENTATIVES, MONDAY, JULY 19th, 1897

HON. J. W. BABCOCK

of Wisconsin

In the House of Representatives, Monday, July 19th, 1897

The House having under consideration the conference report on the bill (H. R. 379) to provide revenue for the Government and to encourage the industries of the United States—

Mr. BABCOCK said:

PREDICTIONS REALIZED.

Mr. Speaker: Something over a year ago I ventured the prediction in this place that free coinage, except by international agreement, when properly understood by the people, would be unable to maintain itself at the polls in a fair contest of American intelligence, and I furthermore ventured to predict that the advocates of this interest could not bar the Fifty-fifth Congress from enacting such wise protective-tariff laws as would furnish ample revenue for the needs of the Government and protection to all the great agricultural, laboring, and industrial interests. Both of these predictions have been realized, and I am now here to add to my forecast of events the further prediction that the era of prosperity, so long delayed by the result of four years of maladministration by the Democratic party in all branches of the Government, will soon be upon us in all its fullness, and will be felt in every home and hamlet of the United States.

None but those selfishly or constitutionally organized to find fault and to obscure the clear vision of the American people to the future can deny that the pulse strokes of a healthy revival of confidence and business energy have already manifested themselves, and that the vigorous constitution of the country is rapidly shaking off the effects of the past four years of free trade, free-coinage agitation, and bond sales, which fastened a new taxation of $262,330,692 upon the workingmen and business interests of the country.

AN ERA OF CHEAP THINGS.

It has been a typical era of "cheap things," putting the farmer and the laborer, the mechanic and the small business men, in the condition of being hardly able to provide the comforts, often the necessities, of life with the cheapened proceeds of their industry. We have learned the bitter lesson, I think, that cheap goods mean cheap labor. We have tried four years of Democratic tariff policy, and it has nearly put our workingmen on a par with the pauper labor of Europe.

Under Republican tariff laws, during the period from the 1st of September, 1865, up to the time President Cleveland was inaugurated in 1893—

twenty-seven and one-half years—the Government debt and obligations were reduced $1,881,367,873, or an average of $68,632,000 per year. The per capita debt in 1865 was $78. In 1893 it had been reduced to $12.55. This is certainly a fair showing, for it covers the whole period from the close of the war until the Democrats secured full control of all branches of the Government. Notice the great difference between the financial policies of the two parties. Since the 1st of March, 1893, until the 1st of March, 1896—a period of three years—the interest-bearing debt increased over $262,000,000, or an average of more than $87,000,000 per year, against a decrease of nearly $69,-000,000 per year under Republican Administrations for the previous twenty-seven years.

THE EFFECT OF DEMOCRATIC LEGISLATION.

The proceeds of these bond transactions were used to pay the running expenses of the Government; to cover deficits which the famous Wilson bill had created. Not all the Democratic leaders were so frank as Representative Dockery, of the Appropriations Committee of the House, when he admitted, in a speech April 29, 1896, that—

"During the last fiscal year the current income was inadequate to meet current liabilities by $42,805,223.18, and it is now estimated that the deficiency in current revenues for the present fiscal year will not be less than $25,-000,000."

Such has been the admitted effect of Democratic legislation as exposed by its own friends, while the prostrate condition of labor-employing industries throughout the United States has been a sad reminder of the truthfulness of their admissions.

Its enemies, Mr. Speaker, will attempt again to blind the vision of the people to the blessings of the bill which the Fifty-fifth Congress has enacted into law; but Republicans everywhere may be proud of the first substantial step in four years to disperse the black vapors of misery and to bring back the era of universal industry and prosperity which marked Republican administrations almost unbrokenly for thirty years. This bill has commanded the full strength of the Republican representation in Congress, and 33 votes from the South were cast for it at different stages of its career. For the first time in the history of Republican tariff legislation Democrats have broken away from their party creed to vote for protection, convinced that thereby alone can they hope to restore living wages, fair returns for capital and industry, and better times for the farming class.

THE BLESSINGS OF TARIFF LAWS.

The bill may not be a perfect measure; perfection cannot be achieved at one stroke; but it was designed to fit the conditions that exist to-day and is a great stride in the direction of a tangible and substantial betterment of the condition of all classes of producers. If left to work out its own salvation it will soon increase the revenues of the Government, so that no more bonds will have to be issued to pay our current expenses, while at the same time it will reopen industrial channels long closed to honest toil and put our workingmen back on the pay rolls of the shops and factories that were closed by the Wilson bill.

In my opinion, Mr. Speaker, we must look for our greatest blessings to judicious tariff legislation, and not allow ourselves to be misled by specious arguments of financial revolution. What shall it benefit the farmer, the mechanic, and the laboring man if we open to them the opportunities to earn wages and, on the other hand, disturb our hitherto unassailable system of finance and pay them in a depreciated currency? In this connection I propose to review briefly the financial history of the United States, so that he who runs may read the fallacy of many of the popular arguments employed to convert the unwary to free coinage of 16 to 1, and also to show how its advocates have perverted facts and history to strengthen their otherwise untenable cause.

A REVIEW OF OUR FINANCIAL LEGISLATION.

Thirty-six years ago the Republican party, confronted by the gravest exigency in our national life, originated and adopted a system of currency and credit.

This system was subjected to the severest of all tests—civil war in its most tremendous form—but achieved a success and earned a place among the monetary systems of the world far greater than any ever instituted by any government on the face of the earth.

The Republican party has steadfastly maintained the high standard of this system through all the years of its ascendancy; has held firmly to an interchangeable currency based upon coin, every dollar of which has been maintained and redeemed according to the original pledge.

The same party is to-day, as ever, in favor of the same sound money, and will continue to maintain, by prudent legislation, the same wide use of gold, silver, and paper with profit and security to all the people.

OUR METALLIC MONEY.

Under the Confederation of 1778, Congress was given the exclusive right and power to regulate the alloy and value of the coin struck by their own authority, or by that of the respective States; but, having no power to enforce its laws in the States and no revenues with which to carry out its own right of coinage, nothing was done.

Under the Constitution, Congress was given the exclusive power to coin money, to regulate the value thereof and of foreign coins. It was expressly provided that no State shall coin money, and Congress exercised this power by the passage of the act of April 2, 1792, establishing a mint and regulating the coins of the United States,

In this act the "dollar" of gold or silver was adopted as the unit money of account, with the dollar coin of 371.25 grains of pure silver as the base.

FROM SILVER TO GOLD BASIS.

Between 1792 and 1834 we were under a bimetallic system, with the silver dollar as the actual unit on a basis of 15 to 1. Spanish dollars until 1816, and other foreign coins of both metals until a later date, were also a legal tender, but, as our lighter-weight silver dollars were exported to the West Indies, where they passed at par, we were without a sufficient national currency of either or both metals.

Legislation was therefore necessary, and by the laws of 1834 and 1837 the weight and fineness of the gold coin—and by the latter act the weight and fineness of both coins—were changed so as to make the ratio 16 (15.98) to 1, and to establish the double unit, viz.: the eagle of gold and the dollar of silver.

COINAGE AND EXPORT OF SILVER TO 1853.

This change undervalued silver, as the act of 1792 had undervalued gold, and as a result silver went out of the United States to countries where it was worth more than with us.

In 1847 our coinage of gold was $20,202,325, which fell to $3,775,513 in 1848; while silver in 1847 was $2,374,450, and $2,040,050 in 1848.

The effects of the California gold output were felt in 1850 and its coinage increased, while that of silver decreased.

In 1850 the gold coinage was $31,981,739; in 1851, $62,614,493; in 1852, $56,846,188; while silver in 1850 was $1,866,100; in 1851. $774,397, and in 1852, $999,410.

CONDITIONS IN 1853.

By 1853 (in spite of an annual coinage of over a million dollars in halves, quarters, etc.) there was not enough subsidiary silver for small change, and we were practically on a gold basis. By the act of this year the values of the minor silver coins were reduced so as to stop their exportation, and, what was a still more important act, these were made a limited legal tender for all' amounts not exceeding $5. This was the first step in the impairment of the double standard, established by the gold act of 1834.

CAUSES.

There were good reasons for this action. Silver was scarce, gold was plentiful, and it had been found necessary to coin silver in small denominations and with smaller proportionate values than the standard dollars to keep them at home for domestic use.

INCREASED GOLD OUTPUT.

The world's supply of gold had suddenly increased because of the California and Australian output. From an annual product of about $13,482,000 in the period from 1831 to 1840 it reached $132,500,000 after 1850. The natural result was to raise the value of silver and to lower that of gold.

NO SILVER IN CIRCULATION.

Then, too, we had no silver dollars in the country, or at least not in sufficient quantities to figure largely as a circulating medium. We had coined none from 1806 to 1836. In 1806 President Jefferson, the demigod of the silver Democracy of the present day, stopped the coinage of the silver dollar at the mints of the United States, and from 1836 to 1853 we had only coined of dollars 1,067,373, all the other silver coinage in this period being of minor money.

GOLD THE ACTUAL STANDARD.

While, therefore, after 1853, except for the minor coins, the double standard was the law, yet the actual condition was that of a single gold standard.

RESUME.

Let us briefly review.

The act of 1792 made the silver dollar the unit, at 15 to 1; those of 1834 and 1837 changed the ratio to 16 to 1; that of 1853 reduced the values of the minor silver coins and limited their legal tender to $5.

While the acts of 1834 and 1837 made the eagle of gold a co-unit with silver, they did not repeal the act of 1792, which based the unit of a bimetallic money on the silver dollar.

But from the causes already named 1853 found us practically with a single gold standard, with gold as the cheaper and more plentiful metal. While silver dollars were a full legal tender, they were not greatly used, because they were usually worth more abroad than at home, and were exported. Gold was the chief and sole base for coin currency.

SILVER DOLLARS COINED UP TO 1853.

We could not, indeed, have had many silver dollars then, because the total coinage of these up to 1853 had been only $2,506,890. This condition obtained until the exigencies of the civil war drove all coin money out and gave place to bonds, greenbacks, and national bank notes.

GOLD STANDARD INTENDED.

There is no doubt as to the intention of the lawmakers at that time on this point. They were legislating for a single gold standard, although they left the silver dollar as a co-unit. That this was the end sought is shown by the remarks made by the chairman of the Committee on Ways and Means:

"We mean to make gold the standard coin, and make these new coins" (the subsidiary silver of proportionately less value) "applicable and convenient, not for large but for small transactions."

Another member of the same committee said:

"We have had but a single standard for the last three or four years; that has been and now is gold. We propose to let it remain so, to adapt silver to it, to regulate it by it."

In 1861 came the civil war, the tremendous expense account of the Government, the exhaustion of our current money, and later the issues of paper money in Treasury notes and bonds and national bank notes.

HISTORY OF THE ACT OF 1873.

This act, concerning which so much has been said, was introduced in the Senate April 25, 1870; was considered through five sessions of Congress, and became a law February 12, 1873.

IT HAS BEEN CHARGED THAT THIS BILL DEMONETIZED SILVER, NOT OPENLY, BUT BY MEANS OF AN AMENDMENT NOT FULLY KNOWN OR UNDERSTOOD EXCEPT BY A FEW. Let us follow the course of this bill,

THE ORIGINAL BILL.

As originally presented, April 25, 1870, section 14 made the gold dollar of 25.8 grains the standard of value, the unit of computation.

Section 15 provided that the weight of the silver coin should be for the half dollar 192 grains (the dollar was not mentioned), with proportionate values for the quarter, 25-cent piece, and dime; and that these should be legal tender for $1.

Section 18 enacted that no coins other than those mentioned (that is, gold and minor silver) should be thereafter coined.

SILVER DOLLAR PIECE DISCONTINUED.

On page 11 of the report which accompanied this original bill are the following words:

"The coinage of the silver dollar piece is discontinued."

The discontinuance of the silver dollar piece is pointed out by the committee three times in other places in this report. In all the discussions and in every form of the bill these two features, making the gold dollar the standard unit of value and the omission of the silver dollar (of 412½ grains), remain unchanged. Indeed, sections 14 and 18 (afterwards section 17) were never changed, but passed absolutely as first presented in the original bill.

SILVER SECTION.

Section 15 passed through enough changes to warrant the idea that its every provision was understood by all fully. In the Senate it first went through unmodified—36 to 14—(January 10, 1871), Senator Sherman voting against and Senator Stewart, of Nevada, voting for it.

LEGAL TENDER $5.

In the House committee this section was amended to make the legal tender $5; but owing to lack of time, the bill went over.

On March 9, 1871, Mr. Kelley, in the House, reported the same bill as amended by the previous House committee; that is, with the legal tender raised to $5; and, except for the 5-cent piece, it was an exact reproduction of the law of 1853. No silver dollars were to be coined, and this minor coinage was to be a legal tender for $5 only.

A 384-GRAIN DOLLAR.

In the discussion it was shown that some desired to have a silver dollar included, although all agreed that its legal tender should be limited, and that its contents should be not 412½ grains, but twice that of the proposed half dollar, or 384 grains.

On February 13, 1872, Mr. Hooper reported it back as H. R. 1427, with these provisions:

"Sec. 16. That the silver coins of the United States shall be a dollar, a half dollar, a quarter dollar, and a 10-cent piece, and that the weight of the dollar shall be 384 grains, the half and other coins in proportion, and that these shall be legal tender for $5."

This passed the House May 27, 1872. It will be noted that this is not the old standard dollar of 412½ grains, but a subsidiary coin for change and of limited legal tender.

TRADE DOLLAR.

There were some who desired to attempt a competition in the East Indies with the Mexican dollar, and through these the bill was still further modified. As it was finally passed, in the Senate January 17, 1873, and House February 7, 1873, the silver clauses were as follows:

A trade dollar of 420 grains for this export trade, although it was made a legal tender and so remained until July 22, 1876, for $5 at home; a half dollar of 12½ grams (on the basis of a silver dollar of 396 grains), and minor coins of proportionate value.

All these were made legal tender for $5 only. A 5-cent piece was included in the copper and nickel coins.

412½-GRAIN DOLLAR NEVER IN THE BILL.

FROM THE FOREGOING IT IS PLAIN THAT THE SILVER DOLLAR OF 412½ GRAINS, "THE DOLLAR OF THE FATHERS," WAS NOT DROPPED OUT SURREPTITOUSLY, BECAUSE IT WAS NEVER IN THE BILL TO BE DROPPED OUT. No one wanted it there. First they had a half dollar (no dollar), then a dollar of 384 grains, then a trade dollar for the Pacific coast trade to the East Indies, and a half dollar of 12½ grams, or 192.9 grains (at the rate of 386 grains for a dollar), and all this silver was, from first to last, a limited legal tender for from one to five dollars.

WHY WAS SILVER DROPPED OUT?

The law of 1853 had abolished the coinage of our minor silver coins for private account, but by a ruling of Mr. Guthrie, Secretary of the Treasury under President Pierce, the Mint was ordered to receive silver from private individuals and coin it.

This ruling furnished the opportunity for an immense profit to the coin and bullion broker, and he did not fail to take advantage of it. Our silver dollars, having a nominal value of 100 cents, were collected by him, taken to the mints, and coined into minor coin; every two dollars yielded four half dollars, a dime, and almost a half dime. Here was a profit of 7 per cent. Silver bullion coined into our minor coin yielded a profit of 4 per cent. From a quarter to a half million dollars were made in this way yearly, with a prospect of many millions profit when we should resume specie payments.

INTEREST OF THE COIN BROKERS.

Following the explanation of the various sections of the bill by Mr. Hooper came a general discussion of the bill, in which was shown a determined effort to secure its defeat. This effort was especially manifest on the part of some of the members from New York.

Mr. Brooks went so far as to move to strike out section 1, for the purpose, as he frankly avowed, of putting an end to the bill. Both Mr. Potter and Mr. Brooks objected to provision after provision of the bill, usually without specific reason, simply declaring that for the present the existing laws were sufficient.

5

MR. KELLEY'S EXPLANATION.

Goaded to desperation by the persistent attempts to defeat the measure, Mr. Kelley, of Pennsylvania, took the floor and very pointedly called the attention of the House to the fact that any legislation, however general in character, which assails existing abuses and would abolish opportunities for illegitimate profits to speculators, is met with zealous and organized opposition.

"Let me, Mr. Speaker, hastily point out some of the interests that are on this floor seeking to protect themselves by preventing the passage of this bill. One silver bullion dealer in New York during the last Congress admitted to Mr. Hooper that under one defect in existing laws he was making at the cost of the Government from $75,000 to $100,000 a year. His profits— and he is but one of those who are growing fat and greedy upon the defects in our mint laws—arise in this way: Our country, like every other civilized government, should procure its own metal out of which to make subsidiary coinage. Now, sir, every coin of ours that is not gold is subsidiary. Our silver dollar, half dollar, and every other coin that is not gold is subsidiary. All other governments pay the expense of minting by the difference between the intrinsic value of subsidiary coins and the value at which they circulate. And such was the law of this country until by a ruling of Mr. Guthrie the mint was ordered to receive silver from private individuals and coin it. Now, it so happens that a constituent of the gentleman from New York has been taking advantage of that ruling and deposited silver to be made into half dollars and other silver coins. He has, as he stated to my colleague (Mr. Hooper, of Massachusetts), and myself, been doing a business of from $1,800-000 to $2,000,000 per annum, giving him as profit an annual income equal to the salary of the President for the Presidential term."

In his speech (House, April 9, 1872, Congressional Globe, pages 2306-2308, vol. 102, one of ten columns, by the way), Mr. Hooper, for the committee, said:

SILVER DOLLARS NOT A CIRCULATING COIN.

"Section 16 re-enacts the provisions of the existing laws defining the silver coins and their weights, respectively, except in relation to the silver dollar, which is reduced in weight from 412½ to 384 grains, thus making it a subsidiary coin in harmony with the silver coins of less denomination to secure its concurrent circulation with them. The silver dollar of 412½ grains, by reason of its bullion or intrinsic value being greater than its nominal value, long since ceased to be a coin of circulation, and is melted by manufacturers of silverware."

MR. STOUGHTON SAYS SILVER DOLLAR IS TOO VALUABLE.

On the same day, Mr. Stoughton, of Michigan, made a speech of seven columns, in which he said (same volume, page 2308):

"The silver dollar as now issued is worth for bullion 3¼ cents more than the gold dollar, and 7¼ cents more than two half dollars. Having a greater intrinsic and nominal value, it is certain to be withdrawn from circulation whenever we return to specie payment, and to be used only for manufacture and exportation as bullion."

MR. POTTER DECLARES LEGAL TENDER SHOULD BE GOLD.

Mr. Potter, in discussing this part of the bill, said:

"This bill provides for the making of changes in the legal-tender coin of the country and for substituting as legal-tender, coin of only one metal, instead, as heretofore, of two. I think myself this would be a wise provision, and that legal-tender coins, except subsidiary coin, should be of gold alone." (Page 2310, volume 102.)

MR. KELLEY FAVORS GOLD AS STANDARD AND SILVER AS SUBSIDIARY MONEY.

And Mr. Kelley, who is reported as having said afterwards that he "did not know that the bill omitted the standard silver dollar," said on this same day (Globe, volume 102, page 2316):

"The values of gold and silver continually fluctuate. You cannot determine this year what will be the relative values of gold and silver next year. They were 15 to 1 a short time ago; they are 16 to 1 now.

"Hence all experience has shown that you must have one standard coin which shall be a legal tender for all others, and then you may promote your domestic convenience by having a subsidiary coinage of silver, which shall circulate in all parts of your country as legal tender for a limited amount and be redeemable at its face value by your Government. But, sir, I again call the attention of the House to the fact that the gentlemen who oppose this bill insist upon maintaining a silver dollar worth 3½ cents more than the gold dollar and worth 7 cents more than two half dollars, and that so long as those provisions remain you cannot keep silver coin in the country."

SENATOR STEWART DECLARES FOR GOLD.

Speaking on another subject a few months afterwards, Mr. Stewart, then, as now, a Senator from Nevada, said (page 1392, volume 2, part 2, Congressional Record):

" I want the standard gold, and no paper money not redeemable in gold."

About two weeks later, on February 20, 1874, Senator Stewart said (same volume, page 1677):

"By this process we shall come to a specie basis; and when the laboring man receives a dollar, it will have the purchasing power of a dollar, and he will not be called upon to do what is impossible for him or the producing classes to do, figure upon the exchanges, figure upon the fluctuations, figure upon the gambling in New York; but he will know what his money is worth. Gold is the universal standard of the world. Everybody knows what a dollar in gold is worth."

These are the words of Senator Stewart before he became simply the representative of a special interest.

SENATOR JONES EXTOLS GOLD.

Senator Jones, of Nevada, took the same position. In the Senate April 1, 1874, he said:

" Does this Congress mean now to leave entirely out of view and to discard forever a standard of value? Did any country ever accumulate wealth, achieve greatness, or attain a high civilization without such standard? And what but Gold can be that standard? What other thing on earth possesses these requisite qualities?"

PUBLIC DISCUSSION OF ACT OF 1873.

It has been charged that very little was said in the public press about this legislation. To this the answer is that in 1873 neither metal was in circulation; and it was also simply a reiteration of what had been a commercial condition for more than twenty years. The bill itself had been before Congress three years. From the date of its introduction in the Senate it was printed, by order of Congress, with amendments, thirteen times, and was considered during five different sessions by the Senate and House. The debates on the bill in the Senate covered 66 pages and in the House 78 pages of the Congressional Globe. It was finally passed with only the addition of the trade dollar, and there was not much worthy of extended comment.

THE PRODUCTION OF GOLD AND SILVER.

The legislation of 1853 and 1873 was based on commercial conditions, which in turn were largely caused by the variation in the output of the two metals both in the United States and in the world. Let us briefly study these and see why from 1853 to 1873, and even for a few years afterwards, gold was the more plentiful and cheaper; why later the price of silver fell so that the two were on a parity; why it kept on falling to far below this limit; and finally why in recent years the change in the ratio of production has tended and still tends strongly to induce the belief that a few years more will see them near the former parity.

GOLD IN THE UNITED STATES.

Up to the year 1848 our annual output of gold had never exceeded a million, except a trifle in two years. In that year it suddenly rose to ten millions (an amount equal to the total annual world product up to 1840); in 1849, to forty millions; in 1850, to fifty millions, and ranged from that figure to sixty-five millions up to 1860. Then for five years it ranged from forty to forty-six, and from 1865 to 1870 averaged over fifty millions. For the next five years it averaged under forty, to go to fifty-one millions in 1878, and ranged from thirty millions in 1883 to $39,500,000 in 1894. It did not touch the forty-million mark after 1871, except $51,200,000 in 1878.

The recent increase dates from 1892, when it was at the low-water mark of $33,000,000. In 1893 it went to $35,900,000; in 1894 it reached $39,500,000; in 1895 it went to $46,610,000, and in 1896 to $53,088,000. The Director of the Mint estimates that but for the great strikes at Leadville, Cour d'Alene, and Cripple Creek the output for 1897 would have been greatly in excess of what the figures for that year are likely to show.

GOLD IN THE WORLD.

The gold product of the world had averaged for many years before 1840 a little over ten millions per year. In the ten years from 1841 to 1850 this suddenly rose to the then unprecedented figure of $36,393,000. Despite this enormous gain, the next five years, 1851 to 1855, showed a product of more than three and a half times as great, $132,513,000, or the immense sum of $662,566,000 for the five years.

From 1856 to 1860 it averaged $134,083,000; fell off eleven millions in the next five years; rose to $129,614,000, 1866 to 1870; fell to $115,577,000, 1871 to 1875; to $114,585,000, 1876 to 1880, and to $99,116,000, 1881 to 1885.

This was the gold low-water mark for the world for the past forty years. Since that time it has steadily increased, until for the year 1892 it reached a sum higher than ever before known—the enormous total of $146,815,100. For 1893 there was a further increase of nearly eleven millions, to $157,287,-600, while the amount for 1894 was twenty-three millions more—to the vast quantity of $180,626,100. The product for 1895 was $200,406,000; that of 1895, as computed by Rothwell, $220,600,000; while conservative estimates put the world's gold product within five years at $300,000,000 per ánnum.

COUNTRIES OF INCREASE.

It may be well to see whence this great increase has come. It will also enable us to estimate as to the future. The principal gold-producing countries for the years 1894, 1895, and 1896 were, in order and amounts, as follows:

COUNTRY	1894	1895	1896
United States	$39,500,000	$46,610,000	$53,088,000
Australasia	41,760,800	44,798,300	45,182,000
Africa	40,271,000	44,554,900	44,000,000
Russia	24,133,400	28,894,400	*31,000,000
Mexico	4,500,000	6,000,000	6,513,090
China	8,556,800	3,521,000	*5,000.000
Total from 6 countries	$158,722,000	$174,378,600	$184,783,000

The figures marked with an (*) are those of Mr. Rothwell, of Mineral Industry, who estimates the gold product of the world for 1896 to have been $220,600,000.

Of the above, China shows a small increase; it of all other nations remains about the same year by year. The recent and future increases are to be found and expected in Africa, Australasia, United States, Russia, and Mexico. These increases have been as follows:

COUNTRY	1893 OVER 1892	1894 OVER 1893	1895 OVER 1894
United States	$2,900,000	$3.545,000	$7,110,000
Australasia	1,529,600	6,072,200	3,037,500
Africa	4,711,500	11,328,500	4,233,900
Mexico	176,100	3,194,700	1,500,000
Russia			4,761,000
Increase	$9,317,200	$24,140,400	$20,692,400

The Director of the Mint and leading European authorities agree in ascribing the comparatively small increase in Africa to the political disturbances in the Transvaal, which were brewing some time prior to their actual eruption in an attempt at revolution.

SILVER IN THE UNITED STATES.

From 1792 to 1834 the product of silver was insignificant; from 1834 to 1844 it is estimated at a total of $250,000; from 1845 to 1857 both inclusive, it is given at $50,000 per year. In 1858 it went to $500,000; in 1859, fell tó $100,000; 1860, $150,000; in 1861 it rose suddenly to $2,000,000; went to $4,500,-000 for 1862; $8,500,000 in 1863, and ranged from eleven millions to sixteen millions up to 1871. In that year it reached twenty-three, and varied from twenty-eight to forty-eight millions up to 1885.

Demonetization, so called, took place in 1873; resumption and the use of coin money took place in 1879. From 1874 to 1884 there was only a slight increase, the highest figure, in 1884, being $48,800,000. In 1885 it reached $51,-600,000; rose to fifty-three in 1887; to fifty-nine in 1888; to sixty-four in 1889, and touched seventy millions in 1890. In 1891 it went to $75,417,000; in 1892 it reached the high-water mark—the highest ever known, $82,101,000—only to fall off in 1893 to $77,576,000, and to $64,000,000 in 1894, increasing to $72,056,000 in 1895, and to $76,069,000 in 1896.

COMPARATIVE INCREASE.

From 1874 to 1895 silver increased $34,751,000; in the same time gold increased a little more than thirteen millions, but there was no appreciable increase in silver until 1885.

SILVER IN THE WORLD.

The annual average coinage value of the silver produced in the world has been: From 1545 to 1761, $12,450,000 to $22,162,000; from 1761 to 1860 it ranged from $19,144,000 to $37,618,000; 1861 to 1865, it was $45,772,000; 1866 to 1870, $55,663,000; 1871 to 1875, $81,864,000; while from 1876 to 1880 it rose to an annual average of $101,851,000, and from 1881 to 1885 to $118,955,000.

The value for 1886 was $120,626,800, and for 1887 it was $124,281,000. It continued to rise steadily some twelve millions per year to 1893, when it was $213,944,400. The year 1894 only showed a slight decrease, a trifle over $1,114,800 for that period. The returns for 1895 again show an increase of $4,781,200.

COINAGE vs. COMMERCIAL VALUE.

The foregoing figures as to silver being based on the United States coinage value, are not a true guide as to the actual market value. From 1833 to 1850 the average price of a fine ounce of silver was about $1.31, or 60 pence. In 1850 and up to 1872 it ranged about $1.33, or 61 pence, only touching $1.36, or 62 pence, in 1859.

AVERAGE BULLION VALUE.

In 1873 the average bullion value of a silver dollar was $1.004, making it more valuable than a gold dollar. For 1874 it was $0.988; 1875, $0.964; 1876, $0.894; 1877, $0.929, and has not reached the $0.90 mark since. In 1886 it got into the seventies, rose to $0.81 in 1890, to fall to $0.764 in 1891, to $0.674 in 1892, to $0.603 in 1893, to $0.491 in 1894, rising to $0.505 in 1895, and to $0.522 in 1896, falling to $0.44 in July, 1897. In other words, in 1873 the ratio was 1 to 15.92; and in 1897 it is 1 to 39.66.

1873 AND 1896.

In 1873 a silver dollar containing 371.25 grains of pure silver would purchase only 369.77 grains of the same silver. The coined value was 1½ grains less than its commercial value.

In 1894 this same dollar would purchase 756.04 grains, or twice itself and 5½ grains over; in 1895 it would purchase 733.87, and in 1896, 711.93.

WHY WHITE METAL FELL IN VALUE.

Did silver fall or did gold get scarcer and grow dearer? I have shown that in the United States the gold product held steadily at over thirty and (except in 1877-78) under forty millions from 1874 to 1894, going from $39,-500,000 in the latter year to $46,610,000 in 1895; that in the world for this same period it had steadily increased from $115,577,000 to $200,406,000. Evidently during this period gold did its full duty and earned the repute of a metal of stable and sufficient increase in output.

Silver first came to be a factor in the United States in 1861, when $2,000,-000 was produced; in 1864 it was $11,000,000; in 1874, $37,300,000; in 1884, $48,-800,000, with from fifty-one to eighty-one millions per year thereafter.

The world product had gone from an annual average coinage value of $81,864,000 in 1874 to $118,955,000 in 1884, and $212,829,600 in 1894.

From 1874 to 1894 silver did not make nearly so great a proportional gain as did gold from 1841-1850 to 1851-1855.

PROPORTION OF METALS.

For three hundred years, 1545-1840, during which time Spain had poured the wealth of her American silver mines into the markets of the world, the general average proportion of the value of the two metals produced had been about 33 per cent. for gold and 67 per cent. for silver. From the period 1841-1850 up to that of 1876-1880 this proportion was about 66 per cent. for gold and 34 per cent. for silver—much greater than the three-century average. From 1881 to 1894 gold was still 44 per cent., while for 1894 it was 46.3, and in 1895 it had increased to 47.7 per cent. It is interesting to note that the percentage of production by value from 1492 to 1895, inclusive, was 45.9 of gold to 54.1 of silver.

SILVER LEGISLATION IN THE UNITED STATES.
Kelley-Bland Bills.

In 1876 Mr. Kelley (Pennsylvania) introduced a bill for the coinage of standard (412½ grains) dollars, and to make them an unlimited legal tender. The same year Mr. Bland (Missouri) introduced a bill for the unlimited issue of Treasury notes in exchange for gold and silver bullion.

Both these measures were considered, and in March, 1877, a commission of Senators and Representatives made a report on the relations of gold and silver.

The Kelley bill, as modified and championed by Mr. Bland, passed the House November 5, 1877. It provided, with the Bland amendment, for the free and unlimited coinage of 412½-grain dollars, and made these an unlimited legal tender, except 'where otherwise specified by contract.

Bland-Allison Act.

The Kelley-Bland bill was modified in the Senate, and became known as the Bland-Allison act. As modified in the Senate and as finally passed it restricted the coinage to the 4,000,000 ounces per month which the Secretary of the Treasury was to purchase, and it gave to the public Treasury the seigniorage or profit on these purchases and coinage. The silver thus to be coined was made an unlimited legal tender except for certificates of deposit of gold and silver bullion under the act of 1863 and in cases where other money had been stipulated by contract. Section 3 authorized the deposit of these dollars and the issuance of (silver) certificates therefor. It became a law over the President's veto February 28, 1878.

Bland and Conger Bills.

In 1886 Mr. Bland again introduced a bill for the free and unlimited coinage of silver—

That is, giving to the mine owner and bullion producer the whole profit of the seigniorage or difference between the actual cost and the legal-tender value of the dollar when coined.

Mr. Conger introduced another bill, embodying the views of Secretary Windom, allowing owners of silver to deposit it and receive Treasury notes to the amount of its then market value, these to be redeemed when presented at its then value.

The Sherman Law of 1890.

The Conger bill, as modified, was finally passed, and became a law July 14, 1890, and is known as the Sherman law.

It directed the purchase of 4,500,000 fine ounces of silver each month at not to exceed $1 for 371.25 grains of pure silver, and the issue of Treasury notes therefor. These notes were to be redeemable on demand in coin, and could be reissued. They were made legal tender for all debts, public or private, except where otherwise expressly stipulated, and for customs, taxes, etc., and when so received could be reissued. They could also be counted as part of the lawful money reserve of national banks.

The act further provided that upon demand of holder the Secretary of the Treasury should redeem such notes in gold or silver, at his discretion, it being (says the act) the established policy of the United States to maintain the two metals on a parity with each other upon the present legal ratio or such ratio as may be provided by law.

Section 3 provided for the coinage until July 1, 1891, of $2,000,000 per month; after that date as much as needed to redeem Treasury notes issued under this act.

Any gains or seigniorage arising from such coinage was to be accounted for and paid into the Treasury.

WHAT IS GAIN OR SEIGNIORAGE ?

The Bland bill as it passed the House November 5, 1877 (it did not become a law), allowed any owner of silver bullion to deposit it and receive for every 371.25 grains of pure silver (412½ grains of standard silver) a coined dollar which should be an unlimited legal tender. He was only to pay the half per-cent. mint charge for this great privilege. All the profit in this transaction was to go not to the Government, not to the people, through the Government, but to the mine owner, the bullion producer. In 1886 Mr. Bland introduced another bill with the same provisions. Mr. Plumb's amendment to the Conger bill, adopted by the Senate June 10, but which also failed to become a law, had the same provisions.

SENATOR STEWART'S FREE COINAGE AMENDMENT.

Another attempt was made in January, 1891, when Senator Stewart, of Nevada, offered a free-coinage amendment providing that at the "owner's option he may receive therefor (silver bullion) an equivalent in such standard dollars or Treasury notes," having "the same legal qualities as the notes provided for by the act approved July 14, 1890." This was designed to leave the Government no option as to the mode of payment for this bullion, and to enable the silver mine owners to take the most valuable mode of payment, which would probably be Treasury notes redeemable in "coin." July 1, 1892, Mr. Stewart offered another measure in the Senate, providing for free coinage and making the standard silver dollar legal tender for all debts and dues, public and private, "provided that foreign silver coins, or silver coins bearing the impress of foreign mints, and bullion formed by melting down such coin, shall be excluded from the provision of this act."

In this measure Senator Stewart sought to fasten legislation upon the country by which it would have been obliged to take the product of the Western silver barons as it was offered for free coinage. Commenting upon this purpose, Senator Vest, of Missouri, declared that he was for free coinage, "not to give a market to the mine owners of the West, but because it is a money metal," and the foreign clause was stricken out.

All of these measures were in the direct interest and to the sole advantage of the mine owners. All profits or gains in the business went, not to the Government to help to lighten the burden of the people, but for the profit and gain of a particular class.

PROFITS OF SEIGNIORAGE.

Let us see what these profits were. Under free coinage, on an average, in 1878 bullion worth 89.1 cents when deposited by the mine owner would have entitled him to receive from the mint a legal-tender dollar worth 100 cents in silver or in gold. He would have made a net profit, not counting the small charge for coinage, of 10 cents—a profit gained at the expense of the whole people.

In 1886 this same bullion was worth only 76.9 cents, giving to this same class a net profit of 23 cents and making a net cost to all the people of

23 cents for the inestimable privilege of allowing the mine owners the chance of using the Government and people of the United States as a stalking horse. It would make their dollars cheaper to the mine owners, of course. How would it help those who had to buy these same silver dollars by the sweat of their brows and at the full price of 100 cents on the dollar?

WHAT FREE COINAGE WOULD HAVE COST.

Let us calculate the result of such financial legislation; let us see what it would have cost the people of the United States to have given the free coinage at the dates stated.

In 1878 the average cost of silver bullion, enough to make a standard silver dollar, was 89 cents. In that year we coined 22,495,550 of these dollars. At 11 cents on the dollar it would have cost the country just $2,474,510.50 to have thus accommodated the silver-mining interests of the country.

A statement prepared at the Mint Bureau shows that the number of silver dollars coined at the United States Mints during the fiscal year ended June 30, 1897, was 21,203,701, on which the seigniorage or profit to the Government amounted to $6,336,104.25. This profit was turned into the Treasury from time to time as the coinage progressed, and was used to reduce taxation instead of wandering into the pockets of the silver producers, as would have been the case under free coinage. A more monstrous instance of attempted diversion of public money was never attempted.

THE SHERMAN LAW.

Under the operation of the Sherman law of 1890 it was found that the Government was purchasing 54,000,000 ounces of silver per year, or nearly all that was produced in the United States. This silver was stored in the Treasury vaults, and Treasury notes issued for the same, which were redeemable in gold on demand. It can be readily seen that it would be only a question of time when the Government would be obliged to suspend gold payments and reach a silver basis if this were continued.

REPEAL OF THE SHERMAN LAW.

At a special session of the Fifty-third Congress, called in August, 1893, after a long and spirited debate, the so-called Sherman law, on November 1, was repealed.

AMOUNT OF SILVER IN USE AS MONEY.

There is a widespread misunderstanding as to the actual amount of silver in use as money by the Government. According to the statistics of the Director of the Mint for 1897, there was coined into silver dollars, which are either in circulation or lodged in the Treasury vaults, silver bullion to secure Treasury notes, and subsidiary silver, the enormous amount of $634,-509,781, all of which is in actual use as money. The total amount of gold in use in the United States July 1, 1897, was $696,270,542, and of greenbacks $346,681,016.

So it will be seen that there is almost as much silver in use as any other kind of money, and I believe it would be greatly to the interest of the Government and of the people if all paper money under $5 could be retired and the silver dollar put in its place to do its work, instead of being stored in the Government vaults. This is the case in France, Germany, and England, where but very little, if any, paper or gold can be found of a less denomination than £1 in England, 20 marks in Germany and 20 francs in France, practically approximating $5 of American money.

REPUBLICANS TRUE TO THEIR PRINCIPLES.

These are official figures, from which every intelligent citizen should be able to draw his own conclusions without further comment. They embody to a great extent the record of the Republican party on the wisest legislation now on our statute books dealing with our finances and the elements of permanent prosperity. The Republican party has again taken the initiative in bringing order out of chaos, and, under the leadership of an able, patriotic, and statesmanlike Chief Executive, President McKinley, is loyally carrying out the principles of the platform adopted by the St. Louis convention in 1896.

In harmony with the spirit of that platform, and in response to the demands of nine-tenths of the suffering business interests of the United States, the President called Congress together in special session to repeal the Wilson bill. Congress enacted the Dingley bill, which is now in full force and effect, and its beneficial influence is already making itself felt in every section of the country.

The President, as one of the first acts of his Administration, appointed a commission to go to Europe to seek the establishment of an equitable arrangement with the leading commercial powers of the world for the use of both silver and gold within the limits of a safe and stable international policy, while he has also sent to Congress a message urging the appointment of a non-partisan monetary commission to recommend supplementary legislation for the improvement of our banking and currency system along necessary and expedient lines. The House of Representatives promptly adopted a resolution in harmony with this message. Thus the Republican party is loyally and fearlessly living up to its principles.

I have endeavored, Mr. Speaker, in these few remarks, to give a history of the finances of this Government since the war; also showing the production of silver and gold for the past three hundred and fifty years, believing that the enormous production of silver during the past twelve years has had much to do with its present bullion value.

OUR PENSION LAWS

What the Fifty-Fifth Congress Has Done

A SLANDER REFUTED

FROM THE SPEECH OF

Hon. GEORGE W. RAY,

OF NEW YORK.

IN THE HOUSE OF REPRESENTATIVES,

July 7, 1898.

OUR PENSION LAWS.

Mr. Ray said:

During the Fifty-fifth Congress 3,825 private pension bills have been introduced in the House alone and referred to the Committee on Invalid Pensions, and 629, and possibly some more, have been introduced and referred to the Committee on Pensions. The most of the 629, however, refer to service in wars other than the war of the rebellion.

March 31, 1898, the number of army and navy invalid pensioners under general law (soldiers and seamen) was..................	334,624
The number of army and navy invalid pensioners under act of June 27, 1890 (soldiers and seamen), was..........................	409,051
Total	743,675
At least 20,000 of those pensioned under the general law did not serve in the war of the rebellion, therefore deduct ,.........	20,000
Soldier and seaman pensioners of rebellion	723,675

A SLANDER REFUTED.

As the survivors of that war number at least 1,064,524, it will be seen that THE OFT-REPEATED SLANDER THAT MORE MEN ARE DRAWING PENSIONS AS SURVIVORS OF THE WAR OF THE REBELLION THAN THERE ARE LIVING OF THAT CLASS IS FULLY ANSWERED AND REFUTED.

About one-third, 340,849, of the surviving soldiers, sailors, and marines who served in the war of the rebellion are not on the pension rolls.

WHAT THE FIFTY-FIFTH CONGRESS HAS DONE.

During the present Congress the Senate has passed and sent to the House 313 private pension bills referred to the Committee on Invalid Pensions.

During the Fifty-fifth Congress, and we now approach the close of the first regular session, during which all of our pension work has been done, the Committee on Invalid Pensions, of which I have the honor to be chairman, has reported to the House 478 private pension bills, of which 403 have passed the House, and 254 have already passed both Houses, been signed by the President, and are now laws. There has been no contention over the bills reported and no man on either side has claimed the amount reported to be excessive or undeserved except in two cases.

The Committee on Pensions of the House has reported and passed 77 private pension bills, of which 61 have passed both Houses and are now laws. The total number of private pension bills that have been reported favorably to the House during the Fifty-fifth Congress is 555, and the total number passed is 485, of which 322 have already become laws. Some 26 await the signature of the President.

As some of our Democratic friends for political effect have spread the false report that this Republican Administration and this Republican Congress are unfriendly and unfavorable to the old soldiers, it is well to compare the work of this, the Fifty-fifth Congress, in special pension legislation with the work of the Fifty-second and Fifty-third Congresses, both of which were Democratic.

The Fifty-third Congress (Democratic) passed a grand total of only 119 special pension bills during its three sessions, its entire life.

The Fifty-second Congress (also Democratic) passed a grand total of 217 private pension bills during both its sessions, its entire life. These two Democratic Congresses during their five sessions passed a grand total of 336 pension bills.

The House in the Fifty-fifth Congress (Republican) has in seven months of one session reported and passed 485 private pension bills, or 149 more than did both the two preceding Democratic Congresses during their five sessions and their entire unfortunate existence. The Fifty-fourth Congress during its entire life, both sessions, only passed a total of 378 private pension bills that became laws, 107 less than have already passed the House in the Fifty-fifth Congress,

Mr. RIDGELY. Will the gentleman tell us the number of bills introduced?

Mr. RAY of New York. I am going to give it to you. There were more introduced than now or about the same number.

It is hardly proper or consistent or honest for our Democratic friends, in view of these facts, to claim that this Congress is unfriendly to the soldiers and their widows and orphans or that it is a do-nothing Congress in pension legislation. NO FAVORITISM HAS BEEN SHOWN; AND PENSION BILLS INTRODUCED BY DEMOCRATIC AND POPULIST MEMBERS HAVE HAD THE SAME ATTENTION AND CONSIDERATION ACCORDED THOSE INTRODUCED BY REPUBLICANS.

PENSIONS NOW PAID.

On the 31st day of March, 1898, we had on the pension rolls the following pensioners:

Under general law:
Army invalid (soldiers).................................. 329,787
Navy invalid (seamen, etc.)............................. 4,837
————— 334,624
Under act of June 27, 1890:
Army invalid.. 394,702
Navy invalid.. 14,349
————— 409,051

Total soldiers, sailors, and marines........................ 743,675

Under general law:

Army widows and dependent relatives..........	93,376
Navy widows and dependent relatives...........	2,320
	95,596

Under act of June 27, 1890:

Army widows and dependent relatives..........	118,056
Navy widows and dependent relatives...........	5,907
	123,963

Total widows and dependent relatives........................219,561
Army nurses..	644

Total pensioners, war of the rebellion........................963,880
Revolutionary pensioners..	16
War of 1812 pensioners...	2,523
Mexican war pensioners...	18,293
Indian wars pensioners..	6,262

Total pensioners March 31, 1898...............................	990,974

In truth, about 1 person out of every 70 of our population draws a pension from the General Government.

In 1897 we paid pensions to the amount of...................	$139,949,717.35
Paid pension agents for disbursing.............................	572,439.41
Paid expenses of Pension Bureau...............................	3,415,343.66

Total expenses, year ending July 1, 1897...............	143,937,500.42

During the fiscal year ending July 1, 1898, we have paid, in round numbers, $148,000,000 to our pensioners.

WORK OF THE PENSION BUREAU.

Much has been said importing that the present Administration in its administration of the pension laws through the present Commissioner of Pensions, Hon. H. Clay Evans, has been and is unfriendly to the pension system and to the old soldiers and their widows and orphans. A certain class of pension agents and attorneys and Democrats (called statesmen) have been exceedingly busy spreading this report. For a year or more during the last of the Administration of President Cleveland pensioners were advised to hold back their claims pending the approaching election and to present and press claims for pension and increases as soon as the new President (certain to be a Republican) should be inaugurated.

The result was that Commissioner Evans found the Bureau "swamped" under a mass of new applications. The eager and expectant applicants could brook no delay. They seemed to expect the immediate allowance of every claim filed, whether for original pension, increase, or restoration to the rolls. They did not pause to consider that such action would be impolitic, unwise, and unjust. The propriety and necessity of a thorough examination of each individual case was a consideration not to be entertained, and as a result there was considerable friction between pension attorneys and the Commissioner.

6

BUT THE WORK OF THE BUREAU, IMPEDED AS IT IS BY THE PRESENCE OF MANY INCOMPETENT CLERKS PLACED THERE BY A DEMOCRATIC ADMINISTRATION, UNFRIENDLY TO THE OLD SOLDIERS AND TO THE PENSION SYSTEM, HAS GONE ON UNCEASINGLY, LABORIOUSLY, AND FAITHFULLY. A comparison of work done and of results obtained under the last Administration and the present will best tell the story.

Comparison of pension claims allowed and disallowed for years 1894, 1895, and 1896, and 1897 (nine months only included).

Year.	Allowed per month.	Rejected per month.
General law—original.		
1894	845	1,653
1895	662	1,582
1896	650	1,307
1897 (9 months)	a 803	1,089
Act of 1890—original.		
1894	b 2,655	4,271
1895	c 2,710	3,777
1896	d 3,341	3,171
1897 (9 months)	e 4,118	2,358
General law—increase.		
1894	913	1,892
1895	810	1,639
1896	1,050	1,887
1897 (9 months)	961	1,165
Act of 1890—increase.		
1894	177	864
1895	288	1,431
1896	844	1,059
1897 (9 months)	743	1,071
General law—original.		
1894, 1895, 1896	f 719	1,514
1897 (9 months)	g 808	1,089
General law—increase.		
1894, 1895, 1896	924	1,806
1897 (9 months)	961	1,165
Act of 1890—original.		
1894, 1895, 1896	2,899	3,740
1897 (9 months)	4,118	2,358
Act of 1890—increase.		
1894, 1895, 1896	270	1,119
1897 (9 months)	742	1,071

a Or 31 per day.   d Or 128 per day.   f Or 27 per day.
b Or 102 per day.   e Or 158 per day.   g Or 31 per day.
c Or 104 per day.

It thus appears that during each of the years 1894, 1895, and 1896, up to March, 1897, when President McKinley was inaugurated, the Democratic Administration was allowing original claims under the general law at the rate of 27 per day and rejecting such claims at the rate of 58 per day. It was allowing original claims under the act of 1890 at the rate of 111 per day and rejecting them at the rate of 143 per day.

Under both laws it was allowing 138 original claims per day and rejecting 201 per day.

The Republican Administration has been allowing original claims under the general law at the rate of 31 per day and rejecting at the rate of 41 per day. It has been allowing original claims under the act of 1890 at the rate of 158 per day and rejecting at the rate of 90 per day.

Under both laws it has allowed 189 original claims per day and rejected 131 per day.

ORIGINAL CLAIMS.

	Allowed per day.	Rejected per day.
Republican Administration	189	131
Democratic Administration	138	201

The above figures relate simply to original claims adjudicated.

Now let us take claims for increase.

The Democratic Administration allowed 35 claims for increase under the general law per day and rejected 69 per day. It allowed of claims for increase, under the act of 1890, 10 per day and rejected 43 per day. In other words, it was allowing 45 increase claims per day and rejecting 112 per day.

The Republican Administration has been allowing 37 increase claims per day under the general law, and 28 per day under the act of 1890, a total of 65 per day, while it has rejected 44 increase claims under the general law per day and 41 of such claims under the act of 1890, a total of 85 per day.

INCREASE CLAIMS.

	Allowed per day.	Rejected per day.
Republican Administration	65	85
Democratic Administration	45	112
INCLUDING BOTH CLASSES.		
Republican Administration	189	131
	65	85
Total	254	216
Democratic Administration	138	201
	45	112
Total	183	313

It is seen that while the Democratic Administration was adjudicating 496 claims per day, as against 470 per day adjudicated by THE REPUBLICAN ADMINISTRATION SINCE THE RETURN OF THE REPUBLICAN PARTY TO POWER, THE PENSION OFFICE UNDER COMMISSIONER H. CLAY EVANS HAS ALLOWED 71 CLAIMS PER DAY MORE THAN WERE ALLOWED UNDER THE FORMER ADMINISTRATION, WHILE IT HAS REJECTED 97 LESS PER DAY.

This proves beyond any controversy whatever that while the Pension Bureau has been a little slower in adjudicating pension claims since March 4, 1897, than prior to that date, the work done has inured wholly to the benefit of the old soldier and of his widow and orphan. Every day for the nine months covered by these figures in 71 cases more than under the last Administration has happiness been carried to the family of some old soldier. The rates allowed have been much larger also.

Those who complain of tardiness at the Bureau and who are inclined to suggest that the Administration is against the old soldier should study the figures well before indulging in such unwarranted and undeserved criticism.

Our Democratic friends who, now they are out of power, would pose as the soldier's friend, when in power and when they had an opportunity to do something for the needy old soldier and his widow and orphan, were slow to act in Congress and granted pensions and increases with a hesitating and niggardly hand, as we have seen.

At the Pension Bureau they struck from the rolls the names of thousands of needy and deserving pensioners. In passing on claims they were swift to adjudicate unfavorably but exceedingly slow to allow pensions. Let the old soldiers remember the few bills passed; the many vetoed; the fact that at the Bureau of Pensions in 1894 and 1895 the Democratic Administration allowed 34 per cent. of the claims examined and rejected 66 per cent; that in 1896, when it did its best, trying to influence the election, it only allowed 42 per cent. and rejected 58 per cent.

During the entire year since H. Clay Evans became Commissioner of Pensions 154,445 pension claims have been finally adjudicated, and of these 79,298, or 52 per cent, have been allowed, and 75,147, or 48 per cent, have been rejected or held for further evidence. The Bureau has proceeded with great care, and in thousands of the cases not allowed the Bureau has held and is holding them for additional necessary evidence. There has been no veto of a special pension bill, and every patriotic citizen knows that President McKinley, himself an old soldier, will not tolerate an illiberal pension policy or an injustice to an old comrade in arms.

During the first nine months of the present fiscal year the pension roll was increased by the addition of 15,000 more names than were lost by death, remarriage, and the arrival of minors at the age of 16 years. During the year ending April 1, 1898, the loss to the roll was as follows:

From death	37,855
Remarriage	1,421
Minors arrived at age	2,284
Failure to claim pension	3,563
Other causes	3,194
Total	48,317

During the year ending June 30, 1895, 37,060 original claims were filed. For the year 1896, 33,749 such claims were filed, while for the year ending April 1, 1898, 61,613 original claims and 164,438 claims for increase—a total of 226,051—were filed. It is easy to see how impossible it has been for the Commissioner to examine and adjudicate all of these claims, and when we consider the rejections and failure to reach claims, and the consequent disappointments, in connection with the misrepresentations made by politicians of the opposing political party for partisan purposes, it is not difficult to understand how undeserved is the criticism to which the Pension Bureau has been subjected.

Common prudence suggests and demands that every case be thoroughly examined. If by inadvertence or neglect an undeserved pension is allowed, the enemies of the pension system and of the old soldiers themselves seize upon the fact and herald it far and wide as an evidence of laxness and corruption in the Pension Bureau and of frauds on the part of the pensioners themselves.

A ROLL OF HONOR.

No class of citizens in our great country is more interested in a just and an honest administration of the pension laws than the old soldiers. The pension roll always has been, now is, and always must be maintained "a roll of honor." The fact that an old soldier's name appears on that roll should guarantee that he was a loyal man, that he was a brave man, that he served faithfully and honorably, and that he received wounds or incurred disabilities in the service and in the line of duty, or that he is now suffering from disabilities that prevent his earning a support by his manual labor.

The generous hand of a just Government will always be open to such as these; and our patriotic people, loving liberty and good government, determined that our institutions shall endure, proud of our past and confident of our future as a nation, admiring the defenders of the national honor and life and ever willing to give them encouragement and recognize their brave deeds and care for those who defended the flag when it needed defenders, or who shall hereafter inscribe additional glorious victories upon its broad and ample folds, will not fail to maintain and perpetuate our pension system.

But honors are for those to whom honor is due, and pensions are for the deserving. The pension laws should be so framed and so executed as to create confidence in the minds of all our citizens that the $150,000,000 annually expended under their provisions is given to those who have just claims upon the resources and generosity of a grateful Republic.

This large amount of money to meet the just claims of our pensioners will be required but a few years longer. Year by year the soldiers and sailors and marines and their widows are answering to the last roll call. In a very few years the last survivor of the Mexican and Indian wars will be in his grave, and fifty years hence the last survivor of the war of the rebellion will have passed over the river to his eternal rest under the shade of the trees on the evergreen shores.

Nearly all who incurred pensionable disabilities in the service are now on the rolls and the main additions by reason of past service will come in under the act of June 27, 1890, where the maximum allowed is $12 per month.

THE DEATH ROLL.

During the last five years pensioners have died as follows:

1893	25,005
1894	28,070
1895	27,816
1896	29,393
1897	31,960

As only two-thirds of the survivors are on the rolls, it is safe to say that at least 25,000 of the comrades of the war of the rebellion die each year.

By reason of deaths and other causes the decrease in pension payments in 1897 was $5,684,081. The increase in the figures before given was caused by the addition of new names and the granting of increase applications. It will be seen that when the addition of new names in considerable numbers ceases the decrease in the amount of pension payments will be very rapid.

A SAMPLE OF PLAIN MISREPRESENTATION.

As a sample of plain evasion of truth and misrepresentation I insert the following letter, written by a Democratic member of this House, who, at the writing, had had three of his own bills favorably reported and one passed and become a law by the approval of the President. As the cases were meritorious, the committee is proud of its action, but must express its regret that the beneficiaries of the bills referred to are represented by a gentleman whose attainments in a certain direction indicate that he is a lineal descendant of Ananias and Sapphira, and that he is fully able and willing to maintain the reputation of the Ananias family.

[Fifty-fifth Congress. Josiah D. Hicks, Pa., chairman; Edward Sauerhering. Wis.; Winfield S. Kerr, Ohio; John M. Mitchell, N. Y.; Walter Reeves. Ill.; William C. Lovering, Mass.; James H. Davidson, Wis.; William L. Ward, N. Y.; William Sulzer, N. Y.; Champ Clark, Mo.; Thomas Y. Fitzpatrick, Ky.; James R. Campbell, Ill.; John H. Stephens, Tex. T. S. Davis, clerk.]

COMMITTEE ON PATENTS,
HOUSE OF REPRESENTATIVES UNITED STATES,
Washington, D. C., April 28, 1898.

DEAR MADAM: I have your letter of late date. If there is any earthly way to pass a pension claim through this Congress, I have failed to discover it. Occasionally a Republican Congressman gets one through for the rich widow of some officers, but for a Democrat to get one allowed for some worthy poor woman or man seems impossible. I do not expect to get one bill passed out of sixty-five introduced by me. The Dingley bill does not bring in enough money to run the Government, and the Republicans are trying to make the pensioners pay the balance by keeping them out of their just dues.

Yours, very truly,

CHAMP CLARK.

Mrs. LYDIA LOLLAR, Sullivan, Mo.

Remember, the gentleman from Missouri had had three of his own bills favorably reported and one passed and approved by the President.

The Dingley bill has done remarkably well in bringing in money, and this Congress has done more for the old soldiers and their widows and orphans in seven months than the Democratic party did in four years. The Dingley tariff bill will more than support the Government, aside from the expenses of the war, and even Democrats know or ought to know the fact.

It may be that the gentleman who wrote that letter had not discovered any "earthly way" to pass a private pension bill through the Fifty-fifth Congress; but the Committee on Invalid Pensions had discovered the way, and had steadfastly and patriotically pursued it.

PENSION TO RELIEVE THE PRESSING NECESSITIES AND WANTS OF THE NEEDY AND DESERVING.

At the time that letter was written its author knew that more than 250 private pension bills had already been reported favorably to the House, and that more than 150 had passed. He also knew, or ought to have known, that nearly every one was in aid of a private soldier, a private soldier's widow, or a dependent child or parent of some defender of the flag long since dead. He also knew, or might have known, that in every case the pension or increase of pension had been given to relieve the pressing necessities and wants of the needy and deserving claimant. He also knew, or might have known, that the Fifty-fifth Congress has reported 115 pension bills introduced by Democratic and Populist members of this House, many more than their proportion.

If the gentleman pleads ignorance of the facts, he still stands before the bar of public opinion convicted, for he who asserts as a fact something he does not know is equally guilty with the one who wilfully misstates a fact within his knowledge. I regret the necessity of calling attention to this letter, but in no other way can I defend the Fifty-fifth Congress against this gross and outrageous slander. In no other way can I reach the ten hundred thousand old soldiers whose minds the gentleman would seek to poison by such misrepresentation. The baseness of the slander will the more fully appear as I proceed.

CHARGES FALSELY AND EVIDENTLY MALICIOUSLY MADE.

I shall be pardoned for exhibiting some considerable feeling on this subject for, as I am charged, as chairman of the Committee on Invalid Pensions, with caring for the rights of the old soldiers, my comrades of thirty-three years ago, and with whom I marched and "drank from the same canteen," the statement is a personal reflection on me, and the Committee on Invalid Pensions, as well as the Republican party and the Fifty-fifth Congress. I regret being compelled by this letter and many more of the same false tenor now in my possession, to give any partisan tinge to these remarks, but, sir, when such charges are falsely and evidently maliciously made, my plain duty as a citizen, and as a member of this House demands that the truth be plainly and fearlessly spoken.

More than 1,500 private pension bills, with all the papers on file at the Bureau and the great mass of testimony filed with the committee, have been carefully examined and considered by the Committee on Invalid Pensions alone. But one bill allowing a pension or an increase of pension in excess of $50 per month has passed the House, and that was given to a private soldier. Only two bills granting pensions or increasing the pensions of general officers have been reported, and only twelve bills granting pensions or increasing the pension of general officer's widows have been reported.

One bill has been reported and passed increasing the pension of a widow of a commander in the United States Navy, and one increasing the pension of the widow of a captain in that service.

CAREFUL ATTENTION TO THE CLAIMS OF PRIVATE SOLDIERS AND OF THEIR WIDOWS AND HELPLESS CHILDREN.

Particular and careful attention has been given to the claims of private soldiers with good records and of their widows and dependent, helpless children, and in every case where a pension or an increase has been asked for any person, recognition has been refused unless the necessitous circumstances of the applicant justified and demanded action. It should be remembered by the old soldiers, officers and privates alike, and by the Representatives in Congress, that the Government has not undertaken, does not undertake, to fully support the old soldiers, seamen, or marines, or their widows, but only to afford a reasonable degree of aid. This is all any nation assumes to do.

Mr. FARRIS. May I ask the gentleman a question?

) Mr. RAY of New York. Certainly.

Mr. FARIS. I should like to ask my friend to state to the House if it is true that he has received the original of that letter which he read.

Mr. RAY of New York. I have seen the original letter. It is on file at the Pension Bureau. But I will not call the names of other gentlemen of this House. This is the wickedest letter of them all, but I have five more written by Democratic members of this House making the same charge and to the same effect.

Mr. CANNON. Mr. Speaker, if it does not discommode my friend I would like to ask him just in that connection if it is not true that in the Pension Office, under the general pension laws, in the lately expired fiscal year, in the settlement of pension claims, there has not been $8,000,000 more expended than was expended during the prior year?

Mr. RAY of New York. I have that here and I am coming to it in just a moment.

PROSPERITY
SINCE McKINLEY'S ELECTION

REPUBLICAN PLEDGES KEPT

HELP FOR CUBA

FROM THE REMARKS OF

Hon. Thaddeus M. Mahon

OF PENNSYLVANIA

IN THE HOUSE OF REPRESENTATIVES

Part of Congressional Record, August 3, 1898

PROSPERITY SINCE McKINLEY'S ELECTION.

Mr. MAHON said:

Mr. CHAIRMAN : I desire to incorporate as part of my remarks the following article from the columns of the New York Tribune:

It is just two years since the Republican party in its convention at St. Louis nominated William McKinley and promised in its platform to do certain things in case it should be again intrusted with the control of national affairs. These things were, in brief, the adoption of a protective tariff, which should benefit the American manufacturer and producer; reciprocity, which would add to the profits of the agriculturist; a sound currency and international bimetalism, if possible, and that the Government of the United States should "use its influence and good offices to restore peace and give independence to the island of Cuba." It is interesting at this time to see how these promises have been kept and what has been the result.

TARIFF.

President McKinley was inaugurated on March 4th. He immediately called Congress to meet in extra session, beginning on March 15th. The President's message dealt wholly with the tariff and urged immediate action. The tariff bill was introduced in the House on the first day of the session, and passed that body fifteen days later, March 31st. Owing to the fact that the Republicans did not control the Senate, it was impossible to make as rapid progress in that body as in the House, but notwithstanding this fact the bill passed the Senate on July 7th and became a law on July 24th. No Administration since that of Washington has brought about the enactment of a tariff law within so brief a period after its inauguration.

TEN MONTHS' RECORD UNDER THE DINGLEY ACT—RECEIPTS
$1,000,000 A DAY.

Now, as to the course of the commerce and national finance since the enactment of this new and thoroughly protective tariff law, compared with the conditions under the tariff act which preceded it. The new law has now been in operation ten months. In spite of the fact that excessive importations in the few months immediately preceding its enactment passed to the credit of the Wilson law, probably $40,-000,000 which would have been collected under the new law but for these anticipatory importations, the receipts of the Treasury have been in these ten months of its operation more than $30,000,000 in excess of those of the corresponding ten months of the history of the Wilson law. That the new law was able, under normal conditions, to produce sufficient revenue to meet the current expenses of the Government is shown by the fact that the receipts during the last four months, in the face of war and the consequent disarrangement of commerce, have averaged $1,000,000 a day.

The ordinary expenditures of the Government during the last few years, aside from the postal service, which is practically self-sustaining, average $1,000,000 a day the year round, and the fact that the Dingley law has produced an average of $1,000,000 a day since the effect of the anticipatory imports ceased to be felt shows that its framers were fully justified in their belief that it would meet the ordinary expenses of the Government, and that the additions which have recently been made have been necessary only because of the extraordinary expenses resulting from the war. The following table shows the receipts of the Government in the first ten months of the Dingley, Wilson, and McKinley laws : · .

A COMPARISON OF RECEIPTS. '

Total receipts of Treasury (exclusive of Pacific Railroad sales), in months, as follows :

First ten months McKinley Law.		First ten months Wilson Law.		First ten months Dingley Law.	
Date.	Amount.	Date.	Amount.	Date.	Amount.
Oct., 1890...........	$39,222,174	Sept., 1894.........	$22,021,229	Aug., 1897........	$19,023,615
Nov., 1890........	28,678,675	Oct., 1894.........	19,139,240	Sept., 1897........	21,933,098
Dec., 1890........	31,106,165	Nov., 1894.........	19,411,404	Oct., 1897..........	24,391,415
Jan., 1891........	36,810,233	Dec., 1894.........	21,866,137	Nov., 1897..........	25,168,987
Feb., 1891........	29,273,173	Jan., 1895.........	27,804,400	Dec., 1897..........	27,931,494
Mar , 1891........	29,027,455	Feb., 1895.........	22,888,057	Jan., 1898	28,795,227
Apr., 1891........	25,465,232	Mar., 1895.........	25,470,576	Feb., 1898.........	28,572,358
May, 1891........	27,289,800	Apr., 1895.........	24,247,830	Mar., 1898.........	29,307,251
June, 1891.........	31,631,850	May, 1895.........	25,272,078	Apr., 1898..........	30,361,443
July, 1891..........	34,158,245	June, 1895.........	25,615,474	May, 1898..........	30,074,818
Total............	$312,662,508	....	$234,336,431	....	$265,559,70

A GAIN OF $157,000,000 IN SALES ABROAD DURING TEN MONTHS.

When the Dingley bill was under consideration the free traders insisted, as they always do, that the adoption of the protective system would affect commerce disadvantageously—would reduce American markets abroad. Let us see how much truth there was in this claim. The new law went into effect during the first month of the present fiscal year, so it is fair, in discussing this question, to consider the entire fiscal year, so far as completed, and compare it with the corresponding months of the preceding fiscal year. Our total sales to other parts of the world during the first eleven months of the fiscal year amount to $1,135,485,618, against $977,800,422 in the corresponding months of the preceding year. Here is a gain of over $157,000,000 in our sales to other parts of the world in eleven months under the new tariff law. Does this look as though the protective system was hampering our foreign trade or reducing our sales to other parts of the world?

EXPORTS OF MANUFACTURED GOODS SHOW AN INCREASE OF $1,000,000 A MONTH.

Not only have American manufacturers been able under the Dingley law to continue their competition in the world's markets, but they have actually increased their sales of American manufactures more than $10,000,000 in the first ten months of the fiscal year. Thus, in spite of the assertion of the low tariff advocates that the protective-tariff system would disadvantageously affect our foreign commerce, we have increased our exports of manufactured articles at the rate of $1,000,000 a month since the enactment of the new law, and our total exports to other parts of the world at the rate of $15,000,000 a month, making a total much greater than in any corresponding period in the history of the country. Indeed, the exports of the eleven months of the fiscal year just ended are greater than in any entire fiscal year in the history of the country, and the balance of trade is much larger than in any preceding year. In the eleven months ending May 31, 1898, our total exports were $1,135,485,618, while the largest exports of any full fiscal year prior to this were (1897) $1,050,993,556.

COMPETITIVE IMPORTS REDUCED.

Not only has the Dingley law fulfilled the promises of its framers in supplying, under normal conditions, sufficient revenue to meet the ordinary expenses of the Government, and show an increase of our exports of manufactures and our general sales to other parts of the world, but it has at the same time reduced the imports from other parts of the world which came into competition with our manufacturers. The imports in the first eleven months of the present fiscal year amount to only \$563,596,581, against \$679,547,391 in the corresponding months of the preceding year. Thus, while we have been increasing our exports \$157,000,000, we have decreased our imports \$116,000,000.

.   The net result of the improvement of our foreign commerce since the enactment of the Dingley law may be stated in a sentence, as follows : For the first time in our history we are exporting more manufactured articles than we are importing, and for the first time in our history our total exports are more than double our total imports. These figures, it should be remembered, relate to the eleven months ending May 31, 1898.

TRADE BALANCES COMPARED.

The following table shows the balance of trade in the eleven months just ended, and compares the figures with those of the corresponding eleven months in each year since 1891 :

BALANCE OF TRADE IN OUR FAVOR DURING ELEVEN MONTHS OF FISCAL YEAR 1898, COMPARED WITH CORRESPONDING PERIOD IN PRECEDING YEARS :

Eleven months ending June 1—	Imports.	Exports.	Excess of Exports.
1898	\$563,596,581	\$1,135,485,618	\$571,889,037
1897	679,547,391	977,800,522	298,253,131
1896	723,560,934	815,901,067	92,340,133
1895	670,307,921	752,570,335	82,262,114
1894	603,210,910	834,636,085	231,425,175
1893	796,706,378	782,218,625	* 14,487,753
1892	755,385,894	965,389,811	208,003,917

* Excess of Imports.

One feature of the discussion of the Dingley law which attracted much attention was the protests from foreign countries, which were more numerous than in any preceding tariff discussion and which were pointed out by those opposing the protective tariff theory as an evidence that the adoption of the new law would result in the loss of our trade with those countries. As the countries making those protests included nearly all of the leading commercial nations of the world, the effect of the adoption of the protective tariff in the face of these protests has been watched with much interest.

The following table shows our exports to the countries in question in the first ten months of the preceding year. It will be seen that in nearly every instance our sales to those protesting countries have been greater since the adoption of the Dingley law than in the corresponding months of last year under the low-tariff Wilson law, the total sales to the fourteen countries in question being nearly $130,000,000 greater in the first ten months of the present year than in the corresponding months of the preceding year:

EXPORTS FROM THE UNITED STATES TO COUNTRIES WHICH OFFERED
PROTESTS AGAINST THE DINGLEY TARIFF.

	Ten months, April, 1897.	Ten months, April, 1898.
United Kingdom and Canada.	$472,203,608	$523,556,877
Germany	107,587,265	129,721,280
France	51,376,430	74,301,932
Netherlands	42,444,677	53,178,788
Belgium	27,900,403	39,572,347
Italy	18,476,062	20,318,564
Japan	11,233,594	17,126,289
Denmark	8,761,664	10,111,635
China	8,997,685	7,871,099
Argentina	5,435,311	5,417,851
Austria-Hungary	3,325,006	4,821,394
Turkey	324,678	736,895
Switzerland	52,136	226,927
Greece	106,981	122,659
Total	$758,225,500	$837,084,837

One effect of the new tariff law which will be of especial interest is the reduction in the importations of wool which followed the enactment of the new law. The following table compares the importations of wool, by months, during the eleven months of the fiscal year with the corresponding months of last year :

IMPORTS OF WOOL DURING EACH MONTH OF FISCAL YEAR 1897 COMPARED WITH 1898.

	1897.	1898.
	Pounds.	Pounds.
July...	5,458,803	23,140,431
August...	4,651,009	2,877,877
September	4,795,176	2,505,673
October..	6,543,287	7,154,542
November...	10,202,004	10,320,644
December...	26,220,650	17,857,218
January..	20,784,829	11,070,126
February	31,650,782	16,083,340
March..	54,229,939	11,944,104
April...	98,547,736	13,148,376
May...	45,857,220	7,586,438
Total, 11 months..	312,941,435	123,688,769

FARMER'S PRICES INCREASED, WHILE ARTICLES HE BUYS HAVE FALLEN.

The effect of the improved conditions among manufacturers and of our foreign market has been felt by the farmers not alone in the increase in the price of wheat, but in the price of practically every article which they have to sell, while in many articles which they must buy prices have fallen.

The following table presents the price of articles of farm production and farm consumption on July 1, 1896, and June 1, 1898, as shown by the publications of Bradstreets, an accepted authority, which was widely quoted by Democratic campaigners in 1896. The comparison of prices of farm production and of articles of farm consumption is followed by a comparison of prices of silver on the two dates mentioned :

PRICES OF ARTICLES OF FARM PRODUCTION.

Products.		July 1, 1896.	June 1, 1898.
Wheat, No. 2, red, winter	per bushel	$0.64⅜	$1.18
Corn, No. 2, mixed	do	.33¾	.37½
Oats, No. 2, mixed	do	.21½	.32¼
Barley, No. 2, Milwaukee	do	.30	.47½
Rye	do	.37⅛	.56½
Beef, carcasses (Chicago)	per pound	.05⅛	.07½
Hogs, carcasses (Chicago)	do	.03⅞	.05
Mutton, carcasses (Chicago)	do	.05½	.08¾
Lard	do	.04¼	.06¼
Potatoes	per barrel	.75	2.00
Hides, dry	per pound	.17	.21
Wool, Ohio X, washed	do	.16	.26
Hops	do	.07	.12

PRICES OF ARTICLES OF FARM CONSUMPTION.

Products.	July 1, 1896.	June 1, 1898.
Nails, wire, per keg	$2.80	$1.70
Pine, yellow, per M	17.00	16.50
Standard sheetings, per yard	.05¾	.04¼
Petroleum, refined, per gallon	.07¾	.06¾
Coffee (Rio No. 7, per pound)	.13	.06½
Phosphate, per 2000 pounds	5.25	5.00
Bar silver, per ounce	.692	.586

Upon this question of the relation of the price of silver to the price of farm products the following table showing the prices of wheat, mess pork, wool and silver at various dates during the last two years is interesting, indicating, as it does, a steady fall in silver and a steady rise in these three representative articles of general farm production:

PRICES OF SILVER AND FARM PRODUCTS.

Date.	Wheat. No. 2, red.	Mess pork, per bbl.	Wool, Ohio, per lb.	Silver, per oz.
	Cents.		Cents.	Cents.
July 10, 1896	63.5	$7.75	17.0	69.2
September 26, 1896	74.5	8.25	18.0	68.0
November 1, 1896	85.0	8.50	19.0	65.6
April 17, 1897	96.5	8.75	21.5	62.5
September 16, 1897	100.5	9.50	26.5	57.4
December 17, 1897	102.2	9.00	27.5	56.6
February 25, 1898	104.2	10.75	27.7	55.6
March 10, 1898	106.5	10.75	28.0	54.3
June 1, 1898	118.0	11.50	26.0	58.6

One feature of the new tariff act which caused especial complaint among those opposed to the protective theory was the assertion that the duty which was placed on hides would increase the price of shoes.   In answer to this it is only necessary to say that price tables recently published in Dun's Review quoting the prices of boots and shoes from January 1, 1897, to June 2, 1898, show that in almost every class the prices of shoes are now lower than they were six months before the adoption of the Dingley law, which placed a duty on imported hides.

That the improvement in our commerce and manufacturing industries following the new tariff law has resulted advantageously to business is shown by the following table from Dun's Review, showing amounts of the liabilities of the commercial failures during the first five months of 1898 as compared with those of the corresponding months of the preceding years since 1893 :

COMMERCIAL FAILURES FIRST FIVE MONTHS.

Calendar Year.	Liabilities.	Calendar Year.	Liabilities.
1898	$52,208,302	1895	$69,007,748
1897	76,940,777	1894	87,344,680
1896	82,209,180		

EXCESS OF GOLD IMPORTS OVER EXPORTS $102,026,989 IN ELEVEN MONTHS.

The enormous balance of trade which the country has enjoyed during the last eleven months has resulted in the largest importations of gold in its history.   The total importations of gold, including ore and bullion, amounted during the eleven months just ended to $117,057,851, and deducting the exports of gold, which are $15,030,862, leaves an excess of imports of $102,026,989 for the eleven months.   This is a larger sum than the total net imports in any full fiscal year in the history of the country, and is in marked contrast with the conditions during the preceding Admistration, in which every year showed a net exportation ranging from $4,500,000 to $87,500,000, as is indicated by the following table, which shows the net exports and imports of gold (including bullion and ore) for the fiscal years since 1892 :

THE MOVEMENTS OF GOLD.

Fiscal year.	Excess of exports of gold.	Excess of imports of gold.
1893	$87,506,463	
1894	4,527,942	
1895	30,083,721	
1896	78,884,882	
1897		$ 44,653,200
1898 (11 months)		102,026,985

The effects of these enormous gold importations and of this general business improvement are felt in the increased amount of money in circulation in the United States, as shown by the official statements of the Treasury Department. This statement is especially interesting, since the assertion was made so frequently during the campaign of 1896 that there could be no material increase in our currency without the free and unlimited coinage of silver. It will be observed that in spite of the fact that free coinage has not been adopted, the money in circulation on June 1, 1898, was greater than on July 1, 1896, by $333,463,290.

MONEY IN CIRCULATION IN THE UNITED STATES.

	July 1, 1896.	June 1, 1898.
Gold	$454,905,064	$649,571,881
Standard silver dollars	52,110,904	57,596,423
Subsidary silver	60,204,451	64,042,000
Gold certificates	42,198,119	35,883,209
Silver certificates	330,657,191	391,225,265
Treasury notes	95,245,047	100,226,855
United States notes	224,249,863	290,202,987
Currency certificates	31,890,000	26,540,000
National-bank notes	215,168,122	224,609,636
Total	1,506,434,966	1,839,898,256

That the farmers of the country have had their share of this general prosperity and have utilized it with a wisdom which characterized their course in the campaign of 1896, as well as on other occasions, is shown by the recently published statement that the farm mortgages in Nebraska, which increased $1,635,000 in 1896, were reduced by $2,923,000 in 1897. The figures published in the early months of the present year—and their accuracy has not been called into question—show that the farm mortgages filed in Nebraska in 1896 were $12,033,000; releases, $11,398,000; increase in indebtedness, $1,635,000; while in 1897 there were filed $11,-844,000; released, $14,767,000—a decrease of indebtedness of $2,923,000.

In only a single instance have the farmers failed to realize improved prices, and that instance is cotton. That this continued low price of cotton is due to causes other than currency is indicated by the following table, which shows the cotton production of the United States at various years since that preceding the date of the crime, so called, against silver.

PRODUCTION OF COTTON IN THE UNITED STATES.

Year.	Bales.	Year.	Bales.
1872	2,975,000	1895	9,901,000
1876	4,632,000	1897	11,100,000
1886	6,575,000		

Not only is the improvement in prices felt in general articles of farm production, but also in farm stock, which, according to the estimates of the Department of Agriculture, has increased about $240,000,000 in value during the year 1897, the increase being distributed as follows:

INCREASE IN FARM STOCK.

Mules	$6,000,000
Hogs	8,000,000
Farm horses	25,000,000
Milch cows	65,000,000
Other cattle	104,000,000

ADMINISTRATION'S POLICY WITH REGARD TO CUBA.

That the Administration has fully carried out the pledges, expressed or implied, of the platform in regard to Cuba can not be doubted by anybody. The platform said : " The Government of Spain having lost control of Cuba, and being unable to protect the property or lives of resident American citizens, or to comply with its treaty obligations, we believe that the Government of the United States should actively use its influence and good offices to restore peace and give independence to the island."

The first step taken by President McKinley upon assuming the duties of his office was for the protection and release of American citizens in Cuba held in Spanish prisons. A statement sent to the Senate by President Cleveland on January 25, 1897, showed that seventy-four American citizens had been arrested in Cuba since the beginning of the insurrection. Seven of these had been tried and appeals taken in two cases; seven others, correspondents of American newspapers, had been banished from the island. The case of Dr. Ruiz, who had died in prison and whose death was believed to be due to inhuman treatment by his jailers, was made the subject of a special inquiry by President McKinley during the first two weeks of his Administration, and in the other cases such vigorous steps were taken to obtain their release before many weeks of the new Administration had passed, that every American citizen so confined was released.

PROTEST AGAINST WEYLER'S POLICY OF CRUEL PERSECU-
TION OF CUBANS.

Another prompt step taken by the President was to bring about the cessation of cruelties inflicted upon prisoners taken by Spanish officials in the war in Cuba. The President served notice upon the Spanish Government shortly after his inauguration that the United States Government recognized conditions in Cuba which demanded a different treatment from that being followed by General Weyler, and this demand on his part was complied with.   On May 17th he sent to Congress a message calling attention to the fact that American citizens in Cuba were suffering as the result of the war, and recommending an appropriation for their relief, which was promptly adopted by Congress, and money and provisions were sent.

Another result of the protests of the Administration against the methods pursued in Cuba was seen in the decree of April 20th, proposing certain reforms in the government of Cuba.   The protests of the United States against the cruelties practiced by General Weyler were followed by his recall October 8th, and on November 27th by a decree tendering what professed to be a system of autonomy, but which soon proved unsatisfactory and delusive.

Meantime the cruelties, especially with reference to the treatment of the reconcentrados, continued so great under General Blanco, who had succeeded General Weyler, that President McKinley finding all peaceful methods and efforts to bring about the cessation of these cruelties and independence of the Cubans unsuccessful, found himself justified in utilizing the last resort upon which the nation has now entered and the success of which is already assured.

Silver and Wheat

Bryan's Argument in the Light of Experience

FROM THE SPEECH OF

Hon. JESSE OVERSTREET,

OF INDIANA

IN THE HOUSE OF REPRESENTATIVES

Friday, April 29th, 1898.

SILVER AND WHEAT.

I now propose, Mr. Speaker, to refer briefly to some of the arguments advanced in favor of the free coinage of silver, and to point out the interests that are at work trying to undo the work of prosperity in order to create a market for silver. I shall show from unassailable sources that an ounce of silver, for which we are asked to pay $1.29, in order to enjoy the inestimable blessings of free coinage, can be produced for less than 25 cents.

COST OF THE PRODUCTION OF AN OUNCE OF SILVER— IMMENSE PROFIT OF THE SILVER BARONS.

It is generally admitted by those who are not wedded to the theory that all national blessings flow from the free and unlimited coinage of silver that the price of silver bullion has been largely reduced because the supply has outgrown the capacity of consumption or demand. For the four-year period 1871-1875 the annual average of the world's product of the white metal was but 63,317,014 ounces, while for the year 1896 it was 165,100,887 ounces, and for 1895 it was still larger.

This increased production was due to large discoveries of silver ore and to the constantly increasing cheapness of the method of production, refining, transportation, etc. It is shown that silver can be produced profitably at prevailing market prices, because the production continues. It must follow, then, that if we restore silver to $1.29 an ounce it would mean the payment of a bonus to the silver barons of the difference between the actual cost of production and the price to which they wish silver restored. It is interesting to review some of the official reports made on the cost of the production of silver as long as ten years ago, when an ounce of silver was worth 93.97 cents as contrasted with 44 cents at the present time.

Professor Austen, of the royal mint in London, carefully investigated the cost of production of fine silver in this country, and he testified to that effect before the royal monetary commission December 9, 1886.

The testimony of Professor Austen is in the first report of the royal commission, pages 62 to 67, and appendix in same volume, page 325. From his testimony it appears that the cost of production of silver was as follows ten years ago:

COST OF PRODUCTION PER OUNCE FINE.

	Cents
Arizona	83.2
California	51
Colorado	60.2
Montana	43.3
Utah	47.7

Average cost of production in the United States, 51.1 cents per ounce fine.

The cost of production of silver in Mexico, according to the report of Mr. Stewart Pixley, of the firm of Pixley & Abell, in London, in the same document, page 325, averages for **an ounce of pure silver 1s. 6d. per ounce fine, or 37 cents.**

According to Professor Austen's returns (same report, volume 1, page 329), the cost of production of an ounce fine silver in Mexico averaged about 44⅜ cents, or 1s. 8d. per ounce of 0.925 fine, English standard.

In south and Central America Professor Austen gives the cost of production of an ounce of fine silver at 1s. 5d., or 34⅝ cents per ounce fine. (Same report, page 328.)

In Germany, the product of the Mansfeld copper mines, according to Professor Austen (see same report, page 328) in 1883, the amount of silver produced annually in the treatment of copper ores is given as 7,200,000 ounces. **Of this quantity 6,500,000 ounces were obtained during the ordinary smelting of copper ores, at a cost of 9 1-2d. per ounce, English standard of 0.925 fine, or 21 5-8 cents per ounce fine silver. It also states in the same article that by the improved process of Claudet 328,000 ounces were recovered in Great Britain from copper ores, at 5d. per ounce standard (0.925 fine), or at 10 7-8 cents per ounce fine silver.**

In Australia the cost of production of pure silver is given by Professor Austen (same report, volume 1, page 328) as follows:

The report for the year 1886 of the Broken Hill mine, Barrier Ranges, New South Wales, a mine of considerable importance, has been published. It states that during the year 1886 the smelting of 10,397 tons of ore yielded 1881 tons of lead and 871,665 ounces of fine silver, at a cost, including mining charges, of £4 12s. ½d. per ton of ore, or at the rate of 1s. 1d. per ounce of silver produced (equal to 28⅝ cents per ounce fine silver) if the lead be considered of no value, but the lead sold at £12 per ton ($58.32 per ton).

Later reports give the production of the Broken Hill mine for 1889 at over 10,000,000 ounces of pure silver and the cost of production not quite 8 pence per ounce, or about 16 cents per ounce fine.

For the nine months of 1890 the production of the Broken Hill mine was 17,000,000 ounces of pure silver, which according to the bullion cost, at

16 cents, would be about $3,000,000, while at the price we paid for it it would be over $20,000,000.

In Director Kimball's report of 1887, page 112, on the cost of production of silver, appears the following statement, showing that the Granite Mountain mine, at Granite, Mont., produced in 1886—

Nineteen thousand three hundred and sixteen tons of silver ore; that the average amount of silver in each ton was 150 ounces of pure silver, and that the total amount extracted was 2,897,754 ounces of fine silver; that the cost of mining was $6.06 per ton, and that the reduction of each ton cost $13, or a total of $19.06 per ton as the cost of production.

This statement was officially furnished by the Granite Mountain Mining Company to the Director of the Mint in 1887, and is, no doubt, correct; and here it is worked out by the Director of the Mint:

19,316 tons of silver, cost of mining, at $6.06 per ton.............$117,054.96
19,316 tons, cost of reduction, at $13 per ton.................... 251,108.00
   Total $368,162.96

The product of these 19,316 tons of silver ore amounted to 2,987,754 ounces of fine silver, at a cost of production of $368,162.96, equal to 12 3-4 cents per ounce.

Thus in this single case, where the cost of production was a little over $368,000, the price that would have been paid for it under free coinage at the prevailing market price ten years ago would be over $3,500,000.

In the report of this company itself to the Director of the Mint for 1887 they give the sale of their silver bullion at 96 cents per ounce. That was the market price per ounce. **Upon their own showing the percentage of labor to profit was, for labor, 13.28 per cent.; profit, 86.72 per cent.**

SILVER AND WHEAT—BRYAN'S ARGUMENTS IN THE LIGHT OF EXPERIENCE.

William J. Bryan and other advocates of free coinage at the ratio of 16 to 1 have based their strongest plea upon the assertion that "wheat and silver" are "linked together" by some mysterious sympathy that causes the price of wheat to decline in accordance with the depression of the price of silver. Mr. Bryan preached this theory to the farmers throughout the national campaign of 1896, when wheat was unusually low, owing to the lessened demand for wheat abroad and the lessened demand at home because of hard times, the result of four years of Democratic misrule. He preached this theory in season and out of season, on the stump and in Congress. In the course of his remarks in the House, Wednesday, August 16, 1893, on the bill to repeal the purchasing clause of the Sherman Act, he said:

But, as I said, the producers of wheat and cotton have a special grievance, for the prices of those articles are governed largely by the prices in Liverpool, and as silver goes down our prices fall. * * * If it is possible to do so, it is no more than fair that we restore silver to its former place, and thus give back to the farmer some of his lost prosperity.

The Democratic campaign book of 1896, prepared by Hon. BENTON McMIL-LIN, of Tennessee, and circulated by the Democratic National Committee, elaborated and illustrated this theory by extensive quotations and statistics. Thus, on page 84, " Decline in farm prices:"

" There is no better illustration of the ruinous consequences flowing from the adoption by the United States of the single gold standard than a comparison of the prices of agricultural products at the date of the demonetization of silver with the price now (1896). * * * It will be observed that since the demonetization in 1873 there has been a decline in every line of farm products. * * * The demonetization of silver was a bold stroke in the interest of capital that has reduced the value of every product in the world. This is conclusively proven by the fact that just as silver has depreciated, in like proportion have all other values fallen in the scale."

This beguiling argument, which made the judgment of so many farmers tremble in the scale, has time and again been proved to be the purest fallacy and the most supreme species of political hypocrisy on the part of Messrs. Bryan, Towne, Jones, and other free-coinage leaders; but the vicious error was brought home to every producer of wheat in the United States when, soon after Major McKinley's election, wheat and silver suddenly parted company, and while the former went skyward the great white metal took a tumble in the markets that knocked all the dignity out of it as an inflexible standard of value.

On September 1, 1896, 1 bushel of wheat and 1 ounce of silver were of equal value. On September 1, 1897, 1 bushel of wheat equaled 2 ounces of silver in value. The following table shows the fallacy of the free-silver argument at a glance:

Date.	Wheat, per bushel	Date.	Silver, per ounce.
	Cents.		Cents.
Sept. 1, 1896..	67.2	Sept. 1, 1896..............	67.2
Sept. 17, 1896.................	70.6	Sept. 26, 1896...............	66.8
Sept. 24, 1896........	76.1	Oct 24, 1896,..............	65.6
Oct. 8, 1896..................	78.8	Mar. 6, 1897.................	64.3
Oct. 15, 1896.................	80.1	Mar. 13, 1897.................	63.4
Oct. 24, 1896	82.2	April 10, 1897..............	62.4
Oct. 29, 1896	83.7	May 1, 1897.................	61.8
Nov. 5, 1896.................	87.1	June 26, 1897..............	60.4
Mar. 11, 1897.................	92.7	July 24, 1897..............	59.7
Mar. 18, 1897.................	93.8	July 31, 1897..............	58.4
Apr. 15, 1897.................	94.2	Aug. 4, 1897	57.1
Apr. 29, 1897.................	96.7	Aug. 6, 1897	56.4
May 6, 1897...	98.1	Aug. 11, 1897..............	55.5
Aug. 20, 1897.................	99	Aug. 16, 1897..............	54.3
Aug. 25, 1897	100.7	Aug. 17, 1897..............	53.1
Aug. 27, 1897	102.5	Aug. 23, 1897..............	52.1
Sept. 1, 1897........	103.2	Sept. 1, 1897..............	51.2

SILVER DOLLARS COINED BEFORE AND SINCE "THE CRIME OF '73"—THE RECORD OF 1897.

The total coinage of standard silver dollars during the year 1897 amounted to $21,203,701.

This is significant considered side by side with Table XLIII, contained in the report of the Director of the Mint, giving the total coinage of silver dollars from 1792 to 1873, the year in which it is alleged "silver was struck down." This table shows the coinage of silver dollars to have been:

From 1792 to 1853..$2,506,890
From 1853 to February 12, 1873. 5,524,348

    Total coinage in eighty-one years..........................$8,031,238

It will be seen that the coinage of silver dollars during the single year of 1897 exceeded the total coinage for the eighty-one years from 1792 to 1873 by $13,172,463, or 164 per cent:

Coinage of 1897...$21,203,701
Coinage from 1792 to 1873................................... 8,031,238

    Excess $13,172,463

The coinage of silver dollars since "the crime of '73" foots up the enormous total of $487,959,666 down to June 30, 1897. This is what Republican legislation has done to "discredit" the "money of the people." Not a dollar was coined from 1806 to 1835, inclusive, operations in that direction having been suspended by order of President Jefferson. The total coinage of silver dollars from 1793 to the beginning of the war, when the Democratic party had been in power continuously for many years, is shown in the following table:

Year.	Value.	Year.	Value.
1793–1795	$204,791	1845	$ 24,500
1796......................	72,920	1846	169,600
1797......................	7,776	1847	140,750
1798......................	327,536	1848	15,000
1799......................	423,515	1849	62,600
1800......................	220,920	1850	47,500
1801......................	54,454	1851	1,300
1802......................	41,650	1852	1,100
1803......................	66,064	1853	46,110
1804	19,517	1854	33,140
1805......................	321	1855	26,000
1836......................	1,000	1856	63,500
1839......................	300	1857	94,000
1840......	61,005	1858	....
1841......................	173,000	1859	636,500
1842......................	184,618	1860	733,930
1843......................	165,100		
1844......................	20,000	Total................	4,140,070

Instead of having struck down silver, it will be seen from the foregoing comparison of official figures that the Republican party is the real friend of the "dollar of our daddies."

DEMOCRATIC POSITION ON SILVER IN 1876.

That the clamor for the white metal is of comparatively recent origin, and that "the crime of '73" itself did not for some years after provoke the great indignation which the would-be saviors of the country of the present day pathetically affect, is proved by the speeches of Senators STEWART and JONES, who were still busy in 1874 praising the unfailing blessings of the gold standard.

But late as 1876 the Democratic leaders of the House were still sanction-ing the "crime of '73" by proposing legislation prohibiting the Secretary of the Treasury from purchasing silver bullion for coinage, restricting silver coinage to subsidiary coinage, fixing the price of silver by the market rate, providing for the transfer of the seigniorage to the Treasury, and finally limiting the legal tender of the standard silver dollar to amounts not exceed-ing $50. Witness the following:

[Forty-fourth Congress. Act to redeem fractional currency. Proceedings in
House.]
A bill (H. R. 2450) to provide for a deficiency in the Printing and Engraving
Bureau in the Treasury Department, and for the issue of silver coin of the
United States in place of fractional currency. Reported from the Com-
mittee on Appropriations.

March 27, 1876, Mr. Holman submitted the following as a new section:

"SEC. 3. The Secretary of the Treasury is hereby prohibited from making any further increase in the interest-bearing debt of the United States by the issue and sale of bonds for the purchase of silver bullion for coinage. But silver bullion shall, under regulations to be prescribed by the Secretary of the Treasury, be received by the several mints for fabrication into sub-sidiary coins, and paid for in such coins at a rate or price per ounce to be fixed from time to time, according to the market rate, by the Director of the Mint with the approval of the Secretary of the Treasury, on the basis of the difference between the par value of such coin and the value of such bullion, and an addition not exceeding 1 per cent, in the discretion of the Secretary of the Treasury, shall be made to the purchasing price as an allowance for the transportation of coin. And the excess of the par value of such coin over the value of the bullion so deposited, less the amount that shall be allowed for transportation, as aforesaid, determined as above provided, shall be from time to time covered into the Treasury, as the Secretary of the Treasury shall direct: *Provided, however*, That such silver coins of the denomi-nations aforesaid, and the silver bullion now owned by the United States, shall not exceed in par value the par value of the fractional currency now authorized by law."

Mr. E. Wells (Democrat) moved the following proviso to the proposed new section:

"*Provided*, That if silver bullion is not provided for coinage in sufficient quantity for the redemption of fractional currency, the Secretary of the Treasury may, under the provisions of the act entitled 'An act to provide for the resumption of specie payments,' approved January 14, 1875, purchase silver bullion for the purpose of coinage as provided in said act."

Which was agreed to—yeas 118, nays 100.

Yeas—Democrats, 45; Republicans, 72; Independent,1.

Nays—Democrats, 88; Republicans, 16; Independent, 2.

Mr. Reagan (Democrat), of Texas, offered the following amendment:

Insert as section 4 the following:

"That the silver coins of the United States of the denomination of $1 shall be a legal tender at their nominal value for any amount not exceeding $50 in any one payment; and silver coins of the United States of denominations of less than $1 shall be a legal tender at their nominal value for any amount not exceeding $25 in any one payment."

Which was agreed to—yeas 122, nays 94.

Yeas—Democrats, 99; Republicans, 22; Independent, 1.

Nays—Democrats, 28; Republicans, 65; Independent, 1.

March 31, 1876, the amendment offered by Mr. Holman, as amended on motion of Mr. Wells, was disagreed to—yeas 68, nays 77.

The bill as amended by the amendment of Mr. Reagan was then passed—yeas 122, nays 100.

Yeas—Democrats, 50; Republicans, 70; Independent, 2.

Nays—Democrats, 80; Republicans, 18; Independent, 2.

(For foregoing proceedings see CONGRESSIONAL RECORD, volumes 14 and 15.)

SENATOR MILLS, OF TEXAS, ON FREE COINAGE AT 16 TO 1.

Senator MILLS, of Texas, United States Senator and ex-chairman of the House Committee on Ways and Means, on March 6, 1898, in his letter withdrawing from the Senatorial race, declared that free silver coinage at the ratio of 16 to 1 by the United States alone is impossible. He said:

"Now that the great body of the commercial world has taken its stand against silver, I do not believe it in the power of the United States alone, by its independent action, to restore the value of silver to par with gold at 16 to 1. I believe that the United States can restore the demand which they withdrew, but do not believe that they can restore the demand which was withdrawn by other countries when they closed their mints against silver."

THE STANDARD DOLLAR FALLS TO 39.66 CENTS.

In August, 1897, the silver contained in the standard dollar, which the Government is now keeping at par with gold, fell to a fraction below 40 cents, as shown by the following Associated Press telegram:

NEW YORK, *August*, 24, 1897.

Silver broke all record again to-day, falling to 23⅞ pence in London, which is one-eighth penny below the previous low point, and to 51½ cents in New York, which is one-fourth cent below the previous low record. Mexican dollars sold at 39½ cents.

At to-day's New York price for bars, the value of the silver in the standard silver dollar is 39.66 cents.

SEIGNIORAGE ON THE SILVER COINAGE FISCAL YEAR 1897.

A statement prepared at the Mint Bureau shows that the number of silver dollars coined at the United States mints during the fiscal year ended June 30, 1897, was $21,203,701, on which the seigniorage or profit to the Government amounted to $6,396,104.25. This profit was turned into the Treasury from time to time as the coinage progressed, and was used to reduce taxation instead of wandering into the pockets of the silver producers, as would have been the case under free coinage.

WAGES AND PENSIONS—HOW FREE COINAGE WOULD AFFECT THEM.

The Journal of the Knights of Labor, published at Washington on October 15, 1896, during the national campaign, told workingmen in a half-page article, entitled " A recapitulation—Have the opponents of Mr. Bryan made out a good case? " that the value of all workingmen's deposits in savings banks, the pensions of old soldiers, and " money in all forms "' would be cut in two by free coinage.

The paper said on this head:

" Third. That the purchasing power of pensions and savings-bank deposits would be cut in two by free coinage. This is the only true contention made by the gold men, and it is fully agreed to by all candid advocates of an increased volume of money. Fixed incomes, bond mortgages, and money in all its forms, whether in savings banks or national banks, would have much less purchasing power."

The article was from the pen of Mr. H. B. Martin, the editor of the paper and a member of the general executive board of the order.

PER CAPITA WEALTH.

Is the amount of money in a country an index of its prosperity, as free-coinage men insist? The per capita metallic wealth of the United States, according to the report of the Director of the Mint, was $23.70. According to this theory the people of Aden and Perim, Ceylon, Hongkong, Labuan, and Straits Settlements ought to be the most prosperous in the world, for theirs is nearly three times that of the people of the United States, their per capita share of the world's money stock being $63.680.

Any American ought to be glad to exchange places with the natives of Hawaii, whose per capita wealth is $60, chiefly gold; or the Siamese, whose per capita is $42.68; or the people of the South African Republic, with $38 per capita. Great Britain's per capita is but $20.65; Germany's but $18.95, yet the export commerce of these nations is enormous. Reducing their per capita share in the money stock of the world to a table, giving their export commerce in juxtaposition, will show how little relation one bears to the other:

Country.	Per capita.	Exports, 1896.*
Great Britain	$20.65	$3,870,500,000
Germany	18.95	2,026,500,000
France	34.68	1,389,600,000

* Figures of Mr. Jules Roche, formerly French minister of finance and commerce.

Great Britain, with a per capita metallic money wealth 14.03 less than France, has a world commerce nearly three times as great as that of France, while Germany, with a per capita metallic stock 15.63 less than France, conducts nearly twice as much foreign business as France.

CONSUL-GENERAL CRITTENDEN ON CONDITIONS IN MEXICO.

Ex-Governor Thomas T. Crittenden, of Missouri, was consul-general to Mexico under the last Cleveland Administration. Mr. Crittenden is an ardent free-silver man and vigorously advocated the election of Mr. Bryan in 1896. Yet this is what Mr. Crittenden sets forth in an official report to the State Department, dated September 1, 1896, touching the financial question as bearing upon the industrial conditions of Mexico. Speaking of these conditions in 1873 as compared with 1896, he says:

" Then again (1873), gold and silver were on a par and Mexican money was almost the equal of the money of all other nations, while to-day, as compared with a gold dollar, it is worth but 52 cents. * * * Finally, it can be generally proven that the cost of living and of wearing apparel of the native was as low, and in many instances lower, in 1873 than at the present time."

Mr. Crittenden then submits the following report on wages and salaries paid in and about the City of Mexico at the present date:

WAGES.

Employment.	Mexican currency.	United States currency.
Agents, railway ....per month..	$75.00 to $150.00	$39.00 to $78.00
Boiler-makers ....per day..	4.00 to 8.00	2.08 to 4.16
Brakemen.................per month..	35.00 to. 75.00	18.20 to 39.00
Bricklayers (natives) ....per day..	1.00 to 1.50	.52 to .78
Clerks (office) ....per month..	40.00 to 200.00	20.80 to 104.00
Cooks, women................... do ..	6.00 to 12.00	3.12 to 6.24
Cooks, men .... do ..	25.00 to 75.00	13.00 to 39.00
Carpenters...................per day..	1.50 to 4.75	.78 to 2.37
Conductors, passenger ....per month..	100.00 to 160.00	52.00 to 83.20
Conductors, freight .... do ..	100.00 to 200.00	52.00 to 104.00
Conductors, street-car ....per day..	.50 to 1.00	.26 to .52
Coachmen, private (native) ......per month..	15.00 to 30.00	7.80 to 15.60
Coachmen, public (native) ...... do ..	15.00	7.80
Division (railway) superintendents, do ..	250.00 to 350.00	130.00 to 192.00
Drivers, street-car ....per day..	.50 to 1.00	.26 to .52
Engineers:		
Locomotive ....per month..	150.00 to 250.00	78.00 to 130.00
Stationary, with board .... per day..	2.50 to 3.50	1.30 to 1.82
Stationary, without board .... do ..	3.50 to 5.00	1.82 to 2.60
Engravers .... do ...	5.00 to 10.00	2.60 to 5.20
Firemen, locomotive...........per month..	75.00 to 100.00	39.44 to 52.00
Firemen, ordinary .... do ..	20.00 to 50.00	10.44 to 26.00
Furnace men...................per day..	1.00 to 1.50	.52 to .78
Harness-makers, etc. .... do ..	.50 to 2.00	.26 to 1.04
Iron workers.................... do ..	3.00 to 2.50	1.04 to 1.30
Jewelers...................... do ..	2.00 to 5.00	1.04 to 2.60
Laborers, in large cities.......... do ..	.37½ to .67½	.19½ to .353
Laborers, in the country .... do ..	.10 to .15	.052 to .078
Laborers in factories (10 to 11 hours) do ..	.50 to 1.00	.26 to .52
Laborers, skilled (10 to 11 hours) do ..	1.50 to 2.00	.78 to 1.04
Mechanics .... do ..	3.50 to 5.00	1.82 to 2.60
Machinists (shop)................. do ..	3.50 to 5.00	1.82 to 2.60
Miners, skilled................. do ..	1.00 to 1.50	.52 to .78
Miners, ordinary .... do .	.50 to .80	.26 to .416
Maids, house ....per month..	4.00 to 7.00	2.08 to 3.64
Operators, telegraph............ do ..	50.00 to 150.00	26.00 to 78.00
Plumbers:		
Native........................per day..	2.00 to 2.50	1.04 to 1.30
American .... do ...	6.00 to 8.50	3.12 to 4.16
Printers:		
Native ....per week..	7.00 to 8.00	3.64 to 4.16
Pressmen..................... do ..	8.00 to 11.00	4.16 to 5.72
Compositors .... do ..	10.00 to 12.00	5.20 to 6.24
Policemen...................per month..	30.00 to 50.00	13.60 to 26.00
Switchmen...................per day..	1.50	.78
Blacksmiths .... do ..	3.50 to 4.50	1.82 to 2.34
Gold and silversmiths.............. do ..	2.25 to 3.50	1.17 to 1.82
Stone masons .... do ..	1.00 to 1.50	.52 to .78
Seamstresses................. do ..	.37 to .50	.29 to .26
Trainmasters ....per month..	150.00 to 175.00	78.00 to 91.00
Tailors:		
Repairers ....per day..	1.00 to 1.25	.52 to .65
Coat makers................... per coat..	5.00 to 12.00	2.60 to 6.24
Vest makers.................per vest..	1.35 to 1.50	.71 to .78
Pantaloonists ....per pair..	1.75 to 2.50	.91

A SOUTHERN EDITOR ON "MEXICAN PROSPERITY."

Throughout the South much interest has recently been manifested in the published statement of Mr. Pleasant A. Stovall, editor of the Savannah Press, who has been making a tour of observations in Mexico. He says that every branch of business in Mexico suffers greatly because of the fluctuations in the price of silver. But his most important testimony relates to the effect of the silver standard on wages. He says:

" Men who went to Mexico years ago and invested money while silver was at a premium are bankrupt, now that silver has gone down to 45 cents on the dollar. Ask the American in business in Mexico; ask the trainmen, the yard-master, the laborers from the States. They will tell you they want the sound, hard, honest dollar of the American eagle. I talked to a score of these people, and to a man they advocated sound money. It is the old story. The laboring man wants to be paid in the best dollar the market affords, and he should be. He gets his wages now in silver, whose fluctuation is like the tide in the Bay of Fundy.

I found no complaint among the bankers. They make plenty of money discounting currency and speculating in the rise and fall of exchange. An American banking house in Calle San Francisco figures out a probable 30 per cent every year. It is not hard to see that the working people and business men must pay this dividend and sustain this loss. I could not help thinking what a panic Wall street would have in this country if the United States were upon a silver basis."

INDUSTRIAL CONDITIONS IN MEXICO.

Side by side with the glowing encomiums which Mr. W. J. Bryan sheds upon the prosperous condition of labor prevailing in Mexico under the silver standard, gentlemen will be interested in the following interview with ex-Congressman John A. McShane, himself a Democrat, who represented the Omaha district in the House of Representatives:

[From the Washington Post (Independent), February 8, 1898.]

" I will not deny that there is a kind of prosperity in evidence in the Republic of Mexico," said Mr. John A. McShane, of Omaha, at the Arlington. Mr. McShane is at the head of a large mining concern that has been engaged in silver production in the Mexican State of Chihuahua for the past ten years.

" It is of this sort: The Government is largely back of it, and to the paternal fostering of the Diaz administration it is mainly due. The government subsidizes breweries, railroads, industrial plants, and aids in every way to build up the material resources of the country. Money is used with a liberal hand, and as a consequence there is much activity and great apparent prosperity. The fact that Mexico is on a silver basis does not figure; it can't help being on that kind of a basis, but I should be sorry to see the United States resort to any such policy.

" Ten years of experience in that country has forever set me against the adoption of a monetary system which is not only in disrepute among the leading nations of the world, but which is about to be discarded by countries like Japan, Brazil, and some of the smaller Spanish-American governments that were formerly on a silver basis. The masses in Mexico are in a worse condition than I trust will ever befall our laboring population. This I can explain by referring to matters that have come under my personal observation.

" When the Sherman purchasing act was in force some seven years ago, silver was worth $1.21, and a United States dollar was worth in Mexico 100 cents in Mexican money. The dollars of the two countries were on a parity. At this time we employed about 300 men in our mines, their pay ranging from $1 to $2.50 per day. It took approximately $10,000 a month to meet the pay roll. The money to cancel this expense was shipped from Omaha, and it was exchanged for $10,000 of Mexican coin. We operated general merchandise stores along with our mining concern, and at the time I speak of sold to our Mexican employees bacon for 20 cents a pound.

" What are the conditions to-day? We still hire 300 men and give them exactly the same scale of wages that obtained prior to the slump in silver caused by the repeal of the purchasing clause of the Sherman Act. Our pay roll still aggregates $10,000 a month. To meet this we have shipped us a like sum of United States money, and here is where the point of difference comes in. Instead of exchanging that amount at our bank for its nominal equivalent, we get for it not $10,000, but $22,000 of Mexican money.

" We have here made a clear gain of $12,000. Our employees still render us 100 cents' worth of work, for which they used to get 100 cents, and do yet, as far as the name goes, but in reality they receive less than half of what should be theirs, seeing that the Mexican coin in which they are paid has shrunk to less than half of its former value.

" But there is more still. When the Mexican miner goes to buy bacon he finds that in tendering payment he cannot buy it with depreciated money for 20 cents a pound; the price is now 45 cents. It would still be so if he could tender a dollar as good as that given him for his labor at the time of the repeal of the Sherman law. The $12,000 I spoke of simply comes out of the labor of the country, and when the toiling class of any nation is forced to such a condition, it is stretching a point to call the people prosperous.

" If the fair and right thing were done by these hard-working miners, their wages would be doubled. The man that now gets $2 a day is justly entitled to $4, but labor will bring only what price is fixed in market, like any commodity, and employers are not yet far enough advanced in philanthropy to voluntarily give more than the customary rate.

" So the talk about the prosperity of Mexico, in so far as it applies to the vast body of its citizens—the common people—is a myth. If there is prosperity at all, it is not due to the silver standard, but in spite of it."

MODERN WAR CRIES AGAINST "THE MONEYED CLASSES" WERE SOUNDING PHRASES IN WASHINGTON'S DAYS.

It must not be supposed that the hue and cry, of Democratic origin, about "the moneyed classes," and the arraigument of class against class, also of Democratic birth, are comparative novelties in American politics. They were just as prevalent under the first Administration as they have been under recent Administrations. The term most popular in the early days of the Government to designate those who were supposed to be inimical to the "plain people" was "aristocrat."

Washington was accused of being an "aristocrat." His neutrality doctrine was decidedly unpopular, and the same element which in the present generation vociferously denounces conservatism in our Government denounced President Washington for refusing to take part in the wars between England and France. His policy was characterized as a betrayal of the masses, who were clamoring for war. But when that policy was vindicated by time and the neutrality doctrine was shown to have brought prosperity to the people of the United States, the Democrats of that day conveniently forgot their former hostility to Washington's wise statesmanship, and Jefferson, the leader in this hostile attitude, officially proclaimed a policy against "entangling alliances."

"A curious phase of prejudice, as already noted, was instilled into the minds of the unintelligent Democracy of that day—"

Writes J. Harris Patton, M. A., in his Short History of the Democratic Party (1884)—

"They were often led by the insinuations and hasty assertions of their leaders to suspect the well-to-do and the educated portion of the community of being hostile to themselves. These leaders at first, as we have seen, characterized those who sustained the policy of the Government for the first twelve years of its existence as "aristocrats," and that term of presumed reproach was used until superseded by that of the "moneyed power," meaning by the latter epithet those who continued to sustain the financial principles introduced by Alexander Hamilton and embodied in the policy of Washington's Administration.

"The policy of neutrality in the meantime became popular. The epithet "aristocrat," as originally used, was no longer available. But in relation to financial measures, taxes, tariffs, banks, etc., 'moneyed power' suited their purpose admirably, and every 'poor man' who worked for wages was impliedly invited to look upon the well-to-do and the intelligent as having but little sympathy for him.

"In order to secure more fully their ends, the leaders in these societies (Democratic) endeavored to array one portion of the community against another. Those who were in favor of neutrality they characterized as 'aristocrats;' every lover of order or supporter of the National Government was

denounced as such and as an enemy of the 'poor man,' a favorer of the
hated aristocratic England and not of democratic France.

"It has been the policy of the leaders of that political organization from
that day to this to proclaim themselves preeminently the friend of the 'poor
man,' as they affectionately designate those who obtain a living by working
in any form for wages, but more especially those engaged in manual labor
or as employees in manufacturing establishments. They imply at the same
time the men of wealth or capitalists—in a word, those who employ work
people—are the enemies of the latter.

"The epithets which they then used had a meaning and a purpose. The
term 'aristocrat' in that day had a peculiarly unpopular significance, and
was designed to excite prejudice against those who were in favor of Washington's policy. By this term they meant to imply that the advocates of
neutrality were imitators of the English aristocracy."

In this connection it is but fair to ask workingmen, who are the special
object of the appeals of the Democratic party to-day, how they can reconcile
this interest in their behalf with the record of the Democratic party in the
past, which for many years preceding the war was officered and manned by
the aristocratic slave owners of the South. It was this party that put a stain
on freelabor by maintaining slavery, and it is this party in the South to-day
that still looks with scorn and contempt upon factory labor, unable to find
a more respectful term than "poor whites" for those who are compelled to
make their living by manual labor.

Where labor is respected is in the strongholds of the Republican party, or
at least where the Republican party has been able to make its policies felt—
not in the Democratic South.

I have thus shown, Mr. Chairman, that the Republican party at the special
session of this Congress placed upon the statute books of our country an
act which in the natural course of events provided ample revenues to run
the Government, and did what it promised in restoring that degree of prosperity which we enjoyed before the late Democratic Administration came
into power with its destructive policies.

The measure now before the House is called for by extraordinary circumstances, which all recognize as being absolutely independent of normal
conditions and which could not be provided for in an ordinary tariff bill.
The Dingley Act is doing its work faithfully and well. We may regard that
part of our work as a closed chapter. But other duties still confront us.
Let our next efforts be directed to the enactment of legislation looking to currency reform. With the wisdom which has governed this Congress in the
passage of a satisfactory and patriotic tariff bill, we may face with confidence the duty of placing our currency plan upon a safe and enduring basis
that shall challenge the admiration of the world.

(No. 9.)

DINGLEY ON THE TARIFF BILL

Revenue, Protection

AND

Commercial Prosperity

SPEECH OF

Hon. NELSON DINGLEY, JR.

IN THE HOUSE OF REPRESENTATIVES,

Monday, July 19, 1897.

Hon. NELSON DINGLEY, Jr.

OF MAINE.

In the House of Representatives, Monday, July 19, 1897

The House having under consideration the conference report on the bill (H. R. 379) to provide revenue for the Government and to encourage the industries of the United States—

Mr. DINGLEY said:

Mr. Speaker: The statement which has been read presents in general terms the result of the action of the conferees on the disagreeing amendments to the tariff bill.

The duty on lead ore, which was placed by the House at 1 cent per pound, was raised by the Senate to $1\frac{1}{2}$ cents per pound, and the House conferees, after considerable contention in reference to the matter, acceded to the Senate amendment so that that duty is raised to $1\frac{1}{2}$ cents per pound. I may add that this is the same as the duty in the act of 1890.

The duty on pig lead was placed by the House bill at 2 cents, but in consequence of the increase in the duty on lead ore the rate has been increased in conference to $2\frac{1}{8}$ cents per pound, which was the best that could be obtained. The duties on white lead and other lead products have been adjusted to the duty on lead.

Most of the other amendments in the chemical schedule are slight reductions, so that the average ad valorem on that schedule is less than it was in the bill as it passed the House.

CROCKERY AND GLASSWARE, ETC.

The duties on earthen and crockery ware have been agreed upon as they stood in the House bill and as they stood in the tariff of 1890, and the provisions remain the same as in the bill which passed the House.

In glassware there have been a few reductions from the House schedule, but in the main the rates of the House schedule have been adopted. The reductions, reluctantly agreed to, are in the paragraphs relating to bottles, molded and pressed glassware, and cylinder and crown glass.

Cement was placed by the House at a duty of 8 cents per hundred pounds, and the Senate increased the rate to 11 cents per hundred pounds; but in conference the Senate receded and accepted the House rate of 8 cents per hundred pounds.

Gypsum rock was placed on the free list by the action of the House, but the Senate placed upon that article a duty of $1 per ton. In conference the duty has been reduced to 50 cents per ton, and the duty on crude and calcined plaster has been raised to $2.25 per ton to correspond with the duty thus laid upon gypsum rock.

The duty on china clay, which is a product used largely in the manufacture of paper, was placed in the House bill at $2 per ton and was increased by the Senate to $3 per ton. In conference the Senate receded from its amendment and accepted the House rate of $2 per ton.

The duty on fuller's earth, both in the crude and in the ground forms, has been slightly raised above the House rate and below the Senate rate.

The duty on marble has been slightly raised in accordance with the Senate amendments.

The duty on freestone and granite in the block has been raised from 10 to 12 cents per cubic foot, and that on dressed granite has been raised to 50 per cent., as proposed by the Senate.

IRON AND STEEL AND COTTON TIES.

In metals and manufactures of metals the duties remain in general as fixed in the House bill. The duty on tin plate is precisely the same as in the House bill. There has been, however, a reduction in the rates on structural iron of one-tenth of 1 cent per pound.

Cotton ties, which were placed on the dutiable list by the House at a rate consonant with the duty imposed upon hoop iron, were placed by the Senate upon the free list. In conference they have been restored to the dutiable list, but at the reduced rate of five-tenths of 1 cent per pound.

The Senate amendment on pocket knives, which is substantially the same as the paragraph passed by the House, is agreed to, and compromise rates have been adopted upon guns.

Nickel ore and nickel matter were placed on the free list by the House. The Senate placed both on the dutiable list, but in conference both have been restored to the free list.

WOOD, AND MANUFACTURES OF.

In general the schedule of wood and manufactures of wood has been left almost exactly as it passed the House. All sawed lumber, except timber exceeding 8 inches square, is placed at $2 per thousand, and the reduction which the Senate made in the rates on dressed lumber has been receded from and the House rates in every case adopted.

SUGAR.

The House differential between raw and refined sugar and the general features of the House schedule have been preserved, and the Senate amendment increasing the differential to one-fifth and reducing the duties one-tenth on sugars of 87 degrees and below (which would have made a difference of thirteen-hundredths between 88-degree and 87-degree sugar) have been rejected in conference. In deference to the wishes of those interested in beet-sugar production, the Senate rate of 1.95 on refined sugar has been retained as an encouragement to that industry, but the duty on raw sugar has been increased seven and one-half one-hundredths, precisely the same as the increase on the refined, so as to leave the differential between the raw and refined at the initial point of 100 degrees the same as in the House bill, and secure so much additional revenue.

To meet the objection that the House bill provided for larger equivalent ad valorem duties on the lower than on the higher grades of sugar, the conference agreement commences with 75 degrees at ninety-five one-hundredths of a cent instead of 1 cent, and then raises the duty on each degree of raw sugar from three one-hundredths to three and a half one-hundredths, so that when the one hundredth degree is reached the duty will be 1.82½ and the duty on refined 1.95, leaving the 12½ differential between raw and refined sugars of 100 degrees test, as it stood in the schedule which passed the House.

Under the bill as it passed the House the duty on raw sugar of 100 degrees purity would be 1.75, and the duty on refined 1.87½, leaving twelve and a half hundredths differential at this point. Under the conference schedule the duty on raw sugar of 100 degrees purity would be 1.82½, and the duty upon refined sugar 1.95, leaving the differential at this point precisely the same, 12½ cents per hundred, in both schedules.

BEET SUGAR PROTECTED.

By this arrangement the revenue will be increased about two and a half million dollars on the sugar schedule, because the increased duty has been placed not simply on refined sugar (as proposed by the Senate), but also upon raw sugars, the point where revenue will be received; and those who are endeavoring to develop the production of beet sugar in this country will have seven and a half hundredths greater protection than they would have had under the bill as it passed the House, but the differential as between refined and raw sugars will remain precisely the same at the 100-degree point.

It must be borne in mind that the countervailing duty applies only to export-bounty-paying countries like Germany, and not to non-bounty-paying countries like Holland, and therefore plays no part in the protection of the refining industry against the competition of non-bounty-paying countries. Moreover, it must be remembered that this countervailing duty as against refined sugar from export-bounty-paying countries is not the entire bounty on refined sugar, but the difference between the export bounty on refined sugar and the export bounty on the amount of raw sugar required to make 100 pounds refined, and this difference is only 9 cents per hundred pounds.

NO INCREASE IN DIFFERENTIAL.

Inasmuch as it is contended for partisan purposes that the proposed sugar schedule increases the "differential," that is, the difference between the duty on sufficient raw sugar below 100 degrees test to make 100 pounds of refined sugar and the duty on 100 pounds refined sugar, above that of the Wilson tariff of 1894, I desire to point out the falsity of this claim; and I will select sugars of 92 degrees test for this purpose, as that was the average test of the importations of raw sugar last year, and is the point chosen for assault.

Let it be borne in mind, in the first place, that while the initial point for estimating the differential is 100 degrees raw and 100 degrees refined sugar—where, as I have already stated, this differential is 12½ cents per hundred pounds, or one-eighth of 1 cent per pound, yet in all tariff bills this differential necessarily increases as sugars of a less polariscopic test are selected, for the reason that the percentage of hard sugar obtainable in the process of refining diminishes and the percentage of less valuable soft sugars and cost of refining increases faster than the polariscopic test goes down. But this increase of differential is adjusted to the basis of 12½ cents per hundred fixed for sugars of 100 degrees test, so that in effect the differential is equal to only the 12½ cents on such basis.

Thus, according to the official figures of the Treasury Department, the differential between the duty on refined and the duty on 107.47 pounds raw sugars of 96 degrees test required by the Treasury drawback regulations to make 100 pounds refined, is, under the present Wilson tariff, 19.82, taking the average of 96-degree sugar (2.12), or 21.02 if St. Croix 96-degree sugar (valued at 2.10) is taken as the basis, and 13.91 under the proposed schedule. This compares with German fine; but compared with Dutch refined, which is the only sugar imported anywhere near the equal of American refined (Dutch costing 13 cents per hundred pounds more than German fine), the differential would be 25.2 per hundred under the present tariff and only 13.91 under the proposed tariff.

COMPUTATIONS VARY UNDER THE TARIFF OF 1894.

It will be seen that the computations vary under the tariff of 1894 according to the kind of raw sugar and refined sugar selected, because the duties under the present law are ad valorem, while under the proposed schedule they are fixed.

But I started to make the comparison on the basis of 92-degree sugar, which gives a larger differential because of the increased labor of refining and the lower proportionate yield of hard sugars.

The average dutiable value of St. Croix 92-degree sugar, which is the medium sugar of 92 degrees, was 1.85 in the first four months of the present year. The duty (40 per cent.) on 1 pound of this sugar is, therefore, .74, and the duty on 114.94 pounds of such sugar required, according to the Treasury drawback regulations, to make 100 pounds refined, is therefore 85 cents.

Dutch refined sugar, the quality which comes near our American refined, was valued at 2.60 in the same period, and German fine, which sells for nearly half a cent less in our markets than our refined because of its inferior quality, was valued at 2.47. The duty (40 per cent. plus 12½ cents) on 100 pounds Dutch refined under the present tariff is, therefore $1.16½, and on 100 pounds German fine $1.113. Deducting 85 cents, and the differential under the present tariff as against Dutch refined sugar is 32 cents per hundred pounds, and against German fine 26.24 cents; or if the average value of all 96-degree sugar (1.95) imported is taken as the basis, then each differential is reduced a little over five-tenths of 1 cent.

DIFFERENTIAL LESS THAN UNDER WILSON BILL.

Inasmuch as the duty on 92-degree sugar in the proposed tariff is 1.54½ per pound, or $1.77½ on the 114.94 pounds of 92-degree sugar required to make 100 pounds of refined, and the duty on both Dutch and German refined $1.95, the differential in the proposed tariff is not quite 17½ cents on both kinds of refined, which is more than 40 per cent. less than the differential under the present or any prior tariff—a fact which our friends on the other side who support the tariff of 1894, and who are denouncing, for partisan purposes, the proposed differential on refined sugar as a surrender to the sugar trust (which refines 70 per cent. of our product as against 30 per cent. by independent refiners), should keep in mind as a check on their new-born zeal against trusts. Let me repeat, AT EVERY POINT THE DIFFEREN-TIAL ON REFINED SUGAR IS FROM 25 TO 50 PER CENT. LESS THAN THE DIFERENTIAL GIVEN BY THE TARIFF OF 1894.

BEET SUGAR INDUSTRY HELPS THE FARMERS AND CRIPPLES THE TRUST.

It should be borne in mind that the general increase of duty on sugar made in the proposed tariff has been made not only to increase the revenue, but also to further encourage the production of beet sugar in this country and furnish a new crop for our farmers, who are being sorely pressed as to our large wheat surplus by Russian and South American competition. I believe that the time has come when the production of our own sugar from the beet ought to be and can be successfully entered upon, and thus the seventy-five millions—soon to be one hundred millions—sent abroad for the purchase of our sugar ultimately distributed here to our own farmers. Already, indeed, it has been demonstrated that we can successfully produce beet sugar here, and the proposed duty placed on that article will gradually bring this about, while for the time being affording increased revenue.

CERTAINLY NOTHING CAN BE DONE TO SO SUCCESSFULLY CLIP THE WINGS OF THE SUGAR TRUST AS TO DEVELOP OUR BEET-SUGAR INDUSTRY. SUGAR-BEET FACTORIES TURN OUT THEIR PRO-DUCT IN A REFINED FORM, AND THUS BECOME THE EFFICIENT COM-PETITORS OF OTHER REFINERS. THE SUCCESSFUL ESTABLISH-MENT OF THE SUGAR-BEET INDUSTRY IN EVEN HALF OF THE TWENTY-SIX STATES WHICH CAN AND WILL SUCCESSFULLY GROW SUGAR BEETS UNDER THE PROPOSED TARIFF WOULD SPEEDILY END ANY SUGAR TRUST, AND WOULD AT THE SAME TIME CONFER IMMENSE BENEFITS ON OUR FARMERS AND ALL OF OUR PEOPLE.

TOBACCO.

On wrapper tobacco the House fixed a duty of $2 per pound—the same as in the tariff of 1890—which the Senate amendment reduced to $1.75 per pound, the rate in the present tariff being $1.50. After more or less con-tention in the conference, a compromise agreement was reached placing the duty on wrapper tobacco at $1.85 per pound, which seemed to adjust the disagreeing views that existed not only among the conferees, but among Senators and others who had placed particular stress on this provision.

The duty on filler tobacco has been agreed to at the Senate rate of 35 cents per pound instead of the House rate of 65 cents per pound.

AGRICULTURAL PRODUCTS, FISH AND COTTON.

On agricultural products in general the duties of the act of 1890 have been restored. The main change has been in oranges and lemons, on which the rate as fixed by the House was three-fourths of 1 cent per pound. The Senate fixed the duty at 1 cent per pound, and the House conferees have receded and agreed to the Senate amendment. In general, the duties on citrus fruits, raisins, and other products competing especially with California fruit products have been raised.

Fish are placed at rates a little higher than those which were provided by the act of 1890, but a little lower than those provided in the House schedule. The conferees on the part of the House insisted as strenuously as possible on the House schedule, regarding the rates as fixed by the House as reasonable and fair, but the Senate conferees were insistent on the point; and with a compromise upon one paragraph, the Senate rates on fish were agreed to.

The duty of 20 per cent. on imported cotton, as proposed by the Senate, has been receded from by the Senate conferees, leaving cotton upon the free list. With reference to this I desire to say that careful investigation by the conferees made it clear that a duty upon cotton would be simply a duty upon Egyptian cotton, and would merely obstruct our cotton manufacturing interests and benefit no one, because Egyptian cotton is of a grade between our uplands and Sea Island cotton, and has certain qualities possessed by no other cotton. If a duty should be placed on this cotton, the effect would be to transfer abroad the manufacture of goods made from Egyptian cotton, without benefiting anyone.

It seemed, therefore, to the House conferees to be wise to leave this matter as it had been left in all previous tariffs. If a duty had been placed upon cotton, as the cotton goods imported are mainly manufactured from Egyptian cotton, it would have been necessary to raise the cotton schedule all along the line. It was not thought wise to do this. It was not believed that a duty upon Egyptian cotton under those circumstances could be of any possible benefit to anyone. Therefore cotton is left on the free list as heretofore.

The Senate rates on spirits, wines, etc., are adopted in the main.

TEXTILE MANUFACTURES.

Compromise rates on manufactures of jute, flax, etc., have been adopted with the purpose of developing the growth of flax in this country for textile purposes and establishing here the linen manufacture, first by taking the lower grades and subsequently the higher grades, so that in the main this schedule as to manufactures has, with certain reductions, been preserved as passed by the House.

Cotton bagging, burlaps, bags, and straw matting, which the Senate placed on the free list, are restored to the dutiable list at reduced rates.

WOOL AND WOOLENS.

The House rates on wool of classes 1 and 2 (which comprise the clothing wools), 11 cents upon the great body of that wool and 12 cents upon the small amount of combing wool that there may be, have been agreed to, so that in this respect the bill stands precisely as it left the House and precisely as provided in the tariff of 1890.

The Senate increased the duties on carpet wools by first placing specific duties on them—duties of 4 cents on wools ranging in value up to 10 cents and 7 cents on those valued above 10 cents--the effect of which was to increase the duties on carpet wool to a considerable extent. In the conference the Senate has receded from a large part of this increase by fixing the dividing line at 12 cents instead of 10 cents; so that while there is a slight increase on carpet wools, yet it is much less than was proposed by the Senate. The House provision transferring six kinds of wool from class 3 (carpet wools) to clothing wools has been agreed to. This removes the irritation which was caused by the use of these so-called carpet wools for clothing purposes.

MANUFACTURES OF WOOL.

The Senate rates on manufactures of wool have been in the main adopted, and they are substantially the same as in the tariff act of 1890. The House, it will be remembered, provided a specific schedule on manufactures of wool. The House conferees endeavored to preserve that specific schedule; but the Senate conferees have objected, for reasons that seemed proper to them. The House has receded, and with slight amendments to the Senate schedule, have adopted it as it passed the Senate.

It is believed that the transfer of wool from the free list, where it was placed by the tariff of 1894 to the dutiable list, with the rates of the tariff of 1890 as to clothing wool, will make wool-growing again profitable to our farmers and stop the destruction of our flocks.

The duties on silk—Schedule L—remain substantially at the same rate as provided by the House bill, and are increased from 5 to 10 per cent. above the present law. The only material difference is in reference to a paragraph relating to what is known as Jacquard silk, or silk made on Jacquard looms. With reference to these, a rate of 50 per cent. ad valorem is fixed instead of the specific rate provided by the House bill on all piece silks. In other respects the silk schedule is the same as adopted by the House.

The sundries schedule is slightly changed from the form adopted by the House. In one particular—that is, in reference to coal—there has been a change. The House provided for a duty of 75 cents per ton on bituminous coal. The Senate has fixed that duty at 67 cents, which is the Canadian duty, the object being to make our duty correspond with theirs, for purposes that will be generally understood upon the floor; and further have reduced the duty on culm to 15 cents per ton. A provision was inserted which is intended to apply to coal commercially designated as anthracite coal, coming in on the Pacific coast, but approximating the condition of bituminous coal. Such anthracite coal as is produced in this country is left on the free list.

PROTECTION TO HIDES.

The House placed hides of cattle on the free list, where they have been in previous tariffs since 1873, but the Senate placed them on the dutiable list with a duty of 20 per cent. The difference between the two Houses was adjusted by reducing the duty to 15 per cent., with a proviso allowing a drawback of the entire duty paid on hides used in tanning leather actually exported.

Paintings and statuary for private use were placed on the dutiable list at 20 per cent., and those for public exhibition were left on the free list.

THE FREE LIST.

The free list which passed the House has been agreed to in conference with very slight changes. Bolting cloths and some of the essential oils have been added to the list. The provision of the House relating to the bringing in of wearing apparel and personal effects by tourists was agreed to. This provision is inserted to break up the abuses arising from the practice of tourists returning from Europe bringing with them wearing apparel in large quantities, clothing, and other articles of personal property which are dutiable under our laws.

This abuse has grown to such an extent that a recent investigation by the Treasury Department disclosed the fact that about $40,000,000 of dutiable goods, classified as wearing apparel and personal effects, escaped duty during the past year under the operation of existing statutes. It is estimated by Treasury officials that this will add at least $10,000,000 to the revenues of the Government, and will be just to dealers in this country, who pay duties on the articles they import for sale to our own people.

Mr. CUMMINGS. Will the gentleman from Maine allow me to ask him a question? What was done with the duty on precious stones? I refer particularly to diamonds.

Mr. DINGLEY. The duty is placed at 10 per cent. I should have been very glad, for myself, to have put even a very much heavier duty on articles of that kind; but it was the unanimous opinion of all the present administrative officers, as it was the opinion of the administrative officers under the last Administration, that whenever the duty on diamonds is placed above 10 per cent. ad valorem, then they are smuggled, and instead of obtaining revenue from them we fail to obtain revenue. The officers presented statistics clearly establishing the fact that the largest revenue from diamonds had been obtained when the duty was placed at 10 per cent.; that this was not the smuggling point; but that when it went above that, then smuggling went on by wholesale.

RECIPROCITY.

I am reminded, Mr. Speaker, that I have omitted to give a statement of the reciprocity features of the bill as agreed to, which I had intended. In substance, the agreement of the conferees combines the reciprocity clause of the House and that incorporated in the bill by the Senate, with certain amendments, which substantially unite the two plans, so that both may be made available if desired. One of the amendments which has been adopted is vital in its effect.

The Senate provided that the President might enter into commercial treaties with foreign countries, and when ratified by the Senate they should become binding on the country. The House conferees insisted upon an amendment that they should not become binding until ratified by Congress. In other words, the House conferees maintained that the House should approve as well as the Senate before any such commercial treaties should take effect, and the Senate conferees conceded the point. (Applause.) Otherwise, in general, the Senate as well as the House plans have been adopted with certain modifications, so that both plans if desirable may be used in securing acceptable commercial arrangements.

Mr. OVERSTREET. How does this compare with the provision of the law of 1890?

RECIPROCITY FEATURES EXPLAINED.

Mr. DINGLEY. The provision of the law of 1890 covered sugar and hides, which have been omitted because they have been made dutiable. We have added to coffee and tea, tonka beans and vanilla beans, which are on the free list, as articles to be used by the President under the provision of the act of 1890, and we have included certain dutiable articles that may be used. Under the Senate provision there would be the delay of obtaining the two-thirds vote of the Senate after the President had made the arrangement, and then the delay in securing the approval of the House of Representatives; and it was thought desirable that the House provision, which put in the President's hands the important powers of using certain articles without going to Congress, should also be adopted. The conferees of both the House and Senate have unanimously agreed on the joint plans, which combine all that appears to be practicable in both provisions.

Mr. OVERSTREET. Is it regarded as a broader measure than that of 1890?

Mr. DINGLEY. Oh, very much broader.

INTERNAL REVENUE PROVISIONS.

Mr. Speaker, I come now to the internal revenue features of the bill which the Senate has added. The Senate increased the internal revenue tax on cigarettes, and this has been agreed to by the House with an amendment covering cigarettes wrapped in tobacco, and amendments to facilitate the collection of the tax. The Senate provisions changing the law so as to allow no rebate on the tax on beer has been agreed to. Under the present law, as gentlemen know, a rebate of over 7 cents is permitted, so that the tax of $1 provided by law amounts only to about 92 cents. The amendment fixes the tax at a full dollar, and will add about $2,000,000 to the revenue of the Government from this source.

The Senate provision for a stamp tax upon the issue and transfer of stock certificates, bonds, etc., is omitted from the bill, for the reason that on careful investigation it has been found that the class of persons whom it was originally supposed we should be able to reach cannot be reached, and therefore whatever small amount of revenue might be received as the result of this tax would be collected from men who are doing legitimate business upon a small scale. It was found that it would be almost impossible to execute the law so far as it endeavored to reach such persons. Then, again, it was found not only that it would be very difficult of enforcement, but that the amount of revenue to be obtained from it would be exceedingly small, and it was thought, at least in the present tariff bill, without opportunity to examine thoroughly in reference to legislation of that character, that it would be unwise to hastily enter upon it without careful investigation under all the circumstances. There was also some question as to the constitutionality of certain provisions in the scheme.

The administrative sections which were added to the bill by the Senate, and which have been agreed to with certain amendments by the House conferees, are almost exactly the same as two sections that were in the administrative bill passed by the House in the Fifty-fourth Congress, which the House therefore had previously accepted.

THE RETROSPECTIVE CLAUSE.

Mr. TERRY. What became of the retroactive clause of the bill?

Mr. DINGLEY. I regret to say that the Senate declined to concur in that, and made this decision known within a few weeks after the bill passed the House in March. I think it was exceedingly unfortunate that the action of the House with reference to that retrospective clause was not concurred in; or at least, if not concurred in finally, that it was not left to stand until the present time. If that had been done, it would have saved more than $25,000,-000 of revenue to the country.

The wisdom of the action of the House in that matter seems to me to have been clearly established by subsequent events. Since the 1st of March there have been imported into this country, in anticipation of an increase of duty on articles on which we have raised revenue, goods which, if they had been imported as required for consumption during the fiscal year upon which we have just entered, would have yielded not far from $40,000,000 of revenue. Of course there are no means of avoiding these difficulties, unless by some such retroactive provision as was contained in the bill as it passed the House.

Mr. OLMSTED. I would like to ask, with reference to the action of conferees on the bill with regard to rails made wholly or in part from imported iron, whether any provision is made for a drawback?

Mr. DINGLEY. The old provision with reference to drawback continues in force. There is no modification. In other words, the administrative officers cannot see a method of determining whether the exported article is made of an imported product or not except under existing regulations, and a drawback provision of the character desired by some is, in the opinion of these officers, susceptible of very great fraud. I may state to the gentleman from Pennsylvania, however, that this matter was not in conference at all.

TWO HUNDRED AND TWENTY-FIVE MILLIONS REVENUE.

Setting aside the effect of the anticipatory importations, there is no doubt that the bill as agreed to by the conferees will yield not less than two hundred and twenty-five millions per annum, an increase of at least $75,000,000 above the present law. The present law in the fiscal year 1896 yielded $160,-000,000 of revenue, but that revenue was increased abnormally by large importations of manufactures of wool. In the previous year the present tariff had yielded a revenue of about $144,000,000. In the last fiscal year, ended the 30th of June, if it had not been for the fact that a new tariff, imposing to a certain extent higher duties, was under consideration, the revenue under the present law would not have exceeded $140,000,0000.

As it is, the revenue from customs under the present law in the last fiscal year was about $174,000,000. But $32,000,000 of that at least was caused by anticipatory importations and withdrawals from bond; for if the revenue from customs had continued for the last four months of the last fiscal year as it had continued during the eight months previous, the revenue would not have exceeded $140,000,000. This makes the average annual revenue-producing quality of the present Wilson tariff about $150,000,000.

LOSS BY ANTICIPATORY IMPORTATIONS.

As I have already stated, it is probable that the Treasury has lost by anticipatory importations of wool, sugar, manufactures of wool, and certain other articles on which the duty has been increased, at least $40,000,000. Now, this $40,000,000 must be deducted from this $225,000,000 which this bill will yield. That leaves $185,000,000. So that this bill, including the internal revenue provision, notwithstanding the loss of $40,000,000 by anticipatory importations, is estimated by the members of the Senate Finance Committee as likely to yield $185,000,000 during the current fiscal year. The Treasury officials, however, put the revenue from the proposed tariff for the present year at one hundred and seventy-seven millions—eight millions less. It must be borne in mind also that thirty-two millions paid into the Treasury in the last four months on anticipatory importations and withdrawals, and credited to the last fiscal year, really belong to the revenue for the present fiscal year.

Now, it is estimated that the revenue from all other sources—ordinary internal revenue tax and miscellaneous sources outside of postal revenue—will be in the neighborhood of $180,000,000, probably $185,000,000. Now, these two estimates give us a revenue in the neighborhood of $370,000,000, or, accepting the Treasury estimate, $362,000,000. The expenditures of the Government during the last fiscal year, aside from the postal expenditures paid by postal revenues, were $365,000,000. But there were undoubtedly some expenditures paid after the 1st of July that belong to the last fiscal year. So that the expenditures may be placed at $370,000,000 per annum.

ENOUGH REVENUE INSURED.

Now, if the Senate Finance Committee have correctly estimated the anticipatory importations at $40,000,000 loss only, then there would be enough revenue, notwithstanding the loss of $40,000,000 during the current fiscal year, to meet the expenditures. But if from any cause the effect of these anticipatory importations shall prove to be greater than estimated, then unquestionably there can be taken with safety from the cash in the Treasury, obtained by the issue of bonds under the last Administration, at least $30,000,000; so that, with the cash in the Treasury and with the revenue that will come from this bill, there is no doubt that the expenditures of the Government for the current fiscal year will be fully met. And after this fiscal year, when this bill shall have become law, the revenue will be increased to that point where every expenditure will be met, and there will be a surplus left (applause on the Republican side) with which can be resumed the reduction of the principal of the public debt. (Loud applause on the Republican side.)

LOW GRADE SUGARS.

Mr. LACEY. I should like to ask the gentleman a question in reference to sugar. I notice the compromise increases the rate on low grades of sugar.

Mr. DINGLEY. The lowest grades are less than in the original House bill up to 84 degrees. Eighty-five-degree sugar is the same, and from that point the new rates are more—at 96 degrees, five and a half hundredths more; and at 100 degrees, seven and a half hundredths more; and on refined sugar, seven and a half hundredths more.

Mr. LACEY. What quantity—how many millions of pounds or how many tons—have been imported?

Mr. DINGLEY. If you refer to low grades of sugar, below 84 degrees, then there is scarcely 2 per cent. of such sugar imported into this country; certainly not over 4 per cent. under 84 degrees test.

Mr. LACEY. Then this change does not give any premium to those who have imported this kind of sugar pending the contest between the two Houses?

Mr. DINGLEY. Not at all. As a matter of fact, these low grades of sugar cannot be used in making hard sugars, and the importations of them are very small.

THE NET RESULT AS TO SUGAR.

Mr. COOPER, of Wisconsin. I should like to ask the gentleman what the net result is as to sugar. Does the rate agreed upon by the conferees lessen or increase the rate of protection, the amount of protection given to the sugar trust by the original House bill?

Mr. DINGLEY. The differential as between raw and refined sugars is precisely the same in this bill on 100-degree sugar as when it passed the House. Under the bill as it passed the House a duty of 1 cent was placed upon sugar polarizing 75 degrees, and an increase in duty of three one-hundredths of a cent for each degree running up to 100. Now, that left a duty of 1.75 on raw sugar of full purity——

Mr. COOPER, of Wisconsin. What do you mean by that—100 degrees?

Mr. DINGLEY. One hundred degrees is full purity, which is, of course, what refined sugar is. That left a duty on raw sugars of full purity, of 100 degrees, of one and seventy-five one-hundredths of a cent.

Mr. JOHNSON, of Indiana. But the duty on raw sugar in this conference report is higher than in the bill as it left the House?

Mr. DINGLEY. Certainly. It has been raised from 84 degrees up, so that the increase at 100 degrees amounts to seven and one-half one-hundredths of 1 cent per pound in order to give that additional encouragement to beet-sugar production.

REFINED SUGAR UNDER THE DINGLEY BILL.

Mr. JOHNSON, of Indiana. What is the duty placed upon refined sugar in this bill as compared with the existing rate?

Mr. DINGLEY. The duty on refined sugar is 40 per cent on both raw and refined, with one-eighth of 1 cent additional on refined in the present Wilson tariff, which amounts to 1.113 cents per hundred pounds, and the duty on raw sugar of 100 degrees purity is 89.48, leaving a differential of 4.82. And in this bill the duty is 1.95 on refined sugar and 1.82½ on raw sugar of 100 degrees test, making a differential of 12½ cents per hundred at that point, with a slight increase as the polariscopic test goes down to cover the increased cost of refining and the loss.

Mr. JOHNSON, of Indiana. Therefore there is a marked reduction in duty on refined sugars.

Mr. DINGLEY. Certainly; an average of 40 per cent.

Mr. SIMPSON, of Kansas. I desire to ask the gentleman a question. While this conference agreement does not increase the duty on refined sugar, does it not have the effect of decreasing the duty on low grade raw sugars, thus giving the manufacturers cheaper raw material?

Mr. DINGLEY. Not at all. Hard sugar, that is, granulated sugar, cannot be made from those low grade sugars. In fact, I may say with reference to that question that careful investigation has shown clearly that the rate we fix, making a slight reduction on these few lower grades, gives an almost exact equivalent ad valorem duty to that placed on the higher grades.

FORTY PER CENT. LESS THAN WILSON RATES.

In general, it may be said that the differential on refined sugar under the schedule which has been presented, which is but a slight modification of the original House schedule, except that it increases the duty on raw sugars, is exactly the same at the 100-degree point in the schedule here proposed as in the bill passed by the House. THERE IS A SMALL INCREASE AS THE POLARISCOPIC TEST GOES DOWN FOR THE REASONS I HAVE STATED; BUT IT IS ABOUT 40 PER CENT. LESS THAN THE DIFFERENTIAL UNDER THE EXISTING LAW AT ALL POINTS.

Mr. DOCKERY. The statement is made that the bounty to the sugar trust has been reduced by this bill; and I sincerely hope that is an accurate statement.

Mr. DINGLEY. The differential on refined sugar is considerably less than under the present Wilson tariff.

Mr. DOCKERY. Then, as I understand, you claim that the bounty carried in this bill is less than under existing law?

Mr. DINGLEY. Certainly. The gentleman means the differential I suppose?

Mr. DOCKERY. Yes, sir.

Mr. DINGLEY. The differential, as the gentleman knows, is the difference between the duty imposed on such a quantity of raw sugar as will make a pound of refined sugar and the duty imposed upon the refined sugar when imported.

NO BOUNTY TO THE SUGAR TRUST.

Mr. DOCKERY. BUT DISCARDING ALL TECHNICAL TERMS AND COMING RIGHT DOWN TO "BED ROCK," THIS BILL GIVES TO THE SUGAR TRUST A CERTAIN BOUNTY——

Mr. DINGLEY. IT GIVES TO NO SUGAR TRUST ANY BOUNTY.

Mr. DOCKERY. WELL, IT GIVES THEM A CERTAIN MEASURE OF "PROTECTION."

Mr. DINGLEY. IT GIVES TO THE REFINING INDUSTRY OF THIS COUNTRY A PROTECTION THAT IS 40 PER CENT. LESS THAN THAT GIVEN BY THE WILSON BILL OF 1894. (Applause on the Republican side.)

Mr. MOODY. I wish to ask the gentleman from Maine what has become of Senate amendment 850, on page 225, providing for an additional duty where an export bounty is paid by a foreign country?

Mr. DINGLEY. A general provision at the close of the bill covers that matter.

Mr. MOODY. There is nothing in the bill, so far as I can see, which indicates whether that provision has been retained or not.

Mr. DINGLEY. It was struck out in the Senate and a general counter-vailing-duty provision put in at the close of the bill, obviating the necessity for the other provision.

Mr. MOODY. But nothing in this printed bill indicates whether that general provision of the Senate has been retained or not.

Mr. DINGLEY. The way to ascertain that is to find the provision as agreed to in conference in the reciprocity section of the bill.

Mr. MOODY. There is nothing to indicate what action has been taken by the conference.

Mr. DINGLEY. If the gentleman will look at the beginning of the bill, he will notice the explanation of these various marks; and when he comes to examine further, I think he will see that the House recedes from its disagreement to that provision and agrees to the general provision of the Senate relating to countervailing duties where there is a bounty on exportation, thus practically accomplishing what was accomplished by the House amendment.

THE INCREASE IN DUTIES.

Mr. Speaker, I desire to call attention to the nature and extent of the increase in the rates of duty in the proposed tariff. The largest increase has been made in the duty on sugar, partly for revenue and partly for the purpose of encouraging the production of our own sugar. It is this increase which raises the average equivalent ad valorem apparently above that of the tariff of 1890, in which sugar was free. The changes which have been made in the bill in conference reduce the average equivalent ad valorem. estimated on the basis of the values of 1893, to about 50 per cent., including the duty on sugar. Excluding sugar, the average equivalent ad valorem, on the basis of the values of 1893, does not exceed 48 per cent., against 49½ per cent. under the tariff of 1890 and 40 per cent. under the tariff of 1894. But the difference between the 40 per cent. of the present tariff and the 48 per cent. (excluding sugar) proposed, properly distributed on protective lines, is the difference between life and death.

We have heard much reckless denunciation of the proposed tariff as "the highest ever known," but, as a matter of fact, the average ad valorem of the tariff of 1824 was 50½ per cent., and 61¾ per cent. in 1830, 48½ per cent. in 1867, and this, too, before undervaluation became a science.

PROTECTIVE DUTIES AND REVENUE.

Mr. Speaker, before considering the second object had in view in framing the proposed tariff measure—that of encouragement to our domestic industries—I desire to correct an impression which exists in some minds that a tariff constructed on protective lines is antagonistic to revenue.

It would be a sufficient answer to such a contention to point to the fact that all our revenue tariffs since 1861 had been greater revenue producers than any tariffs for revenue only ever put into law in this country. The tariff of 1890, notwithstanding it surrendered from fifty to sixty millions of revenue by placing sugar on the free list, yielded nearly one hundred and seventy-seven and one-half millions of revenue from customs in the fiscal year beginning July 1, 1891; two hundred and three and one-third millions in the fiscal year beginning July 1, 1892, and would have undoubtedly yielded two hundred and twenty millions revenue in the fiscal year beginning July 1, 1893, if it had not been for the result of the November elections of 1892, which proclaimed the overthrow of our protective policy and disarranged our industries and impaired the consuming power of our people, and thus cut down revenue, while the present tariff, heralded as a revenue tariff, with 40 per cent. duty on sugar, yielded only one hundred and fifty-two millions in the fiscal year ended June 30, 1895, and would not have yielded in the fiscal year just ended over one hundred and forty millions if it had not been for anticipatory importations to avoid the new duties.

THEORIES vs. EXPERIENCE.

To one who regards theories more conclusive than experience, it might seem as if duties on imports which can be produced or made here without natural disadvantage equal to the difference of cost of production or manufacture here and abroad, with the necessary result of encouraging production here of such articles because of the fact that such duties give our own people an equitable chance to compete for our own markets, would cause a falling off of revenue.

But this conclusion omits to take note of results which flow from such encouragement of production and manufacture here, and of certain habits of a portion of our people: First, the increased purchasing power and higher standard of living of the masses of our people, in consequence of which they buy and consume more imported luxuries, or articles in the nature of luxuries, than ever before, and, second, the presence of a large number of well-to-do citizens who regard it as "the thing" to use imported articles of foreign make, especially wearing apparel, and who are willing to pay high duties on them.

A striking illustration of the influence of these two facts is to be found in a comparison of the revenue-producing qualities of the wool and woolens schedule of the tariff of 1890, framed on protective lines, and the same schedule of the tariff of 1894, framed on non-protective or supposed revenue lines. This schedule of the former tariff yielded under protection in the fiscal year 1893 a revenue of about $44,500,000 on an importation of 40,000,000 pounds of clothing wool and the usual quantity of carpet wool, together with $36,000,000 worth of woolen goods, mainly fine goods, consumed by the well-to-do, and in the fiscal year 1896, under a tariff for revenue, yielded only $23,000,000 revenue under an increased importation of 127,000,000 pounds of clothing wool and the usual quantity of carpet wool, together with nearly $60,000,000 of woolen goods.

ANTI-PROTECTIVE SCHEDULES DIMINISH REVENUES.

In other words, a change from a protective to an anti-protective schedule diminished the annual revenue of the Government $21,000,000. And worse still, it took away from our farmers the opportunity to grow at least 80,000,000 pounds of wool, and by reducing the price of wool 10 cents per pound, diminished their purchasing power at least $30,000,000 annually, which diminution of purchasing power on their part was felt by every class of our citizens. And besides this, it shut down nearly all the woolen machinery in this country and sent into the streets many thousands of operatives, who were obliged to cut down their purchases of the products of the farm, the loom, and the shop.

The fact is that revenue from duties on imports rises and falls with the consuming power or prosperity of the masses of the people, and it is for this reason that a protective tariff so framed as to encourage domestic production and manufacture, and consequently so as to increase the earning and consuming power of the masses, always affords the largest revenue, because it encourages a higher standard of living and a larger consumption of imported luxuries or articles of voluntary use, from which the revenue under a protective tariff is largely derived.

INCREASED REVENUE FROM LUXURIES.

Mr. Speaker, I desire to call special attention to the fact that at least thirty millions of the additional revenue which the proposed tariff bill will yield • after the effect of anticipatory importations has been overcome will come from the restoration in the main of the duties of the McKinley tariff on imported luxuries or articles in the nature of luxuries, duties which were unwisely reduced by the tariff of 1894 in the wild crusade of our free-trade friends against what they denounced as tariff taxation of the masses.

Some of the items which go to make up the thirty-five or forty millions of revenue from luxuries thrown away by the tariff of 1894 and restored by the pending tariff bill are as follows:

On liquors	$1,000,000
On Habana cigars and wrapper tobacco	1,000,000
On silk, linen, and cotton laces and embroideries	3,000,000
On silks and silk plushes and velvets	3,000,000
On kid gloves and jewelry	3,250,000
On ostrich feathers, downs, artificial flowers, etc	1,275,000
On trimmings of beads, glass, etc	400,000
On braids and plaits of straw, etc	400,000
On plate glass and chinaware	890,000
On paintings and statuary	1,000,000
On personal effects (mainly luxuries) of American tourists returning from Europe	10,000,000

TWENTY-FIVE MILLIONS SAVED ON LUXURIES.

HERE ARE OVER $25,000,000 REVENUE FROM LUXURIES THROWN AWAY BY THE SO-CALLED "REVENUE TARIFF" OF 1894 AND RESTORED BY THE PENDING BILL.

If the object of our so-called tariff-reform friends in throwing away this revenue—as gentlemen on the other side declared—was to remove the burdens of the masses—assuming, as our friends assert, that a duty is always added to the price—what rejoicing there must have been among the toiling people when three millions of burden was removed from them by a reduction of the duty on laces and embroideries! And what hallelujahs of praise must have gone up when a burden of three and a quarter millions was lifted from their bills for kid gloves.

No wonder gentlemen on the other side grow red in the face in their bursts of indignation at the proposition embodied in this bill to save $25,-000,000 revenue by placing higher duties on these luxuries, and thus render it no longer necessary to issue and sell interest-bearing bonds to meet the expenditures of Government in time of peace.

But these are by no means the only imported luxuries or articles of voluntary use (on which statesmen have heretofore thought it wise to impose the heaviest duties) on which duties were reduced and revenue thrown away by the tariff of 1894, and which this bill restores.

WOOLENS FOR THE WELL-TO-DO.

It will be observed that of the $36,000,000 woolen goods imported in 1893 under the act of 1890, on which a revenue of about $34,000,000 was paid into the Treasury, more than three-fourths were composed of fine woolens used by the well-to-do, and especially by that class of our people who buy foreign goods because of the impression that it is more fashionable to do this, and who are willing to pay for the gratification of their "fad." Unquestionably three-fourths of the twelve millions of revenue on woolen goods surrendered by the act of 1894 and restored by this bill came from the well-to-do.

Then, undoubtedly, three-fourths of the three millions revenue on cottons surrendered by the tariff of 1894 came from fine goods, which were in the nature of luxuries. And the same remark may be made of many other schedules.

Unquestionably between thirty-five and forty millions of revenue from articles in the nature of luxuries were thrown away by the tariff of 1894. The proposed tariff is framed to recover this revenue.

PROTECTION AND EXPORT TRADE.

Mr. Speaker, I desire in passing to briefly notice the claim, which is being studiously pressed, that the present tariff has increased our exports of manufactured goods. It is true that our exports of manufactured articles have been increased—largely, however, in such articles as mineral oils and specialties, in which export tariff legislation bears no part; but to whatever extent there has been an increase of exports of ordinary manufactures, it is due to the fact that our own consumption has so far fallen off as to force manufacturers to sell wherever they could for less than cost, a result which emphasises our distress rather than illustrates our prosperity.

IT WAS THE BOAST OF THE FRAMERS OF THE TARIFF OF 1894 THAT IT WOULD AT ONCE LARGELY INCREASE OUR EXPORTS OF WOOLEN GOODS BY PLACING THE FARMERS' WOOL ON THE FREE LIST AND THUS GIVING OUR MANUFACTURERS FREE WOOL. YET THERE HAS BEEN NO INCREASE OF OUR EXPORTS OF WOOLEN GOODS, BUT SUCH A DESTRUCTION OF THE PURCHASING POWER OF OUR FARMERS THAT OUR WOOLEN MANUFACTURERS HAVE SEEN THE HOME DEMAND FOR THEIR GOODS LARGELY DECLINE, AND FOREIGN WOOL MANUFACTURERS HAVE BEEN ABLE TO TAKE POSSESSION OF OUR MARKETS TO AN EXTENT NEVER BEFORE KNOWN.

Experience has shown that our foreign trade is largest under the protective policy, for the reason that our imports and consumption of luxuries and of such other goods as we do not make rise with the prosperity of our people, and our ability to compete in foreign markets is increased as American inventive genius is stimulated by a brisk demand for products in our domestic markets.

THE PROTECTIVE POLICY.

Mr. Speaker, the title of the tariff bill under consideration sets forth the two ends which have been steadily kept in view: "To provide revenue for the Government and to encourage the industries of the United States." It is noteworthy that the preamble of the first tariff bill under the Constitution, framed by Madison and approved by Washington—a bill passed on the 4th of July, 1789, a day sacred to every American patriot—declared that that tariff bill was "for the support of Government, for the discharge of debts of the United States, and for the protection and encouragement of manufacturers."

The proposed tariff bill has been framed not only to secure adequate revenue, but also on protective lines with a view of encouraging American industries.

I do not propose at this time to enter into any elaborate argument to demonstrate the wisdom of the protective policy in tariff legislation. The almost uninterrupted prosperity experienced by this country under the protective policy from 1861 to 1893—a prosperity unexampled from 1879, when our currency was placed on a sound basis, up to the close of 1892, when a majority of our people, misled by the assaults and glittering promises of free-trade Democracy, declared for the overthrow of protection, contrasted with the sad experience of the country during the past four years under first anticipated and then partially realized free trade or tariff for revenue only, is a more potent and convincing argument in favor of a return to the protective policy than anything I can say here.

ENLARGED OPPORTUNITIES FOR LABOR.

The object of the protective policy is to enlarge the opportunities for labor and to maintain a high standard of wages, and its yokefellow, a high standard of living for the masses. It rests on the assumption that that country is the most prosperous in which the standards of wages and of living are the highest. It assumes that the standard of living or purchasing power of the masses, which creates the demand for products and sets in motion the intricate machinery of production and distribution in modern civilized society, is dependent on the opportunities to use their labor at good wages, and that these opportunities widen and wages rise as diversified domestic industries multiply and the production of whatever we want which can be made or produced here without natural disadvantage goes on at home rather than abroad. An economic policy which tends to destroy home industries in which no more labor is required for production here than abroad, or to reduce wages under the plea that the products of such industries can be purchased at a lower price abroad simply because our labor is paid higher wages, is destructive to prosperity, for the reason that nothing is cheap which deprives our own people of opportunities for employment of their labor and reduces the wages paid to labor.

CAUSE OF HARD TIMES IN 1893 AND '94.

What took place in 1893 and 1894 in consequence first of anticipated and subsequently partially realized tariff reductions? First, every industry began to shorten sail and stop machinery, and then to reduce wages. Second, the workingmen, discharged or reduced in wages, began to buy and consume less of the products of the farm, the shop, and the mills. And third, the falling off of consumption resulted in gorged markets and unremunerative prices under the inevitable law that prices fall when there are two sellers to one buyer, producing, with other causes, that dislocated condition of production, distribution, and consumption which has continued nearly four years, and which is denominated industrial and business depression, or "hard times." We have had the free trader's paradise of "cheap" goods, but the cheapness has been secured at a fearful cost. I venture to say that, notwithstanding the apparently cheap prices of the past four years, the masses of this country have not for many years paid so much in labor—with which all products are ultimately bought—as they have paid during this period.

A FREE TRADE KINDERGARTEN.

Our people have been attending a free-trade kindergarten, in which we have learned lessons that will not be forgotten for some time. The tuition has come high, but the experience will make it difficult for gentlemen on the other side to again mislead voters by assaults on protective duties as "robbery" or as the "levying of new burdens," when their object is simply to place competition here on the basis of our high wages rather than on the basis of the low wages of Europe.

The end aimed at in the protective policy is not the benefit of the producer or the manufacturer as such, for as such either is as well off under free trade with European wages as under protection with American wages, barring the advantages which flows from the increased market caused by the high purchasing power of the masses. The object in view, I repeat, is to enlarge the opportunities of labor through the diversification and growth of domestic industries, to elevate the standard of wages and the standard of living, and thus promote the prosperity of all classes.

Now, Mr. Speaker, the majority of the committee who have framed this proposed tariff bill believe that any economic measure whose effect is to transfer to Europe or other countries the making of articles which can be produced here without natural disadvantage can never produce anything but ruin to any country. (Loud applause.) We believe that when the protective principle is applied of imposing duties equivalent to the difference of the cost of production and distribution arising from our higher wages of labor, as proposed in the pending bill, and thus increased opportunities are offered to American labor, giving the masses a purchasing power which they have lost under the conditions of the past four years—a purchasing power which enables them to buy more of the farmer, more of the merchant, more of the manufacturer, and more of every producer in the land—then confidence will begin to return, prices will begin to rise to a paying point, and prosperity begin to set in upon the land. (Loud applause on the Republican side.)

Government Obligations.

We are unalterably opposed to every measure calculated to debase our currency or impair the credit of our country.—*Republican National Platform of 1896.*

Contracts based on a 100-cent dollar should be held as valid and binding as contracts based on a 12-inch foot or a 3-foot yard.

SPEECH OF

Hon. EDWARD L. HAMILTON,

OF MICHIGAN.

IN THE HOUSE OF REPRESENTATIVES,

Monday, January 31, 1898.

SPEECH

OF

Hon. EDWARD L. HAMILTON.

The House having under consideration concurrent resolution No. 22, declaring that all bonds of the United States issued or authorized to be issued under certain acts of Congress are payable, principal and interest, at the option of the Government of the United States, in silver dollars of the coinage of the United States containing 412½ grains each of standard silver, and that to restore to its coinage such silver coins as a legal tender in payment of said bonds, principal and interest, is not in violation of the public faith nor in derogation of the rights of the public creditor —

Mr. HAMILTON said:

Mr. SPEAKER: This resolution proposes that bonds issued or authorized to be issued under the acts enumerated in the preamble thereto are payable, principal and interest, at the option of this Government in silver dollars containing 412½ grains each of standard silver.

The resolution further proposes that to restore to coinage—meaning now unlimited coinage—such silver coins as a legal tender in payment of said bonds is not in violation of public faith nor in derogation of the rights of the public creditor.

This resolution stands on the defensive from the outset.

It hastens to deny that the payment of the public debt in silver dollars coined without limit at the ratio of 16 to 1 is dishonest.

It proposes in effect that sovereign Government shall take silver, now standing temporarily at the ratio of about 33 to 1 with gold, coin it into dollars without limit arbitrarily at the ratio of 16 to 1, and pay its debts with the money which it has so created.

(3)

The question resolves itself into one of honesty and good faith, and was passed upon at the last election.

The Republican party, in its platform, pronounced against every measure calculated to debase our currency or impair the credit of our country, and therefore against the free coinage of silver except by international agreement with the leading commercial nations of the world.

It declared in favor of maintaining "our silver and paper currency at parity with gold," and the people of the United States indorsed the Republican platform.

The American people are sensitive to any imputation of public or private dishonor and they pronounced against legalizing the payment of honest obligations in depreciated dollars and thereby violating the pledge of the nation to maintain the parity between gold and silver.

They pronounced against the clipping of coin by legislative enactment.

They pronounced in favor of a silver dollar worth a gold dollar.

In favor of a silver dollar that will not shrink when exposed to salt water while crossing the ocean.

In favor of a dollar worth a dollar the whole world round, and not a dollar fluctuating from day to day in the markets of the world.

In favor of gold and silver, and paper at parity with them—plenty of gold, plenty of silver, and plenty of business to keep them both in use and circulation.

They pronounced in favor of a dollar true to name and true to the value stamped upon it.

COINAGE AND ITS OBJECT.

What is the object of coining money? Simply to certify to the world the weight and fineness of the piece.

Coinage was first resorted to by individuals for business convenience, and then monopolized by governments.

It has been said that if money were not coined every business man would have to carry a pair of scales and be a chemist.

The commercial world does carry scales and does understand chemistry, and the gentlemen on the other side carry scales, but they carry them over their eyes.

Every coin "rung on the counters of this world" must pass either upon its own intrinsic worth or upon the credit of the nation which stamps it, and when the commercial world distrusts a nation's power to keep its money, whether paper or metallic, up to the value stamped upon its face, then such money must pass upon its own merit, sink to its actual value, or seesaw up and down from day to day, subject to the caprice of public confidence.

So the commercial world weighs the Mexican silver dollar, which contains about 6¼ more grains than our own, and says, "This dollar is worth the silver it contains. For it we will give you about 50 cents:" and thus it weighs the money of all the world.

This nation has kept its silver dollars at parity with gold, (1) because behind every silver dollar has stood the nation's pledge to keep and maintain silver and gold at parity; (2) because by coinage on Government account it has wisely limited the output of silver dollars within its powers of redemption; and (3) because it receives them in payment of tariff and taxes.

The difference in the slumping capacity of silver and paper is defined by the difference in the material composing them.

A paper dollar may decline from its face down to nothing, because the paper is worth nothing, while a silver dollar may decline from its face down to the value of the silver composing it.

MONEY AND PRICES.

The quantative theory of money, elementary and old as political economy, was paraded in the last campaign like a new discovery. It was truthfully urged that more money makes higher prices; but the twin truth that it is only money in circulation that affects prices was not dwelt upon.

In the language of John Stuart Mill, "Whatever may be the quantity of money in the country, only that part of it will affect prices which goes into the market of commodities and is there actually exchanged against goods." Substitutes for money, even credit used in making purchases, have the same effect on prices as money itself. This explains why prices are substantially the same in France and England notwithstanding France has twice the volume of coin money that England has.

Money driven to cover by panic and hidden away in fear builds up no enterprise and furnishes no employment.

Confidence makes business, and business makes prosperity.

With confidence fled and business dead, it was said that what the country needed was more money, as if by some sort of legislative legerdemain our population could be enriched without effort.

The way to have "more money," it was said, was to dig down the mountains and coin them into silver dollars at the arbitrary ratio of 16 to 1.

But why coin at 16 to 1? Why not coin at 8 to 1 or 1 to 1, or why not stamp paper, "cheap in material, worked by steam, and signed by machinery?"

If the touch of the Government stamp creates value, why waste silver?

Why not coin pig-iron dollars, as they did in the days of old Lycurgus?

If the touch of the Government stamp can make value, the philosopher's stone is outdone, mankind can be rich without work, rich without thought, and rich without value received; and carking care and the struggle and grind of poverty will be no more.

Let us proceed to stamp and do nothing but stamp.

"FREE AND UNLIMITED COINAGE."

It is said that a free, open mint would create an unlimited demand and pull the price of silver up to parity with gold; that an increased output of silver would increase its value, and somewhere in dim perspective silver and gold would meet at the ratio of 16 to 1.

What is a free, open mint? Simply a place run by the Government where bullion would go into the hopper and come out coin, and the coin would not belong to you nor to me nor to the Government, but would belong to the man who brought the bullion to the mint, and we could not get a dollar of it except for value received.

If this Government should offer to buy wheat at $5 a bushel, and be able to purchase all wheat offered at that price, wheat would be worth $5 a bushel. If this Government should offer to buy whitefish at $5 apiece, and be able to purchase all whitefish offered at that price, every whitefish in the lakes would be worth $5 so long as the market was open. But if this Government should simply say to the owners of whitefish, or wheat, or silver, "Gentlemen, we have exceptional facilities for counting; bring on your commodities and we will count, weigh, label, and stamp them," it is not to be supposed that a rise in value would follow. Eliminating the legal-tender proposition by which silver would have a temporarily enhanced value for payment of past-due debts, a free open mint would give it no value.

If a free open mint would create an unlimited demand and pull the price of silver up to parity with gold, then a free open thrashing machine would raise the price of wheat and a free open sawmill would raise the price of basswood up to that of rosewood or mahogany.

CHARACTER OF MONEY.

It is laid down as an axiom that more money makes higher prices, and it is true. But the money must be in use and circulation, and the quality of the price depends upon the quality of the money in which it is measured and the character of the people among whom it circulates.

More than $450,000,000 of paper money was issued by the colonies and the Continental Congress, which shrunk to nothing in the hands of the last possessor.

Confederate money grew more worthless as time brought Appomattox in sight.

The greenback fluctuated to as low as 38 cents on the dollar, and was restored to parity with gold by the power of this Government to redeem it.

Measured in greenbacks, Confederate or continental money, prices were high, but the seller was not enriched thereby. He became poorer the longer he held the price. That is the price which depreciation exacts. Depreciation levies another tax, also, when the merchant takes toll for uncertainty and charges a percentage for possible loss.

It is true that money circulated in those days, because every man sought to unload on his neighbor.

CLASH OF DEMOCRATIC THEORIES

It was once said by Mr. Cleveland, then at the head of an undivided Democratic party, that the "price is increased to the consumer by precisely the amount of the duty exacted." This argument that "the tariff is a tax," and that prices are too high by reason thereof, has done Democratic duty down to date and has followed prices down to bed rock, when the tariff is under discussion.

No self-respecting Democrat ever alludes to tariff duty as duty; he always speaks of it as a tax, with the peculiar and indescribable intonation and inflection, the result of long habit, which has a tendency to prejudice the casual thinker and lead him to prefer to raise money to pay expenses by running in debt instead of charging the foreigner a license to sell in our markets.

But when money is under discussion the gentlemen on the other side plant themselves on a new premise, viz, that prices are too low.

Their argument runs thus: Prices are too high, therefore let us have free trade. Prices are too low, therefore let us have free silver at 16 to 1.

PRICES AND PROTECTION.

The demonetization of silver by the leading nations of the world may have had its effect on prices; but the world over, man's invention, the cunning of machinery, division of labor, and increased supply are the visible, tangible, undebatable causes of lower prices. And in this country the loom, the spinning frame, the spinning jenny, and the cotton gin, the transition from sickle to harvester, from flail to thrashing machine, from treadmill to steam engine, the enlarged use of steam and electricity have reduced prices, whitened the fields of the South with cotton, covered the Western plains with golden grain, planted cities, laid rails for traffic, and strung wires for communication.

Still another cause has contributed to lower prices. Protective duties have increased the number of factories, which, by competition among themselves, have reduced prices. The more factories the more labor employed; the more labor employed the more consumers; the more consumers the bigger the town; the bigger the town the better the market for the farmer, and the better the market for the farmer the more valuable the farm.

SILVER AND WHEAT.

The country had an opportunity to note the logic of partisan oratory in the last campaign.

Ignoring the law of supply and demand;

Ignoring invention;

Ignoring the fact that the extension of Western railroads in the United States and Canada had carried seeds to unsown lands; that vast wheat fields had sprung up along the way; that mighty harvests had year after year been brought away to glut the world's supply, and that the same is true of Russia, India, and Argentina; it was said that wheat and silver had been going downhill, side by side, joint victims of the same inexorable law.

But in the heat of the last campaign, when this argument had been blazoned in pamphlets and blared on rostrums, wheat went up and has continued to go up and silver went down and has continued to go down.

Facts are eternal; words are words.

RATIO.

The ratio of 16 to 1 has been talked of as if fixed by Omnipotent edict; as if at the dawn of creation silver and gold were yoked in the ratio of 16 to 1 in the moon's eclipse with weird incantation, while the "lakes of bitumen rose boilingly higher and the slumbering earthquake lay pillowed on fire;" and since that time no other ratio is genuine! no other ratio is blown in the metal; every other ratio is a hoodoo!

Beyond the plains that rise toward the setting sun stand the mountains veined and seamed with wealth untold; but when the mountains were lifted up and metals were fused in volcanic fires, no power decreed that silver and gold should vein the rocks at 16 to 1.

And when men followed the overland trail, and railroads climbed the western grade and tunneled out toward the Pacific, and the sound of the miner's pick rang among the solitudes of the mountains, no power prescribed that silver and gold should be found at the ratio of 16 to 1.

And when silver and gold were found, no power prescribed that they should be used at the ratio of 16 to 1.

And when silver and gold are used, no mere paper statute of any single nation, which may happen to decorate or mar the map of the world for a few hundred years, can compel the two metals to go yoked in an arbitrary mint ratio which is not the commercial ratio.

Silver and gold have been the money of all time, but the ratio of their usage and coinage has changed with the changing years.

As well try to keep the deck of a ship level in a rolling sea as to try to make one ratio stand through time and change.

Congress can do much.

A united Republican majority is strong.

It can roll away the clouds of commercial gloom.

It can make the horizon blaze with the sunrise of returning prosperity and the wind vocal with the clatter and song of industry.

I repeat, Congress is powerful, but it is not in the power of Congress to make a half equal to the whole.

It can not change the multiplication table.

It can not fix the value of commodities.

It can not fix by law the relative value of silver and gold.

It is no more in the power of Congress to make this nation richer by calling 50 cents a dollar than it is in the power of Congress to make the this nation bigger by calling half a mile a mile.

It is no more in the power of Congress to make me richer by calling

50 cents in my pocket a dollar than it is in the power of Congress to make me 12 feet tall by calling 6 inches a foot.

It is no more in the power of Congress to make the farmer richer by calling 50 cents a dollar than it is in the power of Congress to make the farmer's farm bigger by calling half an acre an acre.

Neither the Congress of 1792, nor 1834, nor 1853; neither Washington, nor Hamilton, nor Jefferson, nor Jackson, nor any Administration in the United States; nor princes, potentates, or powers outside of the United States, have ever been able singly and alone to make a mint ratio control a commercial ratio. Yet now, in the closing years of the nineteenth century, ignoring history, encouraged only by conjecture, comes a party proposing to repeal the Gresham law by the unlimited coinage of silver and gold at the ratio of 16 to 1, and make silver so coined legal tender in payment of all debts, public and private, "without the aid or consent of any other nation."

It was discovered long ago, first by Oresme, counselor to Charles V, next by Copernicus, next by Thomas Gresham, master of the mint under Queen Elizabeth, that with unlimited coinage of both metals at a fixed ratio the metal worth more at the mint than elsewhere will go to the mint and be coined, and the metal worth less at the mint than elsewhere will stay away.

THE GRESHAM LAW IN OUR HISTORY.

If gold or silver is worth more uncoined than coined, it will not be coined, or, if already coined, it will not circulate.

Our own history has demonstrated this.

Congress has the constitutional power to "coin money, regulate the value thereof, and of foreign coin."

Pursuant to this power the coinage act of 1792 was passed.

The coinage ratio was then fixed by Hamilton, Secretary of the Treasury, and agreed to by Jefferson, then Secretary of State, not in reliance upon any supposed power in Congress to keep and maintain the two metals in circulation by law, but by looking abroad and ascertaining the existing commercial ratio and seeking to make the mint ratio conform thereto.

And there were "struck and coined" at the mint coins of silver and gold at the ratio of 15 to 1. But a mistake had been made. The legal ratio did not conform to the commercial ratio.

Silver was overvalued at the mint, and so came to the mint, but gold remained away.

Nor did our silver dollars remain long in circulation, but went to Mexico and the West Indies in exchange for Spanish dollars, which were about three grains heavier than our own.

Their dollars were brought to our mint and recoined for re-exchange, and this endless chain of coinage and exchange went on without commercial benefit to us till 1806, when the further coinage of the silver dollar was stopped by order of Thomas Jefferson, then President.

By the acts of 1834 and 1837 Congress provided for the coinage of silver and gold at the ratio of 16 to 1, but again the legal ratio did not conform to the commercial ratio. This time gold was overvalued at the mint and so went to the mint to be coined, while silver went abroad, because 16 ounces of silver were worth more than an ounce of gold.

Up to 1853 silver subsidiary coin, viz, half-dimes, dimes, quarters, and halves, had been coined at the ratio of 16 to 1; but persons without regard for the Goddess of Liberty and the American eagle had melted them down and sold them for bullion, because 16 ounces of silver were worth more than 1 ounce of gold, and so worth more uncoined than coined. Therefore in 1853 the coinage of subsidiary coins for private account was stopped. Subsidiary coins were denied legal tender beyond $5 and the bullion composing them was cut down more than 6 per cent.

From 1834 down to the Bland-Allison Act of 1878 the country was on a gold basis, except during the period of our civil war, when we were on a greenback basis, and cheap paper drove both silver and gold out of circulation and went down at times to 38 cents on a dollar.

Because silver drove gold out under the law of 1792, because gold drove silver out under the laws of 1834 and 1837, and because cheap paper drove both silver and gold out, we can not hope to be exempt from the operation of the same law now. Instead of bimetallism we would have silver monometallism, and instead of more money, less money, until the void left by our departed gold could be filled by depreciated silver—time enough for ruin, havoc, and disaster.

PRODUCTION AND COINAGE OF SILVER.

From the founding of our mint in 1792 down to 1873 there were coined about eight millions of silver dollars and about one hundred and thirty-six millions of fractional and subsidiary coin.

Under the law of 1873 about 36,000,000 trade dollars were coined.

Under the Bland-Allison Act of 1878 not less than two million nor more than four million dollars' worth of silver was purchased monthly and coined until $378,166,793 were coined, but silver went down from 92 to 74 cents on the dollar.

The Sherman law of 1890 provided for the purchase at the market price and coinage of 4,500,000 ounces of silver per month, or so much thereof as should be offered. Under this law 168,674,682.53 fine ounces of silver were purchased at a cost of $155,931,002, for which Treasury notes were issued. The coinage of this bullion from 1890 to January 31, 1898, is 73,822,857 silver dollars, and there remains now uncoined in the Treasury (January 31, 1898) silver bullion which cost $101,-379,158, for which certificates are outstanding. In addition to coinage under the Bland-Allison and Sherman laws, the coinage of subsidiary silver has gone on, so that from February 12, 1873, to January 31, 1898, $93,961,181.05 in subsidiary silver have also been added to our circulation. And yet, notwithstanding this tremendous use of silver in the United States since 1873, the price of silver has continued to go down.

The total coinage of silver in the United States from 1792 to February 12, 1873, was $143,813,598.70, while the total coinage from February 12, 1873, to January 31, 1898, was $581,916,755.05.

In 1896 the Director of the Mint reported that the value of all the silver money in all the world in 1873 was estimated at $1,816,565,657, while in 1894 it had grown to $4,000,000,000, a gain of over two billions one hundred millions in twenty-one years.

There had been added to the full legal tender of the world, then, in twenty-one years, from 1873 to 1894, an amount of silver equal to the accumulation of all the nations in all the ages down to that time.

In 1860 we had a per capita circulation of $13.85; in 1872 we had a per capita circulation of $18.19; in 1896 we had a per capita circulation of $21.10, and in 1897 we had a per capita circulation of $22.49.

If the quantative theory of money can be made to apply to a single nation and prices rise, fall, or stand according to the amount of money in circulation within its boundaries, then prices should have been sustained within the United States.

PRICES GOVERNED BY INTERNATIONAL MONEY SUPPLY.

The per capita money of the nations of the world varies. It is absurd to suppose that the circulation of money will be restrained by national boundary lines.

No matter how many dollars per capita a single nation may have, no matter how many dollars in which to measure its property, real and personal, its money will run beyond its borders and seek the general level, and the price of commodities in any single nation will have relation to the general international supply of money, and not alone to the money of that single nation.

In these days when factories touch ends the world over, and freight by sea is less than freight by land, and distance is annihilated, no single nation can by mere coinage legislation raise prices within its borders measured in money of international circulation.

It is true that a nation may raise the price of its products locally by putting cheap money into circulation—for illustration, continental, Confederate, or greenback money—because the cheaper the money the less it takes in commodities to buy a dollar; but no man can be compelled to part with his property except for value received, and he may name the price and the money in which it shall be paid.

It is true also that a nation may perpetrate upon its citizens the wrong of legal-tender laws compelling them to receive in payment of past-due debts money worth less than the money loaned, and governments may repudiate their debts or pay them in depreciated money. But history denounces kings who have borrowed good money of their subjects and repaid them in bad, and when government "of the people, by the people" goes into the business of paying good debts in cheap money, it means cheating "of the people by the people."

Contracts based on a 100-cent dollar should be held as valid and binding as contracts based on a 12-inch foot or a 3-foot yard.

To say in swelling terms that this or any other nation, single handed and alone, without the aid or consent of any other nation, can maintain silver and gold in circulation, yoked in the arbitrary ratio of 16 to 1, when the commercial ratio is something else is mere conjecture, even if it be said so eloquently that phonographs are set rasping the saying the country over.

Hence the Republican platform of 1896 says: "We are unalterably opposed to every measure calculated to debase our currency or impair the credit of our country; we are therefore opposed to the free coinage of silver except by international agreement with the leading commercial nations of the world."

SILVER MONOMETALLISM.

Incident to silver monometallism is partial repudiation, by which—

1. The laborer would be paid for a full day's work in clipped dollars—in dollars big in his pocket, but small at the grocery.

2. The pensioner who fought for the stability of our Government would be paid in unstable money.

3. Life-insurance policies would be cashed to widows and orphans in dollars worth less than the face of the policy.

4. Savings deposits and loan investments slowly paid to maturity would be repaid in clipped dollars, worth less than the dollars invested.

5. Guardians, executors, and administrators would file their final accounts and be discharged on payment of less than the trust estate.

Incident to silver monometallism, too, is the question whether this nation, which stands now in the forefront of the progressive civilization of the world, shall begin to pattern its finances after those of Mexico;

whether we shall slump to a semicivilized money standard or still maintain our proud place among the nations of the world, with coin the image and superscription of which tell no lie, and with flag not lowered to commercial half-mast.

Around the banner of delusion raised at Chicago demagogues recruited an army of ignorance and vice, with plunder more than suggested.

Very few of the rank and file of Democracy, perhaps, aimed to be dishonest. The great mass of the people, of whatever party, advocate their honest convictions and strive by their political acts to bring benefit to themselves and to their country. But the leaders of the free-silver crusade of 1896 openly avowed their purpose of repudiation, clamorously appealing to the ignorant and to the vicious, seeking also by subtle suggestion to enlist the sympathy and cooperation of conscientious farmers and workingmen in the contest for a debased currency.

The successful business man was denounced as a criminal autocrat with whom the laboring man ought to get even, forgetting that poverty can give no employment to poverty; that the closed factory furnishes no work, and the man out of work spends no money at the store.

Class was arrayed against class.

Firebrands were scattered from rear car platforms.

The doctrine of discontent was disseminated.

The policy of enriching all by the ruin of each was broached.

With such arguments it was sought to elect a President of *all* the people.

THE PUBLIC WEALTH.

What is the public wealth of America? It is not what the Government owns, because the Government owns but little beyond a few forts and arsenals, some public buildings and lands, and the graves of its soldiers.

The public wealth of America is made up of the fortunes of its citizens.

It increases as population increases; it fluctuates as people plant and build and traffic more or less, as new industries and new inventions give new value to lands, mines, and forests, as the seasons bring harvests or famines, as mutual confidence and common prosperity extend credit from man to man, as money goes freely from hand to hand or hides for fear of disaster.

When threats and fears of spoliation have caused money to go into hiding instead of investment, and public confidence is shaken, then public wealth is reduced beyond calculation.

Nations may coin money of silver and gold, but the best mint is the mint of public confidence; and confidence is founded on order, and order is not built upon an earthquake.

The Gold Standard

ITS EFFECT ON

MONEY and WAGES

SPEECH OF

Hon. EBENEZER J. HILL,

OF CONNECTICUT.

IN THE HOUSE OF REPRESENTATIVES,

Tuesday, April 12, 1898.

I have shown—

FIRST. That the actual volume of money has enormously increased under the gold standard.

SECOND. That this increase has exceeded the increase of population.

THIRD. That gold alone is now nearly threefold more abundant compared with other money than gold and silver together were in 1873.

FOURTH. That gold alone is as capable of carrying the credit system of the country as gold and silver were in 1860.

THE GOLD STANDARD—ITS EFFECT ON MONEY AND WAGES.
A STATEMENT OF FACTS.

SPEECH OF

Hon. EBENEZER J. HILL,

OF CONNECTICUT.

IN THE HOUSE OF REPRESENTATIVES,
Tuesday, April 12, 1898.

Mr. HILL said:

The oldest financial transaction of which I can find any account is recorded in the sixteenth verse of the twenty-third chapter of Genesis, where we are told that, nearly four thousand years ago, Abraham, in buying a burial place, weighed to Ephron in payment "400 shekels of silver, current money with the merchant."

Abraham was a stranger and a sojourner in that land and paid his debt in a money of commerce, an actual weight of silver bullion, for it was a thousand years before governments had learned to coin money or fix by law ratios between silver and gold.

But the Bible throws a curious side light upon this transaction, showing that human nature was the same then as now, and that Abraham did as all mankind have since done, took advantage of the customs of the country and paid out of his poorest metal money, for the second verse of the thirteenth chapter tells us that Abraham was very rich in cattle, silver, and gold.

GOLD THE NATURAL STANDARD.

We have no knowledge as to the relative value of the two metals at that time, but the position of the word "gold" in the sentence clearly demonstrates its greater importance, and from that day to this, no matter what the coinage of any nation has prescribed or what change in values may have been attempted by legislation, the world's standard of value has been gold, and gold has been the "1," the unit of value by which all ratios have been fixed.

Not only that, but to this day, whatever the law of any country may declare to be legal tender, the money of commerce, the money current with the merchant, the money used in adjustment of international balances, is weighed as Abraham weighed his, and quantity and quality alone measure values, without reference to any marks that may be stamped upon it.

A while ago I saw in the Bank of England the judgment day of the coinage of the world.

A half dozen automatic scales were receiving the coins in hoppers, and, sliding down long grooves, each coin rested a moment in a balance.

If light weight, the arm lifted and tossed the coin to the right.

If full weight, the arm dropped and the coin was thrown to the left.

It was justice working automatically.

The intrinsic worth of each piece preserved it as it was or sent it to the melting pot.

(3)

Passing down into the vaults of that famous institution, I saw in one room was $20,000,000 of American coin that had been run into gold bars.

They looked like copper ingots.

Each one was tagged with the assayer's certificate of weight and fineness and was ready for sale, as iron or coal or copper would be, by weight.

Last year alone more than thirteen millions of foreign gold coin were received by the mint of the United States, and, without reference to the form and stamp upon them, were melted into bars and valued by their weight and fineness only.

Through all recorded time the intelligent choice of all mankind has made pure gold the final measure of values, even though its tools of exchange may have been, from time to time, cattle, corn, metal, paper, or any other of the many things used as currency which temporary convenience may have suggested.

I do not believe that any people ever advanced far enough in the path of civilization to become familiar with metallic money but that, consciously or unconsciously, its coinage or token system bore some recognized relation to gold as the standard of value.

There certainly is no nation in the world to-day which does not thus recognize it.

Why this is so I need not stop to explain, for natural selection needs no argument to justify itself.

It is enough that it is so and that every advocate of silver or any other standard acknowledges it when he urges the use of anything else as money on any other basis than 1 to 1, or an exact equality with gold.

* * * * * * * * *

ARTIFICIAL STANDARDS.

Starting, then, with the assumption that the universal measure of value is and always has been gold, the question naturally arises, Why should anything else be used as money, and why should an artificial standard be set up?

And here the second attribute of money appears as a tool of exchange.

As a standard measure of value quality alone is required, and a unit of its kind would suffice for all the world, but as a tool of exchange a convenient number of units are needed, and, strange as it may seem, the ruder and less developed society is, the greater the number required to effect exchanges.

Hence it is that, as the nations of the earth have one after another passed from barbarism to civilization, they have left behind them the wampum, the cattle, and the slaves; then the iron, the lead, and the copper, and reached out for the precious metals, silver and gold, as better fitting their changed conditions, always striving for the best that was attainable.

During the past hundred years this process of evolution has gone forward more rapidly than ever before until practically the whole world, and actually all of the commercial world except Mexico, has suspended the free and unlimited coinage of silver as standard money, and either adopted the single gold standard, or a limited bimetallism such as obtains in the United States, where silver is being coined on Government account, but limited in quantity to our ability to maintain its parity with gold.

The reason for this great and sweeping change in the monetary systems of the world is neither mysterious nor strange.

In my opinion it is simply the enormous increase in the production of gold, the universally accepted measure of values, so that it not only promises to be but actually is now in the possession of mankind in sufficient quantity to become under the more highly organized commercial methods the best tool of exchange of which the world now has any knowledge.

Think for a moment what this increase has been.

INCREASE OF GOLD SUPPLY.

During the three hundred and fifty years from the discovery of America to the opening of the California mines in 1850 the entire world's product of gold had been but little more than three billions of dollars' worth ($3,121,830,000), or an annual average of eight and three-quarter millio₁s (8,726,200).

It was only just before the beginning of this period that the art of printing had been discovered, and during the greater part of these three and a half centuries the steam engine, the steamship, the railroad, the telegraph, and the telephone were unknown.

None of the means of communication which now bring nations and individuals the world over into daily and hourly touch with each other in their business relations were even thought of.

Checks, notes, drafts, and bills of exchange, by which 90 per cent of the commercial transactions of the nineteenth century have been carried on, had no existence then, and the modern system of banking had not been developed.

Goldsmiths and jewelers were the bankers and brokers of that time, and the actual gold and silver passed from man to man and nation to nation in the settlement of all transactions.

During the same period the world's production of silver was a little over six billions of dollars ($6,196,504,000), or an annual average of seventeen and one-third millions each year, or about double the product of gold.

Both together added but twenty-six millions per year to the world's stock of money, and even from this must be deducted the amount used in the arts, and it is by no means improbable that this amount was greater in proportion to the population than now, when we have the process of electroplating fully developed.

Is it not easy to understand, in view of these facts, how that both metals were a necessity as money, and that the more abundant was accepted as a measure of value and means of exchange?

With both in use domestic trade was largely barter and international trade was greatly hindered.

CHANGE TO GOLD STANDARD BEGUN.

But the gold accumulation of the centuries gradually forced its way into the channels of trade, and in 1798 England stopped the free coinage of silver, and in 1816, in the face of a sharp decline in gold production, adopted the single gold standard, and declared her purpose to thereafter build up her financial system under it.

For forty years she stood alone, but with the best tools of trade in her possession, she could afford to wait, and while she waited she became the leader of commerce and the financial center of the world.

From that day to this the English pound sterling has known no geographical limit, no national boundary lines, but among every people the world around has silently pursued its mission of adding to England's wealth and increasing England's power.

But in 1850 something happened to gold.

Suddenly from the rocks and hills of California and Australia the stores of golden treasure were poured out, and in a single bound the world's average production went from eight to one hundred and twenty-seven millions of dollars, and in the forty-seven years since the aggregate addition to the world's tools of exchange in gold alone has been $6,101,490,600, as against three billions one hundred millions in the entire three and a half centuries preceding.

Is it any wonder that the nations of the earth have fallen into line and one after another, discarding the costly and cumbrous methods of the past, with a worldwide unanimity have chosen gold as their measure of value and tool of exchange?

To me the wonder is that in these closing days of the nineteenth century a great political party in this progressive Republic should stand before the people upon a theory rejected and thrown aside by all the world within the memory of those now living and, ignoring the addition of over three billions of gold to the world's stock since 1873, should now ask us to go back to the double standard and the unlimited coinage of both metals, and thus put ourselves at the mercy of other nations to plunder us of either at their pleasure.

It would seem as though the frozen sands of the Klondike and the quartz reefs of South Africa would melt with indignation at such a proposition.

This nation will go forward, not backward, in the path of progress, and on that march the rightful place of the United States is in the front rank.

THE DOUBLE STANDARD WITH FREE COINAGE IMPOSSIBLE.

A double standard with free coinage of both metals is an impossibility, but the enlarged use of silver as the willing servant of gold is not only possible, but is even demonstrated as an established fact.

Through all recorded time its value has decreased.

History tells us that 4 ounces of silver were once the equal of an ounce of gold.

It was 8 to 1 under Julius Cæsar, 11 to 1 when America was discovered, 15 to 1 when this nation began its coinage, 16 to 1 in 1837, 22 to 1 in 1890, and 40 to 1 in September, 1897.

Its steady course has been downward, unhindered by legislation, influenced in part by its larger production, but far more by the accumulating and annually increasing supply of gold.

The anomaly is in the fact that the lowest price is concurrent with the largest use, for since 1873 there has been an increase in the silver monetary stock of the thirteen principal nations of the world of $670,900,000, and the bulk of this has been full legal-tender coinage.

In fact, the claim that silver has been demonetized, either in the sense that its monetary function or its legal-tender quality has been taken away, is utterly wrong, for this is true of only a total of $163,430,460 sold by Germany, Roumania, and Scandinavia, and probably this silver was recoined into subsidiary money.

Whether it was or not, is of no consequence, for it was less than a year's product, and the aggregate legal-tender coinage has increased as shown.

The only quality that it has lost is that of the standard, and that it was never fit for and never would have received but for the insufficient supply of gold.

Neither is it true, as claimed by some, that depriving silver of its function as a standard has materially helped to reduce its value.

*   *   *   *   *   *   *

No metal with a production in excess of requirement, or of limited production concurrently with another better fitted for monetary purposes, can have one particle of value given to it by a free and unlimited coinage.

Not an ounce of it is taken from the world's market.

The bullion in the coin and the ingot will be precisely the same in price, and the one adapted to and available for the same uses as the other.

A limited coinage, with the value of the coin maintained at parity with gold by governmental credit, does remove that exact quantity from the general stock, and in proportion to such decreased supply will tend to increase the market price.

All experience proves that fact, and the Mexican dollar is the best possible evidence of it to-day.

*   *   *   *   *   *   *   *   *

TWO CLASSES OF FREE SILVER ADVOCATES.

Mr. HILL. I fully understand that there are two classes of advocates of the free and unlimited coinage of silver.

One class believes, and believes honestly, that by an unlimited demand working upon a limited supply, additional value will be given, which will bring it to an equality with gold.

While I am willing to concede their honesty of purpose, I must totally disagree with their conclusions.

I heard once of a man who, on retiring for the night, found the blankets too short to properly cover his person, with the result that he suffered all night long from cold feet.

The next night, with the enthusiasm born of a new idea, he cut a strip from the upper end of the blanket and pinned it to the lower end and then retired in the firm belief that his troubles were all over.

He was doubtless honest, but had poor judgment.

I would remind these gentlemen who would legislate value into silver of the old conundrum which I used to hear when I was a boy: "If you call a dog's tail a leg, how many legs would a dog have?" and, to save them any waste of gray matter in guessing it, will state that the answer was "Four; for calling the tail a leg does not make it one."

The second class is made up of those who do not believe that silver can acquire added value from legislation, but who desire free coinage purely as an inflation scheme.

As an illustration of that class, I cite the last Democratic candidate for the Presidency, who some time ago, in a speech in Brooklyn, said: "We do not want to change the ratio. It is not because we produce silver that we want 16 to 1, but because we own property and owe debts."

It is further illustrated by the action of forty-two United States Senators who, when a short time ago the question of paying the Government bonds in silver was under consideration, voted down the Nelson amendment, which declared that—

"It is the duty of the Government of the United States, under existing laws, to maintain the parity of its gold and silver money, so that a dollar of the one metal shall for all monetary purposes always be the equal in value to a dollar of the other metal."

And who made a still more specific declaration of their views and purposes by defeating the Caffery amendment, which provided that—

"If at the time of payment of the principal and interest on the bonds herein mentioned the market value of silver is not on a par with gold at the ratio of 16 to 1, the principal of said bonds shall be paid in gold or silver at the option of the creditor."

For such declarations and for the principle or lack of principle on which they are based I have neither sympathy nor respect, nor do I believe that any man or party acting in accordance therewith will ever receive the indorsement of the honest people of this country. [Applause on the Republican side.]

VOLUME OF MONEY AND PRICES.

The recent manifestoes issued jointly by the chairmen of the Democratic, the Populist, and the Silver-mine parties declare in effect that the adoption of the gold standard by the principal nations of the world has largely reduced the volume of money, and that as a result prices have declined, development has been checked, and wages have been reduced.

As an unanswerable argument against this, I submit the following table showing the approximate stock of gold, silver, and uncovered paper money in the principal countries of the world in 1873 and in 1897, with the changes between these dates:

Approximate stock of gold, silver, and uncovered paper money in the principal countries of the world in 1873 and 1897 and changes between those dates, expressed in millions.

[Compiled from pages 40, 41, and 42 of the Report of the Director of the Mint for 1897.]

Country.	Gold.			Silver.			Uncovered paper.		
	1873.	1897.	Increase.	1873.	1897.	Increase.	1873.	1897.	Increase.
Great Britain.........	160	584	424	95	121.7	26.7	59.8	112.1	52.3
France..................	450	772	322	500	443.9	*56.1	385.3	119.2	*265.1
Germany...............	160.2	654.5	494.3	306.2	212.8	*93.4	90.8	123.8	33
Russia	149.1	586.9	437.8	18.6	74.2	55.6	618.4	467.2	*151.2
Italy.....................	20	96.9	76.9	23	45.4	22.4	87.8	161	73.2
Belgium................	25	35	10	15	57	42	35.1	72.5	37.4
Netherlands..........	12	21.9	9.9	37.3	56.1	18.8	15.3	37.9	22.6
Austria Hungary....	35	178.5	143.5	40	63.7	23.7	265.8	177.6	*88.2
Australasia............	50	132.1	82.1	3	7	4	....	22.5	22.5
Denmark...............	4.1	15.4	11.3	7.5	5.4	*2.1	6.5	6.4	*.1
Sweden	1.8	10.6	8.8	4.3	4.9	.6	6	19	13
Norway.................	7.6	7.5	*.1	1.6	2	.4	2.3	3.8	1.5
United States.........	135	696.3	561.3	6.2	634.5	628.3	749.4	397	*352.4
Total.............	1,209.8	3,791.6	2,581.8	1,057.7	1,728.6	670.9	2 322.5	1,7.0	*602.5

Net increase, $2,650,200,000.

I would especially call attention to the footings, which show that these nations in 1897 had $2,581,800,000 of gold and $670,900,000 of silver more than they had in 1873, while the uncovered paper money—the demand obligations of these nations—shows a decrease of $602,500,000, making a net increase of currency in twenty-three years of $2,650,200,000.

But not only is it true that the actual monetary stock of the world has been largely increased, but it is also true that this increase has outstripped the increase of population.

Take as an example our own country.

In 1873 we had per capita $3.24 of gold as against $9.55 now, 0.15 of silver as against $8.70 now, and $17.97 of paper as against $5.45 now, making a total per capita of all forms of money of $21.36 in 1873 against $23.70 now.

England has increased her per capita from $9.90 to $20.65, Germany from $13.59 to $18.95, Belgium from $14.44 to $25.70, Italy from $4.88 to $9.69, the Netherlands from $16.56 to $23.65, Sweden from $2.75 to $6.90, Denmark from $10.05 to $11.83, Australasia from $20.38 to $32.32, and Norway from $6.39 to $6.65, while Russia has decreased 61 cents, Austria 16 cents, and France $2.31.

But not only do these figures show conclusively that there has been no shrinkage in the volume of money, but it is found that the actual increase far exceeds the entire world's production of silver, less the amount used in the arts since 1873.

I am well aware that in response to this showing of the increase of the world's volume of money the advocate of free coinage will still claim that such increase is not in what he calls "money of final redemption."

While I deny that there is any such thing as a particular money of final redemption in our system where we have four kinds of legal tender with the right of exchange of one for the other indiscriminately under the parity clause of the act of 1893, yet I am willing to concede that what is meant is "standard" money and will test this claim on that basis only.

* Decrease.

In 1873, under the double standard, the United States had:

[See Mint Report, 1897, page 42.]

Gold	$135,000,000
Silver	6,150,000
Total specie	141,150,000
Paper	749,445,610

Taking silver and gold together, the money of final redemption was 18.83 per cent of the money to be redeemed.

In 1897 the United States had:

[See Mint Report, 1897, page 37.]

Gold	$696,300,000
Silver	634,500,000
Paper	731,772,151
Silver and paper	1,366,272,151

So that in gold alone the money of final redemption is now 50.96 per cent of the money to be redeemed.

Mr. SHAFROTH. You count silver as redemption money?

Mr. HILL. No; I am taking your view of the case. And though counting silver and paper as subject to redemption in standard money, yet we are nearly three times as well prepared for this as we were in 1873, with both metals in use for that purpose.

Again, the loans and discounts of State banks in 1860 were $706,333,272.22; specie held (gold and silver), $82,638,510.09.

* * * * * * * * *

There is no better way of testing this question of business requirements than from loans and discounts. Loans and discounts of national banks February 18, 1898, were $2,138,078,280.43; gold held, $222,855,516.77. So that it appears that, according to the population at each period, the gold held by national banks in 1898 was $3.06 per capita, and the specie—gold and silver—held in 1860 was $2.69 per capita.

Not only that, but where, in 1860, the specie holdings of banks were 11.6 per cent of the loans and discounts, in February, 1898, notwithstanding an enormous expansion of the credit system and the use of other legal tender as bank reserves, the gold alone was 10.42 per cent. of the loans and discounts.

I have shown—

First. That the actual volume of money has enormously increased under the gold standard.

Second. That this increase has exceeded the increase of population.

Third. That gold alone, or the money of ultimate redemption, now is nearly threefold more abundant compared with other money than in 1873.

Fourth. That gold alone is as capable now of carrying the credit system of the country as gold and silver were in 1860.

In view of these facts, what becomes of this triplet proposition that the shrinkage in the volume of the world's money has reduced prices and checked development?

The truth is, and it is coming to be more and more accepted, that it is the quality rather than the quantity of money that influences prices, conditions of supply and demand being unchanged, and that the quantitative theory ignores rapidity of circulation, improved facilities of exchange, and the modern use of credit instruments.

BANK CREDITS IGNORED.

Mr. HILL. I am quite sure that in considering the subject of the volume of money our free-silver friends forget the bank credits of this and other countries, which amount to more than $16,000,000,000 ($16,051,137,349), consisting of capital, surplus, circulation, and deposits of commercial banks and banks of issue only, all savings banks being excluded both here and abroad.

This enormous sum is to all intents and purposes available as money and performs all of the functions of a tool of exchange.

As against the $23.70 per capita of money here, there is a banking power of $72.61; in Great Britain, $110.66; Australasia, $136; Switzerland, $86.71; Denmark, $67.64; Canada, $57.10; Sweden, $46.95; Straits Settlements, $39.60; Netherlands, $19.22; France, $24.23; Belgium, $19.15; Austria, $13.68; Germany, $8.94; Italy, $8.76; Russia, $6.33; Mexico, $3.88; Turkey, $1.12; Japan, $6.88. (Compiled from the Report of the Comptroller of the Currency for 1897, pages 594, 595, 596.)

Add the deposits of savings banks to the rating of the United States and it will carry us to over a hundred dollars per capita ($102.52).

This is a factor in the financial problem that must be reckoned with.

Compared with the volume of money, it exceeds it fourfold here and fivefold in Great Britain.

It is a structure built up from the bed rock of confidence in a fixed and unchanging unit of value—gold.

Undermine this, cut this in two by legislation for fiat money, and "the subsequent proceedings will interest us no more," for there will not be enough left to worry over. [Loud applause on the Republican side.]

THE REPUBLICAN PARTY AND THE WAGE-EARNER.

There is one claim in this recent manifesto which I confess is a surprise to me.

For the past three years we have been told again and again that in order to meet the competition of the silver-standard nations we must adopt the same policy and pay our labor in depreciated money, and the rapidly increasing dangers of Oriental competition have been sounded in our ears as something which could not be overcome by a protective tariff and which would yield to no treatment but the heroic one of free silver coinage.

I had begun to breathe freer and to think that perhaps the danger was over when Japan and India adopted the gold standard and thus voluntarily surrendered all of the advantages of low wages paid in cheap money which they formerly possessed, but I never expected to see our Democratic and silver-mine party friends face squarely about and charge the reduced wages of the past four years, which it was one of their main objects to perpetuate, to the present financial policy of this nation.

For forty years the pride and boast of the Republican party has been that American labor has been the best-paid labor in all the world, and, since the resumption of specie payment in 1879, paid in the best money of the world.

The very inception of that party was an organized protest against human slavery, and it poured out its blood and treasure in 1861 that labor might be free, for it knew that when the lower stratum was lifted all would rise.

In the providence of God and amid the storm of war slavery died, and from that day this nation marched on and up, till, in 1892, a single day's wages would bring to the home of the American workman more of the comfort and luxuries of life than mankind had ever dreamed of for like service since the fall of Adam; and then, intoxicated by our success and fooled by the very men who now preach the gospel of free silver and fiat money, we opened wide the doors of this great nation to the unrestricted competition of other lands, and in a single day lost all the fruits of a struggle which had lasted thirty years.

But four years of hardship and privation have not blotted from the memory of the toilers of this nation the achievements of the past; and while I can not speak for other portions of the land, I do believe that this fall, as in 1896, the workingmen of New England will march in solid column to the polls to sustain that party which has stood by them.

Mr. Chairman, out of all the misery and wretchedness of that useless sacrifice of four years of American progress one scene comes back to me which I can never forget.

In the town of Torrington, the banner Republican town of my State, a few days after the splendid political victory of '94, a jubilee was being held. The whole town was ablaze with bonfires and illuminations.

As the procession passed down the street between the separate cottages of American workingmen we came to one house lighted from garret to cellar and decorated in every conceivable spot with American flags.

It was the home of a mechanic who, strange to say, had always before voted the Democratic ticket.

The front door stood wide open, and in the bright light which streamed forth the mother stood watching the passing crowd.

Halfway between the door and the street a large box had been placed, and standing on it was a little girl dressed in white and waving the flag as the procession passed.

It was a beautiful sight, but what attracted my attention most was this inscription on the front of the box at her feet:

"Papa is in the parade; mamma and I are happy."

It was only the expression of a thought of a child, but it told the glad story that hope had come to them again.

Mr. Chairman, the working men and women of New England are looking forward to the day when the full old-time prosperity shall come again, when every man shall be at work and every child shall be at school and every mother shall be at home singing the song of happiness and content.

When that time does come and protection wages are fully restored, I want them paid in gold or its full equivalent, as they have been for twenty years.

You planters in the South and miners in the West may vote for fiat money and free silver if you will. I want the shining gold, with the highest possible purchasing power, for New England workingmen.

WAGES IN THE UNITED STATES.

Two years ago the Secretary of State sent instructions to our consular officers all over the world to report, among other things, the effect of the then existing currency system in the countries where they were stationed upon the rates of labor.

Every word of this testimony is from Democratic sources, for they were all appointees of the party then in power.

It is an unanswerable argument from our political opponents in favor of the single gold standard as the one system which will best conserve the welfare of the American workman and establish and maintain a permanent prosperity within our borders.

At the very beginning of these quotations I will place a table showing the relative wages in gold in all occupations in the United States from 1840 to 1891.

The time covered includes every system of finance which the nation has had—first, the double standard nominally; second, the irredeemable paper money of the war time, and third, from resumption in 1879 to 1891.

It is taken from the Senate Finance Committee Report on Prices, Wages, and Transportation, printed in 1893.

It shows two things. First, a slow but steady advance before the war, a sharp decline, but gradual recovery during the paper-money period, and a uniformly upward tendency thereafter.

There are no statistics since 1892, and I am glad of it, for they would have been neither satisfactory nor creditable to the American people for the four years succeeding.

HUMAN LABOR THE BEST MEASURE OF GOLD.

The second point to which I would call attention is, that human labor is the most uniform and most reliable in supply of anything which the Lord has put on this planet.

The chinch bug, the weevil and the potato bug, frost, drought, and storm may all affect the product of the field.

The area of cultivation may be extended or decreased.

Invention, improved machinery, new mines discovered, oil fields exhausted, all these things serve to increase or decrease the products of our farms and shops, and in these modern days the "gold bug" must take all the blame, but human labor in this table measures gold and proves beyond dispute the stability of the existing standard and the wisdom of its continuance.

Relative wages in gold in all occupations, 1840 to 1891, grouped by different methods.

Year.	Simple average.	Average according to importance.	Year.	Simple average.	Average according to importance.
1840	87,7	82.5	1866	108,8	111.1
1841	88	79.9	1867	117,1	121,8
1842	87.1	84,1	1868	114.9	119.1
1843	86,6	83	1869	119.5	123.5
1844	86,5	83,2	1870	133,7	136.9
1845	86.8	85.7	1871	147.8	150.3
1846	89.3	89,1	1872	152.2	153,2
1847	90,8	91.3	1873	148.3	147.4
1848	91.4	91.6	1874	145	145.9
1849	92.5	90.5	1875	140,8	140.4
1850	92.7	90.9	1876	135,2	134.2
1851	90,4	91.1	1877	136,4	135.4
1852	9·,8	91,8	1878	140.5	139
1853	91,8	93,2	1879	139 9	139,4
1854	95,8	95,8	1880	141.5	143
1855	98	97,5	1881	146,5	150,7
1856	99,2	98	1882	149,9	152,9
1857	99,9	99,2	1883	152,7	159,2
1858	98,5	97.9	1884	152,7	155,1
1859	99,1	99,7	1885	150,7	155,9
1860	100	100	1886	150,9	155,8
1861	100,8	100,7	1887	153,7	156,6
1862	10·,4	101,2	1888	15·,4	157,9
1863	76,2	81,9	1889	156,7	162,9
1864	80,8	86,2	1890	153,9	168,2
1865	66,2	68.7	1891	160,7	168.6

With this table before him, how any man can claim that there has been any appreciation in the value of gold since 1866 is something I can not understand.

CONSULAR REPORTS ON WAGES.

The reports to follow will generally cover the ten years previous to 1896, and refer to Europe and North America only.

England.—Single gold standard.

The opinion seems rather to be that industry may be impeded by a bad system of money, and great social mischief and confusion produced; but a good monetary system can do no more than let the various forces of industry work unchecked. It is held also that the English monetary system is of this sort. There is no doubt about the standard money; there is an abundant and even indefinite amount of currency for all payments and transactions; credit is vastly developed. But the system has been in existence for generations the same as now, and there could not be any noticeable stimulus due to a monetary cause between the dates mentioned, as there has been no change in the system in the interval.

Rates of wages in the principal occupations were somewhat higher than in 1886, except in agriculture.

The record of changes in wages now made by the labor department from year to year shows that the general wage level changes very slowly.

Canada.—Single gold standard.

In the census taken in 1891, the average wages paid in manufacturing and mechanical industries are shown. These industries were classified as follows:

Industries having an annual output of $25,000 and more:

Wages per employee, 1881	$296.20
Wages per employee, 1891	346.60
Increase in ten years	50.40
Percentage increase	18.30

Industries having an annual output exceeding $500 and less than $25,000:

Wages per employee, 1881	216.68
Wages per employee 1891	244.24
Increase in ten years	27.56
Percentage increase	12.07

Belgium.—Double standard, but no coinage under it for twenty years.

The rates of wages were practically the same in 1886. Since that date wages have not undergone any sensible variation.

Netherlands.—Double standard, but mints open to gold only

A slight advance in wages.

France.—Double standard, but mints open to gold only.

For the last fifteen years wages, both for skilled and unskilled labor, have slowly but regularly increased in France.

Germany.—Single gold standard.

A general advance. In Rhenish Westphalia textile industries wages increased from about $143 per capita in 1886 to about $163 in 1895.

Day labor shows a general slight advance.

In many trades the advance is marked from 1886 to 1892.

Rates of wages of the workingmen in shops of railroads under Government control.

Year.	Laborers, not including officials.	Annual wages paid or expenses incurred for laborers.		Average wages paid per head.	
		Marks.	United States currency.	Marks.	United States currency.
1884–85	47,048	42,838,066	$10,199,539.15	910.50	$216.78
1885–86	47,402	43,306,825	10,311,148.80	913.60	217.52
1894–95	58,145	59,630,899	14,197,833.09	1,025.50	244.16

Austria.—Gold standard since 1892; formerly silver; free coinage abolished in 1878.

During the period embraced between the years 1886 and 1896 manufacturing industries have been stimulated, owing, it is considered, to the development and improvement of foreign trade. Wages have likewise increased during the above period. The expressed opinion of the leading manufacturers seems to be that the increase in wages is due to political reasons rather than to any changes in the currency. To meet the demand of the labor party for a legal working day of eight hours, a compromise was effected by increasing the rate of wages and making the working day ten hours.

Switzerland.—Double standard; mints open to gold only.
It is universally known and recognized that the wages for all classes of labor have very appreciably increased within the last ten years and the condition of the laboring man greatly improved. This, however, is attributed almost exclusively to the better organization of labor, their unions enabling them to demand higher wages.

Italy.—Double standard; mints open to gold only.
According to statistics got together and published by the director-general of agriculture, there has been a marked increase in the wages of agricultural laborers. But owing to the minimum wages originally earned in this labor, the increase seemed greater than it has been in fact, if the normal condition of living be considered. A general increase is to be noted, however, and especially in those industries in which inventions have made improvements, yet even this branch has its exceptions, as in the case of silk spinning. At the same time the prices of products in general use have gone down and the hours of labor have generally been lessened.

Mexico.—Nominally, double standard; actually, silver.
As regards wages paid in Mexico, it has been found impossible to obtain any accurate statistics as to the rate which was paid ten years ago. The Government statistics at that time were not very accurate; but from all the obtainable information, derived from hearing the facts and views of well-informed persons cognizant of the conditions existing then and now, it can safely be stated that as regards skilled labor there has been a slight increase, both in the amount paid and in the demand, while as regards unskilled labor the conditions may be said to be substantially the same.

The amount of wages paid varies throughout the Republis, being higher in some sections than in others, and in certain mining districts lower than they were ten to fifteen years ago. This is generally owing to local causes. As a matter of course, owing to the construction and management of 7,000 miles of railroads, the introduction of electricity, and the placing of new and improved machinery in many of the mines and in some of the agricultural districts, there has been an increase in the number of skilled laborers and some increase in the demand for the same; but it is true that, with the great mass of Mexican laborers, there has been but little if any change in the amount of wages paid.

As might naturally be expected, there are some instances where laborers receive more than ten years ago, but these are the exceptions. There are also many instances where less is received. The daily wage paid to the farm laborer hired by the day does not exceed 30 cents per day, taking into account the whole laboring agricultural population. There are instances where the day laborer receives 50 cents per day; but again there are also instances where he only receives 15 to 20 cents. The secretary of the treasury of Mexico estimates the daily wages of farm laborers at 25 cents.

British Honduras.—Gold standard since 1894; formerly silver.
The laboring man has been materially benefited, beyond the shadow of a doubt, and well he knows it, as against his silver wages, as prior to the gold standard his pay was, in silver, from $10 to $14 a month, and what he had to buy and pay for out of his wages was increased proportionately as silver decreased commercially. Now (at the date of writing) he gets paid in gold what he then got in silver, and what he now buys is not subject to the fluctuation of silver. The price of labor ranged pretty evenly from 1886 up to October, 1894. There may have been some little difference in wages during that period, but not of any moment.

The laboring classes, the backbone of the colony, have largely benefited as regards wages, the dollars now earned equaling the number formerly received by them in sols. Savings-bank deposits have increased. Land and house property, whether in town or country, has increased 100 per cent in value, commanding now in gold the same amount received formerly in the money it replaced.

Nicaragua.—Silver standard.

There are few manufacturing industries in Nicaragua, and the existing currency has done nothing to stimulate them. The people prefer agricultural pursuits to manufacturing enterprises. The wages of the working classes occupied in all kins of labor range from 40 cents to $1.50 silver (18.8 cents to 70½ cents gold) per day for unskilled or skilled labor. Clerks and the higher classes of laborers receive from $2 to $6 (94 cents to $2.82 gold) per day.

Costa Rica.—Nominally, double standard; actually, silver.

In 1886 prices of labor may be considered to have been one-third less than they are to-day—in Costa Rican currency.
Wages (peons), 1886, $1; 1896, $1.50.
The increase of wages, measured in gold, since 1886 is apparent only. Peons receive now less gold than they did in 1886.

Denmark.—Gold standard.

I have talked with the director-general of foreign affairs and others on the practical effect of the currency on manufacturing and the wages of labor, etc., and have learned in a general way that, though Denmark is not largely a manufacturing country, industrial enterprise is generally increasing, and the wages of labor have increased here, as they have, happily, throughout Europe; but whether this increase is attributable to the currency—with which the people generally seem satisfied, though there is a large party here which favors a double standard of gold and silver—is a matter of conjecture and argument.
Consul Ryder, in 1884, made an exhaustive report specifying the wages of laborers in many lines of industry. I have been informed that wages have advanced, on an average, about 10 per cent since that time.

Portugal.—Gold standard, but specie payments suspended in 1891.

Since the suspension of specie payments there has been certainly some increase in the manufacturing industries, but not sufficiently marked to attract attention. The average rate of wages paid for labor, skilled and unskilled, has remained about the same as it was when the country was on a specie basis.
In a general way, it can only be said that while labor, both skilled and unskilled, has remained at substantially the same wage, the prices of agricultural products, clothing, groceries, boots and shoes, hardware, drugs, etc., have increased about 25 per cent, which is about the premium of gold.

Russia.—Silver standard at time of this report; since changed to single gold standard.

As to the growth of manufactures, it has long been stimulated by a protective tariff as well as by the ability of the manufacturers to pay their workmen approximately the old scale of wages in the cheaper money of the present system [then referring to silver].
An inquiry into wages does not show that the workmen participate appreciably in the benefits bestowed upon these industries. Official statistics showing the condition of agriculture are lacking, except as respects the rates and course of wages in agricultural pursuits, which will be shown in a later part of this report. It suffices to state here, where the general effect is being considered, that I have not read or heard a word favor-

able to the condition of agriculture; that the universal testimony is of extreme depression, and the wages of the agricultural laborers, as shown by the official table referred to, have had, in the main, a downward tendency.

Spain.—Double standard; mint open to gold only.

All information received from as reliable sources as individual observers can be, indicate two things: First, that so far as unskilled labor is concerned, wages have remained stationary; second, that though among skilled laborers for the same amount of skill wages have remained stationary, yet owing to some of the more recent industrial enterprises undertaken in Spain, requiring greater expertness or specialism, the average of wages for skilled laborers, a considerable number of whom are foreigners, has been raised.

During the last ten years, among the higher class of employees in the service of the railways, the wages or salaries have been raised to some extent, as has been done with Government employees, but any connection between this rise and the shrinkage in the value of Spanish currency has been absolutely disclaimed.

Sweden.—Gold standard. From tables given by the American minister a general advance is shown for past ten years.

Norway.—Gold standard.

The existing currency established by law of June 4, 1873, has not had any practical and direct influence on the manufacturing industries and the wages of labor. The latter have increased during the last decade in this country as elsewhere, but probably from reasons different from the introduction of the gold unit. The last statistics published by the central statistical bureau of Norway do not embrace any later year than 1890, which is compared with the statistics of 1885. But it may be safely said that since the former year the wages of labor have steadily increased, though I am unable to state the actual rates.

No comment upon these quotations is necessary, for the fact is clearly established that under the gold standard business conditions have been settled and a general advance of wages has occurred both in Europe and America; that not only have higher wages been paid, but they have been paid in money of the greatest purchasing power, and that if any decline in wages is found, it is in silver standard countries.

THE GOLD STANDARD THE WORLD'S CHOICE.

Mr. Speaker, within the limit of the century now drawing to a close 855,000,000 of the population of the globe have voluntarily abandoned the free coinage of silver and chosen gold as their standard measure of value.

They comprise the skill, the genius, the intelligence, the culture, the enterprise, the progress, and the wealth of the world.

To every one of the other countries, belated stragglers on the march of time, or not yet emerged from barbarism, we are sending missionaries to-day to lead them up to civilization and a higher life.

The advocate of free silver coinage may turn to such a source for wisdom and counsel on financial methods if he will, but this great Republic will not follow him, for its people have been taught by their own experience that a currency solidly based on gold has not only built up the nation in the days of peace, but is its best defense in time of war.

GROSVENOR

ON

Democratic Opposition to War Measures.

It does seem to me to be a curious fact that no bill can be reported here which looks to the real defense of the country and to the real purpose of defeating the foe with whom we are contending, without adverse criticism being made, and, in my humble judgment, that sort of criticism which ought to have no weight with the members of the House.

Mr. HAY (Dem. of Virginia).

[Record, p. 5611, May 18, 1898.]

Since the outbreak of the Spanish War they have committed—that is, the Democrats in the House—about every error possible. Giving a grudging support to the various imperative measures which followed the original appropriation of $50,000,000 for the national defense, they lined themselves up almost solidly against the War-Revenue Bill, and capped the climax last Wednesday by casting the bulk of their vote in opposition to the annexation of Hawaii.

[Record, June 29, 1898.]

SPEECH OF

Hon. CHARLES H. GROSVENOR,

OF OHIO,

IN THE HOUSE OF REPRESENTATIVES.

WAR EXPENDITURES.

The House having under consideration the conference report on the bill (H. R. 10100) to provide ways and means to meet war expenditures—

Mr. GROSVENOR said:

Mr. SPEAKER: Shortly after the meeting and adjournment of the Republican State convention of Ohio, over the deliberations of which I had the honor to preside, some remarks which I made in that connection were severely criticised in one of the great newspapers of the country, and I was sharply assailed in the House by the gentleman from Missouri [Mr. COCHRAN] and the gentleman from Mississippi [Mr. ALLEN]. The language complained of is, as I understand, contained in the following:

THE ADMINISTRATION'S WAR POLICY.

There came to the country an incident that was not counted upon at St. Louis. There came to the Administration of William McKinley a responsibility never dreamed of when he was elected President of the United States. War came. The mutterings of the coming storm began to be heard across the Gulf of Mexico, almost upon the threshold of the Administration. He found a country unfitted for war, incapable of war, incapable of a respectable effort at war, and he very early found a body of men in the country, and largely in Congress, who were willing to gain a little early bird stolen sentiment in favor of rushing to war without the intelligence to know whether we were ready to go, without the intelligence to know what we were going to war for.

And if you will notice, the passage of the fifty-million war emergency bill in Congress marks the last echo of patriotism of nine out of every ten of those gentlemen. They were willing to gain some sort of popularity before the people of the country by shouting about the suffering reconcentradoes of Cuba. But when the money has been asked for for the suffering soldiers of the Union, nine out of every ten of them have voted "no" on every appropriation bill. They were willing to demand that the President should send his army and his ships to bombard Havana, but when they have been asked to raise the money to carry on the war, all but six of them in the House of Representatives and all but eight of them in the Senate voted "no" upon every proposition.

On the same day of the convention in Ohio, a Democratic newspaper, published in the city of Washington, to wit, the Washington Daily Times, owned, as it is understood, by one of the most distinguished Democrats of the United States (Mr. Hutchins), printed the following:

DEMOCRATIC FOLLY.

We do not think it will profit the Democrats of the House to hold any more caucuses. It will be much better for the minority to go at once into voluntary liquidation and apply for a leader who has the ability to lead and whom they with self-respect can follow. Nothing short of a complete reorganization within the next thirty days will avert the popular wrath to come.

Since the outbreak of the Spanish war they have committed about every error possible. Giving a grudging support to the various imperative measures which followed the original appropriation of $50,000,000 for the national defense, they lined themselves solidly against the war-revenue bill, and capped the climax last Wednesday by casting the bulk of their vote in opposition to the annexation of Hawaii, a consummation devoutly desired by a two-thirds majority in both Houses of Congress and four-fifths of the American people without regard to party.

The result is plain. What was intended to be, and what was originally, a purely American war, has degenerated in the eyes of the country into a Republican war, with all that that implies.

The Republican President stands before the world to-day as one pursuing a patriotic policy in the teeth of unreasoning Democratic opposition. When victory comes to him and Spain is humbled in the dust; when America's possessions are enriched by the addition of Hawaii, the Philippines, Puerto Rico, and perhaps the Canaries, Mr. McKinley can rise and truthfully say: "This is my work—mine and the Republican party's. As we saved the Union in 1861, so now do we glorify it with victory. Ours the triumph, ours the spoils, including a majority in the new House of Representatives."

And the people on the 8th day of November wil cry "Amen."

In this connection, and in order that the representative character of this paper may be fully accredited, I advert to the fact that very recently the national committee of the Democratic party furnished to this paper a certificate that it was the paper recognized as a leading and distinguished organ of the Democratic party of the United States, and this certificate had the approval of the honorable chairman of the national committee, Senator JONES of Arkansas.

Later the Hon. NELSON DINGLEY, chairman of the Ways and Means Committee, in a speech which he made accepting the nomination for Congress in his district, used the following language:

As soon as we were actually plunged into war, its energetic and successful conduct required money to carry it on, and a large amount for the reason, first, that modern ships and guns and engines of war are more powerful and expensive than any known in any previous war; and, second, that for the first time in our history we are compelled to carry on war against a country separated from us by great oceans.

To provide ways and means to meet war expenditures it became necessary not only to impose special taxes, to which resort is had only in time of war, but also to authorize the Government to borrow whatever additional sums might be required; and to issue its promises to pay the amounts borrowed, with interest—in other words, to issue bonds and certificates of indebtedness.

When this measure came before both House and Senate, at once the same Chicago-platform Democracy, who had been so fierce to plunge us into war before we were ready, began to oppose so much of it as provided for borrowing and paying what we desired to borrow, with interest. Imitating the celebrated Ensign Stebbins, they were for war, but practically opposed to providing adequate means for carrying it on in the only way open to us, after we had applied available taxation. They plumed themselves on their readiness to vote appropriations, and voted against the war-revenue bill which provided the ways and means to pay the appropriations. They declaimed against the bloated bondholder, and opposed "mortgaging the future," but were never able to show how the Government any more than an individual, could borrow money without engaging to pay what was borrowed, with interest for its use.

Immediately after the assaults made upon me I gave notice that at the earliest opportunity I would answer the criticisms that were made by the gentlemen to whom I have referred, as well as the newspaper, for which I have always had, and may say have yet, the highest appreciation and regard.

Under the rules of the House, I could not speak only when the House was in Committee of the Whole on the State of the Union. I made haste to be ready, but after my preparations were complete the House did not again go into the Committee of the Whole, and therefore no opportunity was given me except by unanimous consent.

I sought the opportunity to be heard by gaining unanimous consent, but was met by a vociferous opposition, so I am driven to avail myself of printing a speech on the war-revenue bill, and, fortunately for me, in this case it is appropriate, for it was about and concerning the war-revenue measure that I made my speech complained of at Columbus.

Now, in the first place, what did I say and what was the plain meaning of it? Let us see. The language complained of is as given above.

Every fair-minded man will say that my meaning and my purpose and intent was to assail the Democratic majority on this floor, and that the use of the word "appropriation" meant, and was intended to mean, and was understood by every intelligent man to mean the appropriation of revenues of the country as embodied in the war-revenue bill. The language of Mr. DINGLEY means the same thing. The language of the Democratic editor, to whom I have referred, goes a good deal further, and charges the Democratic party with very much more than I had intended or was understood to intend. NO BILL CAN BE REPORTED HERE WITHOUT ADVERSE CRITICISM.

But now, having promised to make clear my vindication, I propose to lay down, as a text for the remarks I make, the language of a Democratic member of this House. I refer to the statement made by the Hon. Mr. HAY, of Virginia, Democratic member of the House of Representatives, made in the House on the 18th day of May, 1898 (see RECORD, page 5609 to 5614).

It was pending the war measure, which had been asked for by the War Department, to prevent spies from giving information to the Spanish of the location, size, and material of our defenses. Bitter opposition had come from the Democrats to the present consideration of the bill, and finally Mr. HAY used the following language:

I say this is a common-sense proposition. I say that it is one that ought to be supported; and it does seem to me to be a curious fact that no bill can be reported here that looks to the real defense of our country and to the real purpose of defeating the foe with whom we are contending without adverse criticism being made, and, in my humble judgment, that sort of criticism which ought to have no weight with the members of the House.

Now, taking these measures in the order in which they came to the House, let us see. As I read the RECORD, April 4, 1898, was the first effort made to place the Government on a strictly war footing, and referring to page 3896 of the RECORD it will be found that the first emergency measure was objected to by the leader of the Democratic minority; and in this connection I beg to call the attention of the members of the House to the words of Mr. BAILEY, on page 3896, after he had killed, for the time being, the measure under consideration. He said:

"ONLY A SHORT TIME AGO WE WERE COMPELLED TO VOTE TO PLACE $50,000,000 TO BE USED AT THE DISCRETION OF THE PRESIDENT OF THE UNITED STATES."

I cite this to justify the Washington Times when it said that vote was a reluctant vote, and that it was given rather in fear than in love.

Here follows the CONGRESSIONAL RECORD with the several pages containing the appropriations of the House on April 4, April 12, May 9, May 12, May 16, May 24, June 1, June 16, June 20, and June 23. It will be seen that on the 4th of April the chairman of the Military Committee, at the request of the War Department, asked to suspend the rules and after a forty-minutes' debate pass an emergency measure, but to this Mr. HANDY, a Democrat, of Delaware, objected. And further on, after efforts at compromise had been made, Mr. SAYERS, of Texas, a Democrat, also objected.

It will be seen that on the 12th of April a bill then before the House fell under the objection of Mr. McMILLIN, one of the Democratic leaders; and let me point to the House that on the 9th of May (RECORD, 5299), after the fall of Manila, and when we were struggling to increase the naval power, that this same bill, coming from a conference was defeated by Mr. BAILEY, who made a point of no quorum. A bill to reorganize the Adjutant-General's Department fell under the objection of the Democrat from Texas. Again, on the 24th of May it will be seen that an effort to improve the Hospital Corps was under consideration and fell under the objection of a single Democrat, Mr. UNDERWOOD.

On June 6 a bill for the improvement of the Quartermaster-General's Department was knocked out by Mr. UNDERWOOD, who asked for the regular order. Again, on the 16th of June, the chairman of the Committee on Military Affairs of the House asked unanimous consent that time be given for a certain emergency bill, and Mr. UNDERWOOD objected. On the same day the chairman appealed for the setting apart of a single day for the consideration of these bills and Mr. BARTLETT, a Democrat, objected.

On the 20th of June Mr. HULL asked that the 23d of June be set apart for the consideration of these bills, and Mr. UNDERWOOD objected. Again, on the 23d of June, another appeal was made to the House, and the honorable chairman of the committee used this language: "They are recommended by the Secretary of War and are necessary for the prosperous business of the war," and two gentlemen objected, one a Democrat and the other a Republican, Mr. BAIRD and Mr. CODDING.

April 4, 1898, RECORD, pages 3896, 3897:

Mr. CANNON. Mr. Speaker, I desire to report from the Committee on Appropriations, with favorable recommendation, and ask that it be considered at this time.

,   *   *   *   *   *   *   *

Joint resolution (S. 129) relative to suspension of part of section 355 of Revised Statutes, relative to erection of forts, fortifications, etc.

Resolved by the Senate and House of Representatives of the United States of America in Congress assembled, That in case of emergency, when, in the opinion of the President, the immediate erection of any temporary fort or fortification is deemed important and urgent, such temporary fort or fortification may be constructed upon the written consent of the owner of the land upon which such work is to be placed; and the requirements of section 355 of the Revised Statutes shall not be applicable in such cases.

Mr. BAILEY. Mr. Speaker, is this presented as a matter of privilege?

The SPEAKER. It is presented, as the Chair understands, for the unanimous consent of the House.

Mr. BAILEY. Well, Mr. Speaker, before any other preparations for war are made, I want to know whether we are going to have war. I object to the immediate consideration of the resolution.

        *   *   *   *   *   *

Mr. BAILEY. Mr. Speaker, I simply desire to call the attention of the House to the fact that on several occasions within the last thirty days this House has been called upon to vote appropriations and permissions to meet extraordinary cases, and yet this House is not in the possession of any fact which warrants it in supposing that the executive department believes that any extraordinary emergency is upon the country.

Only a short time ago we were compelled to vote to place $50,000,000 under the absolute discretion of the President of the United States. The situation at that time appeared so critical that no gentleman on this side was willing to resist that; and we all voted for it.

April 4, 1898, RECORD, pages 3900, 3901:

ARMY REORGANIZATION.

Mr. HULL. Mr. Speaker, I move to suspend the rules and adopt the resolution which I send to the Clerk's desk.

The SPEAKER. The gentleman from Iowa moves to suspend the rules and adopt the resolution which the Clerk will report.

The Clerk read as follows:

"*Resolved,* That the rules be suspended and the bill (H. R. 9253) for the better organization of the Army be considered with forty minutes' debate at the conclusion of the vote to be taken on amendments reported from the committee and then the bill to final passage."

        *   *   *   *   *   *

The SPEAKER. The gentleman from Iowa asks unanimous consent that the bill H. R. 9253 shall be in order after the reading of the Journal on Wednesday morning. Is there objection?

Mr. HANDY. I object.

        *   *   *   *   *   *

Mr. SHAFROTH. Mr. Speaker, I ask unanimous consent again that the time for the consideration of this bill be set for next Wednesday morning immediately after the reading of the Journal.

Mr. COX. Mr. Speaker, I was recognized by the Speaker, and I do not propose that the gentleman from Colorado [Mr. SHAFROTH] shall introduce his point here at this particular time. [Laughter.]. If I am recognized, I will proceed.

The SPEAKER. The gentleman is only recognized under consent of the House.

Mr. COX. Well, if anybody objects, all right.

Mr. SAYERS. If I can get two minutes, I am perfectly willing that the gentleman from Tennessee shall speak in behalf of this bill.

Mr. COX. I do not propose to buy my time of the gentleman from Texas; if he objects, let him object.

Mr. SAYERS. I will object, then, Mr. Speaker.

April 12, 1898, RECORD, pages 4134, 4135:

NAVAL BATTALION, DISTRICT OF COLUMBIA.

Mr. HILBORN. Mr. Speaker, I ask unanimous consent to take from the table Senate bill No. 1316, to provide for organizing a naval battalion in the District of Columbia, and ask for its immediate consideration.

Mr. LEWIS of Washington. Mr. Speaker, I have a privileged resolution——`

The SPEAKER. The Clerk will proceed with the reading of the bill indicated by the gentleman from California, after which the Chair will ask if there be objection.

The bill was read at length.

The SPEAKER. Is there objection to the present consideration of the bill?

Mr. BAILEY. Mr. Speaker, reserving the right to object, I would like an explanation of this bill. But in the first place I should like to ask the gentleman from California this question: Does this bill propose to permanently increase the naval force of the United States?

*   *   *   *   *   *   *

The SPEAKER. Is there objection to the present consideration of the bill?

Mr. RIDGELY. I object, Mr. Speaker.

The SPEAKER. Objection is made by the gentleman from Kansas.

April 12, 1898, RECORD, pages 5440-5443:

NAVAL HOSPITAL CORPS.

Mr. BOUTELLE of Maine. Mr. Speaker, I move that the House resolve itself into Committee of the Whole House on the state of the Union for the consideration of the bill I send to the desk.

Mr. OSBORNE. Mr. Speaker, before that I desire to submit a parliamentary inquiry.

The SPEAKER. Does it refer to the present motion? Otherwise it would not be in order.

Mr. OSBORNE. It relates to the proceedings in the House during the day.

The SPEAKER. The Chair will hear the parliamentary inquiry of the gentleman.

Mr. OSBORNE. I wish to ask, Mr. Speaker, having this morning objected to the consideration of the bill (H. R. 4073) authorizing the appointment of a nonpartisan labor commission, and being desirous of withdrawing that objection, if it would be in order for me now to do so?

The SPEAKER. It could not be withdrawn now, because the objection has had its effect to prevent consideration at the time the measure was proposed.

Mr. OSBORNE. I wish to state, Mr. Speaker, that I desire to withdraw the objection, having examined the bill proposed.

The SPEAKER. The Clerk will report the bill called up by the gentleman from Maine [Mr. BOUTELLE.]

The Clerk read as follows:

"A bill (H. R. 10220) to organize a hospital corps of the Navy of the United States, to define its duties, and regulate its pay."

*   *   *   *   *   *   *

Mr. BOUTELLE of Maine. I ask unanimous consent that the House resolve itself into Committee of the Whole House on the State of the Union for the consideration of this bill.

Mr. McMILLIN. Mr. Speaker, until I can get the information which the report fails to give us, I object.

Mr. BOUTELLE of Maine. The gentleman from Tennessee objects?

The SPEAKER. The gentleman objects.

May 9, 1898, RECORD, page 5281:

INCREASE OF NUMBER OF REAR-ADMIRALS.

Mr. BOUTELLE of Maine. It is not necessary to move to reconsider and lay that on the table. Now, Mr. Speaker, by instruction of the Naval Committee, I offer the resolution which I send to the Clerk's desk:

*   *   *   *   *   *   *

"A bill (H. R. 10251) fixing the number of rear-admirals in the United States Navy.

"*Be it enacted by the Senate and House of Representatives of the United States of America in Congress assembled*, That the number of rear-admirals in the United States Navy now allowed by law be, and is hereby, increased from six to seven, and this act shall be construed and taken as validating and making in force and effect any promotion to said rank of rear-admiral in the United States Navy made heretofore or hereafter and during the existing war and based upon the thanks of Congress."

Mr. BAILEY. Mr. Speaker, before unanimous consent is given I would like to ask the gentleman from Maine if under the existing law Commodore Dewey would not be entitled to promotion by virtue of the fact that the Congress has thanked him by name?

Mr. BOUTELLE of Maine. Under the statute he would not. There is no rear-admiralship to which he could be promoted, and the statute provides that during the time of war promotion to the grade of admiral can only be made under conditions like those of the present. To enable this promotion to be made this bill creates an additional position of rear-admiral, to which this officer, in the discretion of the Executive, may be appointed. I will state further to the gentleman that this action of mine and the Committee on Naval Affairs is based on consultation with the executive department, with the Senate, and ourselves, and is absolutely essential to carry out the purpose which I infer is in the heart of every member of the House, to enable the President to confer upon Commodore George Dewey the well-earned title of rear-admiral in the United States Navy.

Mr. BAILEY. Mr. Speaker, I desire to say that no title and no office that the Congress can confer upon Commodore Dewey will increase the respect in which the American people hold him. I am sure that he would rather enjoy the satisfaction that comes from this well-earned victory than to take any additional honor and emolument which Congress could confer upon him. I do not intend in this case to make an objection, for it is a peculiarly meritorious one; but I think we might as well understand now that the spirit of patriotism so highly commendable is not to be made a pretext for creating a large number of important and highly salaried offices. This particular case I shall not object to; but it must be a very exceptional case if I consent to the creation of any new and permanent office during this war.

May 9, 1898, RECORD, page 5299:

The committee of conference on the disagreeing votes of the two Houses on the amendment of the House to the bill (S. 1316) to provide for organizing a naval battalion in the District of Columbia having met, after full and free conference have agreed to recommend and do recommend to their respective Houses as follows:

That the House recede from its amendments.

The Clerk read the statement, as follows:

"The managers on the part of the House of the conference on the disagreeing votes of the two houses on the amendments of the House to the bill S. 1316, an act to provide for organizing a naval battalion in the District of Columbia, submit the following statement: .

"The first amendment of the House provided that the battalion contemplated by the above-named bill should be a part of the militia already authorized for the District of Columbia, instead of in addition thereto, as in the original bill. The second amendment proposed to strike out the word 'relative,' so that it would give the staff officers absolute instead of relative rank. After full and free interchange of views the House conferees agreed to recede from the House amendments, and as now recommended the bill stands as it was passed by the Senate "

Mr. HILBORN. I move that the House adopt the report of the conferees.

* * * * * * *

Mr. Speaker, I move the previous question.

The previous question was ordered.

The question being taken on agreeing to the conference report, there were on a division (called for by Mr. BAILEY)—ayes 71, noes 45.

Mr. BAILEY. I make the point of no quorum.

The Speaker pro tempore proceeded to count the House.

May 12, 1898, RECORD, pages 5426-5428:

Mr. Marsh. Mr. Speaker, I now ask unanimous consent to take from the table the bill (S. 4567) to organize a volunteer signal corps and put it upon its passage.

The Speaker. The bill will be read, subject to the right of objection.

The bill was read, as follows:

"*Be it enacted, etc.*, That the President is hereby authorized to organize a volunteer signal corps, for service during the existing war, which corps shall receive the same pay and allowances as are authorized by law for the Signal Corps of the Army.

"Sec. 2. The volunteer signal corps shall consist of 1 colonel, 1 lieutenant-colonel, 1 major as disbursing officer, and such other officers and men as may be required not exceeding 1 major for each army corps, and 2 captains, 2 first lieutenants, 2 second lieutenants, 5 first-class sergeants, 10 sergeants, 10 corporals, and 30 first-class privates to each organized division of troops: *Provided,* That two-thirds of all officers below the rank of major and a like proportion of the enlisted men shall be skilled electricians or telegraph operators."

The Speaker. Is there objection to the present consideration of this bill?

Mr. Bailey. Reserving the right to object, I wish to ask the gentleman in charge of this matter what necessity exists for the passage of the bill at this time?

Mr. Marsh. I will answer the gentleman from Texas by having read communications from the Department, which explain.

     *   *   *   *   *   *   *

The Speaker. Is there objection to the present consideration of the bill?

Mr. McMillin. I shall not object to the consideration of this bill, but I hope where we are called upon in matters of this importance that we will at least have a painstaking report from a committee.

The Speaker. Is there objection? [After a pause.] The Chair hears none.

May 16, 1898, Record, page 5546:

ADJUTANT-GENERAL'S DEPARTMENT.

Mr. Hull. Mr. Speaker, I move to suspend the rules and pass Senate bill 4556, to provide for the increased volume of work in the Adjutant General's Department of the Army, now on the Speaker's table.

The Speaker. The Clerk will report.

The Clerk read as follows:

"*Be it enacted, etc.*, That the President is authorized, by and with the advice and consent of the Senate, to appoint one assistant adjutant-general with the rank of lieutenant-colonel and one assistant adjutant-general with the rank of major: *Provided,* That the vacancy created in the grade of colonel by this act shall be filled by the promotion of officers now in the Adjutant-General's Department according to seniority, and that upon the mustering out of the volunteer forces and the reduction of the Regular Army to a peace basis no appointments shall be made in the Adjutant-

General's Department until the number of officers in each grade in that Department shall be reduced to the number authorized by the law in force prior to the passage of this act."

Mr. DOCKERY. Mr. Speaker, I demand a second.

Mr. HULL. I ask unanimous consent that a second may be considered as ordered

The SPEAKER. The gentleman from Iowa asks unanimous consent that a second may be considered as ordered. Is there objection?

Mr. SLAYDEN. I object, Mr. Speaker. I want to say a word in explanation of that

May 18, 1898, RECORD, pages 5609-5614:

PHOTOGRAPHING GUNS OF THE UNITED STATES.

Mr. HULL. Mr. Speaker, I ask unanimous consent for the present consideration of the bill (H. R. 9553) in reference to photographing any guns which would give the strength of any fortification of the United States.

The Clerk read as follows:

"*Be it enacted, etc.*, That it shall be unlawful for any person or persons, corporation or association, to print, publish, photograph, or reproduce by any process whatsoever, so as to make public in any wise, any information giving the power of the guns or the strength of any fortification of the United States.

"SEC. 2. That any person convicted of the offense charged in the first section shall be deemed guilty of a felony and punished by imprisonment for not more than ten years or by a fine of not more than $25,000, or both, in the discretion of the court."

After much opposition, coming principally from Democrats and Populists, Mr. HAY of Virginia (Democrat) said:

I say that this is a common-sense proposition. I say that it is one that ought to be supported, and it does seem to me to be a curious fact that no bill can be reported here which looks to the real defense of the country and to the real purpose of defeating the foe with whom we are contending, without adverse criticism being made, and, in my humble judgment, that sort of criticism which ought to have no weight with the members of the House.

The bill was recommitted.

May 24, 1898, RECORD, pages 5767-5768:

HOSPITAL CORPS OF UNITED STATES NAVY.

Mr. BOUTELLE of Maine. Mr. Speaker, I desire to call up the bill (II. R. 10220) to organize a hospital corps of the Navy of the United States, to define its duties, and regulate its pay.

The bill was read as follows:

"*Be it enacted, etc.*,

* * * * * * *

Mr. UNDERWOOD. I demand the regular order, Mr. Speaker.

Mr. BOUTELLE of Maine. Does the gentleman object to the consideration of this bill? Mr. Speaker, I desire the question put to the House.

The SPEAKER. The gentleman from Alabama demands the regular order, which is equivalent to an objection.

Mr. PAYNE. I desire the Chair to lay before the House the bill——

Mr. BOUTELLE of Maine. I have one more bill I desire the House to act on—a bill of great exigency.

Mr. PAYNE. But the gentleman from Alabama [Mr. UNDERWOOD] has demanded the regular order.

Mr. BOUTELLE of Maine. On that bill.

Mr. UNDERWOOD. I do not care to insist on the regular order generally. I objected to that particular bill.

June 1, 1898, RECORD, page 6035:

POST QUARTERMASTER-SERGEANTS OF THE UNITED STATES ARMY.

Mr. HULL. Mr. Speaker, I ask unanimous consent for the immediate consideration of the bill H. R. 10051, to increase the number of post quartermaster-sergeants of the United States Army.

The Clerk read the bill, as follows:

"*Be it enacted, etc.*, That the number of post quartermaster-sergeants of the Army be increased by the addition of twenty-five post quartermaster-sergeants, to be appointed by the Secretary of War in the manner now provided for by law."

The SPEAKER. Is there objection to the present consideration of the bill which has been reported?

Mr. SIMPSON. Reserving the right to object, I hope we shall have some explanation of it.

Mr. MCMILLIN. I ask that the report be read.

*　　　*　　　*　　　*　　　*　　　*　　　*

The SPEAKER. Is there objection to the present consideration of the bill?

Mr. UNDERWOOD. Mr. Speaker, in consideration of the importance of these bills, and that I do not think they are of such urgent nature as to need to be considered at once, believing that they ought to be considered in the regular way and not by unanimous consent when there is evidently no quorum of the House present, I shall be compelled to demand the regular order.

The SPEAKER. The gentleman demands the regular order.

June 16, 1898, RECORD, page 6726:

ORDER OF BUSINESS.

Mr. HULL. Mr. Speaker, I ask unanimous consent that Saturday next be set apart for the consideration of bills from the Committee on Military Affairs which have received the unanimous support of the committee. There are four or five bills that ought to be considered at an early day. One pertains to the Inspector-General's Department, one to the Ordnance Department, one to the Engineer's Department, and another bill that will fix the status of the chaplains of the volunteer regiments. These bills ought to be considered and passed this week.

* * * * * * *

Mr. HULL. I have stated what the bills relate to.

Mr. SULZER. These bills are all unanimous reports of the committee.

Mr. GAINES. Mr. Speaker, I think it is no more than right and just to the House that these bills should be printed before unanimous consent is asked for consideration.

Mr. HULL. They are already printed. Mr. Speaker, I ask unanimous consent that next Tuesday be assigned for the consideration of these bills unanimously reported by the Committee on Military Affairs.

Mr. UNDERWOOD. I object.

June 16, 1898, RECORD, pages 6740-6741:

* * * * * * *

Mr. HULL. Mr. Speaker, I want again to ask unanimous consent that next Tuesday be set apart for the consideration of the following bills, reported unanimously by the Committee on Military Affairs——

Mr. MAGUIRE. What time?

Mr. HULL. The bill H. R. 10424.

Mr. McMILLIN. Is that the same request that was made this morning?

Mr. HULL. Yes, sir.

* * * * * * *

Mr. BARTLETT. I call for the regular order, Mr. Speaker.

Mr. HULL. I hope the gentleman will let us fix a day for the consideration of these bills; and I want to read the numbers of them, so that members may know what they are.

Mr. GAINES. The reason why I asked the question was because my colleague [Mr. Cox] has been absent for ten days, so that if any bills have been reported since that time, they have not been reported unanimously.

Mr. HULL. Some of these bills were agreed to since he left and others before he left.

Mr. BARTLETT. I call for the regular order.

June 20, 1898, RECORD, page 6923:

* * * * * * *

Mr. HULL. I ask unanimous consent that Thursday, the 23d instant, be set apart for the consideration of bills reported from the Committee on Military Affairs, and that only bills shall be considered which the committee by a vote have instructed the chairman to call up for consideration.

The SPEAKER pro tempore. The gentleman from Iowa asks unanimous consent for the present consideration of a resolution which will be reported by the Clerk.

Mr. BARTLETT. Reserving the right to object—I did not hear the resolution. Let it be read.

The SPEAKER pro tempore. Certainly.

The Clerk read as follows:

"*Resolved,* That Thursday, the 23d instant; be set apart for the consideration of bills reported from the Committee on Military Affairs, and that only bills shall be considered which the committee by a vote have instructed the chairman to call up for consideration."

*   *   *   *   *   *   *

Mr. CANNON. Well, Mr. Speaker, I will have to antagonize that.

Mr. BARTLETT. If it is to be granted by unanimous consent, I object.

Mr. MAHON. Mr. Speaker, we are willing to give up Friday for the consideration of private business, and I ask that next Friday may be substituted for to-day for the suspension of the rules, and that same right shall be given to suspend the rules on Friday as to-day.

Mr. UNDERWOOD. I object.

June 23, 1898, RECORD, pages 7031, 7032:

BUSINESS OF THE COMMITTEE ON MILITARY AFFAIRS.

Mr. HULL. Mr. Speaker, I wish to ask unanimous consent again to fix next Tuesday for the consideration of bills reported from the Committee on Military Affairs, and I will be very glad to read the numbers of the bills and have them placed in the RECORD, so that all members may know what they are and what the commitee proposes to call up at that time. They are reported from the Committee on Military Affairs and are mainly for the better administration of the Army during present conditions; they are recommended, by the Secretary of War and are necessary for the successful prosecution of the business of the war. Their passage is imperatively demanded in the interest of both efficiency and economy.

*   *   *   *   *   *   *

Mr. UNDERWOOD. The gentleman from Iowa does not understand the position I take, which is that during war excitement matters like these are brought——

Mr. STEELE. If we can have an agreement, that is all right; but I do object to taking the forenoon in order to find out whether anybody is going to object. It becomes a very puerile business.

Mr. HAY. I want to make a suggestion to the gentleman from Iowa, if the gentleman will permit me. My suggestion is this——

Mr. FARIS. Mr. Speaker, I rise to a point of order. We can not hear.

The SPEAKER. Is there objection to the consideration of the bills named by the gentleman from Iowa on Tuesday, after the reading of the Journal?

Mr. UNDERWOOD. If we can not come to an agreement with the gentleman from Iowa, I will object.

Mr. HULL. I can not take those bills out, because I am informed, and the whole investigation made shows, that these two corps of the Army need the increase badly now, and would need it badly if the war should close to-morrow.

Mr. UNDERWOOD. Will the gentleman guarantee that he will give us ample opportunity on Tuesday to debate the bills and offer amendments?

Mr. HENDERSON. That ought to be done. There ought to be the fullest opportunity for discussion.

Mr. HULL. Of course; I will do that.

Mr. MAHANY. I would like the chairman to state what he means by "ample time for discussion." Is there not a likelihood that under this arrangement some of these bills may be debated to such an extent that the others will not be reached?

Mr. STEELE. Mr. Speaker, I call for the regular order.

Mr. DOCKERY. I assume that the gentleman will give opportunity for full discussion.

Mr. STEELE. I withdraw the call for the regular order.

The SPEAKER. Is there objection?

Mr. CODDING and Mr. BAIRD objected.

But, Mr. Speaker, all these were not in my mind at the date of the speech complained of, but I think they were in the mind of the gentleman from Maine at the time of his speech, but I confess I had in my mind the vote of the Democrats on the revenue bill, and here we might as well call things by their right names. The war-revenue measure was a measure to provide money to pay for the cost of the war in all the branches thereof. It was a patriotic measure, demanded by the country and indispensable to the maintenance of the honor of our country and the success of our Army. The bill was reported from the Committee on Ways and Means on the 26th day of April, three days after the declaration of war, and debate proceeded until, as appears by the RECORD, page 4855, a vote was taken, and on the passage of that bill 5 Democrats voted in the affirmative and 130 Democrats and their allies voted "no."

On the preceding page of the RECORD it will appear that on a motion to recommit 134 Democrats voted to kill the bill and 170 Republicans voted against that unfriendly proposition. Later on this same revenue bill came back to the House remodeled in some respects, and passed by the Senate. The whole question of amendment had been fought out in the Senate and in conference committee, and on that day the whole question came to a vote in the House, and it is true to say that on that vote turned the whole question of war or peace, and on that question hung every hope of supplying the Army, and on that vote 149 Republicans and 5 Democrats voted in the affirmative, and 106 Democrats and their allies voted "no."

During the progress of this controversy there were propositions raised by the Democrats to raise some money for the use of the Army by a taxation of incomes, but those propositions were not important, for had their income propositions been accepted it would have been but a comparatively trifling addition to the gross amount of revenue necessary for the purpose of the Government, so that the record stands just this way: A majority of the House of Representatives being Republican provided a measure amply sufficient to carry on the war, pay the soldiers, provide for pensions and the defenses of the country, and the Democrats voted "no."

After the measure had gone through a long and weary consideration, and after making compromise after compromise and concession after concession, and a measure had been agreed upon—the best and only thing that could be done, as everybody knows, with the exception of five or six—these Democratic members voted "no" to every proposition, and to that I referred in my Columbus speech, and to that I adhere. It will not do to say that the Democrats were ready to have voted for a provision for the Army if they could have had certain amendments; they had had all these amendments offered and they had all failed. Shall the question of free and unlimited coinage of silver be permitted now to stand across the pathway of the great interest of the Army? Yet upon that question the Democratic party here took its stand, and it will be held responsible. I do not believe that the Democrats of this country indorse this record, and I do not believe that they will indorse it in November.

Now, there was a proposition pending in the House to permit the soldiers in the field to vote for Congressmen. It had the solid vote of the Republicans in the House and a few Democrats joined, but the bulk of the Democratic party, led by its distinguished leader, fought it to the bitter end, and would have defeated it had they had votes enough. It was finally defeated in the Senate by the Democratic Senators, and in this way 250,000 men, just as capable of voting intelligently as any member of this House, are deprived of voting for Congressmen.

They are fighting the battles of their country out in the jungles of Cuba and far out in the seas of the Orient, but the Democratic party in Congress refuses them the right to vote. We shall be permitted to charge, and we will charge, as I now charge, that they were refused the right to vote by the Democrats. So, Mr. Speaker, I am justified by record in all that I said. The last hours of the House witnessed the oft-repeated appeal of the chairman of the Military Committee for action, by the House, on important bills, but his appeal was in vain.

It will be said that the Democratic members would have voted for the annual and special appropriation bills, but what would it have benefited the country to have made appropriations with no money to pay them? The vital support of the Administration was the war-revenue bill. It will take $200,000,000 more than the taxes to carry us to the 1st of January next, and four hundred millions if the war is to last a year.

Could we have put $500,000,000 of taxation upon the people in a single year in addition to the tax now existing it would have crushed the life out of the industries. We took care that the old cry of idle silver should be heard no more in the land, for we have provided for the coinage of the surplus silver in the Treasury.

ISSUE OF

$150,000,000

Additional Treasury Notes

THE TELLER RESOLUTION

TO COIN SILVER DOLLARS ON PRIVATE ACCOUNT AND PAY THE NATIONAL BONDS WITH THEM

SPEECHES OF
HON. KNUTE NELSON
of Minnesota

In the Senate of the United States, January 29 and May 27, 1898

UNITED STATES BONDS PAYABLE IN SILVER DOLLARS.

The Senate having under consideration the concurrent resolution (S. R. 22) declaring United States bonds payable in silver dollars—

Mr. NELSON said:

Mr. PRESIDENT: I offer an amendment to the pending resolution, and in connection with it I desire to submit a few statements. When a witness is sworn in court he is not only sworn to tell the truth, but the whole truth and nothing but the truth. So with the resolution that is now pending before the Senate. It does, to a certain extent, declare the technical truth, but not the whole of it by a great deal.

It is true that under existing laws, technically, the Government can pay its obligations in every instance, except where the law otherwise provides, in either gold or silver. But coupled with that right is a duty—a duty enjoined upon the Government—to maintain the parity of the two metals.

This duty rests upon two grounds—a statutory mandate and changed conditions in the relative value of the two metals. The Government has the technical right to pay its obligations in gold or silver, but coupled with that right is the duty always to maintain the parity of the two metals. I can pay my debt in silver or gold if I have not obligated myself to pay in gold, but I have not the duty to perform that the Government has—that of maintaining the parity. The Government has the right to pay in either silver or gold, but coupled with that right is the duty enjoined upon it by law—by two existing laws, that of 1890 and 1893—under all conditions to maintain the parity in value.

IN 1878 THE SILVER IN A SILVER DOLLAR WAS WORTH 90 CENTS IN GOLD.

Senators have stated on this floor that the conditions are now the same as they were when this resolution was passed in 1878. Mr. President,

(3)

neither as a matter of fact nor as a matter of law is that true. As a matter of fact, in 1878, when the resolution was passed, the silver in the silver dollar was worth about 90 cents in gold. To-day it is worth only 44 or 45 cents in gold. At that time we had no law on our statute book requiring the Government to maintain the parity of the metals. That was not placed in the law of 1878. It was not in existence at the time that resolution was passed.

In 1890, when the so-called Sherman law, providing for the extensive purchase of silver, was passed, the duty of maintaining the parity was first enjoined in that law. Some of the Senators who aided in passing that law are now, in effect, seeking by this resolution to destroy the effect of the parity requirement. This is the provision of the law of 1890:

> That upon the demand of the holder of any of the Treasury notes herein provided for, the Secretary of the Treasury shall, under such regulations as he may prescribe, redeem such notes in gold or silver coin, at his discretion, it being the established policy of the United States to maintain the two metals on a parity with each other upon the present legal ratio, or such ratio as may be provided by law.

Here you have a statutory declaration of duty, a mandatory duty, laid upon the Government in connection with the monetary legislation that was procured at the instance of the advocates of free silver at that time. My objection to the resolution in the present condition is that while it announces the technical right of the Government to pay in either metal, it utterly ignores the duty of maintaining the parity. This same duty was reiterated and enjoined in the act of 1893. If the Government adheres to the duty laid down in both of these acts, and maintains the parity of the two metals, then it will make no practical difference in which coin the bonds are paid.

If this resolution is correct it does not go far enough. If our bonds are payable, as the resolution says, so are our greenbacks and so are the notes issued under the act of 1890. If you add the amendment which I introduced the other day, and shall offer to-day, and attach it to the resolution, in legal effect the two together would be exactly the language of the act of 1890, giving the Secretary of the Treasury the option to pay the Treasury notes issued under that act either in gold or silver, with the condition that it was always the duty of the Government to maintain the parity of the two metals. Unless you object to the maintenance of the parity—unless you aim by indirect means to destroy that parity—you can certainly have no objection to the amendment to which I refer.

"I CAN NOT PAY YOU IN GOLD."

Let me also call attention to the fact that whenever the Government fails in its duty to maintain the parity it is not only the bondholders who suffer, but every one of us who holds any of Uncle Sam's money except gold coin. If the Government of the United States, when a creditor comes and demands payment of any of its obligations, whether it be a bond or a Treasury note, shakes its head and says "I can not pay you in gold; that is the dearest metal; I will pay you in the cheaper, silver"—whenever the Government assumes that attitude and refuses to pay either a greenback, a Sherman note, or a bond to the holder in gold, when he demands it, that moment and in that act the Government discredits its silver money and says it is not as good as gold, and that brings us on a silver basis immediately, when silver will circulate on its bullion value.

What is the difference between our silver dollar and the Mexican silver dollar? Down in Mexico they have a silver dollar with a little more silver in it than ours. There they have the free coinage of silver. Yet that silver dollar is worth only 45 cents in gold, because there is nothing back of it. It circulates upon its value as silver bullion merely.

Our silver dollar is worth 100 cents in gold. Why? Because the Government of the United States, our law, and our policy, and our practice stand back of it and make that silver dollar as good as a gold dollar. By standing pledged to maintain the parity, by being ready to redeem all our paper in gold, and by receiving the silver dollar in payment of all public dues as equivalent to a gold dollar, we maintain the parity. Our American silver dollar can say what the Mexican silver dollar can not say, "I know that my redeemer—Uncle Sam—liveth."

If our friends on the other side seek to pass this resolution without providing that the Government shall maintain the parity, then they are indirectly seeking to bring about a state of silver monometallism, though this may not be their avowed purpose.

Mr. President, if it were only the bondholders they would injure, that would be bad, but not the worst of it. But the bondholders are not the only ones who would suffer. Whenever you cut down our currency by such methods, whenever you Mexicanize our silver, you not only punish the bondholders, but punish every citizen in the United States who has any of our currency, except gold. Every dollar of greenbacks, every dollar of Sherman notes, every silver dollar, and every national-bank note is at that moment cut down to the bullion value of silver.

ONLY $850,000,000 BONDS OUTSTANDING.

There are only $850,000,000 bonds outstanding, while our greenbacks and Sherman notes, our silver and silver certificates, and our national-bank notes exceed, in the aggregate, over $1,100,000,000, nearly all of it outstanding and in circulation. To put us on a silver basis, you would not only reduce the value of the bonds more than one-half, but also the value of all this currency, a loss that would reach every holder of this money. And, in addition to all this, you would further contract the currency, by driving our gold money abroad and out of circulation.

You not only punish the bondholders—if that was the extent of your punishment, though unjust, we might stand it—but you strike at every man who has any of the money of this Government in his possession. You not only strike him down, but you reduce the wages of the laboring man; you reduce the value of saving deposits and of all outstanding money obligations. And thus you would bring about a public calamity much more serious than even you contemplate or intend.

Mr. President, I am not here shedding tears for the bondholders, but I am here to protect the American people from the calamity of silver monometallism.

WAYS AND MEANS TO MEET WAR EXPENDITURES.

The Senate, as in Committee of the Whole, having under consideration the bill (H. R. 10100) to provide ways and means to meet war expenditures—

Mr. NELSON said:

Mr. PRESIDENT: I propose for a few moments to discuss the proposed issue of an additional $150,000,000 of greenbacks—or United States Treasury notes. I regard that as one of the most important matters involved in the pending bill.

The first issue of United States Treasury notes was under the act of February, 1862. The highest amount outstanding was in 1864, when it amounted to $447,300,203. Since 1878 the net amount outstanding has been $346,681,016. There has been issued and reissued in all a total of $2,876,020,-129, or a quantity equal to nearly 8.3 times the amount outstanding at any time since 1878. These notes are receivable in payment of all taxes and public dues except customs. Prior to July 1, 1879, $1,151,572,362 of these notes were redeemed by being received in payment of public dues and taxes.

Since June 30, 1879, $1,477,766,753 have been redeemed, but of this redemption $516,030,273 have been redeemed on demand by direct payment of gold to the holder. Of this direct gold redemption, only $43,310,896 was made between July 1, 1879, and July 1, 1892; and from July 1, 1897, to the present time only $21,523,345 have been redeemed.

But for the period of five years extending from July 1, 1892, to July 1, 1897, $451,196,132 was directly redeemed, on demand of the holders, in gold. An average of $90,000,000 per year, or only $10,000,000 less than the gold redemption fund, thus necessitating its duplication once a year in that time. During this period of hard times, within the memory of all, the Treasury was treated as the reservoir, and the greenbacks as the instrument, for satisfying the excessive gold demand of our people. This excessive and unusual gold withdrawal occurred chiefly from two causes. In the first instance it arose from the fear that the excessive silver inflation under the act of 1890 might destroy the ability of the Government to maintain the parity of our silver currency with gold. This fear of coming to a silver basis led many of our people to seek gold for purposes of hoarding.

GOLD DEMAND TO SATISFY AN ADVERSE BALANCE OF TRADE.

In the next place the gold demand came, to a large extent, for the purpose of satisfying an adverse balance of trade. And by this I mean an adverse balance upon all our transactions with foreign countries, whether arising from commerce or credits; for all international balances are settled and adjusted with gold. Since July 1, 1897, our shipment of breadstuffs and other products abroad at high prices and in great quantities has been so large that it has kept the balance of trade in our favor and brought us a constant inflow of gold, which would have been even greater but for the credit balance against us in Europe.

This large inflow of gold from this cause has reduced the gold redemption of our greenbacks to well-nigh a nominal basis. But the conditions of the past year have been so unusually favorable, especially in the matter of breadstuffs, that we can not well count on their permanent continuance nor make them the basis of our calculation for the maintenance of the gold-redemption fund. Caution and prudence should rather lead us to base our calculation on the recurrence of such times and conditions as we labored under from 1892 to 1897.

Our Treasury notes are not only money of a certain kind, but they are also due bills, evidences of demand loans. As mere loans they are not of very much help or benefit, unless redemption is temporarily stayed as during the late war. If the holder can demand payment at any time, the Government must of necessity always keep on hand an idle fund for redemption purposes. For it occupies, as a mere debtor, the relation to the Treasury notes that a bank does to its depositors or its bill holders. It can not redeem by giving new notes of a similar kind, for that would simply be Micawber-like to give one due bill for another.

THE GOVERNMENT MUST OF NECESSITY REDEEM IN COIN.

The Government must of necessity redeem in coin, and, technically, it can redeem in either coin—gold or silver. If both metals were intrinsically on a parity with each other, then the Government would be justified in availing itself of the technical right to pay in either metal. But, commercially and intrinsically, silver is far below a parity with gold, and hence arises the duty enjoined upon the Government, both by law and morals, of maintaining our silver money on a parity with gold.

The holder of a Treasury note is not only interested in having his note redeemed, but he is also interested in having it redeemed in, and kept up to, the value of our best money, that which is intrinsically highest—gold— for that is of necessity and in the very nature of the case the only true standard of parity. To maintain this parity the Government must always be ready and able to redeem its notes in that money—gold—which is intrinsically the most valuable, if demanded. If the Government refuses to redeem in its best money when demanded, it by that very act discredits its intrinsically cheaper money; and if it insists on redeeming in the cheaper money it in effect makes that the standard and level of value, and the monetary parity of the two metals is gone.

The issue of these demand Treasury notes, then, entails a double duty and a double burden upon the Government: First, the duty and burden of a banker to its depositors or bill holders of always maintaining an ample redemption fund on hand; second, the duty and burden, as the financial and fiscal agent of our nation, to maintain these notes as money on a parity with our best money—gold. In other words, the Government must maintain these Treasury notes both as due bills and as money, and to maintain them as such it must always have on hand an ample gold redemption fund.

But both of these burdens and duties are of a shifting, fluctuating, and uncertain character, dependent on a variety of conditions and circumstances entirely beyond the control or guidance of the Government. A banker can never to a certainty predict or foretell the amount of the demand the depositors or bill holders will make upon him at any given time. In good, prosperous times the demand will be moderate; in hard, bad times it will be excessive, and in times of panic it will amount to a raid and complete destruction. · In good times the reserve can run low, but in bad times it must be large and ample, for the demand upon it will be much greater. Our sound banks never kept such large reserves as they did in the bad times of 1893, 1894, and 1895. Their reserves were so large that they derived no substantial profits from their deposits.

GOVERNMENT AS A MERE DEBTOR TO ITS BILL HOLDERS.

And so it is with the Government as a mere debtor to its bill holders. In prosperous times the call for redemption is slight and the circulation is ample. In hard times the call for redemption is excessive and the circulation is nominal. But there is one anomaly the Government labors under that the bank is free from. The Government is never done with redeeming no matter how much it redeems, for under the law as soon as it redeems a note it must at once reissue it. Redemption relieves the bank from the burden, but with respect to the Government as to its Treasury notes redemption does not redeem.

While the redemption demand upon the bank may be uncertain and fluctuating, it has nevertheless a limit. With the Government the redemption demand is not only uncertain, but it is utterly without limit; and it is this fact which embarrasses and handicaps the Government more than anything else. It places it completely at the mercy of the whims and necessities of the holders of the notes, who, as a rule, are governed by their own selfishness.

But the duty of responding to this illimitable redemption demand is further aggravated by the fact that the redemption fund must be kept in gold, owing to the disparity between the two metals and for the sake of maintaining the parity. The Government can not artificially regulate the inflow of gold except by purchase. Outside of this the inflow or outflow of gold is wholly dependent upon trade and business conditions. If the balance of trade, so called, is, as a whole, in our favor there will be an inflow of gold, more or less, in proportion to the balance in our favor. But if the balance of trade is against us, then there will be an outflow of gold measured by such balance. We are still a debtor nation, and for some years to come the balance on that score will be against us. We shall have to overcome that balance by the balance in our favor upon the sale of our products—raw and manufactured—and it is only the excess of such balance over the credit balance which gives us the substantial balance that brings the inflow of gold.

But it is evident, on reflection, that our trade balance rests upon at least two grounds, is dependent upon at least two contingencies—first, on our productive capacity in any given year; and second, on the demand for our surplus abroad. Barren and scant harvests at home, and ample and bounteous harvests abroad, will infallibly be apt to turn the tide against us. And such unfavorable conditions we can neither predict, stay, nor guard against.

A FACTOR THAT SHOULD BE NOTED.

There is another factor that should also be noted and taken into account, and that is that the inflow of gold from commercial causes does not necessarily bring the gold into the Treasury, for there is no law requiring any gold payments to be made to the Government, not even for customs. There are, and frequently may be, times when our banks and other monetary institutions are in need of increasing their supply of gold to an unusual degree, and hence at these times and for such purpose these institutions may, for the time being, temporarily intercept, divert, and absorb the inflow of gold arising from our trade balance.

Thus it will be seen that our Government, as to its gold-redemption fund, may suffer from a double embargo—an adverse balance of trade or an abnormal domestic demand for gold. All these conditions and contingencies to which I have thus briefly alluded show how fickle, unreliable, and uncertain, and of what perplexing and doubtful character such Treasury notes are, either as loans or as currency.

As there are certain trees of the forest that have the quality of conducting thunderbolts from the storm clouds of heaven to the bosom of the earth, causing havoc and destruction, so with this currency—it can so easily and swiftly be the means of conducting doubt, misgiving, stagnation, and distress from the storm clouds of the business and financial world. It can be made the vehicle for depleting the gold reserve, for destroying the parity of our money, and for reducing us to a fluctuating, shifting, and depreciated silver basis.

The depressed, stagnant, and panicky times of 1893 and 1894 gave us ample proof of this fact. The lesson of those dark and dreary days, with their havoc and distress, wrought and threatened, ought not to be ignored nor easily forgotten. The memory of it ought to admonish us to greater care, prudence, and circumspection. The rule that a sound business man would apply to his own affairs ought to be a guide to us at this juncture.

Would a careful and prudent merchant, in active trade, short of operating capital and wanting to borrow, take the risk, for the sake of probably saving a little interest, of a large loan payable on demand in gold, or would he prefer a reasonable time loan with a low rate of interest? No one can doubt the course he would take under such circumstances. He would prefer the time loan with its interest rather than the doubt, uncertainty, and anxiety of the demand loan. The demand loan might be the means of hurling him headlong without warning into bankruptcy should the heartlessness or necessity of the creditor impel him to demand payment of the loan.

THE INTEREST ON THE TIME LOAN A WELL-INVESTED PREMIUM OF INSURANCE.

The interest on the time loan is a well-invested premium of insurance against such misfortune. The risk of a demand loan is even greater for the Government than for an individual, for it involves the maintenance of an ample gold reserve, and of the parity of our money—duties not resting upon the individual. The greenback issues of the war were noninterest-bearing forced loans, not payable on demand. Th Government in effect said, We can not redeem these notes till the war is over and we have recuperated from its effects, but in the meantime we will accept them as payment for all Government dues except customs.

This loan arose from and was justified by the necessities of the war, but there is no doubt that the burden of it, prior to the resumption of specie payment, resulting from its depreciation in value, was far greater than the interest saved by its circulation. Of all our war loans, from first to last, it was no doubt the most expensive. Its justification was that for the time being it filled a gap that could not have been easily supplied by a time loan.

But this war issue furnishes us no precedent for the issue proposed by the majority of the committee. The war greenback was an indefinite time loan, and it did not at that time and juncture involve the maintenance of the parity of our money, for at that time we were on a pure paper basis. No reasonable man now wants such a greenback. We all want a greenback payable on demand in our standard money. Our past custom and experience show that an additional issue of $150,000,000 of Treasury notes would involve and require an additional permanent gold redemption fund of $43,000,000, so that the net amount of circulation derived from this issue of notes would not be over $107,000,000 at any time.

This amount, however, is more apparent than real. In good times, with a favorable balance of trade like the fiscal year now drawing near its close, this amount would about measure the circulation, but in such times as from 1892 to 1897 the circulation would be much less, for there would be a constant redemption and reissue going on, with a constant shifting and fluctuation in circulation, and the expense of maintaining the gold reserve would be far greater than any possible gain of interest from such circulation. At all events, the slight gain of interest will be no compensation for the great risk and burden of maintaining the gold redemption fund and for the doubt and uncertainty it will tend to throw around our paper currency among our own people and throughout the world.

OUR PER CAPITA CIRCULATION NOW HIGHER THAN AT ANY TIME SINCE 1867.

The issue of these notes is not called for through any lack of currency or deficiency of money. On the 1st day of May last the per capita circulation in this country was $24.33. A year ago it was $23.01. Our per capita circulation is now higher than at any time since 1867, except in 1892, when it was $24.44—only 11 cents more than at this time. There is an abundance of money that can be borrowed at lower rate of interest than ever before. Surely no candid man will contend that the issue of these notes is called for by reason of a dearth of currency. Neither is the contention well grounded that an issue of these notes will obviate the issue of bonds.

On the contrary, if such times should come upon us again as in 1893-94, these notes would be the instruments that would be used by heartless brokers and money changers to withdraw gold from the Treasury and force us to replenish the loss by an issue of bonds to obtain gold. And such an issue of bonds is only measured by the greed and power of the money syndicates. The misfortune is that we are never through redeeming such notes, for under the law they have to be reissued as soon as redeemed. More greenbacks simply furnish Wall street with great means to abstract gold and to force the issue of bonds—bonds, too, that, as a rule, will not go into the hands of the masses of the people. Surely no scheme can be better devised than the issue of these notes to put our Government in complete control of the so-called money power—the Morgans and other syndicates who may desire to raid our Treasury.

Mr. President, I desire to say a few words as to the manner in which the question of the seigniorage strikes me. Under the law of 1890 there were purchased 168,674,682 ounces of silver bullion at a cost of $155,931,002, or an average cost of 92.44 cents per ounce. For this amount of silver Treasury notes have been issued to the amount of $155,931,002, of which $102,394,280 are still outstanding, and these represent the actual cost of the silver at 92.44 cents per ounce; amounting in all to 109,355,514 ounces. Sixty-six million two hundred and eighty thousand ounces have been coined, and the notes have been taken up and replaced by silver dollars.

The only seigniorage that can be fairly considered a matter of legislation and open at this time for consideration is the seigniorage on the silver which has been coined and which has taken the place of those notes, and that does not exceed the amount of $20,000,000.

SILVER AT ITS COST PRICE IN THE NATURE OF A TRUST FUND AS TO ALL THESE NOTES.

Until the silver is coined, so long as these notes are outstanding, that silver at its cost price is in the nature of a trust fund as to all of these notes, because the notes were based not upon the quantity of silver that it takes to make a silver dollar, but they were based upon the cost of the silver bullion purchased; in other words, for every dollar's worth of silver purchased a dollar in notes was issued—no more and no less—and now, in advance of the retirement of these notes of 1890, it would be a matter of bad faith to abstract in any shape or manner the silver which is their basis. But in respect to the amount which has been coined, there is a seigniorage of near $20,000,000 that is loose and is available and could be utilized. My idea, however, is that the safest way of utilizing this without producing any friction in our currency is to coin it into subsidiary silver, if it has not already been coined.

Mr. ALDRICH. Will it interrupt the Senator if I make a suggestion?

Mr. NELSON. Not at all.

Mr. ALDRICH. I wish to suggest that as to the $20,000,000 of which the Senator speaks, that has been covered into the Treasury and has been coined into silver dollars, and certificates issued against it.

Mr. NELSON. If that is true, that covers it.

Mr. ALDRICH. It does, entirely.

Mr. NELSON. If the Senator's statement is true, that will cover it.

Mr. ALDRICH. There is no question about that.

Mr. COCKRELL. I did not understand the Senator from Rhode Island.

Mr. ALDRICH. I said that the seigniorage already accrued upon the purchase of silver under the act of 1890 has been coined into silver dollars, and that there are certificates now outstanding against the whole of it.

Mr. COCKRELL. We coined nineteen millions into silver dollars and covered the balance into the Treasury.

Mr. ALDRICH. That is exactly what I said.

Mr. NELSON. If that is true—and I do not question it—there is no seigniorage that in justice and equity is fairly available. The seigniorage on the uncoined silver will be utilized and coined as fast as the balance of the notes are retired, and that is conformable to the letter and the spirit of the act of 1890. Those notes are based on a given, fixed quantity of silver bullion, and that basis should not be tampered with in advance of their retirement.

Billiges Geld,
oder Bonds?

Auszüge aus Reden der

Achtb. JOSEPH W. BAILEY, von Texas.

Achtb. J. P. DOLLIVER, von Iowa,

Achtb. JAMES K. JONES, von Arkansas.

Achtb. CHAS. W. FAIRCHILD, von Indiana.

Achtb. KNUTE NELSON, von Minnesota.

Achtb. WILLIAM LINDSAY, von Kentucky.

FROM THE CONGRESSIONAL RECORD.

Aus der Rede des
Achtbaren JOSEPH W. BAILEY,
Demokraten von Texas,
Im Repräsentanten = Hause am 26. April 1898.

Geld für den Krieg.

Wenn die Herren behaupten, daß sie $100,000 000 haben müssen, ehe die Steuern erhoben werden können, so wollen wir diese Summe auch anschaffen. Wir haben im Schatzamte eine Summe von über $42,000,000, die wir zu ihrer Disposition stellen wollen. Wir wollen nicht nur den Finanzsekretär anweisen, die Silber-Seignierage in Silberdollars prägen zu lassen, sondern wir wollen ihn ermächtigen der Prägung vorzugreifen und ihn Silber Certificate dafür ausgeben zu lassen, womit die Kriegskosten bestritten werden können, wie es nothwendig wird. (Applaus auf der demokratischen Seite.) Wenn das nicht genug ist — und nach Ihrem Gutachten wird es nicht genug sein — so wollen wir weiter gehen; wir wollen den Finanzsekretär anweisen, den Rest der $100,000,000, die, wie Ihr sagt, sofort nothwendig sind, durch Ausgabe von $58,000,000 Greenbacks anzuschaffen. (Applaus auf demokratischer Seite.) Es giebt keinen Mann, der bezweifelt, daß die Regierung ihre Circulation um $58,000,000 ohne Gefahr vermehren kann. Ich bin so weit entfernt an Fiatismus zu glauben wie irgend Jemand, ich habe nie zu der Ansicht gehalten, daß der Congreß etwas aus nichts machen kann, aber ich weiß, daß diese Regierung, in einer Zeit wie diese, ihre „Demand“-Noten leicht und sicher um $58,000,000 vermehren kann, und auf der andern Seite sitzt jetzt kein Mann, der das Gegentheil behaupten wird.

Mit diesen $42,000,000 Seignorage u. den $58,000,000 Schatzamtsnoten würden wir nicht nur die Kriegskosten decken, sondern wir würden die Geschäftswelt von einem Drucke befreien, den sie anderweitig, durch das Entziehen des Goldes aus der Circulation, erleiden würde. Wir müssen uns erinnern, daß, wenn unsere Schiffe nach dem Auslande gehen, sie nicht unsere Noten mitnehmen können. Wenn überhaupt Noten mitgenommen werden, werden sie nur als Bankpapier gelten und zur Collection zurückgeschickt werden. Unsere Offiziere müssen Münze mitnehmen und die Entziehungen von den Geschäftswegen müssen innerhalb der nächsten vier Monate unfehlbar mehr als die hundert Millionen Dollars betragen, welche wir beabsichtigen zu liefern. Unser Vorschlag löst die Frage also nicht nur vom Standpunkte der Sparsamkeit, sondern auch vom andern, wichtigeren Standpunkte, dem, die Geschäftsinteressen des Landes vor ungenügender Circulation zu wahren.

Aus der Rede des
Achtbaren J. P. DOLLIVER,
Republikaner von Jowa,
gehalten im Repräsentanten=Hause am 26. April 1898.

Was für Steuern schlagen wir vor?

Ich hatte beabsichtigt, die verschiedenen Bestimmungen der Bill, welche jetzt vor dem Hause ist, etwas eingehender zu besprechen, allein der Vorsitzer des Ausschusses (Herr Dingley) hat jede derselben, sowie die mit den verschiedenen Sektionen der Bill verknüpften Umstände so vollständig erklärt, daß es für irgend Jemanden auf der einen oder andern Seite des Hauses unnöthig ist, das Thema weiter zu berühren. Der Vorsitzer des Ausschusses hat dem Hause eine vollständige Erklärung über unsere Vorschläge gegeben. Die gesammte außerordentliche Revenue, welche dadurch dem Schatze zugeführt wird, ist auf nahezu $100,000,000 geschätzt und, wenn diese Bill ein Gesetz wird, wird sie das Schatzamt in den Stand setzen, seine Lasten zu zu tragen, ohne dieselben meist unsern Nachkommen zu vererben.

Der Ausschuß hat alles erwogen, was über die Berechtigung und Billigkeit dieser Steuern gesagt worden ist. So weit ich in Betracht komme, muß ich sagen, daß ich nicht sehen kann, wie $140,000,000 mit weniger Lasten und Bedrückung vom Volke der Vereinigten Staaten erhoben werden können. Fünfzig Millionen davon kommen von zwei Artikeln, die in jedem Lande der Welt als passende Steuerobjekte anerkannt werden, und praktisch alle anderen werden von dem Theile des Gemeinwesens bezahlt werden, der am wenigsten davon bedrückt wird. Ich gestehe, daß wir ziemlich viele substantielle Artikel dieser Maßregel erhalten haben.

Nach der Rede meines Freundes von Texas (Herrn Bailey) zu urtheilen, die er soeben gehalten, giebt es keine besonderen Einwände gegen die Bill, ausgenommen gegen das, was sie nicht enthält. Nach sorgfältiger Erwägung werden von denen, deren Pflicht es ist, in Vereinigung mit uns diese Bill vor das Haus zu legen, keine wichtigen Klagen gegen irgend welches Item in derselben erhoben. Was thun? Sie sagen, daß sie der Vermehrung der Bondschuld der Vereinigten Staaten opponiren, außer wenn es nöthig ist den Credit und die Zahlungsfähigkeit des Schatzamts der Vereinigten Staaten zu wahren.

Woher soll das Geld kommen?

Aber Sie wissen, und jeder Geschäftsmann weiß, daß, so viel Geld auch von diesen Steuern erhoben werden mag, wir von heute an praktisch mit einem Schatze in den Krieg gehen, der nicht im Stande ist, die nöthigen Gelder zu liefern und daß, wenn nicht Geld geborgt wird, das Schatzamt angesichts dieser Bedürfnisse hülflos sein wird. Was ist der wirkliche Stand des Schatzamts?

Wir besitzen eine Baarsumme, laut Bericht vom 26. April 1898 von $219,157,981.80 wovon die folgenden Posten als nicht verfügbar abgezogen werden müssen:

Fällige Schuld, zahlbar auf Verlangen am 1. April	$ 1,283,780.26
National-Banknoten Einlösungsfonds	31,946,933.50
Bonds und Interessen zahlbar im laufenden Monat	5,129,121.85
Scheidemünzen außer Curs	5,000,000.00
Bank-Bilanzen	18,512,936.22
Zusammen	$61,872,771.83

Von den $219,157,981.80 müssen deswegen diese $61,872,771.83 abgezogen werden und es verbleiben $157,285,209.97, wovon die Goldreserve von $100,000,000 abgezogen werden muß, wonach am 26. April 1898 eine wirklich verfügbare Bilanz von $57,285,209.97 verbleibt. Gegen diese ist nun praktisch die ganze Verwilligung von $50,000,000 vom letzten Monate zu setzen, wovon ein Theil schon ausgegeben, der Rest bald ausgezahlt worden sein wird.

Diese Zahlen zeigen, so daß jeder Mann von Geschäftskenntniß es verstehen kann, daß, wenn wir die Goldreserve abziehen, jetzt weniger als $60,000,000 für die Kosten des eben begonnenen großen Unternehmens vorhanden, von denen $50,000,000 schon zur Zahlung angewiesen sind. So daß, weil wir das Schatzamt nicht hülflos lassen wollen in dieser großen Zeit, wir die Bestimmung über den Verkauf von Bonds, wie in dieser Bill vorgeschlagen, befürworten.

Ich glaube, daß das Schatzamt der Vereinigten Staaten die Macht haben sollte, das Geld zur Deckung des Deficits in den laufenden Einnahmen zu borgen. Ich glaube nicht, es ist weise oder patriotisch, das Schatzamt der Vereinigten Staaten angesichts seiner Verbindlichkeiten hülfloser zu lassen als die gewöhnlichen Geschäftshäuser in den Vereinigten Staaten sind. Ich weiß nicht, ob die Beträge, welche wir vermittels dieser Anleihen zu erlangen suchen, zu groß sind oder nicht, ich wünsche nur, daß ich fühlen könnte, daß wir Autorität suchen zuviel zu borgen. Nun, was schlagen diese Herren (die Demokraten) vor? Sie schlagen dreierlei vor. Zuerst, daß wir das Einkommensteuer-Gesetz in mutilirter Form wieder passiren.

Ungleich meinem Freunde werde ich mich auf kein Argument über den Werth dieser Steuer einlassen. Mir ist klar, daß dieselbe zwei Seiten hat. Viele Herren auf dieser Seite haben die Ansicht ausgesprochen, daß diese Einkommensteuer, wenn sie gesetzlich erhoben werden könnte, eine gerechte und produktive Steuer sein würde. Es ist aber nicht nöthig, hier diese Frage zu beleuchten.

Wir stehen großen Ausgaben gegenüber. Wir fordern die Bürger der Vereinigten Staaten, die jungen Männer jedes Staates in der Union auf, ihr Geschäft zu verlassen und sich in Militär-Lagern einzuüben, um diesen Krieg zu führen, und unsere Freunde auf der anderen Seite beginnen die Erneuerung einer Streitfrage, die seit Jahren nicht mehr vor dem Publikum gewesen ist, und bieten für die Unterhaltung der Armee und Flotte die Einnahmen einer gerichtlichen Klasse an, die, wie Gouverneur Dingley so trefflich gesagt hat, schon im Voraus gegen uns entschieden ist.

Ich erhebe keinen Einwand gegen die Wiederaufnahme des Einkommensteuer-Prozesses. Ich habe mit vielen prominenten Männern gesprochen und gefunden, daß viele Ansichten über die Einkommensteuer bestehen. Mein Freund von Texas (Herr Bailey) sagt, unsere Väter welche die Verfassung zimmerten, hatten nur eine sehr unbestimmte und unvollständige Idee über die Natur einer direkten Steuer. Er hat uns auch glauben lassen, daß das Bundes-Obergericht heute noch eine sehr unbestimmte und unrichtige Idee darüber hat was eine direkte Steuer ist, und der allgemeine Ton und die Richtung seiner Bemerkungen machten auf mich den Eindruck, daß es gewaltig wenige Leute in diesem Lande giebt, welche wissen, was eine direkte Steuer in Wirklichkeit ist. (Gelächter auf der republikanischen Seite.)

Die Prägung der Silber-Seigniorage.

Dieser Ungewißheit wegen, weil wir Geld und nicht Gesetzbücher brauchen, weil wir Einnahmen und keine Prozesse in den Gerichten nothwendig haben, opponire ich der Vermischung dieses Vorschlages mit der Einkommensteuer-Controverse vom Jahre 1894. (Applaus.)

Zunächst schlägt er vor die Seigniorage in dem Schatze der Vereinigten Staaten auszuprägen. Das sieht ebenfalls aus, wie die Wiederkehr in diese Kammer eines alten Freundes. Ich habe seit fünf Jahren versucht auszufindiren, was die Seigniorage eigentlich ist, und nach Allem, was ich darüber gelernt, glaube ich, daß Gouverneur Dingley es gerade richtig hat. Es ist der Profit aus der Prägung von Geld, der in dem Unterschiede zwischen dem bezahlten Werthe des Materials und dem nominellen Werthe der Münze besteht.

Dennoch machen die Herren nicht den Vorschlag, die Silberbarren im Bundesschatze auszuprägen. Wenn sie den Vorschlag machten, möchte er etwas werth sein. Ich wäre bereit sein, mit ihnen für ein Gesetz zu stimmen, das die Bundes-Münzstätten anweist $50,000,000 der vorhandenen Silberbarren in Scheidemünze auszuprägen. Aber was ist dies für ein Vorschlag? Es ist ein Vorschlag, die Vereinigten Staaten aus dem Profit unseres Silbergeschäfts während der letzten zehn Jahre zu erhalten.

Was sind die Thatsachen? Wir haben im Bundesschatze $119,864,515 Unzen fein Silber. Wir bezahlten dafür $99,319,752. Es ist heute kaum halb so viel werth als wir dafür bezahlt haben. Dennoch schlagen diese mit charakteristischer Scheinheiligkeit vor, diesen Krieg mit dem Profite einer Transaktion zu führen und unsere Armee im Felde und unsere Flotte auf dem Meere damit zu erhalten, wenn diese Transaktion uns schon den erwähnten Verlust gekostet hat.

Meine Freunde, ein Vorschlag wie der, soweit ich ihn verstehen und ergründen kann, läßt bei Euch einen Gemüthszustand vermuthen, der in Humbug schwimmt wie ein Fisch im Wasser. (Gelächter.) Es ist kein Verstand darin. Angenommen diese eingebildete Seigniorage von $42,647,336 würde zur Prägung bestimmt, so würden alle unsere Münzstätten wenigstens sechzehn Monate brauchen, um die Arbeit zu thun.

Was wollen sie sonst noch thun? Sie wollen, wie der Herr von Texas sagt, „Gebrauch von dem unverzinslichen Credite der Vereinigten Staaten machen." Mit Verbindlichkeiten, die auf Verlangen eingelöst werden müssen und nahezu eine Billion Dollars betragen, ausstehend, fordern sie von uns, daß wir diesen Krieg mit Zahlungsversprechungen führen. Und doch wissen sie, was jeder intelligente Geschäftsmann in den Vereinigten Staaten weiß, daß es kein Mittel giebt und in der Handelsgeschichte der Welt nie eines gegeben hat, den Werth eines Zahlungsversprechens aufrecht zu erhalten, wenn dieses nicht bezahlt wird oder jeden Augenblick bezahlt und eingelöst werden kann. Und es giebt keinen Weg, auf dem eine Regierung diese Zahlungsversprechungen, welche unter solchen wie den uns jetzt umgebenden Umständen ausgegeben worden, einlösen kann, der nicht am Ende kostspieliger wäre als die Ausgabe von verzinslichen Bonds.

Ich sage dem Herrn von Texas, daß eine Geschäfts-Panik, eine Störung, welche durch einen Werthmesser Wechsel in die amerikanische Geschäftswelt kommt, indem die Goldzahlungen suspendirt werden, durch die Werthverschlechterung unserer Münzen, durch die Weigerung die Verbindlichkeiten der Vereinigten Staaten bei Präsentation einzulösen, in dreißig Tagen mehr Schaden und Unrecht verursachen wird, als alle Armeen und alle Flotten der Welt in fünf Jahren anrichten könnten. (Applaus.) Deswegen verlangt der gesunde Verstand, daß wir für die Verbindlichkeiten Sorge tragen die wir jetzt haben, anstatt sie noch zu vermehren.

Zwei Wege, auf denen wir das Geld erlangen können.

Es bleiben uns also zwei Wege auf denen wir das Geld erlangen können — durch Besteuerung und durch Anleihen. Ich befürworte beide Wege, jeden benutzend, je nachdem die Bedürfnisse der Regierung und der Regierungs-Credit es nöthig machen. Ich weiß, es giebt viele Leute, welche behaupten, daß das Volk der Vereinigten Staaten es sich nicht gefallen lassen wird, daß die Zeit kommen, und bald kommen wird, wenn es sich erheben und die Lasten und Ungerechtigkeiten dieser neuen Steterauflagen abwerfen wird. Ich glaube es nicht.

Wenn es je der Fall gewesen, daß eine Kriegserklärung direkt auf den Wunsch und die Forderung eines Volkes erfolgte, so ist dies der Fall jetzt. Es gereicht dem Volke der Vereinigten Staaten zur Ehre, daß es während dieser ganzen erregten Periode von Motiven die höher als Parteipolitik und edler als Förderung eigener materieller Interessen, geleitet worden ist.

Der Präsident hat uns nicht in den Krieg getrieben.

Dieses Volk wußte im Voraus, was die Lasten und Kosten des Krieges sein würden, und alle diese Sachen hat das amerikanische Volk in seinen Herzen erwogen, während die mächtige Woge der öffentlichen Meinung emporstieg, welche die Nation auf die Wellen eines Enthusiasmus erhoben hat, den keine Parteiführerschaft controliren oder unterdrücken konnte.

Es kann nicht gesagt werden, daß der Präsident der Vereinigten Staaten sein Land in den Krieg gestürzt hat.

Hätte er das gethan, die Wohlfahrt eines Landes wie dieses rücksichtslos in Gefahr gebracht, würde er anstatt den Respekt und das Vertrauen der Welt zu genießen wie er es thut, verdienen, daß ein Mühlenstein an seinen Hals gelegt und er im Meere versenkt worden wäre, wo es am Tiefsten ist. Er hat sich keines solchen Vergehens gegen die Wohlfahrt seines Landes schuldig gemacht.

Anstatt die öffentliche Meinung zu entflammen zu suchen, hat er versucht sie zu mäßigen und zu lenken. Anstatt die Aussichten auf ein friedliches Abkommen wegzuwerfen, hat er sich mit jedem gutem Einflusse zu Gunsten einer solchen Lösung der gefährlichen Angelegenheit verbunden. Er ist von seinen Feinden geschmäht worden und seine Freunde haben ihn mißverstanden, weil er die Weisheit besaß, zu erforschen, die Klugheit vorzubereiten, und die Staatsklugheit das Vorher und das Nachher zu erwägen.

Wenn je die Zeit kommen sollte, da das amerikanische Volk, unter den Lasten, welche unser Protektorat über Cuba ihm auferlegt, sich auflehnen und beklagen sollte, so giebt es wenigstens einen Mann im öffentlichen Leben dieser Zeit, der im Stande sein wird, seinen Landsleuten gerade ins Gesicht hineinzuschauen und ihnen zu sagen: „Ich that mein Bestes, meinen Mitbürgern diese Leiden zu ersparen." (Applaus.) . . . . . .

Aber als einer der seine Weisheit oder Patriotismus nie für einen Augenblick bezweifelt hat, wage ich die Behauptung, daß wenn diese Tage fieberischer und geschwätziger Critik vergessen sind, die Welt mit wachsender Achtung auf den braven und guten Mann blicken wird der, inmitten unvergleichlichen Lärmes, seine Lippen durch die Natur seiner Pflicht gesiegelt, den moralischen Heldenmuth besaß, festzustehen, so lange die geringste Hoffnung vorhanden war, a s der Magistrat eines christlichen Volkes, den Einfluß seines Amtes zu Gunsten eines ehrenhaften Friedens zu benutzen. (Lauter Applaus auf republikanischer Seite.)

Aus der Rede des
Achtbaren JAMES K. JONES,
Demokrat von Arkansas.
Gehalten im Bundessenate am 16. Mai 1898.

Ich will nicht den Vorschlag besprechen, $42,000,000 Noten gegen die $42,000,000 Silber-Seigniorage auszugeben, welche der Regierung der Vereinigten Staaten gehört, die bezahlt ist, und deren Eigenthum sie ist. Wir haben dies einmal durch eine Bill angeordnet, die von beiden Häusern passirt wurde, allein sie wurde vetirt..............

Eine andere Bestimmung dieser Bill, wogegen Einsprache erhoben wird, ist der Vorschlag $150,000,000 Greenbacks auszugeben. Ein Senator sagte mir gestern, offenbar sehr erregt, „Was, Fiatgeld ausgeben!" Herr Präsident, Gold und Silber mag Fiatgeld sein, aber eine Greenback-Note ist ein Versprechen zu bezahlen, und ein Versprechen auf Verlangen den Betrag zu zahlen, der auf der Note genannt wird; es ist ein Schuldschein. Der Senator von Iowa erzählte uns gestern, wie wunderbar dieses Land gewachsen ist welche glänzenden Entwickelungen stattgefunden haben, und er illustrirte es mit der Erwähnung der Zunahme des Verkaufs von Postmarken seit 1882. Er hätte einen Schritt weitergehen und sagen können, daß die Schätzung des Reichthums des Landes in 1860 vielleicht $16,000,000,000 betrug und daß sie jetzt $80,-000,000,000 beträgt.

Wir hatten am Ende des Krieges verzinsliche und unverzinsliche Schulden im Gesammtbetrage von mehr als siebenundzwanzig hundert Millionen Dollars. Wir haben der Welt unsere Fähigkeit gezeigt, selbst in jener Zeit unserer Schwäche, diese große Schuld abzutragen. Wer will dann sagen, daß unser Versprechen, die armselige Summe von $150,000,000 zu zahlen, nicht gut ist? Das Volk würde diese Greenbacks gern und bereitwillig in Zahlung irgend eines Guthabens annehmen. Vielleicht würden reiche Männer kein Gold oder Silber darauf leihen, wie auf Bonds, aber sie können dem Volke ausgezahlt werden; sie werden als Geld gebraucht werden; sie werden nicht zur Einlösung an das Schatzamt geschickt werden, sondern einen Theil des Circulationsmediums bilden, zur Hebung des bestehenden Geldmangels führen und Gutes thun anstatt Böses, so lange sie bestehen.

Aus der Rede des

Achtbaren CHARLES W. FAIRBANKS,

Republikaner von Indiana.

Gehalten im Bundessenate am 2. Juni 1898.

Damals und Jetzt.

Als die Ausgabe von Greenbacks im Jahre 1862 autorisirt wurde, war dies durch die Umstände gerechtfertigt welche unsere Staatsmänner umgaben und die ernste und unabweisbare Nothwendigkeit, welche sie confrontirte. Damals hatten verschiedene Staaten Secessions-Ordinanzen angenommen und versuchten sich aus der Union auszutreten; die Zukunft war voller Zweifel und Ungewißheit; Niemand als der Allmächtige wußte, was das Resultat des Conflictes sein würde. Baarzahlungen waren aufgehoben, der Bundesschatz war leer, die Regierung besaß nicht den Credit, wodurch sie ihn hätte füllen können und wir hatten praktisch kein Courantgeld. Jetzt aber ist das Land einig und durch unlösbare Bande verbunden; der Credit ist, wie es scheint, grenzenlos; wir haben Courantgeld genug im Umlaufe, so viel, ungefähr, wie wir je gehabt, ein Courant, das nichts entwerthen kann als unser eigener Leichtsinn und Thorheit, und Niemand ist so pessimistisch an der Zukunft zu zweifeln...............

Als die erste Greenback-Bill berathen wurde, erklärte der Vorsitzer des Finanz-Ausschusses, daß es nur beabsichtigt sei $150,000,000 Vereinigte Staaten-Noten auszugeben und daß seiner Ansicht nach nicht mehr nöthig sein würden. Doch, entgegen dieser ausgesprochenen Ansicht, mußten eine zweite und eine dritte Ausgabe der gleichen Summe bald folgen und innerhalb eines Jahres vom 25. Februar 1862 wurden $150,000,00 Greenbacks autorisirt.

Schnelle Entwerthung der Greenbacks.

Die schnelle und große Entwerthung dieses Courantgeldes und die allgemeine Veränderung aller Werthe alles Eigenthums ist wohlbekannt.

Es sollte doch scheinen als ob die Uebel eines solchen ungewissen Courants während des Bürgerkrieges so groß waren und vor so kurzer Zeit bestanden, um jeden Versuch zur Rückkehr zu rem Systeme, das sie hervorbrachte, unmöglich zu machen. Was unter dem Zwange des Bürgerkrieges weise und nothwendig zu sein schien, sollte jetzt unnöthig und unweise erscheinen.

Die Urheber der ersten Greenbacks fühlten die Nothwendigkeit sie einzulösen, und da es an den nöthigen Münzen dafür fehlte, wurde verfügt, daß sie für Münz (Coin-)Bonds angenommen und umgewechselt werden könnten. Die schnelle Entwerthung dieser Noten, trotz sogar dieser Garantien, ist ein Theil einer wohlbekannten Geschichte. Die Nothwendigkeit sie einzulösen und dadurch den öffentlichen Credit zu stärken, stellte sich schnell heraus und das Werk der Einlösung wurde bald nach dem Ende des Krieges in Aussicht genommen...............

Nach der Wiederaufnahme der Baarzahlungen in 1879 wurde das Vertrauen in den Werth der Greenbacks so allgemein, daß sie nicht die Quelle ernster Befürchtungen oder Gefahren wurden bis während der zweiten Administration des Präsidenten Cleveland, als in Folge der schnellen Zunahme unsres Vorrathes an billigem Gelde durch die Ankäufe von Silber unter dem Gesetze von 1890 und der Verminderung der Regierungseinnahmen, Zweifel an der Zahlungsfähigkeit des Schatzamts und der Fähigkeit der Regierung, Gold für Greenbacks und andere „Demand"=Noten zu geben, auftauchte...............

Was wieder kommen könnte.

Zwischen dem 1. Juli 1892 und dem 1. Juli 1897 wurden $155,025,817 in Goldmünze auf Verlangen von Inhabern von Greenbacks aus dem Schatzamte gezogen. Obgleich die Regierung mehr als den Werth der Noten in Gold ausbezahlt hat, ist das Volumen derselben unvermindert. Dies ist eine Illustration der Arbeit der „endlosen Kette", und illustrirt was sich wieder ereignen mag, wenn der Credit unserer Regierung in Zukunft geschwächt sein, oder ein Zweifel über ihre Absichten und Fähigkeiten, die Auswechselung von Gold gegen ihre „Demand"=Noten vorzunehmen, entstehen sollte...............

Billiges Geld.

Es ist eine bezeichnende Thatsache, welche dem intelligenten Beobachter nicht entgeht, daß die Befürworter von mehr Papiergeld die Leute sind, welche an die Freiprägung von Silber glauben und sie befürworten. Die Politik, mehr Greenbacks auszugeben, hat ihre Wurzeln in demselben Zwecke, und der ist: „Billiges Geld." Die Ausgabe von uneinlösbarem Papiergelde, dem Zwangszahlungskraft verliehen, in genügenden Quantitäten, würde seinen Gleichwerth mit Gold verlieren, Gold auf ein Prämium und folglich aus der Circulation vertreiben. Das würde den Weg zur freien Silberprägung eröffnen. Es scheint mir, daß diese Absicht, unser Courant übermäßig zu vermehren, nicht nur aus dem angeblichen Wunsche entstanden ist, Zinszahlung auf Bonds zu vermeiden, denn die Interessen sind verhältnißmäßig nicht von hohem Betrage, sondern in der Hoffnung und bestimmten Erwartung, daß die Sache des freien Silbers durch die Zerstörung unseres Courants gefördert werden würde. Das würde ohne Zweifel die direkte, natürliche, logische Folge der vorgeschlagenen Maßnahme sein.

Rede des

Achtbaren KNUTE NELSON,

Republikaner von Minnesota.

Gehalten im Bundessenate am 26. Mai 1898.

Wie Gold durch Greenbacks aus dem Bundesschatze geholt wurde.

Herr Präsident, ich möchte für einige Augenblicke die vorgeschlagene Ausgebung von weiteren $150,000,000 Greenbacks als Vereinigte Staaten Schatzamtsnoten erörtern. Ich betrachte dies als einen der wichtigsten Punkte, um die es sich in der vorliegenden Bill handelt, und um das, was ich über den Gegenstand zu sagen habe, in gedrängter Kürze vorzubringen, habe ich es zu Papier gebracht.

Die erste Ausgabe von Vereinigten Staaten Schatzamtsnoten geschah unter dem Gesetz vom Februar 1862. Der ausstehende Betrag war am höchsten in 1864, als er sich auf $447,300,203 belief. Seit 1878 beträgt die ausstehende Nettosumme $346,681,016. In allem ist ausgegeben und wieder ausgegeben eine Gesammtsumme von $2,876,020,129 oder eine Quantität, welche beinahe 8.3 Mal den zu irgend einer Zeit seit 1878 ausstehenden Betrag erreicht. Diese Noten mußten als Zahlung angenommen werden für alle Steuern und staatlichen Abgaben, ausgenommen Zölle. Seit dem 30. Juni 1879 sind 1,477,766,753 eingelöst worden, aber von dieser Einlösung sind $516,030,273 auf Verlangen durch directe Goldzahlung an die Inhaber eingelöst worden. Seit dieser directen Goldeinlösung wurden nur $43,310,998 in der Zeit zwischen dem 1. Juli 1879 und dem 1. Juli 1892 gemacht, und seit dem 1. Juli 1897 bis zu dem gegenwärtigen Zeitpunkt sind nur $21,523,315 eingelöst worden.

Dagegen wurden in dem fünfjährigen Zeitraum vom 1. Juli 1892 bis zum 1. Juli 1897 auf Verlangen der Inhaber $451,196,132 direct in Gold eingelöst. Das macht im Durchschnitt $90,000,000 im Jahr oder nur $10,000,000 weniger als der Goldeinlösungsfond, der infolgedessen in jener Zeit einmal im Jahre verdoppelt werden mußte. Während dieser, Allen erinnerlichen Periode schlechter Zeiten wurde das Schatzamt als das Reservoir und die Greenbacks als das Werkzeug behandelt, um die übermäßige Nachfrage unseres Volkes nach Gold zu befriedigen. Diese übermäßige und ungewöhnliche Goldentziehung hatte ihren Grund vornehmlich in zwei Ursachen. Sie entsprang zunächst der Furcht, daß die übermäßige Silberanschwellung unter dem Gesetz von 1890 es unserer Regierung unmöglich machen könnte, die Parität unserer Silberumlaufsmittel mit Gold aufrechtzuerhalten. Diese Furcht, daß wir auf einer Silberbasis anlangen könnten, führte viele Leute dazu, Gold für Aufbewahrungszwecke zu suchen.

Sodann lag der Goldnachfrage zum großen Theile der Zweck zu Grunde, eine ungünstige Handelsbilanz gut zu machen. Und dabei meine ich eine ungünstige Handelsbilanz von allen Transactionen mit auswärtigen Ländern, ob sie vom Handel oder von Krediten herrühren, denn alle internationalen Bilanzen werden mit Gold ausgeglichen. Seit dem 1. Juli 1897 ist unser Versandt von Brodstoffen und anderen Produkten nach dem Auslande zu hohen Preisen und in großer Menge so stark gewesen, daß dadurch die Handelsbilanz sich zu unseren Gunsten gestaltet und uns einen bedeutenden Goldzufluß gebracht hat, der noch größer gewesen sein würde wenn nicht die Creditbilanz in Europa gegen uns gewesen wäre.

Dieser große hierdurch bedingte Goldzufluß hat die Goldeinlösung unserer Greenbacks beinahe auf eine normale Basis heruntergebracht. Allein die Verhältnisse des verflossenen Jahres waren so ungewöhnlich günstig, namentlich was Brodstoffe anbetrifft, daß wir täglich nicht auf ihre Fortdauer rechnen und sie auch nicht zur Basis unserer Berechnungen betreffs der Aufrechterhaltung der Goldreserve machen können. Vorsicht und Klugheit sollten uns eher dazu leiten, unsere Berechnungen auf die Wiederkehr solcher harten Zeiten und solcher drückenden Verhältnisse zu basiren, wie wir sie von 1892 bis 1897 hatten.

Was unsere Noten sind.

Unsere Schatzamtsnoten sind nicht nur eine gewisse Art von Geld, sondern sie sind auch Schuldscheine, Darlehensnachweise. Als bloßes Darlehen helfen oder nützen sie wenig, es sei denn, daß die Einlösung zeitweise eingestellt ist, wie es während des Rebellionskrieges der Fall war. Wenn der Inhaber jederzeit Zahlung verlangen kann, so ist die Regierung gezwungen, allerzeit einen brachliegenden Fond für Einlösungszwecke an Hand zu halten. Denn als bloßer Schuldner nimmt sie den Schatzamtsnoten gegenüber dieselbe Stellung ein, wie eine Bank ihren Depositoren oder ihren Rechnungsinhabern gegenüber. Sie kann nicht dadurch einlösen, daß sie neue Noten ähnlicher Weise gibt, denn das hieße einfach, a la Miawer, einen Schuldschein für einen anderen geben.

Noten in Münze zahlbar.

Die Regierung muß nothgedrungen in gemünzten Geldern einlösen, und technisch kann sie in beiden Münzarten, entweder in Gold oder in Silber einlösen. Wären die beiden Metalle in sich selbst gleichwerthig, dann wäre die Regierung gerechtfertigt, wenn sie von dem technischen Recht, Zahlungen in dem einen oder dem anderen Metall zu machen, Gebrauch machte. Nun steht aber Silber, seinem innerlichen wie seinem Handelswerth nach, unter dem

Goldwerth, und daraus ergiebt sich für die Regierung die rechtliche und die moralische Verpflichtung, unser Silbergeld gleichwerthig mit Gold zu erhalten.

Dem Inhaber einer Schatzamtsnote kommt es nicht nur darauf an, daß seine Note eingelöst wird, es kommt ihm auch darauf an, daß dieselbe eingelöst und einlösbar gehalten wird zu
dem Werth unseres besten Geldes, dasjenige, welches von sich selbst aus am höchsten steht,
und das ist Gold. Gold ist nothwendigerweise und dem wahren Sachverhalt nach, der einzige
wahre Werthmesser der Parität. Um diese Parität aufrechtzuerhalten, muß die Regierung stets
bereit und im Stande sein, ihre Noten auf Verlangen mit diesem Geld — Gold — das in sich
selbst den vollkommen Werth besitzt, einzulösen. Wenn die Regierung sich weigert, mit ihrem besten
Gelde einzulösen, wenn solches verlangt wird, so bringt sie schon durch diese Handlungsweise ihr
Geld von geringerem innerlichem Werth in Mißcredit, und wenn sie darauf besteht, mit
billigerem Gelde einlösen zu wollen, so macht sie thatsächlich dieses zu dem stehenden Werthmesser, und mit der Parität der beiden Metalle als Geld ist es vorbei.

Noten sind Goldschulden.

Demnach legt die Aussendung dieser Nachfrage-Schatzamtsnoten der Regierung eine
doppelte Last auf: erstens die Pflicht und Last eines Bankiers, der für seine Depositoren und
Rechnungsinhaber stets einen ausreichenden Einlösungs-Fond an Hand haben muß, zweitens
die Pflicht und die Last des Finanz- und Fiscus-Agenten unserer Nation, der diese Noten als
Geld auf gleichen Werth mit unserem besten Geld, Gold, erhalten muß. Mit anderen Worten:
die Regierung muß diese Schatzamtsnoten sowohl als Schuldscheine wie als Geld aufrechterhalten
und, um sie als solche aufrechtzuerhalten, muß sie stets einen ausreichenden Goldreserve-Fond an
Hand haben.

Diese beiden Lasten und Pflichten sind jedoch von einem schwankenden und unsicheren
Gepräge von allerhand Bedingungen und Umständen abhängig, welche sich der Controle und
Leitung der Regierung vollkommen entziehen. Ein Bankier kann nie mit Bestimmtheit den
Betrag der Forderungen voraussehen, welche die Depositoren und Rechnungsinhaber zu einer
bestimmten Zeit an ihn stellen werden. In guten, glücklichen Zeiten werden die Forderungen
mäßig, in harten, schlimmen Zeiten werden sie übermäßig sein, und zur Zeit einer Panik werden
sie auf eine vollständige Verheerung hinauslaufen. In guten Zeiten darf die Reserve zusammen-
schmelzen, aber in schlechten Zeiten muß sie stark und reich sein, denn dann pflegen größere
Anforderungen an sie gestellt zu werden. Unsere gesunden Banken hatten niemals so starke
Reserven wie in den schlechten Zeiten von 1893, 1894 und 1895. Ihre Reserven waren so groß,
daß ihre Depositen ihnen keine substantiellen Profite einbrachten.

Und so ist es mit der Regierung als bloßem Schuldner ihren Rechnungsinhabern gegenüber. In Zeiten allgemeiner Wohlfahrt kamen wenig Anfragen wegen Einlösung vor, und die
Circulation ist stark; in schlechten Zeiten laufen die Anfragen wegen Einlösung im Uebermaße ein,
und die Circulation ist nominell. Eine Anomalie aber giebt es, welche der Regierung zu schaffen
macht, während die Bank davon frei ist. Die Regierung mag einlösen so viel sie will, sie wird
mit dem Einlösen niemals fertig, denn nach dem Gesetz muß sie jede Note, sobald sie dieselbe
eingelöst hat, wieder ausgeben. Der Bank nimmt die Einlösung eine Last ab; für die Regierung bedeutet in Bezug auf ihre Schatzamtsnoten Einlösung daraus keine Erlösung.

Bei der Bank mag die Einlösungsnachfrage unruhig und schwankend sein; sie hat aber
ihre Grenze. Bei der Regierung ist sie nicht nur ungewiß, sondern auch geradezu grenzenlos,
und es ist diese Thatsache, welche unserer Regierung mehr Hemmungen und Verlegenheiten
bereitet, als irgend etwas anderes. Sie übergiebt sie auf Gnade und Ungnade vollständig den
Launen und Bedürfnissen der Noteninhaber, die in der Regel sich von ihrem eigenen selbstsüchti-
gen Zwecken leiten lassen.

Die Verpflichtung, diesen grenzenlosen Einlösungsnachfrage zu befriedigen, wird dadurch
noch erschwert, daß infolge der Werthverschiedenheit der zwei Metalle und um die Werthgleich-
heit aufrechtzuerhalten, der Einlösungsfond in Gold gehalten werden muß. Die Regierung ver-
mag den Goldzufluß nicht künstlich zu regeln, ausgenommen durch Ankauf. Abgesehen von diesem
hängt das Einströmen und Ausströmen des Goldes lediglich von dem Handelsverkehr und von
den Geschäftsverhältnissen ab. Wenn die sogenannte Handelsbilanz im Gange und günstig ist,
werden wir nach Maßstab dieser Bilanz einen Goldabfluß haben. Wir sind noch immer eine
schuldende Nation, und auf eine Reihe von Jahren hinaus wird in diesem Betracht die
Bilanz gegen uns sein. Wir werden diese Bilanz überwinden müssen durch die uns günstige
Bilanz aus dem Verkauf unserer Producte, Rohproducte und Fabrikserzeugnisse — und erst

der Ueberschuß solcher Bilanz über die Creditbilanz giebt uns die substantielle Bilanz, welche den Goldzufluß bringt.

Nachdenken lehrt uns jedoch, daß unsere Handelsbilanz auf mindestens zwei Grundlagen ruht, von mindestens zwei Zugehörigkeiten abhängt, erstens von unserer Productionsfähigkeit in jedem gegebenen Jahr, und zweitens von der Nachfrage nach unserem Ueberschuß im Auslande. Dürftige und knappe Ernten daheim, und reichliche, ausgiebige Ernten im Ausland sind unfehlbar dazu angethan, uns eine Ebbe zu bringen. Und derartige ungünstige Verhältnisse können wir weder voraussehen, noch aufhalten, noch uns gegen sie schützen.

Woher die Regierung Gold erhält.

Und da ist noch ein anderer beachtenswerther Factor, mit welchem gerechnet werden muß, ich meine den, daß der Goldüberfluß aus Handelsursachen nicht nothwendigerweise Gold in das Schatzamt bringt: denn ein Gesetz, welches verlangt, daß die Regierung in Gold bezahlt werde, besteht nicht, nicht einmal für Zölle. Es giebt Zeiten und sie mögen sich häufig wiederholen, wo unsere Banken und Geldinstitute sich genötigt sehen, ihren Goldvorrath auf eine ungewöhnliche Höhe hinaufzubringen, und zu diesem Behufe mögen diese Institute vorübergehend den aus unserer Handelsbilanz kommenden Goldzufluß abfangen, abladen und aufsaugen.

Man sieht also, daß unsere Regierung in Hinsicht ihres Goldeinlösungsfonds an einer Doppelsperre zu leiden hat, einer ungünstigen Handelsbilanz und einer ungewöhnlich starken Goldnachfrage im Inland. Alle diese Verhältnisse und Zufälligkeiten, die ich eben kurz angedeutet habe, zeigen, wie unbeständig, unzuverlässig und unsicher und von was für einem zweifelhaften, Verlegenheiten bereitenden Charakter solche Schatzamtsnoten sind, als Anleihe sowohl wie als Geldumlaufsmittel.

Wie leicht eine Panik kommen kann.

Wie es im Wald gewisse Bäume giebt, welche die Eigenschaft besitzen, aus den Sturmwolken des Himmels Donnerkeile nach dem Busen der Erde herabzuleiten und so Verwüstung und Verheerung anzurichten, so ist es mit diesem Geldumlaufsmittel. Es kann so leicht und so rasch ein Mittel werden, Zweifel, Bedenken, Stockung und Unheil aus dem Sturmgewölk der Finanz- und Geldwelt herabzuziehen. Es kann zu einer Handhabe gemacht werden, um die Goldvasen auszuschöpfen, um die Parität unseres Geldes zu zerstören und um uns auf eine schwankende, veränderliche, entwerthete Silberbasis herunterzubringen.

Die gedrückten, Geschäftsstillstand und Panik mit sich bringenden Zeiten von 1893 und 1894 haben uns diese Thatsache zur Genüge bewiesen. Die Lehre, welche jene dunkle, trübselige Tage, mit ihrer unheilvollen, ausgeführten und angedrohten Zerstörungsarbeit uns ertheilt haben, sollte nicht so leicht in Mißachtung oder Vergessenheit gerathen. Das Andenken an sie sollte uns zu größerer Sorgfalt, Klugheit und Umsicht antreiben. Die Regel, welche ein verständiger Geschäftsmann auf seine eigene Angelegenheiten anwendet, sollte uns in dieser entscheidungsschweren Lage zur Richtschnur dienen.

Die Gefährlichkeit der Forderungs=(Demand=)Noten.

Würde ein bedächtiger, vorsorglicher Kaufmann, dem es an Betriebskapital fehlt und zu borgen wünscht, um einer wahrscheinlich kleinen Zinsersparniß willen eine große Anleihe riskiren, die auf Forderung in Gold zahlbar ist, oder würde er ein vernünftiges Zeitdarlehen zu einem niedrigen Zinsfuß vorziehen. Niemand kann darüber im Zweifel sein, welchen Weg der Mann unter solchen Umständen einschlagen würde. Er würde das Zeitdarlehen mit seinen Zinsen dem von Zweifel, Ungewißheit und Besorgniß umgebenen Forderungs=Darlehen vorziehen. Das Forderungs=Darlehen könnte dazu dienen, ihn kopfüber und unversehens in Bankerott zu stürzen, falls die Herzlosigkeit oder das Bedürfniß des Gläubigers ihn zwingen sollte, Zahlung der Anleihe zu verlangen.

Die Zinsen für das Zeit-Darlehen sind eine wohlangelegte Versicherungsprämie gegen solches Mißgeschick. Das Risiko einer Forderungsanleihe ist aber für die Regierung sogar noch größer als für ein Individuum, denn es schließt in sich die Aufrechterhaltung einer ausreichenden Goldreserve und der Parität unserer Goldes-Pflichten, welche dem Individuum nicht zufallen. Die Greenbacks-Ausgaben während des Krieges waren erzwungene, nicht zinsentragende Anleihen, die nicht auf Forderung zu zahlen waren. Die Regierung sagte einfach: „Wir können diese Noten nicht einlösen vor Ablauf des Krieges und bis wir uns von den Folgen desselben erholt haben, wollen dieselben aber in der Zwischenzeit für alle Regierungsabgaben, ausgenommen Zölle, in Zahlung annehmen.

Greenbacks waren Zwangsgeld und sehr theures.

Diese Anleihe entstand und war gerechtfertigt durch die Kriegsbedürfnisse, aber es unterliegt keinem Zweifel, daß bis zur Wiederaufnahme der Baarzahlungen ihre Belastung in Folge ihres Wertverlustes weit größer war als die durch die Circulation gesparten Zinsen. Von allen unseren Kriegsanleihen, von der ersten bis zur letzten, war diese ohne Zweifel die kostspieligste. Ihre Rechtfertigung lag darin, daß sie für den Augenblick eine Lücke ausfüllte, die durch ein Zeitdarlehen nicht leicht hätte ausgefüllt werden können.

Aber diese Notenausgabe im letzten Krieg kann uns keinen Präcedenzfall abgeben für die von der Mehrheit des Committees vorgeschlagene Notenausgebung. Die Kriegs-Greenbacks waren ein unbestimmtes Zeitdarlehen und begriffen unter den damaligen Zeitverhältnissen nicht die Aufrechterhaltung der Parität unseres Goldes in sich, denn damals standen wir auf einer reinen Papierbasis. Kein vernünftiger Mensch verlangt heutzutage einen solchen Greenback, der nicht in unserm Währungsgeld zahlbar ist. Unser früherer Brauch und Erfahrung zeigen, daß eine weitere Ausgabe von $150,000,000 in Schatzamtsnoten einen weiteren permanenten Goldeinlösungsfonds von $43,000,000 nöthig machen würde, so daß der Nettbetrag des aus dieser Notenausgabe erwachsenden Geldumlaufs sich auf $107,000,000 belaufen würde.

Dieser Betrag ist jedoch mehr ein scheinbarer als ein wirklicher. In guten Zeiten mit einer günstigen Handelsbilanz, wie in dem jetzt seinem Ende entgegengehenden Fiscaljahr, würde dieser Betrag ungefähr das Maß des Umlaufes abgeben, aber in solchen Zeitläuften wie von 1892 bis 1897, würde der Umlauf weit geringer sein, denn es würde dann ein beständiges Einlösen und Wiederaussenden stattfinden mit einem beständigen Wechsel und Schwanken in der Circulation, und die Kosten der Aufrechterhaltung der Goldreserve würde viel größer sein als irgend ein Zinsengewinn, den eine derartige Circulation möglicherweise bringen könnte. Auf alle Fälle würde der unbedeutende Zinsengewinn kein Ersatz sein für das große Risico und die große Mühsal, den Goldeinlösungsfonds aufrechtzuerhalten, und für die Zweifelhaftigkeit und die Unsicherheit, mit denen es unser Papiergeld bei unserem eigenen Volke und in der ganzen Welt umgeben würde.

Geld genug vorhanden.

Die Aussendung dieser Noten ist nicht bedingt durch Mangel an Umlaufsmitteln oder Geldknappheit. Am letzten ersten Mai betrug der Geldumlauf in diesem Land $24,33 auf jeden Kopf. Ein Jahr vorher betrug er $23,01. Unsere pro Kopf-Circulation ist gegenwärtig höher als zu irgend einer Zeit seit 1867, ausgenommen in 1892, wo sie $24,44 betrug, nur 11 Cents mehr als augenblicklich. Es ist Geld im Ueberfluß da, welches zu einem niedrigeren Zinsfuß als je zuvor geborgt werden kann. Sicherlich wird kein aufrichtiger Mensch behaupten wollen, daß diese Notenausgabe wegen einer Knappheit der Umlaufsmittel geboten erscheine. Auch die Behauptung läßt sich nicht begründen, daß diese Notenausgabe die Ausgabe von Bonds entgegenstehe.

Im Gegentheil, wenn wieder solche Zeit über uns kommen sollte wie in 1893—1894, so würden diese Noten die Werkzeuge sein, deren sich herzlose Makler und Geldwechsler bedienen würden, um Gold aus dem Schaßamt zu ziehen und uns zu zwingen, den Verlust durch eine Bondausgabe, die Gold bringen würde, zu ersetzen. Und eine solche Bondsausgabe findet ihr einziges Maß in der Gier und der Macht der Geldfyndikate. Das Unglück ist, daß wir mit der Einlösung solcher Noten nie fertig werden, denn nach dem Gesetz müssen dieselben, sobald sie eingelöst find, von neuem ausgegeben werden. Mehr Greenbacks liefern einfach Wall Street größere Mittel, Gold an sich zu ziehen und zwar von Bonds, die in der Regel nicht in die Hände der Volksmassen gelangen. Gewiß fein besserer Plan als diese Notenausgabe läßt sich erfinnen, um unsere Regierung vollständig unter die Controlle der sogenannten Geldmacht — der Morgans und anderer Syndikate zu bringen, welche es auf einen Raubzug gegen unser Schaßamt abgesehen haben mögen.

Was die Seigniorage ist.

Herr Präsident, ich will noch ein paar Worte sagen, wie ich über die Münzprofite (Seigniorage) denke. Unter dem Gesetz von 1890 wurden $68,674,682 Unzen Silberbullion zu dem Kostenpreis von $155,931,002, oder zu einem Durchschnittspreis von 92.44 Cents die Unze, gekauft. Für diesen Betrag Silber sind Schaßamtsnoten im Betrage von $155,931,002 ausgegeben worden, von welchen $102,394,260 noch ausstehen, und diese stellen (92,44 Cents die Unze) die thatsächlichen Kosten des im ganzen auf 109,355,514 Unzen sich belaufenden Silbers dar. Sechsundsechzig Millionen Zweihundert und Achtzig Tausend Unzen sind geprägt worden, und die Noten sind eingezogen und durch Silberdollars ersetzt worden.

Der einzige Münzprofit, welcher billigerweise als Gegenstand für die Gesetzgebung jetzt in Frage kommen kann, ist der Münzprofit von dem Silber, welches geprägt worden und an die Stelle jener Noten getreten ist, und dies übersteigt nicht den Betrag von $20,000,000.

Solange jene Noten ausstehen, bildet dieses Silber, bevor es geprägt wird, ihnen gegenüber eine Art von Trust=Fonds, denn die Noten waren basirt nicht auf die Quantität von Silber, welche man braucht, um einen Silberdollar zu machen, sondern sie wären basirt auf die Kosten des gekauften Silberbullions, mit anderen Worten: für jeden Dollarswerth Silber, der gekauft war, wurde ein Dollar in Noten ausgegeben — nicht mehr und nicht weniger — und es würde sich sehr übel ausnehmen, wenn wir jetzt vor der Einziehung dieser Noten von 1890 auf die eine oder anderer Weise das Silber wegziehen wollten, welches ihre Basis ist. Was dagegen den Betrag angeht, der bereits geprägt ist, so ist von diesem eine Münzgebühr von fast $20,000,000 vorhanden; diese ist verfügbar und könnte nutzbar gemacht werden. Ich bin jedoch der Ansicht, daß der sicherste Weg, dieses Silber nutzbar zu machen, ohne eine Störung in unserem Geldwesen hervorzurufen, der ist, daraus, wenn es noch nicht gemünzt ist, Scheidesilbermünze zu schlagen.

Herr Aldrich. Werde ich den Senator unterbrechen, wenn ich ihn auf etwas aufmerksam mache?

Herr Nelson. Durchaus nicht.

Herr Aldrich. Mit Bezug auf die $20,000,000, von welchen der Senator spricht, möchte ich ihn daran erinnern, daß diese in das Schaßamt geflossen, in Silberdollars geprägt und Certificate dafür ausgegeben worden find.

Herr Nelson. Wenn dem so ist, das deckt die Sache.

Herr Aldrich. Vollkommen.

Herr Nelson. Wenn die Angabe des Senators auf Wahrheit beruht, so ist das genügend.

Herr Aldrich. Das ist gar keine Frage.

Herr Cockrell. Ich habe den Senator von Rhode Island nicht verstanden.

Herr Aldrich. Ich sagte, daß die Münzgebühr, die von dem Silberkauf unter dem Gesetz von 1890 abfällt, bereits in Silberdollars gemünzt ist, und daß gegen den ganzen Betrag Silbercertificate ausstehen.

Herr Cockrell. Wir haben neunzehn Millionen in Silberdollars gemünzt und den Restbetrag in's Schaßamt gesteckt.

Herr Aldrich. Genau das sagte ich.

Herr Nelson. Wenn das wahr ist, und ich bezweifle es nicht, so ist kein Münzprofit vorhanden, welcher mit Fug und Recht verfügbar wäre. Der Münzprofit von dem ungeprägten Silber wird verwandt und gemünzt werden, so schnell wie der Rest der Noten eingezogen wird. So stimmt es zu dem Buchstaben und dem Geist des Gesetzes von 1890. Diese Noten sind basirt auf eine bestimmte vorhandene Menge von Silberbullion, und an dieser Basis darf vor der Einziehung der Noten nicht gerüttelt werden.

Aus der Rede des

Achtbaren WILLIAM LINDSAY,

Gold = Demokrat von Kentucky.

Gehalten am 24. Mai 1898.

Die Frage ist, ob wir Bonds verkaufen sollen, um das nöthige Geld zur Bezahlung der Kosten des Krieges anzuschaffen, oder ob wir die Ausgabe der Greenbacks vermehren und die Regierung zwingen sollen, Bonds zu verkaufen, um Gold in den Bundesschatz zu thun, womit wir die Greenbacks auf dem gleichen Werthe mit Gold halten können, sobald es den Spekulanten gefällt einen Angriff auf das Schatzamt zu machen, nachdem wir deren Gelegenheit, es zu thun, um 25 Prozent erhöht haben, vermittelst der Bill, welche Sie zum Gesetze erheben wollen.

Herr Spooner: Das ist der Zweck.

Herr Lindsay: Es ist keine Bondfrage. An jedem Ende der Linie haben wir Bonds. Es ist eine Frage, ob wir die im Minoritätsberichte des Finanz-Ausschusses empfohlenen Bonds verkaufen wollen, oder ob wir Bonds unter dem Gesetze von 1875 verkaufen wollen, und Jedermann weiß, daß dies der Fall ist. Es wird vielleicht keine Attake auf das Schatzamt gemacht werden, wie insinuirt wird. Aber wann haben wir dieses plötzliche Vertrauen in die Mäßigung der Gold-Spekulanten und Schatzamts-Angreifer gewonnen? Was hat sich während der letzten zwei Jahren ereignet, um uns glauben zu machen, daß wenn diese Leute durch den Export von Gold Geld verdienen können, sie nicht einen Angriff auf das Gold im Schatzamte mit den jetzt ausstehenden Greenbacks machen werden und ihn nicht noch erfolgreicher machen würden mit den neuen Greenbacks, welche nach den Bestimmungen dieser Bill noch weiter in Circulation gebracht werden müßten?

Mein Freund von Texas (Herr Chilton) gab vor zwei Jahren, als diese Frage erörtert wurde, seine unqualificirte Zustimmung für Gold als gesetzliches Zahlmittel. Indem er seine Einwände, oder Punkte, die seine Billigung nicht fanden, aufzählte, sagte er:

"Einer derselben richtet sich gegen die vierte Sektion, welche die Wiederausgabe der eingelösten Greenbacks vorschreibt. Ich für meinen Theil kann nicht glauben, daß wir wieder geordnete Finanzverhältnisse haben werden, bis der bestehende Gebrauch, eingelöste ''Demand Notes'' der Regierung wieder auszugeben, abgeschafft ist; und sobald ein gerechter und annehmbarer Plan zur Erreichung dieses Zweckes vor dem Senat liegt, erwarte ich dafür zu stimmen."

Mit dieser Ansicht bin ich in vollem Einklange.

Der Punkt, den ich mache, ist folgender: Wir können gegenwärtig die freie und unbeschränkte Silberprägung nicht einführen. Wir können und dürfen nicht vorschlagen, Silberdollars in den Reserve-Fonds zu thun, um Greenbacks damit einzulösen. Nun, also, wenn es schlechte Politik ist, nachdem wir das Recht haben Noten, die gesetzliches Zahlmittel sind, mit sowohl Gold wie Silber einzulösen, sie wieder auszugeben, so frage ich ob es nicht schlechte Politik ist, sie wieder auszugeben und sie als Forderungen an das Schatzamt ausstehen zu lassen, wenn wir doch nur eine Art von Münze haben, womit sie eingelöst werden können?

Herr Bacon: Ich stimme dem Senator vollkommen zu. Wenn wir lauter geprägtes Geld haben könnten, so würde ich natürlich allem Papiergelde opponiren; da aber die Barriere errichtet ist und Sie sagen, wir sollen kein geprägtes Geld haben, sondern daß das meiste Courant Papier sein soll, dann ist die beste Note die der Regierung.

Greenbacks, um Gold damit aus dem Schatze ziehen zu können.

Herr Lindsey: Nun, lassen Sie uns sehen, wie es mit dieser besten Note steht. Vor zwei Jahren war diese Sache unter Discussion. Ich glaube mein Freund hier (Herr Allen) war dafür verantwortlich. Ein hervorragendes Mitglied des Finanz-Ausschusses, der Senator von Arkansas (Herr Jones) hatte Gelegenheit sich über diese Art von Geld auszusprechen. Ich glaube, mein Freund von Nebraska (Herr Allen) hatte sich zu verschiedenen Behauptungen verstiegen, daß Greenbacks ideales Geld seien und das beste, das wir je gehabt.

Herr Allen: Ich will es jetzt sagen.

Herr Lindsey: Der Senator von Arkansas sagte damals:

„Die Wahrheit ist, daß die Silber-Certificate heute Dienst als Papiergeld für das Land thun. Die Greenbacks thun ihn nicht. Im Gegentheil, die werden von den Banken zurückgehalten, um mit ihnen Gold aus dem Bundesschatze zu holen, sobald sie es wollen, wenn immer sie ihre Goldvorräthe vermehren wollen. Während der letzten sechzig Tage," — ich glaube, es war im Jahre 1895 — „wie ich gerade gesagt habe, sind mehr als $50,000,000 Gold in dieser Weise aus dem Schatze gezogen worden und von diesen $50,000,000 sind nur $15,000,000 nach dem Auslande geschickt worden. Die andern $35,000,000 wurden gezogen, um beiseite gelegt, in Banken gehalten zu werden und dies wird andauern, solange wir dies bequeme Mittel, das Schatzamt zu entblößen, in ihren Händen lassen." —

Nun, wir haben das Mittel bis heute in ihren Händen gelassen und jetzt ist der Vorschlag gemacht, die Macht noch um 25 Proz. größer zu machen, als sie zur Zeit war als diese Erklärung abgegeben wurde —

„Sobald sie einen Bondverkauf erzwingen wollen, können sie es thun, indem sie Gold aus dem Schatze ziehen, bis der Präsident den Goldbestand für gefahrdrohend geschwächt hält, und nachdem die Bonds verkauft sind, kann das dafür bezahlte Gold gleich wieder aus dem Schatzamte gezogen und in den Banken aufgehäuft werden, und nachdem dies ein Dutzend mal geschehen, sind wir nicht besser ab; wenn wir $100,000,000, $200,000,000, oder $300,000,000 Bonds ausgegeben haben, sind wir nicht besser d'ran, als da wir anfingen." —

Das war die demokratische Greenback-Idee im Januar 1895, daß sie ihrem Zwecke nicht dienen, daß sie von den Banken und Gold-Spekulanten zurückgehalten wurden, und daß die Banken und Spekulanten den Bundesschatz mit ihnen ausraubten, wenn immer sie Profit dabei machen und das Schatzamt zwingen konnten, Bonds unter dem Gesetze vom 1875 zu verkaufen. Diese Bill beabsichtigt diesen Leuten $150,000,000 Demand-Noten mehr zu geben als sie in 1895 hatten; sie steht zur Goldwährung, wozu diese Administration verpflichtet ist, zu stehen; sie läßt das Gesetz von 1875 in Kraft, so daß die ausgezeichneten Herren, welche Geld aus Angriffen auf den Schatz machen, diesen 25 Prozent besser und leichter angreifen können, als zur Zeit wo der Senator von Arkansas Sachen aufdeckte die damals kein Mensch bestritt, und deren Existenz kein Mensch jetzt bestreiten kann.

Aber wir wissen so viel: Wenn Sie diese Greenbacks ausgeben, werden sie mit Gold eingelöst werden, und Sie wissen, daß wenn sie eingelöst sind, sie wieder ausgegeben werden, und dann wieder mit Gold eingelöst werden müßten; und Sie wissen, daß wenn es nöthig ist, Gold dafür anzuschaffen, wieder Bonds unter dem Gesetze von 1875 verkauft werden müssen, um es zu bekommen.

PROPOSED

INVESTIGATION

As to the Organization and Equipment

Of All Branches of the Army

Mr. Simpson, of Kansas, Objects

SOLDIERS' RATIONS

BY

HON. JOHN ALLEN, OF MISSISSIPPI

"Slander your Government if you Must"

Supply of Quartermaster and Commissary Stores During

THE SANTIAGO CAMPAIGN

WAS ABUNDANT

From the Congressional Record and Official Reports of the War Department

Resolution Authorizing the House Military Committee to Investigate All Branches of the Army.

[From the Congressional Record, July 8, 1898, p. 7646.]

Mr. HULL (Republican). Mr. Speaker, I want to submit the following resolution and ask its immediate consideration.

The Clerk read as follows:

Resolved, That the Committee on Military Affairs have power to sit during the adjournment of Congress, and make such investigation as to the organization and equipment of all branches of the Army as it may deem advisable, and report to the next session of Congress.

*　　*　　*　　*　　*　　*

Mr. RICHARDSON. Is this resolution recommended by the Committee on Military Affairs?

Mr. HULL. Yes, only by conference with the two Democratic members and several Republican members. I will say to the gentleman that this resolution does not provide for the payment of the expenses of the committee, and they will have to pay their own expenses where they travel. I did not want it, for myself at least, to be thought that we wanted to fix up a job, but I do believe that the House should pass a resolution of this kind, so that the members of the committee, or a part of the committee, should be able to go to Fort Alger, Tampa, and Chattanooga with power to make a proper investigation of the different camps.

HON. JERRY SIMPSON (POPULIST, OF KANSAS) OBJECTS.

Mr. SIMPSON. Mr. Speaker, I want to say to the gentleman from Iowa that we have within the last month passed bill after bill providing for a thorough organization of the Army, inspector-generals without number, and we have all these officers to look after the matters in connection with the Army. I do not see any good to come out of a committee of civilians to investigate it, and I want the party in power that appointed the men to assume the responsibility, and therefore I object to the consideration of this bill.

(2)

HON. CHAMP CLARK (DEM., OF MISSOURI) INCLUDES POPS AND FREE SILVERITES IN THE DEMOCRATIC PARTY.

Mr. CLARK (of Missouri). My Republican friends, we took you by the scruff of the neck and dragged you into it, and that will be the verdict of history.—Record, p. 5017.

Now, Mr. Speaker, I am about through with this business. I said if either party had a right to claim this war as its own, it is the Democratic party. I glory in it, and in that I include the Pops and Free Silverites, because on this war question we are all one substantially. (Laughter on the Republican side.)—Record, p. 5018.

THE SOLDIERS' RATION

BY HON. JOHN ALLEN, DEMOCRAT, FROM MISSISSIPPI.

[From the Congressional Record, Page 7278.]

Being an old and experienced soldier and having had much experience with rations and the want of them [laughter], I might be permitted to express some opinion on this subject. I want to say that my experience was with the rations issued to an army that, judged by its achievements, was as good as the world ever saw. And when I look over the bill of fare now issued as the rations to our soldiers, I can but think of what a banqueting feast it would have been to the soldiers who made such a reputation for soldierly qualities on both sides in this nation thirty-five years ago. Just listen to this bill of fare. This is the daily ration now required by law to be furnished the soldiers:

THE OFFICIAL ARMY RATION

A ration is the allowance for subsistence of one person for one day, and consists of the meat, the bread, the vegetable, the coffee and sugar, the seasoning, and the soap and candle components. (Paragraph 1251, Army Regulations, 1895.) See also paragraph 1258, ibid.

The kinds and quantities of articles composing the ration for troops where cooking is practicable, and the quantities computed for 100 rations, are as follows (Paragraph 1253, ibid.):

Articles.	Quantities per ration.		Quantities per 100 rations.		
	Ounces.	Gills.	Pounds.	Ounces.	Gallons.
Meat components.					
Fresh beef	20		125		
Or fresh mutton, when the cost does not exceed that of beef	20		125		
Or pork	12		75		
Or bacon	12		75		
Or salt beef	22		137	8	
Or, when meat cannot be furnished, dried fish	14		87	8	
Or pickled fish	18		112	8	
Or fresh fish	18		112	8	
Bread components.					
Flour	18		112	8	
Or soft bread	18		112	8	
Or hard bread	16		100		
Or corn meal	20		125		
Baking powder for troops in the field, when necessary to enable them to bake their own bread	$\frac{16}{25}$		4		
Vegetable components.					
Beans	$2\frac{2}{5}$		15		
Or pease	$2\frac{2}{5}$		15		
Or rice	$1\frac{3}{5}$		10		
Or hominy	$1\frac{3}{5}$		10		
Potatoes	16		100		
Or potatoes, 12⅘ ounces, and onions, 3⅕ ounces	16		100		
Or potatoes, 11⅕ ounces, and canned tomatoes, 4⅘ ounces; or 4⅘ ounces of other fresh vegetables not canned, when they can be obtained in the vicinity of the post or transported in a wholesome condition from a distance	16		100		
Coffee and sugar components.					
Coffee, green	$1\frac{3}{5}$		10		
Or roasted coffee	$1\frac{7}{25}$		8		
Or tea, green or black	$\frac{8}{25}$		2		
Sugar	$2\frac{2}{5}$		15		
Or molasses		$\frac{16}{25}$			2
Or cane sirup		$\frac{16}{25}$			2
Seasoning components.					
Vinegar		$\frac{8}{25}$			1
Salt	$\frac{16}{25}$		4		
Pepper, black	$\frac{1}{25}$			4	
Soap and candle components.					
Soap	$\frac{16}{25}$		4		
Candles (when illuminating oil is not furnished by the Quartermaster's Department)	$\frac{6}{25}$		1	8	

Why, Mr. Speaker, when I was a soldier, this ration cooked, as we knew how to cook, would have furnished a feast more tempting than any that could be set before me now by Delmonico. There may be some complaint with some of the volunteers who have never been accustomed to army life, but I understand that the regular soldiers are well satisfied with their rations, and it is admitted that the Commissary Department is opposed to this change. When the volunteers become inured to camp life, I think they will be well satisfied too.

I am willing to do everything necessary for the good and comfort of our soldiers. But if you want good soldiers, you do not want to coddle them too much. You hear a great deal of talk about "hard tack" and "sow belly," but I have not been real hungry since the war that I did not crave hard-tack and bacon. ,

Why, Mr. Speaker, a man with a good appetite who is really hungry, who can get some hard-tack or baker's bread and a piece of bacon, put a stick through it, hold it over the fire and broil it, and drip the grease on his bread and eat it has what is to me a very good repast, if he can get enough of it. When I get hungry, as I have many a time, I think much more about broiled or fried bacon and bread than I do about terrapin and champagne or lobster a la Newberger or punch a la Romani. [Laughter and applause.]

Why, sir, last year I bought a few boxes of hard-tack and took them down to some of my old Confederate friends just as a reminder of old times. [Laughter.] I do not want our soldiers confined to hard-tack and bacon, but you see by this bill of fare they are not confined to it. You do not want to overdo this thing and get your ration too big. Our Army is not going out just for the purpose of eating. [Laughter and applause.] They have other business in hand to which they will properly attend if you will give them a reasonable amount of food and a chance to fight.

Look at the Regular Army, who have been furnished with the rations now prescribed by law. You will not see a finer, healthier, or hardier set of men anywhere. They have plenty of such things as experience has demonstrated was best for them. Let the Government see that the contractors do not swindle them in the quality of the food furnished. I do not care much about this proposition to furnish cheese, but I doubt very much if it is made as much in the interest of the soldiers as it is in the interest of the people who have cheese for sale.

Mr. Speaker, so far as I am individually concerned and those who co-operate with me in this House, we want to give to the Administration every possible facility for the proper conduct of this war. I do not believe there will be found on either side of this House anyone voting to obstruct a successful prosecution of this war; it is not a partisan war.

I do not believe if we had a Democratic Administration that you people would want, for partisan purposes, to hamper or impede that Administration in conducting a war against a foreign country, and I for one protest against the efforts which have been or may hereafter be made to make political capital in favor of or against any political party, especially when there is no more ground for it than exists up to this time.—Record, p. 7278.

DEMOCRATS REBUKED—PATRIOTISM RISES ABOVE PARTY.

Mr. CUMMINGS (Democrat from New York). Mr. Speaker, the gentleman from Washington (Mr. Lewis) for some inscrutable reason has seen fit to embalm me in the honey of his intellectuality. . [Laughter.] He asks above which party does patriotism rise in the House. It rises, Mr. Speaker, above both parties. As a war Democrat, I enlisted in the war for the Union, not because it was Democratic policy, not because it was Republican policy, but because the country was in danger, and I was due. [Great applause.]

The gentleman voted, without talking, for the $50,000,000 appropriation. Why did he not think of "contractors" then? Was not the time to speak beforehand, and not afterwards? Why is it that he is already accusing men in high standing of corruption when the war has hardly begun?

Mr. LEWIS of Washington. But they have. [Laughter and applause.]

Mr. CUMMINGS. Make your statements clear, produce your proof, and then slander your Government if you must. Do not do it under suspicion. [Great applause.]

Now, Mr. Speaker, I did believe, when I voted for the bill proposing to raise revenue to carry on this war, and the Democratic side of the House almost unanimously voted for war, that I was doing fully as patriotic a thing as the gentleman did when he voted for the $50,000,000, to be placed at the disposal of the President without conditions. I believed that if a Democratic Administration was forced to sell $300,000,000 in bonds to run the Government in time of peace, that a Republican Administration might be allowed to sell bonds enough to run the Government in time of war. [Great applause on the Republican side.]—Record, p. 5014.

SUPPLY OF QUARTERMASTER AND COMMISSARY STORES DURING THE CAMPAIGN WAS ABUNDANT.

[From the Official Report of General Shafter on the Santiago Campaign to the War Department.]

My efforts to unload transportation and subsistence stores, so that we might have several day's rations on shore, were continued during the remainder of the month. In this work I was ably seconded by Lieut. Col. Charles F. Humphrey, deputy quartermaster-general, U. S. A., chief quartermaster, and Col. John F. Weston, assistant commissary-general of subsistence, chief commissary; but notwithstanding the utmost efforts it was difficult to land supplies in excess of those required daily to feed the men and animals, and the loss of the scow, mentioned as having broken away during the voyage, as well as the loss at sea of lighters sent by Quartermaster's Department, was greatly felt.

*　　*　　*　　*　　*　　*

Before closing my report I wish to dwell upon the natural obstacles I had to encounter and which no foresight could have overcome or obviated. The rocky and precipitous coast afforded no sheltered landing places, the roads were mere bridle paths, the effect of the tropical sun and rains upon unacclimated troops was deadly, and a dread of strange and unknown diseases had its effect on the army.

At Daiquiri the landing of the troops and stores was made at a small wooden wharf which the Spaniards tried to burn, but unsuccessfully, and the animals were pushed into the water and guided to a sandy beach about 200 yards in extent. At Siboney the landing was made on the beach and at a small wharf erected by the engineers.

I had neither the time nor the men to spare to construct permanent wharves.

In spite of the fact that I had nearly 1,000 men continuously at work on the roads, they were at times impassable for wagons.

The San Juan and Aguadores rivers would often suddenly rise so as to prevent the passage of wagons, and then the eight pack trains with the command had to be depended upon for the victualing of my army, as well as the 20,000 refugees, who could not in the interests of humanity be left to starve while we had rations.

Often for days nothing could be moved except on pack trains.

After the great physical strain and exposure of July 1 and 2, the malarial and other fevers began to rapidly advance throughout the command, and on July 4 the yellow fever appeared at Siboney. Though efforts were made to keep this fact from the army it soon became known.

The supply of quartermaster and commissary stores during the campaign was abundant, and notwithstanding the difficulties in landing and transporting the rations, the troops on the firing line were at all times supplied with its coarser components, namely, of bread, meat, sugar, and coffee.

There was no lack of transportation, for at no time up to the surrender could all the wagons I had be used.

In reference to the sick and wounded, I have to say that they received every attention that it was possible to give them. The medical officers without exception worked night and day to alleviate the suffering, which was no greater than invariably accompanies a campaign. It would have been better if we had more ambulances, but as many were taken as was thought necessary, judging from previous campaigns.

RECOMMENDATIONS FOR PROMOTION OF SURGEONS AND COMMISSARY OFFICERS.

The discipline of the command was superb, and I wish to invite attention to the fact that not an officer was brought to trial by court-martial, and, as far as I know, no enlisted men. This speaks volumes for an army of this size and in a campaign of such duration.

In conclusion, I desire to express to the members of my staff my thanks for their efficient performance of all the duties required of them, and the good judgment and bravery displayed on all occasions when demanded.

I submit the following recommendations for promotion, which I earnestly desire to see made. It is a very little reward to give them for their devotion and fearless exposure of their lives in their country's cause:

B. F. Pope, lieutenant-colonel and surgeon, United States Volunteers, to be brevetted colonel for faithful and meritorious service during the campaign.

John F. Weston, colonel and assistant commissary-general of subsistence, chief commissary, to be brevetted brigadier-general for meritorious service throughout the campaign.

C. G. Starr, major and inspector-general, United States Volunteers, to be brevetted lieutenant-colonel for faithful and meritorious conduct throughout the campaign.

Leon Roudiez, major and quartermaster, United States Volunteers, to be brevetted lieutenant-colonel for faithful and meritorious conduct throughout the campaign.

II. J. Gallagher, major and commissary of subsistence, United States Volunteers, to be brevetted lieutenant-colonel for faithful and meritorious service throughout the campaign.

Captain Brice, commissary of subsistence, United States Volunteers, to be brevetted major for faithful and meritorious service throughout the campaign.

Captain Johnson, assistant quartermaster, United States Volunteers, to be brevetted major for faithful and meritorious service throughout the campaign

* * * * * *

The following general order indicates the manner in which the troops left the transports and the amount of supplies carried immediately with them:

GENERAL ORDERS,   HEADQUARTERS FIFTH ARMY CORPS,
No. 18.   .   ON BOARD S. S. SEGURANCA,
                     At Sea, June 20, 1898.

[Extract.]

2. All troops will carry on the person the blanket roll (with shelter tent and poncho), three days' field rations (with coffee, ground), canteens filled, and 100 rounds of ammunition per man. Additional ammunition, already issued to the troops, tentage, baggage, and company cooking utensils will be left under charge of the regimental quartermaster, with one noncommissioned officer and two privates from each company.

* * * * * *

[From the Official Report of Brigadier General H. W. Lawton.]

To Surg. H. S. Kilbourne, chief surgeon, is due the thanks not only of myself, but of the whole division, for faithful and unremitting attention to the wounded on the field and under fire.

* * * * * *

[From the Official Report of Brigadier General J. Ford Kent.]

The officers enumerated should at least be brevetted for gallantry under fire. I also personally noticed the conduct of First Lieut. F. J. Kirkpatrick, assistant surgeon. United States Army, on duty with the Twenty-fourth Infantry, giving most efficient aid to the wounded under fire.

* * * * * *

[From the Official Report of Major General Joseph Wheeler.]

Major West, my quartermaster, deserves special commendation for his energy and good conduct during the campaign, and Maj. Valery Harvard and Mr. Leonard Wilson have also done their full duty.

* * * * * *

[From the Official Report of Brigadier General J. C. Bates.]

I wish also to add that Major Ives. my chief surgeon, was on the firing line and did efficient service during the progress of the fight and behaved in most gallant manner.

* * * * * *

[From the Official Report of Brigadier General H. W. Lawton.]

During the action I was accompanied most of the time by Maj. Gen. J. C. Breckinridge, Inspector-General, United States Army, as a spectator, and had the advantage of his valuable suggestions and advice during the day, for which I desire to express my sincere appreciation. His horse was shot under him on the advance upon Santiago, the morning of the 2d instant.

THE

Conduct of the War

THE TRUE STORY OF PREPARATION FOR THE CONFLICT, OF DIFFICULTIES OVERCOME, AND OF MAGNIFICENT RESULTS, PLAINLY AND IMPARTIALLY TOLD

How the United States in One Hundred Days Organized, Armed and Equipped and Provided Transportation for an Army of over a Quarter of a Million of Men, Conducted Campaigns Separated by 10,000 Miles of Land and Water, Humiliated and Destroyed the Enemy Wherever Met, Without One Single Reverse.

FROM THE
NEW YORK MAIL AND EXPRESS
October 11, 1898

The
Conduct of the War.

THE MAIL AND EXPRESS BUREAU,

WASHINGTON, October 11.

"I feel that the American people have committed these boys into my hands, and if anybody has wronged them, I want to find it out.

"I do not believe that any army has been watched over more anxiously and continuously than I have watched over this army, for I spent seventeen hours a day in my office looking after it."

These were the words President McKinley used when he asked several members of the Commission, now investigating the war, to undertake that work.

AN AUTHORITATIVE STATEMENT.

It was with the same idea to show the country that the War Department used every effort in its power before and during the war to guard and care for the army that President McKinley granted me permission to prepare for The Mail and Express this article. It has been prepared with his knowledge and consent, and all statements made have been verified by official records.

While the President's words quoted above express his feelings and his desires clearly and concisely, the statement which follows gives authoritatively the true position and condition of the War Department during the last six months.

PRESIDENT'S WISDOM SHOWN.

Already the wisdom of the President in ordering an investigation of the charges made against the War Department has beeen shown. The Investigating Committee has been in session but a short time and but a few witnesses have been examined, but the testimony of officers of high rank has shown how utterly unjust and unfounded have been the charges and criticisms of the majority of the critics. The testimony has shown that where abuses or neglect were pointed out or discovered, every effort was made to correct them.

THE OTHER SIDE OF THE QUESTION.

For the first time the public has had a glimpse of the other side of the question. For weeks the maligners of the Administration and the War Department have been making reckless charges and complaints, and the country has been stirred up and inflamed by sensational reports. There has been no denial of sickness, death or discomfort among our troops. This could not have been prevented. There have been mistakes made, but the records of the Department show that everything possible was done beforehand to prevent these.

But this has been war and not a summer outing, and looking over the results and the victories, the country cannot but be congratulated on the remarkably low death rate; its great achievement in raising an army of over 275,000 officers and men in less than fifty days, and bringing to a successful conclusion a war with a foreign nation within three and a half months.

DEPARTMENT KEPT STEADILY AT WORK.

During the storm of abuse which blew steadily over the country, and was especially directed against the War Department, that branch of the Government, of necessity, was obliged to remain silent. While politicians and newspapers were spreading broadcast sensational and, for the most part, unfounded reports in regard to our soldiers and their camps, the President and the officials of the War Department kept steadily at work, remedying faults, correcting abuses and holding the tight rein of organization over the troops which were threatened with demoralization by the sensational and scandalous abuse. It was at this time that the President decided that if the soldiers who had been committed to his care had been wronged, he would find it out, as it was due to the public and the country to know the truth, and he would give it to them. The only way to do this was to appoint an investigating committee, composed of men beyond reproach, and who would get at the truth. Every one knows now the history of the appointment of the War Commission, and its work so far as it has gone.

OVERCOMING LEGAL OBSTACLES.

While the public is hearing from the officers of high rank exactly what was done for the soldiers and their comfort, nothing has been given to the country in regard to the work of the Administration, especially the War Department, in preparation for the war or the legal obstacles which hampered these preparations. The Mail and Express is enabled to-day to present for the first time a clear and authentic statement of the conditions which confronted the War Department when war was declared; what was done to overcome these obstacles of law and the willful neglect of past Congresses; how the great army was raised, equipped and put in the field; how the Quartermaster, Commissary and Medical departments worked to make the new army fit for the field, and, finally, what was accomplished and the results.

NOT A DEFENSE, FOR THAT IS NOT NEEDED.

In presenting this statement I do not make it as a defense of the War Department, for it needs none. It is simply an official and authentic declaration of facts, founded upon official records and actions. It tells the story of preparation before the war and what the War Department did, and what it accomplished during the war, in language for the people. There are no excuses, no elaborations, no exaggeration. It is simply the truth, as told by the records, and shows for the first time exactly what the Administration and the War Department did.

It is official and authentic. The figures, data and statements can all be proven by records in the Department, while the statements in regard to certain actions, loudly attacked by ignorant critics, clearly and forcibly answer these charges.

HOW PREPARATION WAS HAMPERED.

The story starts with the condition of the army at the beginning of the year and the number of officers and men then on a peace basis. As events of February last made war seem certain, preparations for the inevitable were begun, but legal restrictions and lack of Congressional action did much to hamper these preliminary and necessary steps. Notwithstanding these obstacles, the War Department went on with its work as best it could, but it was not until war was actually declared that authority was given to go ahead with the vast work necessary to put a great army in the field. It is here shown how, in the short period of five weeks, Adjutant-General Corbin, with his four assistants. under the direct supervision of the President, organized, commissioned and assigned to duty over 800 generals and staff officers, and enrolled and mustered into service the regiments of the vast army which sprang into existence in answer to the President's call.

The cry has been that politics had much to do with the appointment of general and staff officers, but it is shown that no party or faction was recognized. The Democrats asked for and were given as much as the Republicans. The South received equal patronage with the North. There was no East or West; all were treated on equality and the best man, no matter where he came from or his politics, was chosen, so far as in the President's knowledge and power.

In making selections from 18,000 applicants a little over 36 per cent were chosen from the regular army.

THOSE SONS OF FATHERS.

A great deal has been said and printed about the appointment of "sons of fathers," grandsons and nephews to staff appointments. The President did appoint less than forty young men who happened to have illustrious ancestors, but they were all bright, accomplished men, who had made reputations in their own sphere and who were anxious to serve their country by going to the front. With less than half a dozen exceptions all of these men did good work after they had a few weeks' experience. The records show that the young men in the army did the best work; were more energetic and efficient than many of the older ones. A few figures will show exactly how many favorite sons the President appointed, and like all other criticisms and complaints the official figures will show how a single example has been taken for the whole.

President McKinley appointed 836 general and staff officers. Of these 33 were sons of distinguished ancestors, 25 were "sons of fathers," as critics have called them, 4 were grandsons, 3 were nephews, 1 was a son-in-law and 4 were appointed, as the yellow journals declare, by social "pull."

Of all the staff appointments 40 were chosen by Senators and appointed on their recommendation. Ten of these Senators were Democrats, and of these more than one asked for and received more than one appointment. Twenty-six staff officers were appointed on recommendations of Representatives in Congress. Certainly if the representatives of the people could not recommend appointments, to whom could the President turn for advice?

Of all the 836 appointments but three were President McKinley's personal appointments, one was personal to Vice-President Hobart; six by personal recommendation of the Secretary of War and one by that of Senator Hanna, but there were 39 other Senators who asked the same favor, and the President granted what they desired.

CONGRESS PARTLY TO BLAME.

A clear statement is made of what the War Department asked of Congress and what Congress granted.

It is interesting to note in this regard that to the failure of Congress to carry out the War Department's recommendation as embodied in what is known as the Hull Reorganization bill can be traced a good deal of the suffering and disease of the troops. The War Department wanted the regular army increased, but the pressure from the country forced Congress to act otherwise, and the volunteer service was made up by giving preference to the State militia.

The comparisons given show that the death rate among the volunteers and the regulars is sadly against the former. This is emphasized by the report from the camp at Chickamauga. There the volunteers and the regulars were camping side by side in the ratio of about two of the former to one of the latter, and there were 425 deaths among the volunteers and only one among the regulars.

The chapter in regard to how and why the camps were chosen is exceedingly interesting, and gives the reasons of the Department for selecting Chickamauga, Alger and Tampa for places of mobilization. That part referring to Camp Wikoff at Montauk, is also full of importance just now.

WORK OF QUARTERMASTER'S DEPARTMENT.

The work of the Ordnance, Quartermaster, Subsistence and Medical Departments is treated under separate heads. The unreadiness of the country for war is especially shown by the Ordnance Department's being suddenly called upon to equip a quarter of a million men with a class of articles not produced by private manufacturers. It is shown why the Springfield rifles had to be used and why smokeless powder could not be furnished. Every means was used to provide the latter in time, but it could not be obtained until the war was practically over and too late to use. The difficulties in providing artillery with equipment are explained by the lack of appropriations provided before the war began.

The heroic work done by the Quartermaster's Department is fully shown, together with exactly what that work consisted of. Considering the too few officers provided by law and the action of Congress for years back in insisting upon economical appropriations for this Department, the way the Quartermaster's Bureau equipped an army of a quarter of a million ought to come in for praise instead of abuse.

The troopship question as well as that of supplying the army with everything that goes to make up an army, except men and food, fell to the Quartermaster's Department, and in a clear and straightforward manner the great work of this bureau is laid before the public for the first time.

SIMILAR DIFFICULTIES.

The difficulties under which the Commissary or Subsistence Department labored for lack of legal power and ability to buy supplies in open market were similar to those of the Quartermaster's Bureau. The law provides that the Subsistence Department shall purchase the food, but it does not allow it to cook it. A great deal of trouble and disease resulted from this and this Bureau has been blamed. It is shown that the Commissary Department furnished sufficient and good food to the soldiers, but it is also shown that they could not compel them to cook or use it properly.

COMPARISON IN DEATH RATE.

One of the most interesting portions of the article is the comparisons made of the death rate of this war with those of former wars in the West Indies, as well as abroad. The first expedition sent to the West Indian Islands was that by the English. The land forces numbered 14,000. In this expedition the losses were 1,790 officers and men killed, wounded and missing, while the losses from disease were about 50 per cent of the total forces. In 1802, during the French expedition to the West Indies, 58,545 men were sent to the islands. In four months the loss from disease reached the astounding figure of 50,207, or a mortality of 585 per thousand. Of the 8,275 survivors 3,000 were reported unfit for duty. Compare these terrific losses with the almost insignificant loss of our own army in Cuba. During the same period as the French expedition our aggregate loss from all causes was but 2,910, out of a total force of 274,717 officers and men, or a percentage of 1.059.

These figures become more significant when it is stated that during the present war Spain has carried to the island 135,000 men, of whom but 85,000 remain.

Disease caused this great havoc, for her losses in battle have been insignificant.

THE MEDICAL DEPARTMENT.

The statement in regard to the medical department shows exactly with what force and lack of preparation on account of legal obstacles that department entered the war; how it was built up, and at the same time clearly explains much of the horrors and discomforts which our soldiers were obliged to suffer. This is but a brief outline of what is set forth fully below.

THE RESULTS OF THE WAR.

The results of the war are too well known to require much attention. To sum them up in a few words the United States, in the short space of 100 days, organized, armed and equipped and provided transportation for an army of over a quarter of a million of men; conducted campaigns separated by 10,000 miles of land and water; humiliated and destroyed the enemy wherever met, without one single reverse. And this with the small loss of but a little over 1 per cent from all causes—an achievement unparalleled in the history of warfare, savage or civilized, and which will be referred to by critics of the future as the military marvel of the century.

ON A PEACE BASIS.

How the Army Was Situated Before the Hostilities Broke Out.

The year 1898 began with the United States at peace with the world; its army on a peace basis, of 2,164 officers and 25,350 enlisted men, embracing (in addition to the general staff corps, and including one battalion of engineers) ten regiments of cavalry, five regiments of artillery and twenty-five regiments of infantry, gathered in various posts throughout the country. The entire force was well armed, well clothed, well housed, well fed, and regularly paid; all of the men in splendid spirits and excellent physical condition. A state of discipline prevailed which knew nothing but loyalty and obedience, awaiting any call, ready for any service.

COAST DEFENSE INCOMPLETE.

An elaborate scheme for coast defense, devised in 1886, was not only incomplete, but just fairly begun; but few guns had been mounted, and the few others made ready for mounting with meagre appropriations had not left their factories, owing to the failure of Congress to provide the necessary funds asked for from time to time by the Chief of Ordnance.

The devastating war in Cuba which had waged for the two and one-half years preceding, occupied the minds of the American people. Neither the Administration, the War Department nor any of its bureaus have anything to excuse, but a few words of explanation touching the obstacles to be overcome, considered in connection with the results obtained, will appeal to the reason of fair-minded people who may have or who would criticise upon imperfect knowledge or false statements.

LACK OF CONGRESSIONAL AUTHORITY.

Many legal restrictions hampered and embarrassed the transaction of business. Indeed, only those conducting the affairs of the war can have any idea of the handicap placed by Congress on the War Department and the serious obstacles which have made it impossible to accomplish ready and effective work at all times.

During the War of the Rebellion the Secretary of War exercised to its fullest extent the power which then lawfully belonged to the heads of the several departments in controlling and directing the appropriations voted and placed under his care. Can it be questioned that the arm of the great Secretary was strengthened by this prerogative which enabled him to maintain complete control and directive power over the expenditures necessary to a successful prosecution of his work? This power over expenditure remained with the Secretary of War until March 30, 1868, when Congress deprived him of it and placed over him the Comptroller of the Treasury, with power to reverse his action and disallow his payments; the effect has made contractors timid and slow.

Nine successive Attorney Generals (Wirt, Berrian, Taney, Butler, Reverdy Johnson, Crittenden, Cushing, Bates and Stanbery), after elaborate consideration of the same question, held that it was essential to the proper and successful administration of the Government that the executive heads of the several departments, in the matter of expenditures of money, should exercise and control authoritative direction, not subject to the reversal of the Comptroller or any accounting officer of the Treasury.

RED TAPE HAMPERED PREPARATIONS.

In the work of organizing, equipping, subsisting, clothing, sheltering, transporting and providing munitions of war, medical supplies and surgical aid, the numerous and varied expenditures incident to military operations, require prompt and decisive action in the matter of expenditures, with prompt and certain payment if satisfactory results are to be obtained.

At the outbreak of the Hispano-American war, no supplies in large quantities could be purchased without advertisement; and copies of advertisements were required to be submitted to and approved before publication, by the Secretary of War, or payment could not be authorized. The newspapers of the National capital were excluded by law from publishing advertisements, except for supplies and services to be used in the District of Columbia.

THE ARMY REGULATIONS.

There has been criticism of the army regulations. It is admitted that as they are now constructed they are cumbersome, but they are the product of thirty years' work and experience. To have changed them materially when war was declared or during the campaign would have created no end of confusion and perhaps disaster. What changes could be made at such a time were made. The army regulations under which the War Department is working were revised under a former Democratic Secretary of War.

CONGRESS OBJECTED TO TRAINED COOKS.

For over twenty years efforts have been made to secure legislative action for the enlistment of trained cooks for the military service, but it was denied until after war was declared.

By the same legal restrictions, the number of cavalry and artillery horses was limited to the number of mounted men in the service, not allowing for a single breakdown, a single death or a single remount; and the number of draft animals was limited to 5,000, a number by no means sufficient to mobilize the small regular army.

No law existed which enabled the War Department to regulate and protect explosive mines and mine fields in the waters of the United States.

HAMPERED BY OLD DECISIONS.

At the present time, a serious embarrassment arises to pay for certain advertisements which were essentially necessary in the matter of procuring recruits and volunteers for the army, and to supply wood for the troops near Tampa, and to provide cavalry horses for the service. Notwithstanding the vouchers for these items were approved by the Secretary of War, the Second Auditor of the Treasury adheres to a decision made in 1876, that written authority of the Secretary of War must be obtained before publication, or payment must be withheld.

Section 3648, Revised Statutes, provides that no advance of public money shall be made in any case whatever, and agents of express companies frequently refuse to forward goods without payment in advance.

UNHEEDED APPEALS TO CONGRESS.

The foregoing are merely a few of the cases in which it became necessary for the War Department to apply to Congress for legislation. Many instances might be shown where the dispatch of public business and the workings of the bureaus of the Department were embarrassed and delayed by reason of its head being deprived of final authority in the matter of allowance of accounts and expenditures.

ATTACKS FROM THE REAR.

The supply departments have been the subject of bitter attack from the rear, though the American soldier at the front has courageously borne the hardships of war, which he expected and knows are unavoidable, with but few complaints. The partisan journals have spread discontent and created sorrowful anxiety at home.

President McKinley and the officers of his Administration, continually since assuming office, had been alert and active to bring the struggle to a close and give peace and stable conditions to Cuba, and sought, if possible, to accomplish the end without recourse to arms.

DRIVEN INTO WAR.

Jaundiced journals and jingo orators manufactured a restless disposition and impatient demand from the people for precipitate action, and the temper of the Spanish people was such that pacific diplomacy became unpopular in both countries. Notwithstanding this public pressure, the President and his associates worked incessantly for, and believed that peace could be maintained, most of them having learned on the battlefield what war meant, what distress and suffering it entailed, and sought to save the nation from its dreadful consequences. Therefore but little was done, and but little could be done in preparation for war, without increasing its chances. The publication of the De Lome letter, speaking disparagingly of the President on February 8, added fuel to a fire which burst into a blaze of wrath and indignation on February 15, when the world was horrified by the destruction of the battleship Maine in Havana harbor.

CONGRESS GIVES A LITTLE AID.

One week following that disaster Congress increased the army of the United States by the addition of two regiments of artillery. This was hardly a war measure, however, but merely an additional force required to care for the extra guns of costly pattern which had been mounted along the sea coast, and the need for which had been shown for a long period previous, though, through political fear, the legislation had not been enacted into law.

THE DEFENSE BILL.

By March 8 the situation had grown so grave that Congress, upon the request of the President, appropriated, by unanimous vote, the sum of $50,000,000 for the National defense. This act, however, was viewed as more of a peace than a war measure, and three days later the new Spanish Minister, Senor Polo y Bernabe, was received by the President of the United States

WAR RESOLUTIONS

It was not until April 11 that the President asked authority of Congress to intervene in Cuba by force to re-establish peace and order in the island. After nearly a week of debate the resolutions were passed. The President signed them on April 20 and sent the ultimatum to Spain.

On the following day, April 21, the war broke out, and two days later came the call for 125,000 volunteers, followed by a second call for 75,000. In the meantime Congress had passed a law increasing the regular army to 61,000 and also providing for sixteen regiments of United States volunteer engineers, cavalry and infantry.

HOW A VAST ARMY SPRANG UP.

Mustering was carried forward vigorously in every State of the Union, and in the short space of one month this vast army of nearly two hundred and twenty-five thousand men were suddenly gathered together, and the staff departments had to be organized and were called upon to equip and supply them.

WORK OF THE ADJUTANT-GENERAL.

In the short period of five weeks the Adjutant-General of the Army with his four assistants, at their desks constantly from 8 in the morning until after midnight week days and Sundays, had organized his working force, issued commissions to and assigned to duty over 800 generals and general staff officers, enrolled and mustered the regiments of this vast army into service of the United States, completed the papers, gathered them into camps of instruction and organized them into brigades, divisions and army corps, and conducted without error the overwhelming correspondence arising from the abnormal conditions, which ran the average of his telegrams to over 500 and his letters to over 1,000 per day, touching every intricate legal question affecting personal and public interests; surrounded too, by throngs of Congressmen pressing the claims of their constituents, newspaper men eager to furnish their papers with accurate and comprehensive reports of proceedings and progress, and a crowd of persistent callers seeking personal advantage.

NO PARTY OR FACTION RECOGNIZED.

There were over eighteen thousand applications for appointment of general and staff officers; the President in his selections and appointments from this vast number recognized no party or faction. Of the 836 appointed, 301,

C of W

or a little over 36 per cent, were chosen from the regular army—a larger percentage than was ever selected to officer any volunteer army organized in the United States; and all would have been taken from the regular army if possible, but so large a number could not be spared without seriously impairing its efficiency. The regular army was recognized by military men, and thoughtful statesmen, as already too small, and its officers had been reduced by the withdrawal of 200 for mustering and recruiting duty.

MAJORITY OF OFFICERS WERE REGULARS.

Of the major-generals appointed, all, with the exception of five, were from the regular army, and of these five three were graduates of the Military Academy and all of them soldiers of distinction and National reputation.

Of the seventy brigadier-generals appointed, forty-two were from the regular army, and of the others, five were graduates of the Military Academy and the remainder men who had won reputations as soldiers on the battlefield.

HOW STAFF OFFICERS WERE CHOSEN.

Of the seven hundred and forty-eight staff officers, two hundred and fifty-six were chosen from the army; of those selected from civil life, many were graduates of the Military Academy, or had seen service, and all were appointed upon the recommendation of chiefs of staff departments, other soldiers, and of the representatives elected by the people to promote their welfare and guard their every interest. Of the remaining four hundred and ninety-two civilian appointments, over one-half are in the Medical Department, Pay Department and the Signal Corps, the only field from which men in such numbers, possessing approximately the required technical knowledge, could be drawn.

The appointment of officers of the staff would have produced at once an efficient service, if equal care had been exercised by the Governors of all the States to appoint none but good regimental and company officers. A staff officer's work is rendered futile by neglect or lack of knowledge on the part of line officers. Over the appointment of the latter Congress gave the President no power, but instead, reserved it to the Governors, and in one State the Governor went so far as to disband the National Guard before mustering began, so that the officers' positions in the volunteers might be more easily bestowed upon political friends.

In all assignments to duty, care was exercised to see that only trained officers of the regular army were put in position of high authority and great responsibility.

WHAT WAS ASKED OF CONGRESS.

Every general commanding the army since the Civil War has included in his annual report from time to time a recommendation to Congress for a reorganization of the infantry arm of the service upon modern lines; and every Congress for the same period has had upon its calendar a bill embodying such features; and in the spring of 1898, when war seemed imminent and apparently near at hand, Mr. Hull, chairman of the House Military Committee, drafted a bill embodying the ideas of the most experienced officers of the army, which provided for an increase of the regular establishment to about 100,000 men. This, it was confidently expected at the War Department, would, as a war measure, be enacted into law; and the thought given to preliminary preparation proceeded with that end in view.

WHAT CONGRESS GRANTED.

The organized militia opposed the passage of such a measure, fearing that if it became a law it would destroy their organization by replacing it, and Congress failed to pass the measure. Had this bill become a law, the splendid recruiting organization of the regular army, with the multitude of applications for enlistments, could have been quickly recruited to the full strength from men chosen with peculiar fitness for military service, without the strong ties binding them to home, school and business, which, when excitement wanes, breed discontent and nostalgia. All of the men so enlisted would have been quickly gathered in companies and regiments of the regular army, where, with their veteran comrades side by side in the same tents and the same messes, they would have quickly adapted themselves to the splendid discipline and thorough instruction under the watchful care of the trained and zealous officers so necessary to the health, instruction and efficiency of an army.

REGULARS AND VOLUNTEERS.

By this failure it became necessary to send the regular army, small as it was, in compact regiments, carefully looking after their own health and comfort, and side by side were regiments of men equally patriotic and zealous but suffering from a lack of knowledge, which rendered the superiority of the one over the other, so apparent.

DEATHS: VOLUNTEERS, 425; REGULARS, 1.

In the camp at Chickamauga, where the volunteers and the regulars were camping side by side, in the ratio of about two of the former to one of the latter, there were 425 deaths among the volunteers and only one of the regulars.

No braver, no more zealous, no more devoted soldiers ever followed a country's flag than the volunteer soldiers in the American army; but putting a gun in a man's hand no more makes him a soldier than putting a plane in his hand makes him a carpenter. Our people and their representatives have indulged in this mistake for thirty years.

The science of arms is a profession which requires a long apprenticeship and careful training under schooling of a master, and no amount of patriotism and no degree of bravery can make up for the lack of such training and apprenticeship. If without it great results are obtained it is at the expenditure of life to a degree so shocking that the true cause is lost to sight for the moment and until reason makes it plain.

CONGRESS ACTS—BUT TOO LATE.

Finally Congress did effect a partial reorganization and about doubled the enlisted strength of the regular army, but did it at a time when the States were organizing their own troops and the influence of friends in regiments already enlisted carried the men into the State organizations rather than the regular army, and delayed its recruitment.

HOW AND WHY CAMPS WERE CHOSEN.

After the State troops were mustered into the United States service it became necessary to gather them into large camps of instruction for the purpose of organization and formation into brigades, divisions and army corps. Several points of concentration were selected, notably Chickamauga, on account of the great extent of country there owned by the United States, and over which 100,000 men had once engaged in the grand mancuvers of a great battle. The selection was influenced by the splendid character of the roads throughout the park, its adaptability to camping purposes on account of abundant shade, open fields, rolling surface and the splendid water supply, as reported by Gen. Boynton, chairman of the Park Commission.

WHY CAMP ALGER WAS SELECTED.

In a great war between two nations the capital of the country is always supposed to be a final objective, and one of the military weaknesses of the United States is the location of its beautiful capital within fifty miles of the sea, and upon a tide-water river.

With an adversary having nearly one hundred thousand troops within eighty miles of our territory, and a navy supposed to be as strong if not stronger than our own, it was but a reasonable precaution to take measures against the possibility of an attack on Washington. For that reason a force of some thirty thousand men were gathered together in the vicinity of that city for the double purpose of organization, instruction and possible defense.

For that reason Camp Alger was established. The site selected was ten or twelve miles from Washington, upon which had camped during the War of the Rebellion frequently an equal and at times a vastly greater force, without inconvenience or more than the average death-rate from disease.

TAMPA WAS NEAR CUBA.

Tampa was selected as a point of embarkation on account of its proximity to the Cuban coast, and with the thought that a sojourn in the Southern latitudes would in a measure prepare the troops for a climate it was known they must endure in a tropical campaign. As soon as possible after the embarkation of a portion, the remainder of the troops were removed. When the danger of attack upon Washington had entirely passed, troops were moved from Camp Alger.

AS TO MONTAUK POINT.

Montauk Point was selected because of its splendid adaptability as a recuperating point, with salt water bathing, fresh ocean breezes, excellent artesian water, good surface drainage and sufficiently isolated to protect the centers of population of the United States from fever infection brought from the tropics by the returning soldiers.

In preparing the camp at that point an experienced medical officer was put upon the ground immediately after the selection of the site, who had authority to call upon the medical supply officer at New York for everything he needed, and that officer was directed to fill all his requisitions without reference to the War Department.

IT WAS THE BATTLEFIELD BROUGHT HOME.

To persons unused to the scenes and horrors of war, it doubtless presented many sights of pity and despair, but it must be borne in mind that it was but the rear of the battlefield of Santiago brought home, where the terrible privations of that struggle would be diminished, and some lives saved, which if the troops had remained long in Cuba, or had been transported farther, would have been lost.

WAR AND PEACE ARE DIFFERENT.

In gathering together large bodies of men it is hard to impress upon them that their daily life must be materially changed. Men from the villages and the rural districts are not able to understand why practicing a mode of life to which they have been accustomed will endanger and develop disease dangerous and fatal. And this, as with many other lessons in life, there seems to be no master but experience, and the only lessons learned and taken to heart are those received in that thorough school.

ALL COMPLAINTS WERE INVESTIGATED.

Many individual complaints were received at the department in various ways—anonymous letters apparently written by soldiers, newspaper articles prepared far from the scene of action, letters from friends and relatives based upon letters received from members of their families in the army, and from members of Congress, generally based upon hearsay evidence. Never was a single complaint allowed to pass without a thorough investigation and report; nearly always with the result that the complaint was trivial and not founded upon fact, but in the few cases which merited remedial measures they were at once applied; and if neglect upon the part of officers was discovered, they were promptly admonished.

. ADVOCATES OF WAR FIRST TO COMPLAIN.

Hardly had the sensational journals of the country ceased their exciting and inflammatory editions crying for war when they began to magnify complaints and utter criticisms as unjust as they were pernicious and harmful, spreading discontent in the ranks and producing alarm at home.

REMEDIAL MEASURES INSTANTLY TAKEN.

Immediately upon receipt of reports at the Department that sickness was prevalent in the camps, measures were taken to remove the men and scatter the commands. Chickamauga and Camp Alger were abandoned, but after supplies and equipment had been sent to those points they could not be entirely given up until the supplies were properly distributed. And, moreover, until the camp lessons were learned, one suitable location was as good as another.

ORDNANCE DEPARTMENT.

How a Quarter of a Million Men Were Armed and Equipped.

The bureaus attracting the most attention are the Ordnance, Quartermaster's, Subsistence and Medical Departments.

When the first call for troops was made, the Ordnance Department was called upon to suddenly equip a quarter of a million of men with a class of articles not produced by private manufacturers. Appropriations of Congress for these equipments for many years had been barely sufficient for replacing those worn out by the regular army, which required about 5,000 sets of equipments per year, and to equip 250,000 men in four weeks required it to increase its business six hundred-fold.

NOT ARTICLES OF COMMERCE.

The supply on hand was necessarily very small, and money for the increase in these classes of equipment was only available a few days before war had actually begun, when upon telegraphic orders the work of manufacture was immediately commenced at the various arsenals, and was supplemented by purchase from contractors; though it must be borne in mind that stores of this character are not articles of commerce, and purchases from contractors were delayed by the time required by manufacturers to acquaint themselves with the requirements, specifications, mode of manufacture and sources of material for producing them; and the degree of excellence required was something for which the contractors were not prepared, notwithstanding the standard was somewhat reduced.

VOLUNTEERS' EQUIPMENT UNFIT.

The first levy of troops being made up largely from the National Guard of the States, it was supposed from reports that most of their arms and equipment, though somewhat worn, were unfit for service. This expectation, however, was not realized, and before the troops were ready to take the field it was found necessary to replace three-fourths of their arms and equipment. Delays, too, were caused by failures on the part of organizations to make requisitions (although the requisition in this, as in all the departments, is very simple, requiring merely to state the number of men, the number of serviceable equipment on hand and the number required to complete the outfit).

Some delays, it is true, were caused by the congestion of railways and the inability to promptly distribute arms and equipment that had been sent to the different camps. Supply depots were established at Tampa, Chickamauga and Benicia Arsenal, near San Francisco, with a view to completing the arming and equipping of regiments before they embarked for foreign expeditions, which was successfully accomplished.

THE WORK ACCOMPLISHED.

Between April 15 and August 31, the Department provided 250,000 sets of infantry equipments, and 30,000 sets of horse equipments, and on the later date was prepared to produce infantry equipments at the rate of 8,000 sets per day, a set including knapsack, haversack, with knife, fork and spoon, a canteen, a meat ration can, tin cup, cartridge belt and bayonet scabbard.

THE SPRINGFIELD RIFLES.

At the outset of the war the Department had on hand an ample supply of caliber 45, Springfield rifles, for arming the new troops, and was able to supplement the supply of rifles, carbines and sabers on hand in sufficient quantities to meet demands.

The propriety of equipping the troops with the 45-caliber rifle was not at first questioned. Its excellence and accuracy had been proven by long service; its simplicity and certainty to keep in good fighting condition under exposure and bad usage were known. Success with a more complicated magazine arm required experience and time for study upon the part of the officers and men, and the troops called out were already familiar with the Springfield rifle, and the work in hand was to complete this armament and replace unserviceable arms with new ones, and, moreover, magazine rifles were not on hand and could not be provided otherwise than by manufacture.

Many unjust criticisms of the Springfield rifle have appeared in the public prints. It may be stated that its rate of fire and extreme range are practically the same as the best-known military magazine arm; and the shock of the blow imparted by the bullet at its extreme range (3,200 yards) is greater. Its disadvantages are summed up in the height of the trajectory and the weight of the cartridge carried, which is nearly double that of the smaller bore.

LITTLE SMOKELESS POWDER.

Prior to the war the Ordnance Department had, after a long series of experiments, arrived at a satisfactory smokeless powder for the 45-caliber cartridges, but no money, though asked for by the department, was appropriated for the manufacture of a large reserve supply. At the commencement of hostilities the private cartridge factories were not prepared to use the smokeless powder in the manufacture of cartridges, and it required time to make preparation. Every resource of the powder manufacturers was consumed in providing smokeless powder for the coast defense and the field and siege artillery, and to meet the demand for this ammunition for the time being it was absolutely necessary to furnish charcoal cartridges. The manufacture of smokeless powder, 45 caliber cartridges, was taken up as soon as possible, and, though an ample supply was provided later, it was not used in any engagement.

After the breaking out of hostilities the Ordnance Department provided about eighty million small arms cartridges of all kinds.

PROVIDING THE ARTILLERY.

The labor of providing the artillery was even more difficult. The armament and equipment of all regular batteries were increased from four to six guns. The volunteer batteries were armed and equipped generally as fast as they were ready to receive their guns, cartridges and equipments.

When the war began the only field and siege artillery ammunition that appropriations had enabled the Department to have on hand was the small supply used annually by the regular army for artillery practice, and a small reserve for emergency. This had been manufactured prior to the adoption of smokeless powder, and for want of better was immediately issued to the batteries that were hastened to the front, and was sufficient in quantity.

The manufacture of this ammunition with smokeless powder in sufficient quantities for a protracted war was commenced at once, and every resource of the arsenals and private establishments throughout the country was brought to bear in providing a quantity more than required to meet the probable demands of a protracted war.

All of the work of the Department was performed by a corps of officers, claimed by the Chief of Ordnance to be too small for the regular army in time of peace.

QUARTERMASTER'S DEPARTMENT.

Hampered by Impossibility of Procuring Supplies at Short Notice.

The Quartermaster's Department is the great general supply department of the army. Its administration touches every branch of army service. Upon this department by law is placed the duty and responsibility, among others, of supplying ovens and cooking appliances, every article of clothing, shelter and storage of all kinds, camp grounds, water and drainage facilities,

16

all cavalry, artillery and draught horses, mules, harness, ambulances, wagons and carts, veterinary service and supplies, forage for animals, and transportation not only for its own but for the supplies of all other departments. It builds wharfs and docks, charters ships and boats of every character and executes contracts for rail and wagon transportation.

TOO FEW OFFICERS.

At the beginning of the war this department contained but fifty-seven officers, a number below the needs of the regular army. It has been necessary for years to supplement its strength by details of officers from the line, the same as in other departments. The commissioned personnel had also to be increased.

UNABLE TO PREPARE.

At its supply depots were sufficient supplies for the wants of an army of 25,000, but no more. Congress having for years insisted upon economical appropriations in all branches of public service, and the Quartermaster's Department had at the time of the blowing up of the Maine been unable to make any advance preparations whatsoever for war. On March 9, it received an allotment from the $50,000,000 appropriated for the National defense, but the entire country was as little prepared for war and the production of war materials as were the staff departments of the army.

Canvas for tents was unobtainable, owing to the great demand to supply the Klondike; light materials for summer uniforms had to be either woven or brought from Europe. A uniform which afterward the Quartermaster's Department bought for from $3.50 to $4, cost officers who wanted them quickly from $20 to $35, and they were obliged to wait two weeks, or even a month, before the tailors could produce them. The wool for cloth uniforms had to be dyed, spun and woven. Open market purchases could only be made in limited amounts on account of legal restrictions.

DEPARTMENT'S HANDS TIED.

Skilled employes could not be hired beyond a fixed rate of pay, and in this way the Department found its hands tied and otherwise hampered in the way of supplying service for a vastly increased force. The limited appropriations made by Congress had deprived the Department of trained wagonmasters and packers. Pack mules and saddles had to be obtained. For service beyond the sea transports had to be purchased and fitted out as best possible in limited time for the transportation of soldiers. The United States never having engaged in foreign war, not a single troopship was available. The neutrality laws prevented their purchase abroad. No vessels except those of American build could engage in the coastwise transportation, even though chartered by the Government, and Congress was averse to granting American registry to foreign bottoms, forcing the Department into the purchase of foreign vessels.

NECESSITY FOR HASTE.

What had to be done must be done quickly. To have waited for the proper fitting up of the troopships would have kept the soldiers who planted the Stars and Stripes over Santiago and Manila in the United States until the present time, for it will be October 10 before the first really modern troopship belonging to the United States will be off the ways at Cramp's shipyards, and another will follow from the yards at Bath, Me., the first week in November. In the short space of time occupied by hostilities the Quartermaster's Department has performed its manifold duties with striking energy, and besides improvising sufficient transports has purchased the following for the use of troops:

Horses	17,119
Mules	21,090
Wagons	602
Ambulances	595
Harness (sets)	26,476
Blankets	516,012
Campaign hats	476,705
Blouses	170,106
Trousers	353,707
Shoes	707,837
Tents of all kinds	224,225
Field ovens	5,130
Bread ovens	150

In many cases it was not what was desired, or what was believed by experienced officers to be requisite, but it was what could be obtained. The old adage "any port in a storm" was the watchword, not only with this Department, but the entire War Office.

SUBSISTENCE DEPARTMENT.

Plenty of Supplies in Bulk Always on Hand for the Troops.

At the beginning of the war the Subsistence Department, being compelled by law to keep provisions for the army on a peace basis only, had thirty days' supplies on hand for the regular army, with no reserve stock, it not being in the interest of the soldiers or the Government to keep large supplies of food on hand for fear of deterioration, and the appropriation for the fiscal year had been almost entirely expended.

At no time has it been claimed that the subsistence supplies in bulk were not present with the troops at all times and in ample quantities wherever they were found, and weekly reports of quantities on hand were rendered, to prevent a shortage, even if requisitions failed to arrive.

GOOD COOKS NEEDED.

The food needed only proper cooking. Gen. Coppinger in his report says: "The regulars lived well. The volunteers in too many cases messed badly, but this was owing to the ignorance and inexperience of the officers, who did not know how to procure and care for the rations, and the ignorance of the cooks, who did not know how to cook them. I have been especially impressed by the comfortable messing of the regular soldiers close to my headquarters, while volunteer troops in the adjoining field were subsisting on chunks of ill-cooked beef and vile biscuit—an excellent field oven lying neglected and unused close by."

The War Department can furnish the articles, but it cannot cook the food and put it in the soldiers' mouths. The components of the ration are fixed by Congress, and its suitability or unsuitability rests with that body, and not with the Subsistence Department.

The rations are ample in quantity and made up of staples which, by careful and skillful use, enables the regular army always to make a considerable saving, which is sold for cash, and the money derived from such sales expended in the purchase of such varieties of food and delicacies as cannot be kept on hand, as the company commander may deem necessary to the health and contentment of his men. The volunteers might have done the same with proper experience and economy.

SMALL NUMBER OF OFFICERS.

At the outbreak of hostilities the Subsistence Department had but twenty-two officers, barely sufficient for the 25,000 men of the regular army, and an increase in the personnel was necessary to supply army corps, divisions, brigades, depots and transports with commissary officers.

Of the thirty-six appointed, sixteen were from the regular army, and to have made a greater number would have stripped some companies of their officers and rendered them inefficient; the new appointees, acting under trained chiefs, it was thought would soon gain experience in the special work that was to be done, and the President took the wise course of leaving the line of the regular army with enough officers to render it effective.

COMPLAINTS INVESTIGATED.

Complaints received at the Department were nearly all of a trivial character, but nevertheless were subjected to investigation, and in each case shown to be untrue and devoid of merit. Frequently it occurred that the men reported to have made complaints denied them when confronted with the evidence, and it was not infrequent that men who made complaint of insufficient food, when placed on the scales, showed that they had gained in weight since their enlistment. Investigation shows that men who subsisted upon the rations had less sickness than the men who ate indiscriminately of various articles for sale by the hucksters, or of other food found in the country.

The men cannot be blamed for this indiscretion; they did not know the danger they ran, nor the necessities for precaution. Six months would have made a regular of the volunteer.

TRANSPORT DISCOMFORTS.

Complaints have been made of the discomforts and lack of food provision on transports. Undoubtedly there is some basis for this; but as stated before, it must be remembered that such transports as were wanted could not be obtained, and many of the sick returning from Santiago knew in advance the hardships they would have to endure on some of the vessels; it was a choice between remaining in fever-ridden Cuba or returning to the United States. Both alternatives presented great hardships, and both the Government and the men chose the lesser to overcome the difficulty, and reduce the danger of death.

The surgeons received 60 cents per day per man to buy articles of diet for the sick, and in Santiago the amount allowed was 75 cents per day.

FAULT WITH THE LAW.

By law the Subsistence Department purchases the food. It is transported from the place of purchase to the place of issue by the Quartermaster's Department, cooked on stoves provided by the Quartermaster's Department, carried on the soldiers' persons and conveyed to their mouths by equipments provided by the Ordnance Department; and these three departments must under the law make connection at the soldiers' mouths. The fault, if any, exists with the law, and not with the departments.

THE MEDICAL DEPARTMENT.

Unjust Criticisms by Those Unaccustomed to the Horrors of War.

The medical department of the army seems to have come in for more than a just share of criticism and blame.

Prior to the blowing up of the Maine it had made no preparation for war. except to place the supplies on hand, which were ample for the existing army, in condition for ready issue; but immediately thereafter prompt steps were taken to increase the enlisted personnel of the medical corps, and to obtain supplies, especially those adapted to field service.

Necessity was at once created for medical, surgical, field and mess chests. litters and litter-slings, medical instruments and various other articles, all of special pattern, not in the market and the manufacture of which required time.

CONGRESS FAILED TO ACT.

The act organizing the volunteer army provided three hospital stewards to each regiment. On April 23, the Surgeon-General asked that twenty-five hospital corps privates be enlisted for each regiment; and for each division. one steward, one acting steward and fifty privates. Congress failed to carry out this recommendation, and it became necessary to increase the number of privates in the United States Hospital Corps sufficiently to meet the needs of the entire volunteer army of two hundred and fifty thousand.

Congress increased the number of hospital stewards to 200, and measures were at once taken to recruit the hospital corps as rapidly as possible. Men were obtained by transfers from the line, and by enlistment to the number of 7,000.

STORES SPECIALLY PREPARED.

Medical stores for use of an army in the field are not such as can be purchased in bulk in wholesale drug houses. They must be specially prepared and specially packed to economize space and withstand the dangers of transportation to which they may be subjected.

The number of medical officers allowed by law is inadequate in time of peace. The total number allowed is 192. There are at present thirteen vacancies. Of the number allowed by law six are required in the Surgeon-General's office and Army Medical Museum. Eleven are on duty at medical supply depots as chief surgeons of military departments. One is at the Soldier's Home, while fifty-six are at general hospitals on hospital ships as garrison posts; four are disabled by sickness, and five are on duty as chief surgeons of the Army Corps. This leaves ninety-seven medical officers available for duty with troops in the field. Of these thirty-five have been appointed brigade surgeons of volunteers and distributed among the various army corps. Since the declaration of war there has been a loss of two by death, and twenty-three are on sick leave. This deficiency in the regular medical officers made it necessary to employ more than 650 contract surgeons.

VOLUNTEER MEDICAL CORPS.

Steps were taken at once to organize the Volunteer Medical Corps. All appointments were made by the President, and every one on the recommendation of the Surgeon-General of the army and of other medical men whose opinions were of value; but the rapidity with which the volunteer army was organized prevented many of the contract surgeons from being subjected to examination, the urgency being so great that it was not practicable to have examining boards pass upon their qualifications. The Surgeon-General, however, endeavored as far as possible to obtain satisfactory professional indorsement before making a contract with an applicant. Most of the contract surgeons have displayed energy and efficiency, though time was insufficient for them to master the peculiar duties and requirements of military surgery and camp sanitation. One thing, however, was strictly enforced. If a contract surgeon, after reaching his post, was found incompetent, he was immediately discharged and his contract canceled.

FAULT WITH THE LAW.

The number of medical officers was fixed by Congress, and, if inadequate, the fault is with the law and not with the Department. True, deficiencies may be made up by employing acting assistant surgeons, but their salary is but $100 per month, and men possessing the great ability required of military surgeons cannot be expected to enter the service in great numbers for such small compensation.

Notwithstanding all these difficulties, requisitions were promptly filled and stores forwarded in abundance. In some cases congested railway travel prevented prompt delivery and early distribution.

INSTRUCTIONS FOR CAMPS

The sanitary condition of camps was under the supervision of the Surgeon-General, and the surgeons of the corps, divisions and brigades. Four days after the declaration of war the Surgeon-General issued a circular prescribing sanitary measures to protect the troops in the field, especially in tropical climates. The subject was treated in detail, and instructions given for the preservation of the health of troops; and again on August 8 attention was invited to the same subject. Camps were constantly and bountifully supplied with disinfectants, and if not used it was the fault of the surgeons in the field. In view of the fact that the army was hastily organized, and the men put into service with the briefest possible delay, the difficulties of providing for their medical wants, coupled with a lack of special knowledge of newly appointed medical officers, the rates of disease and death, as will be shown by the statistics below, were kept at a marvelously low figure. Delays and some confusion were inseparable from existing conditions. The machinery of the entire War Department was working at high pressure, and the human machine, like a mechanical contrivance, will, when working at its fullest speed for a long-continued period, either break down or occasionally produce imperfect results.

It is the history of all suddenly improvised armies that men suffer greatly from disease incident to their unaccustomed mode of life. The prevalence of disease, which, if occurring in civil life, would not attract particular attention, under the peculiar circumstances and the strong light of public scrutiny, become matters of criticism and comment.

Armies as hastily gathered together as that which waged the war with Spain, in a great many instances, bring the seeds of disease with them to the camps, as was evidenced in the cases of many men dying in the State camps before the regiments were mustered in, and many others within a week thereafter.

A DESPERATE TASK.

The task of the Medical Department is a desperate one. It is called upon to deal and come face to face with the horrors of war, in such places that persons entirely unacquainted with such sights and scenes may visit and behold, but are helpless to aid. It is no wonder that the sights of mutilation and carnage and the sounds of delirious moaning, shock the nerves and appal the senses of those who have been spared a view of the dreadful flow of human blood and merciless mangling of human form.

No more horrible place can be imagined than the battlefield hospital, with its gruesome pile of amputated feet and arms, quivering, mangled and bloody, piled without, while the victims within are groaning under anesthetics or wailing with pain in their first awakening moments.

SUCH IS WAR.

But such is war, and those who clamor for it must expect nothing else. Possibly after a great engagement men may lie wounded for two or three days, or even more, without aid. Such cases occur after every great battle. Men fall in hidden places or crawl away to seek shelter from missiles or to avoid capture. Sometimes they are never found. Some of them may die a lingering death of pain and starvation. Read the long list of missing after every battle and drop a tear and utter a prayer. Such cases will occur no matter what the number or how great the ability of the surgeons in attendance. With 10,000 loving comrades searching for fallen heroes in the thorny thickets surrounding Santiago, forty-two men yet are missing. Is it a wonder that with such diligent search a few might be found who had patiently lingered for aid, and when recovered, is it not a case for rejoicing rather than for wrath and criticism?

NO REASON FOR CRITICISM.

If men were carried to hospitals denuded of clothing the mere fact should not excite criticism. The litter bearers perhaps wore but a shirt, trousers and shoes. If because some wounded soldier gave his clothing for bandages to save the life of a comrade in greater danger, or if his clothing was torn from his weakened body by thieves, should he be denied the immediate benefits of hospital or dressing station, or should he wait until clothing can be sent merely to satisfy a sentimentality?

The history of every army is that when untrained men in large numbers are gathered into large camps they are attacked by disease; and no war has ever been waged where disease was not vastly more deadly than the bullet.

STRIKING COMPARISONS.

The deaths from all causes in our army from May 1 to date were 2,910 out of a total force of 274,717, or a percentage of 1.059. These figures when brought in comparison with the losses of former expeditions to the West Indies, show how insignificant our death rate has been. In the English expedition to the West Indies the land forces numbered 14,000. The losses were 1,790 officers and men killed, wounded and missing, and the losses by disease were about 50 per cent of the total force.

The French expedition to the West Indies in 1802 was perhaps the most disastrous in losses from disease. The French army loss in four months from disease alone was 15,207 men, out of a total of 58,545, a mortality of 868 per thousand. Of the 8,275 survivors 3,000 were reported unfit for duty.

The figures as to the loss of the Spanish from disease in this war are not obtainable yet, but one statement alone shows how greatly the Spanish army suffered. Spain has carried to Cuba during the present war 135,000 men. There now remains but 85,000, and thousands of these are incapacitated and will have to be carried back to Spain in the hospitals. Compared with her loss from disease, the losses in battle by the Spanish have been insignificant.

OTHER SOUTHERN CAMPAIGNS.

The death rates of other campaigns in southern climates bring out by comparison our small losses. The loss of the campaign in Algeria, in 1848, was 77.81 per 1.000. The expedition to Tunis, in 1881, suffered a mortality of 61.30 per 1,000. The French losses in Cochin China expedition (1861-62) was 100 men per 1,000. In the French campaign to Madagascar (1884-85) the loss was from 70 to 110 per 1,000. The English campaign in Burmah (1824-26) had a loss of 72 per 1,000.

In Napoleon's campaign to Russia, his loss by wounds and disease amounted to 243,000 men out of 363,000. In Napoleon's campaign of 1813, against Germany, but 85,000 out of his original 500,000 returned. In the Turko-Russian War of 1828-29, the Russians lost 60,000 men, mostly by disease.

CIVIL WAR RECORDS.

In the first year of the War of the Rebellion the sick in some regiments ran as high as 45 per cent. In the Army of the Potomac the average number of constant sick per 1,000 was 61; in the Valley of the Mississippi, 116, and in the Department of West Virginia, 162.

Of the British Army in time of peace, 6½ per cent are in the hospital. The British Army in the Peninsular War, under the Duke of Wellington, had 21 per cent sick in hospital, which increased at one time to 33 per cent.

These rates were exceeded in the British army of the Crimea, where the constant sick rate was 26.6 per cent; the annual rate of mortality being 3 per cent in battle and 20.6 per cent by disease and accident.

DEATHS IN FOREIGN WARS.

The rate of mortality from all causes experienced by our army in the war with Mexico was one-half greater than it was in the War of the Rebellion, and of the British troops in the Peninsula more than double, and in the British War of the Crimea more than three times that experienced by the Union armies in the War of the Rebellion. To sum up from extracts of military statistics of the United States, the deaths in the volunteer forces of the United States (June, 1861, to February, 1862,) under more favorable conditions than those experienced by the volunteer forces of our present army, were from wounds received in action 8.6 per cent, disease and accident 44.6, or a total of 53.2. The annual death rate in both Europe and America of civilians of the military age is nearly one-half the death rate experienced in the army of the United States in the present war, from all causes. During the war with Mexico the mortality was 118 per thousand; 14 from wounds received in action, including killed in battle, and 104 from disease and accidents.

During the Spanish Peninsular campaign under Wellington (1811-1814) the annual death rate experienced by the British forces was 165 per thousand, of which 52 was from wounds and 113 from disease; in the campaign of the allies against Russia in the Crimea the rate experienced in hostilities for the period of the first nine months, not including those killed in battle, was 232 per thousand, 30 being from wounds and 202 from disease.

THIS WAR'S STATISTICS.

Deaths from all causes between May 1 and September 30, inclusive, as reported to the Adjutant-General's office up to date in our army are: Killed, 23 officers and 257 enlisted men; died of wounds, 4 officers; died of disease, 80 officers and 2,485 enlisted men; total, 107 officers and 2,803 enlisted men.

This is an aggregate of 2,910 out of a total force of 274,717 officers and men, a percentage of 1,059, or, if continued for an entire year, would result in a loss of only 4.41 per cent, or, reducing to a basis of actual number of deaths per year, makes a total loss from all causes of but 25.5 per thousand, three from wounds received in action, and 22.4 from diseases and accidents, or considerably less than one-half the death rate for the same period of the Civil War.

THE DIVISION HOSPITAL.

The division hospital became the subject of peculiar and vicious attacks, either from ignorance of its adaptability to a state of war or from jealousies arising in regiments. The best military authorities in the great armies of the world unite in pronouncing it the only successful method of caring for the sick of a great army.

Regiments are organized to move and to fight. If they are hampered by their own sick in their own hospitals, when marching orders are received they must either be delayed by transporting their sick to some other hospitals or be burdened with their care upon the march.

The presence, too, of sick and wounded men so near noise and confusion of a regimental camp is not calculated to hasten their recovery, and the effect of their presence is depressing upon the able-bodied.

VOLUNTEER SIGNAL CORPS.

Its Admirable Work at the Front, Though Belated in Starting.

It was nearly a month after war was declared before authority of Congress was secured for the organization of the Volunteer Signal Corps, but in the short period of time intervening before the opening of the campaign, to the small regular establishment of sixty officers and men had been added a volunteer force of one hundred and sixteen officers and one thousand enlisted men, well organized and so perfectly equipped that in every camp there had been established a complete telephone exchange and telegraphic system; and at Santiago the firing line was so well supplied with means of communication that it took but twenty minutes for a message to pass from the rifle pits to the Executive Mansion in Washington.

In the Philippines they constructed and maintained telegraph and telephone lines in the advance trenches, and wherever the troops were, there was the Signal Corps also present, thoroughly equipped and efficient.

THE ENGINEER CORPS.

Their Work in Coast Defense and During Santiago Campaign.

The duties of the Engineer Corps of the United States Army in time of war may be considered conveniently under two heads: First, in relation to the seacoast defenses of the country; second, in relation to the operations of armies in the field.

Under the first heading the duties of the corps consist in planning and constructing permanent works of defense for the protection of our seacoast towns and cities, and in the planting and operation of submarine mines blocking the entrance thereto.

Under the second heading their duties consist as staff officers in planning, laying out and constructing temporary fortifications, hasty intrenchments, roads, bridges, etc., and in making reconnaissances and military maps. In this latter class of duties engineer troops are largely employed whenever their services can be obtained.

DEFENSES WEAK.

At the outbreak of the war with Spain our seacoast defenses were scarcely in a condition to have withstood a well-directed naval attack upon our coasts. Strenuous efforts were, however, made to mount every available gun in such batteries as were then in progress, and to provide temporary batteries for old-style armament at a number of places otherwise wholly defenseless. In an exceedingly short time a large number of guns, new and old, were in readiness for service, and would have given a good account had any hostile attack. taken place.

TORPEDO WORK.

Deficiency in submarine mining material threatened to render submarine operations futile at the outbreaking of hostilities but by taking advantage of the entire manufacturing resources of the country, and working night and day, torpedo defenses were placed in position and maintained in good order throughout the entire period of. active hostilities at all principal harbors.

ENGINEERS IN SANTIAGO.

In the Santiago campaign the operations of the engineer troops were, in consequence of inadequate numbers, limited to the more technical classes of engineer work, such as road repairs and construction, repairs to railroads, construction of landing piers and military reconnaissances.

The various engineer officers assigned to duty on the staffs of corps and division commanders in the different camps were employed in laying out the sites of camps, providing for water supplies and sanitation, in the instruction of troops in military reconnaissances and map making, and in the construction of hasty field intrenchments.

JOHN S. SHRIVER.

Money, Coinage and Prices

JULY 1896, AND JANUARY, 1898

● ● ●

INCREASE OF WAGES

AND

REVIVAL OF INDUSTRIES

UNDER REPUBLICAN POLICY

● ● ●

From the remarks of

SENATOR SHELBY M. CULLOM

of Illinois

In the Senate, Friday, January 28, 1898

Senator SHELBY M. CULLOM,

OF ILLINOIS.

In the Senate, Friday, January 28, 1898.

———

Mr. CULLOM said:

I wish now to submit a few observations not directly related to the pending resolution. I have gathered some statistics to which I wish to call the attention of the Senate. I hold in my hand the official figures of the Treasury Department showing the money in circulation in the United States July 1, 1896, and January 1, 1898.

	July 1, 1896.	Jan. 1, 1898.
Gold coin	$454,905,064	$547,568,360
Standard silver dollars	52,116,904	61,491,073
Subsidiary silver	60,204,451	65,720,308
Gold certificates	42,198,119	36,557,689
Silver certificates	330,657,191	376,695,592
Treasury notes	95,245,047	103,443,936
United States notes	224,249,868	262,480,927
Currency certificates	31,890,000	43,315,000
National bank notes	215,168,122	223,827,755
Total	$1,506,434,966	$1,721,100,640

Gain in circulation in eighteen months, $214,665,674.

We have heard much about the distress in the country and the disposition on the part of the Republican party and its Administration to neglect the people and to subserve only the interests of the bondholders, and I submit whether we have not done measurably well to increase the circulation of the country in eighteen months since the nomination of the candidates for the Presidency in 1896 $214,665,674.

The addition to the currency of the country by coinage of the United States Mints since July 1, 1896, is as follows:

July 1, 1896, to January 1, 1897	$39,129,305
January 1, 1897, to January 1, 1898	96.041,882
Total	$135,171,187

MR. BRYAN ANSWERED.

I call the attention of the Senate to the fact that Mr. Bryan, in his Greensboro, N. C., speech in 1896, asserted that Senator Sherman had stated that there should be an addition of $42,000,000 per annum to the circulating medium of the country to keep pace with the growth of population, and he said: "What provision has the Republican party made for the supply of the money that we need? None whatever." Yet it will be observed that the amount of money coined by the mints of the United States since the beginning of the campaign of 1896 is more than double the increase named by Senator Sherman and approved by Mr. Bryan in the speech referred to above.

I call the attention of the Senate to another table, compiled from Bradstreet's Journal, comparing the prices of articles mentioned on January 1, 1898, with those of July 1, 1896, the nearest obtainable date to Mr. Bryan's nomination. They show that in practically all articles which farmers produce the prices now received are much higher than when Mr. Bryan was nominated and when his party insisted that improved conditions could only come through the free and unlimited coinage of silver; also, that in a large proportion of the articles which the farmers and others must purchase for daily use the prices have fallen. The figures relate to New York markets, except where otherwise specified.

INCREASED PRICE OF FARM PRODUCTS.

Article.	July 1,1896.	Jan. 1, 1898.
Wheat, No. 2, red winter............per bushel..	$0.64⅜	$0.98¾
Oats ....do....	.21½	.28¼
Barley No. 2 (Milwaukee)................do....	.30	.42
Rye ....do....	.37½	.55
Flour, winter............per barrel............	3.25	4.25
Beeves, best (Chicago)..........per 100 pounds..	4.65	5.20
Sheep (Chicago)	4.00	4.50
Hogs	3.40	3.50
Horses, average (Chicago)......................	65.00	80.00
Beef carcasses (Chicago)............per pound..	.05½	.07
Hogs' carcasses (Chicago).................do....	.03⅞	.05 3-5
Mutton carcasses (Chicago)................do....	.05½	.07¾
Eggs ....per dozen..	.12½	.25
Beef ....per barrel..	8.50	10.50
Pork, mess ....do....	8.25	8.75
Bacon, smoked (Chicago)............per pound..	.04⅜	.05
Lard ....do....	.04 1-5	.05
Butter ....do....	.15	.22
Cheese ....do....	.06⅝	.08½
Beans ....per bushel..	1.15	1.40
Potatoes, eastern..................per barrel..	.75	2.00
Onions	1.50	2.50
Wool, Ohio and Pennsylvania X (Boston)........	.16	.27
Hides	.17	.20
Flax	2.25	3.25
Hops	.07	.16
Tobacco, medium (Louisville)......................	.11	.15½
Cotton seed (Houston)..........................	.08	.09½
Lumber, pine, yellow............................	17.00	15.75
Timber, Eastern spruce..........................	15.00	14.50
Timber, hemlock (Pennsylvania)..................	11.00	11.00
Nails, wire..........................per keg..	2.80	1.75
Tin plates (Pittsburg)..........................	3.65	2.85
Cotton sheeting	.04¾	.04¼
Print cloths	.02½	.02¼
Steel rails (Pittsburg)..................per ton..	28.00	18.25
Coal, anthracite	4.25	4.00
Coal, bituminous (Chicago)......................	2.75	2.75
McConnellsville coke	2.00	1.75
Phosphate rock (South Carolina)........per ton..	5.25	5.00
Quinine ....per ounce..	.30	.28

I present the table because our distinguished friend the Senator from Colorado was talking much about the blistered hand of the farmer, and I desire to show that the farmer did not suffer so badly last year as compared with previous years.

Mr. GEAR. In 1896, during the campaign, our Democratic friends carried in one hand the Democratic platform and in the other Bradstreet's and

Dun's reports, showing that they trusted them implicitly, and now they deny everything therein stated.

Mr. CULLOM. As a matter of fact, I think the country generally, without reference to party politics, regards Bradstreet's report as entirely impartial.

I want to submit a statement showing the resumption of manufacturing activities and increase of wages since the enactment of the Dingley law, taken from Bradstreet's, a generally recognized journal of trade, finance, and public economy:

THE RECORD OF THE MONTH OF AUGUST.

Cleveland (Ohio) rolling mills resume work, employing 2,000 men.

Wages increased 16½ per cent. on Louisiana plantations of Leon Godchau, the largest sugar producer in the United States.

Wheaton & Co.'s glass works, at Millville, N. J., resume work.

Ensign Car and Manufacturing Company, Huntington, W. Va., resume work.

Cotton mills at Lancaster, Pa., resume operations, employing 1,000 hands.

Edge Tools Works at Ogontz, Pa., resume work.

Philadelphia and Reading coal and iron collieries, near Pottsville, Pa., have resumed.

American Watch Company, Waltham, Mass., resumes work.

The Crescent tin-plate mill, Cleveland, Ohio, the second largest mill in the United States, resumes work.

Rolling mills at Lebanon, Ohio, resume operations.

Birmingham, Ala., rolling mills resume work, employing 1,200 men.

Gate City, Ala., rolling mills resume work.

American Wire Nail Company, St. Louis, increase working force from 400 to 1,000 men.

Victor Window Glass Company, St. Louis, increases its plant 50 per cent.

American Tin Plate Company, St. Louis, increases its working force 600 men.

Reading, Pa., iron works resume, giving employment to 700 men.

Richardson & Boynton, stove works, New Jersey, resume.

Norwalk Woolen Mills, Winnipauk, Conn., resume work, notifying employees that night work will also be required.

Birmingham, Ala., rolling mills resume, employing 700 men.

Alabama Pipe Works, at Bessemer, Ala., resume.

East Lake Woolen Mills, Bridgeton, N. J., resume work.

Providence Coal Company Mines, Scranton, Pa., resume after two years' idleness.

Delaware Iron Works, Newcastle, Del., resume, giving employment to 500 hands.

Wall paper factory at Newark, Del., begins operations.

Advance of 20 cents per ton on prices paid miners in Boyd coal mines, Nashville, Ill.

Pottery manufacturers of New Jersey announce advance in wages averaging 12½ per cent.

Southern Railway increases working hours in its shops at Birmingham, Ala.

INCREASE IN WORKING TIME.

Alabama Great Southern Railroad Company increases working time from five hours per day to nine hours, affecting 1,000 men.

Hutchinson, Cole & Co., manufacturers of shirts, Norwalk, Conn., resume, giving employment to 500 operatives.

United States Rubber Company, Millville, Mass., increases working hours.

Hetzel & Co., worsted goods manufacturers at Chester, Pa., restore wages of 1892, affecting several hundred hands.

Mitchell-Lewis Wagon Works, Racine, Wis., increases time to twelve hours per day.

Hartford, Vt., Woolen Company restore wages of 1892 rates.

Methuen, Mass., cotton mills, employing 500 hands, resume work.

Pottstown, Pa., Iron Mills resume work, running night and day.

Whitaker Iron Company, Wheeling, W. Va., resumes work.

Consul-General Osborne reports that leading tin-plate and woolen manufacturers of Great Britain are preparing to transfer their manufactories to the United States.

Heskell & Barker Car Company, Michigan City, Ind., increase time to twelve hours, affecting work of 1,500 men.

Hillsboro, N. H., woolen mills start up on full time.

Britton Tin Plate Company, Cleveland, Ohio, resumes work.

Union Rolling Mills, Cleveland, Ohio, resume work.

All railroad shops at Birmingham, Ala., increase working time to ten hours per day.

Washington Steel and Tin Plate Company, Washington, Pa., resumes work at double its former capacity.

Pennsylvania Railroad locomotive shops at Altoona, Pa., increase working time to ten hours per day.

Girard Union Iron and Steel Works, Youngstown, Ohio, resumes after a long shut-down.

Read Carpet Company, Bridgeport, Conn., resumes operations.

National Tube Works, McKeesport, Pa., increase wages 10 per cent.

Fall River (Mass.) Iron Works, employing 2,700 men, resume work.

American Printing Company, Fall River, increases working hours to full time.

Columbus, Hocking Valley and Toledo Railroad shops increase working hours from half time to 10 hours per day.

Chicago, Rock Island and Pacific Railroad Company adds 30 clerks to its force in auditing office.

Illinois Steel Company, at Chicago, Milwaukee and Joliet, resumes work with increased force.

SEPTEMBER.

Great Falls Manufacturing Company, at Somerville, N. H., resume work with 2,000 hands.

Eight puddle furnaces of Ellis and Lessig Steel Company, Pottstown, Pa., resume work.

Glasgow, Pa., Rolling Mill resumes after a year's idleness.

Philadelphia and Reading machine shops increase working hours to full time.

Schuylkill, Pa., Coal Exchange advances miners' wages 6 per cent.

Sharpsville, Pa., iron furnaces resume work.

Falls Manufacturing Company, Norwich Conn., start up on full time.

Sampson & Williams's woolen mill, Fairfield, Me., increase hours to double time.

New York Herald publishes official estimates of trades union, showing that 36,000 workmen in New York city who were idle in 1896 are employed in 1897.

Reports from 20 large iron plants in Mahoning Valley, Ohio, indicate business 70 per cent. better than one year ago.

Corunna Coal Company, Owosso, Mich., advances miners' wages 5 cents per ton.

Baltimore and Ohio Railroad Company reports the demand for freight cars in excess of supply.

Isaia (Ohio) Cordage Mills, idle several years, resume work on full time.

East Lake Woolen Mills, Bridgeton, Pa., resume work after three years' idleness.

Wead Paper Mill, Malone, N. Y., resumes after two years' idleness.

Advance in wages of coal miners in Ohio, West Virginia, and elsewhere, affecting many thousands of men.

Cleveland Rolling Mill announces sale of 1,000 tons of bar steel in Birmingham, England; and Appleton, Wis., paper mills announce sale of 2,000 tons of print paper for Japan.

American Wire Nail Works, at Madison, Ind., resume work.

Lamp chimney factories at Madison, Ind., employing 800 hands, resume work.

National Rolling Mills, Pittsburg, Pa., resume work in puddling department after long idleness.

American Steel Casting Company, Sharon, Pa., doubles the capacity of its manufacturing establishments.

Bellaire (Ohio) Steel Company resumes work, with new $500,000 blast furnace in operation.

Tip-Top Coke Works, Scottdale, Pa., resume work after an idleness of three years.

Reports from Pennsylvania coke fields show an increase of 886 ovens in operation within twelve days' time.

Monadnock Cotton Mills, Claremont, N. H., increase schedule from half time to full time.

Lindsay & McCutcheon's Iron Mills, Allegheny, Pa., advance wages.

Peninsular Car Works resume operations in all departments, increasing force from 2,500 to 3,500 men.

One of the largest soap manufactories in England announces establishment of a large factory in the United States and construction of a village for its employees.

OCTOBER.

Philadelphia and Reading Company increases working hours in its locomotive departments.

Woolen mill operators at Chambersburg, Pa., advance wages.

Red Stone Coal, Oil and Coke Company begins work in its coke plant, built five years ago, but never operated in full until now.

Brooke Iron Company, Birdsboro, Pa., increase output 20 per cent.

Sharpsville, Pa., furnace works resume after more than one year's idleness.

Reading, Pa., Iron and Pipe Company increases hours to double time.

Cumberland Valley Railroad shops increase to ten hours per day for the first time in several years.

Seyfert Rolling Mills, Naomi, Pa., resume work.

Warren Tube Works, Warren, Ohio, increase wages 10 per cent.

Minnesota Iron Company increases wages of all employees 10 per cent.

Large increase in blast furnaces in operation at Birmingham, Ala., reported.

Hollidaysburg, Pa., iron and nail works resume after a long period of idleness.

Sharon, Pa., iron works resume, including thirty-six puddling furnaces; increase of employees, 25 per cent. over 1896.

Coal miners at Des Moines, Iowa, give a 10 per cent. increase of wages.

Disston Saw Works, Tacony, Pa., resume work on full time, employing 1,000 men, after four years' of partial idleness.

Bellefonte, Pa., glass works resume operation.

Lake Erie, Alliance and Southern Railroad advances wages 10 per cent. and restores employment to all employees laid off during the year.

Reeves Iron Company, Canal Dover, Ohio, resumes after a long idleness.

Wilhelm Bicycle Works, Hamburg, Pa., increases wages 5 per cent.

Wages of cornice and skylight workers in New York and Brooklyn advanced.

Old Dominion Iron and Nail Company, Richmond, Va., resume work in horseshoe rolling plant.

Wages of employees in Howard-Harrison Pipe Works, Bessemer, Pa., advanced.

East Lake Woolen Mills, Bridgeton, N. J., resume work.

Work resumed in thirty-four furnaces of Porkhouse Iron Mills, Allegheny, Pa.

Naumkeag Mills, Salem, Mass., increase time from four days per week to full time.

IRON MILLS RESUME.

Several iron mills at Sharon, Pa., announce resumption after long idleness.

New York beet-sugar factory, Rome, N. Y., announces its first production of beet sugar.

Pennsylvania Railroad Company places orders for 40,000 tons of steel rails to be delivered before January 1, 1898.

Postal authorities at Washington announce increase of 7 per cent. in business of post offices in thirty largest cities, comparing September, 1897, with same month of 1896.

Olneyville, R. I., woolen mills restore 1892 wages, an average of over 20 per cent. increase.

Wages advanced in the Riverside, Weybosset, Manton and Lymansville, R. I., mills.

Lawrence Carpet Mills, Philadelphia, Pa., resume operations on full time, with increased machinery.

Thomas Iron Company, Allentown, Pa., resumes operations.

Frankstown Rolling Mill, Pittsburg, resumes work, employing 1,000 men.

New steel manufacturing plant announced by Standard Steel Company at Pittsburg, to employ 1,000 men.

Columbia Steel Mill, Uniontown, Pa., announces resumption after a long period of idleness.

NOVEMBER.

Basic steel plant in operation at Middlesboro, Ky., for first time in several years.

Vale Mills, Nashua, N. H., resumed work after long idleness.

Tremont Worsted Mills, Methuen, Mass., increased wages from 10 to 20 per cent.

Carpenter Steel Works, Reading, Pa., increased schedule to double time.

Andrew Bros., blast furnace, Youngstown, Ohio, advances wages 10 per cent.

Bachman & Co., Philadelphia, advance weavers' wages 5 per cent., affecting earnings of 1,000 persons.

Mahoning, Pa., blast furnaces advance wages 10 per cent., affecting 3,000 employees.

Allegheny county, Pa., reports every blast furnace within its borders in operation.

Berkshire, Mass., glass works resume operation.

Bethlehem, Pa., steel mills resume work, employing 1,000 men.

Lehigh Zinc Company, Bethlehem, Pa., announces large additions in its manufacturing establishment and increase of employees.

Wages increased from 10 to 20 per cent. at Alice Furnace, Sharon, Pa.

Laconia, N. H., car works resume operations, employing several hundred men.

Wages of 2,000 employees of Wheeling, W. Va., Iron and Steel Company advanced 10 per cent.

East Liverpool, Ohio, potteries announce that their pay rolls have doubled over those of August, most of the establishments running double time.

WAGES ADVANCE TEN PER CENT.

Wages advanced 10 per cent. in Eddy Woolen Mills, Fall River, Mass., affecting several hundred hands.

Moore & Sinnott Distillery, Gibsontown, Pa., resumes after two years' idleness.

Shamokin, Pa., coal mine operators announce their pay roll the largest in several years.

Twenty per cent. advance in wages announced by Bessemer, Carbon, and other limestone companies of Mahoning Valley.

Ten per cent. increase in wages announced by Chapin Mining Company, Pewable Mining Company, the Antoine Ore Company, Aragon Ore Company, and Pennsylvania Iron Mining Company, of Iron Mountain, Mich., affecting over 2,000 men.

British silk manufacturers, A. W. Pierson & Co., of Southfort, England, establish silk works at Passaic, N. J., to employ large number of hands.

Wages of 15,000 employees of Missouri Pacific Railway advanced 10 per cent.

Ten per cent. advance in wages of employees of New York Knife Company, Walden. N. Y.

DECEMBER.

Fifteen per cent. advance in wages at Wyoming Lace Mills, Wilkesbarre, Pa.

Ten per cent. advance in wages in Jones & Laughlin's iron mills, Pittsburg.

President Garland, of the Amalgamated Association of Iron and Steel Workers, reports tin-plate mills generally filled with orders and steady work in prospect.

Work resumed at puddle and nail-plate mills of Chesapeake Works, Harrisburg, Pa.

Work resumed in McKee Bros.' chimney shops, Jeannette, Pa.

Myers Company works, Beaver Falls, Pa., increase schedule to full running time.

Miners wages advanced 20 per cent. at Creede, Colo.

Lackawanna Company resumes work in Avondale colliery, producing 700 tons of coal per day, after a long shut-down.

Northern Illinois coal miners resume work.

Glass factories controlled by the American Glass Company, resume work with an advance of 12 per cent. in wages.

Ten per cent. increase in wages given employees in wire nail works at Newcastle, Ind.

Wages advanced 15 per cent. in mines of Coronna Coal Company and Virginia and Alabama Coal Company, Alabama.

Resumption of work in window-glass factories, giving employment to 15,000 men, with advanced wages in most cases.

JANUARY, 1898.

Advance of 12½ per cent. in wages of pottery establishments in New Jersey and other Eastern States.

Paxton furnaces, Harrisburg, Pa., resume work.

Flint-glass factories in Ohio Valley and elsewhere resume work on full time.

Saxony Knitting Mill, Little Falls, N. Y., increases schedule to full time.

Five per cent. increase given employees of Humaston & Beckley Cutlery Manufacturing Company, New Britain, Conn.

St. Paul railway shops at Milwaukee announce large increase in employees and work, with greater demand than at any time since 1892.

Pennsylvania Railroad Company ordered 100,000 tons of new steel rails.

Illinois Steel Company, South Chicago, announces increase in running hours.

Increase of wages by Metropolitan Iron and Land Company, Ironwood, Mich., affecting 1,000 employees.

Illinois Steel Company announces extension of its works, which will add 1,000 men to its pay roll.

Pennsylvania coke manufacturers report the 1897 output of coke at 6,915,054 tons, valued at $11,409,835.

Mr. BACON. Does the table which the Senator from Illinois has presented take into account the New England cotton factories?

Mr. CULLOM. I do not know whether it does or not. I think it does, and that some of the Southern factories are mentioned in it as well. There are a great number of the factories named where work has begun in which, under the former Administration, nothing was being done whatever, or very little.

Mr. BACON. The former Administration maintained the same financial policy as the present one.

Mr. GALLINGER. If the Senator from Illinois will permit me, in answer to the observation of the Senator from Georgia, I will say that the great Amoskeag corporation in Manchester, N. H., employing 10,000 people, was idle a considerable part of last summer, and is now running at a less rate of wages than was paid two or three years ago, but the operatives are better off, they think, to get reasonably good wages rather than to be entirely idle, as they were for a considerable time under the Wilson Act.

HUNDREDS OF ESTABLISHMENTS RESUMING WORK.

Mr. CULLOM. One would suppose from listening to the debate of the last two or three days that there had been no improvement in the condition of affairs within the last year, while the list I have submitted mentions hundreds of establishments which have resumed work and are now doing business and have been doing business since the Republican party came into power.

I desire to insert a brief paragraph from the speech of the honorable Secretary of the Treasury at Philadelphia a few nights ago in relation to wages:

"This brings the question to the test of fact. It has been asserted upon authority, and I believe it to be approximately true, that within the period 1872-1891 prices have fallen an average of 27½ per cent. I am at liberty, therefore, to adopt the same authority as to the course of wages. It appears from the exhaustive figures of the Commissioner of Labor, the authority cited, that within the period 1872-1891 wages have increased an average of

10 per cent. Taking the greater power of wages to command things by reason of their lower price, the economic advantage gained by labor it still further emphasized.

"In 1872 $100 in gold would buy a certain amount of living; in 1891, prices having fallen, $100 would buy 27½ per cent more than it did in 1872, and wages having increased 10 per cent. in the meantime, the same work which was paid $100 in 1872 received $110 in 1891. From the double advantage of decreased prices and increased wages it follows that in 1891 the same labor would purchase 51.7 per cent. more of living than it did in 1872. Let us apply these advantages by example.

"In 1891 the labor that supported fifteen people supported only ten in 1872. In 1891, from the same labor as in 1872, a man living upon the same scale would have over one-third of his wages to put in bank or better provide for his family.

"I am further borne out in this demonstration by the statistics of savings banks covering the period under consideration. Since 1871 the number of depositors in such institutions has increased from less than 2,000,000 to more than 5,000,000, and the average per capita saving in the United States has increased 86 per cent."

I also submit a statement in relation to exports in 1897:

HEAVY EXPORTS DURING 1897.

"A comparison of the exports of domestic articles during the year 1897 and the preceding year of 1896 shows that notwithstanding the enactment of a protective tariff law our productions have gone abroad in even greater quantities than under a low tariff measure. In the first eleven months of 1897 the value of the exports of agricultural implements was $5,149,000 against $4,527,000 for the first eleven months of 1896. The value of cattle exported in the first eleven months of 1897 was $35,498,000 against $33,621,000 in 1896. The value of the horses exported in these eleven months of 1897 was $5,170,000 against $3,282,000 in 1896.

"The value of sheep exported in the first eleven months of 1897 was $1,259,000 against $1,891,000 in 1896, showing a falling off in the exportation of these animals. This, however, is more than satisfactorily accounted for by the fact that the sheep raisers of the country are building up their flocks, and many farmers are branching out into sheep raising and wool growing. Of barley, the exports increased from $5,555,000 in 1896 to $6,535,000 in the eleven months mentioned in 1897. Some very gratifying figures are found in the exportation of corn, which in 1897 amounted to $53,441,000 against $39.-382,000 in 1896, and corn meal $1,209,000 in 1897 against $551,000 in 1896.

"The exportation of oats has increased from $6,796,000 in 1896 to $11,852,-000 in 1897; oatmeal, from $789,000 to $1,025,000; rye, from $2,038,000 to $4,362,000. Of course in wheat the contrast is marked, the value of the exports of the first eleven months of 1896 being $51,356,000, against $87,412,000 in 1897. The value of the total exportations of breadstuffs was $160,000,000 the first eleven months of 1896, against $222,000,000 in the corresponding period of 1897.

"The exports of carriages, cars, etc., have risen from $5,924,000 in the first eleven months of 1896 to $9,393,000 in the corresponding period of 1897. Of hog products the exports in 1896 were $27,927,000 against $35,566,000 in 1897; of butter, the exports of 1896 were $3,578,000, against $4,412,000 in 1897; of cheese, $3,512,000, against $5,212,000 in 1897; of vegetables, $1,678,000, against $2,231,000 in 1897; of wood manufactures, $7,413,000, against $9,017,000, and of lumber, $10,548,000, against $12,537,000."

THE
TELLER RESOLUTION

FROM THE REMARKS OF

Hon. NELSON DINGLEY, of Maine

Hon. ALBERT J. HOPKINS, of Illinois

Hon. THOS. H. TONGUE, of Oregon

Hon. D. B. HENDERSON, of Iowa

Hon. CHAS. H. GROSVENOR, of Ohio

Hon. J. P. DOLLIVER, of Iowa

IN THE HOUSE OF REPRESENTATIVES

January 31, 1898

THE TELLER RESOLUTION

IN THE HOUSE OF REPRESENTATIVES,

January 31, 1898

MR. DINGLEY ON THE TELLER RESOLUTION.

The House having under consideration Senate concurrent (Teller) resolution No. 22, relating to the payment of the bonded obligations of the Government—

Mr. DINGLEY said:

Mr. Speaker: The pending Senate resolution is not a joint resolution which, when duly enacted and approved, would have the force of law. It is simply a concurrent resolution which does not require the approval of the Executive, and which, even if adopted also by the House, would be only the expression of the opinion of the two Houses of Congress.

Its importance, therefore, lies in the fact that, if concurred in by the House, it would legitimately and inevitably be regarded, not only here but by the world, as the expression of the deliberate judgment of a majority of the American people as to their standard of honor and good faith in the discharge not only of national but also of private obligations.

At the outset it is important to strip from the issue presented by the pending resolution all the subterfuges which have been resorted to to conceal or cloud its real character under the conditions which exist to-day and to obtain a clear understanding of its meaning and significance.

THROWING DUST IN THE EYES OF OUR PEOPLE.

Let it be borne in mind, then, that this resolution is not presented for the purpose of securing an expression by Congress as to the power or legal rights of the Government either as to the payment of its obligations or as to what may be declared legal tender. It is throwing dust in the eyes of our own people and of the world to assume that we are determining a question of power or even of technical legal right. No one denies that this or any other nation has the power to pay in full or in part or none of its obligations, in gold, or silver, or paper, or copper, according to its pleasure. Payment can not be enforced against a sovereign nation. Its obligations are measured by its own sense of honor and good faith.

But even if this sense of honor is at any time blunted, as was Shylock's, by dwelling on a narrow view of the letter rather than the spirit of the obligation, the intelligent selfishness of a nation, which is to live not simply for a generation but for centuries, ought to lead it—and wherever a nation is wisely governed, does lead it—to so scrupulously maintain its pledges in both letter and spirit as to preserve its credit untarnished, and thereby not only make it possible to borrow at the lowest rate of interest, but also to make it easy to obtain loans in exigencies, which are sure, sooner or later, to come to every nation. A nation's honor and credit, I may say to gentlemen on the other side who applauded so jubilantly when the pending resolution was brought into this Hall, are among its most priceless possessions—aye, its title deed to permanence and prosperity.

Gentlemen on the other side, who so exultantly applauded under the impression that they were hitting the hated holder of bonds issued by the Government to fund the debt incurred in defending and saving the Union in its years of adversity and peril, were, in fact, hitting and discrediting the credit of the nation, which stands for every citizen, high or low, rich or poor, and whose flag is the emblem of freedom and civilization.

Mr. Speaker, the sting and dishonor of the pending resolution is in its tail, and that sting, well-nigh harmless twenty years ago under conditions then existing, is made deadly by the changed conditions of to-day.

DEADLY TAIL OF THE RESOLUTION.

All that precedes this deadly tail, declaring what the Government has the power to do, if it regards it just and wise, is denied by no one; and hence this attempt to secure its labored assertion, or rather reassertion, is an absurdity which obtains importance only because those who are pressing this assertion of the existence of the power intend that its reassertion shall be construed to mean that the two Houses of Congress believe it just and wise, under existing conditions, to exercise that power, to wit, to authorize the free and unlimited coinage, by this country alone, of silver at the ratio of 16 to 1, and to pay the outstanding bonds of the Government in the dollars so coined.

The deadly tail of this resolution reads as follows:

That to restore to its coinage such silver coins as a legal tender in the payment of said bonds—

Meaning practically all the bonds of the United States now outstanding—

is not in violation of the public faith nor in derogation of the rights of the public creditor.

This, it will be observed, is not an assertion of the power, or even the technical legal right, of the Government, but a proposed declaration by the two Houses of Congress of the standard of honor and good faith which the American people are prepared under existing conditions to proclaim to the world.

4

OBJECT OF ITS MOVERS.

The declarations of the movers and supporters of this resolution in the Senate during its recent consideration in that body as to its purpose and intent will throw a flood of light on this point, if, indeed, anything more is needed than a reference to existing conditions to understand exactly what is meant now by the phrase "to restore to its coinage such silver coins"—a phrase which in 1878 was with good reason interpreted by many who supported a similar resolution to mean something vitally different from what it must mean now.

The Senator who introduced the resolution into the Senate at this session furnished the country with an authoritative interpretation of its meaning. I read from the Record the following colloquy:

FREE COINAGE PURPOSE ADMITTED.

MR. SPOONER. I ask the Senator whether he means to be understood by the resolution as saying that it will be in consonance with public faith for the Government to open the mints for the free and unlimited coinage of silver at a ratio of 16 to 1 and pay in those dollars as a legal tender the principal of the bonds?

MR. TELLER. The Government absolutely has a right under the law, and a moral right that can not be questioned, in my judgment.

MR. SPOONER. Is not that what this resolution is intended to mean?

MR. TELLER. That is what I intended it to mean.

This frank statement makes so clear the meaning and intent of this resolution at the present time that I need not cite similar statements by other supporters of the resolution.

It is well known, as I have already intimated, that in 1878, when the original Matthews resolution was adopted by both Houses of Congress, the phrase "to restore to its coinage such silver coins," etc., was understood by many who then supported the resolution (but now oppose it) to refer to the standard silver dollars which were proposed by the Allison-Bland bill, that became a law within two weeks thereafter, that the Government should coin on its own account in limited volume and maintain at a parity with gold. Such full legal-tender silver dollars, kept by the Government as good as gold by limitation of the coinage and by indirect redemption in payment for duties and taxes, have since been coined to the extent of four hundred and fifty-six millions, up to January 1, all but seventeen millions of which are in circulation either in the form of coins or certificates of deposit.

Even the seventeen millions owned by the Government—and this small amount is all that the Treasury could use in redemption of bonds—are doing the same service in the Treasury as other forms of money, including gold, and thus practically aiding even in the payment of bonds; and all because the policy of the Government, since formulated into law, has been for twenty years to keep all its currency, whether silver or paper, as good as gold.

$30,000,000 OF BONDS PAID IN GREENBACKS OR CURRENCY CHECKS.

Let me repeat. This resolution cannot have any practical reference to the standard silver dollars coined on account of the Government since 1878, because the small number of these coins which are owned by the Government, as well as the large number in circulation either as coins or in the form of certificates of deposit, are kept as good as gold by the Government, and are practically used for all purposes in such a way as will best secure this parity.

So long as silver dollars and greenbacks are kept as good as gold and confidence is maintained that such parity will not be disturbed, it is found by experience that even bondholders accept both without objection. Indeed, within the past six weeks the Government has paid nearly thirty millions of matured bonds either in greenbacks or currency checks. It is only when confidence is weakened by such propositions as that covered by the pending resolution that public creditors demand gold. In other words, such schemes as this defeat the very end which the proposers profess to be seeking.

When gentlemen on the other side point to the standard silver dollars coined in limited volume on account of the Government as "honest dollars," as they certainly are, so long as the Government maintains the value which they have possessed for twenty years, and then ask the country to infer that standard silver dollars minted under free and unlimited coinage by this country alone at the ratio of 16 to 1 of gold, at a time when the commercial ratio is 33 to 1, will be equally good, they must expect that candid investigators of monetary facts will listen with astonishment, however sincere they may regard those who entertain such a belief.

THE 200 CENT DOLLAR THEORY.

Indeed, Mr. Speaker, the frequent declarations of many of the advocates of 16 to 1 unlimited silver that we have had since 1879, and now have a 200-cents dollar, and that an "honest dollar" is one which has only half the purchasing power, are a practical admission on their part that what they expect to obtain by their policy, if they can secure its adoption, is the depreciation of the dollar—a depreciation of one-half on the basis of their own assertions—and then the use of such a depreciated dollar to pay not only Government but also private obligations.

It is sometimes loosely asserted that a depreciation of our dollar one-half is justified by an alleged appreciation of gold since we got back to a specie basis in 1879. As a matter of fact, this assertion is not supported by any fact. The only evidence that has ever been offered for such an assumption is the decline of prices. Even if it be conceded that a fall of prices necessarily shows a rise in the value of the dollar measure—a concession inadmissible in view of the well-recognized fact that as to most articles there is and has been for a long time a continuous reduction in cost of production by the increased use of labor-saving devices and economies—let it be borne in mind that according to the tables of Commissioner Wright, as presented in the report of the Senate Committee on Finance, the decline of average gold prices in the United States from 1879 to 1891 was only 5 per cent., and even from 1870 to 1879 only 5 per cent., while from 1870 to 1891 wages rose 20 per cent. Since 1891 the unexampled increase of gold production makes it improbable that gold can have increased in value. The great fall of prices between 1893 and 1897 has been brought about in large part by precisely the same causes that produced a fall of prices to the extent of 12 per cent. in 1857-58.

THE MORAL VIEW OF IT.

This brings me, Mr. Speaker to the consideration of the vital question as to whether "the Government has the moral right"—in other words, whether it would be an act which the moral sense of the world would regard as in accordance with honor and good faith—for the United States to pay its outstanding bonded indebtedness in dollars of so materially less value than the dollar which has been the practical standard of value since 1834, barring the war and reconstruction period, and which has been the legal and practical standard of value since 1879, and the dollar in which our bonded indebtedness has been paid thus far—paid by every Administration from Lincoln to McKinley—to wit, the dollar equal in value to 25.8 grains of standard gold.

It is urged that the original act authorizing the issue of all existing bonds for the purpose of refunding the debt, which was passed in 1870, provided for the payment of coin of the then existing standard, and that as the law then stood a coin dollar might be a gold dollar of 25.8 grains of standard gold or 412½ grains of standard silver, coined without limit, and therefore that we may now honorably and with good faith establish unlimited coinage of silver at the same ratio of 16 to 1, when silver has fallen more than one-half, and use such depreciated dollars to pay our public debt.

Bear in mind that we are discussing this question from the point of honor and good faith and not from the point of power or technical legal right, for I have already said that the Government can do as it pleases.

THE MEANING OF "STANDARD COIN."

The fact is, and no one questions it, that in 1870 whenever the words "standard coin" were used, they referred, in the understanding of the markets, to gold coin. Almost no silver dollars had been coined for circulation for years, and none were in actual circulation. The silver dollar was in 1870 worth over 2 cents more than the gold dollar. All the loans under that act were paid into the Treasury in gold or its equivalent, and nobody thought of a silver dollar in that connection.

More than three-fourths of the outstanding bonds were as a matter of fact issued and sold after 1873, when the silver dollar was dropped from the list of coins. Now, in view of these facts, after the Government has sold all its bonds for gold, after it has paid all its matured bonds in gold or its equivalent for so many years without any deviation, after the law providing for the free and unlimited coinage of silver at the ration of 16 to 1 has been repealed for twenty-five years, would it be good faith for Congress, now that silver has so greatly depreciated, to restore its free and unlimited coinage at the ratio of 16 to 1 when the market ratio is 33 to 1, and then use such dollars to pay the bonds which we had sold for gold under such circumstances?

NO TIME FOR TRIFLING.

I do not think it would. I have so high an appreciation of the sense of honor of gentlemen on the other side even that I can not bring myself to believe that they in their hearts believe it would. I fear that many of you are resting on the expectation which you have that nothing of this kind will be done and are excusing your vote for it on the unworthy idea that you are "playing politics."

If so, I beg of you to not trifle with the honor and good faith of the nation for any such miserable end, for rest assured such an expression of opinion as to the sense of honor of the people of this country contemplated by this resolution under existing conditions would seriously injure the credit of the country and tend to weaken reviving confidence.

Let me read to gentlemen on the other side the patriotic utterance of a Democratic Senator, Mr. Caffery, only a few days ago, who said in reference to this resolution:

A DEMOCRATIC SENATOR'S VIEW.

"I do not agree that a great government, having in its power the passage of an act which will depreciate its own coin, and passing the act, has a right to say to the public creditor, 'I have depreciated the coin which I have the option to pay in, and I will pay you the depreciated coin; and that discharges my obligation according to the stipulation of the bond.' If that is morality, I do not know what morality is. If to take advantage of an act of the Government, the Government being the debtor, having in its power to debase its own obligations, is not a violation of the public faith, my feeble mind can not conceive of an instance where public faith could be violated by an act of turpitude or dishonor."

Mr. Speaker, there is another phase of this subject which should not be ignored. The pending resolution refers specifically only to the payment of the interest-bearing obligations of the Government. In spirit, however, it includes the five hundred millions of legal-tender demand notes of the Government which are used as currency. If it be honest and in good faith to pay our interest-bearing obligations in silver dollars coined under unlimited coinage at the ratio of 16 to 1, and therefore worth, as standard silver dollars coined in the same way and at nearly the same ratio in Mexico are worth, less than 50 cents each, then it is also honest and in good faith to use the same kind of dollars in redeeming our demand obligations.

And this step would, of course, depreciate every greenback and Treasury note one-half, as well as all of our present silver dollars and silver certificates, and at once deprive us of all our gold for use as money. What the effect of such a depreciation of our dollar and of all of our currency, and such a loss of all our gold, would have on the industries and business of this country and on the wages which are now paid to the masses of our people in money as good as gold can be faintly imagined, but not fully appreciated until such a disaster should overtake us.

EVERY DOLLAR OF CURRENCY AS GOOD AS GOLD.

The one pivotal principle on which we should stand is that every dollar of our currency, whether silver or paper, shall be kept as good as gold. We favor whatever full legal-tender silver can be maintained at an equality of value or purchasing power with gold, even the free and unlimited coinage of silver at a fixed ratio with gold, whenever an international agreement of the leading commercial nations can be secured to that end, which, in our judgment, is the only way in which, under existing conditions, the concurrent circulation of gold and silver under free and unlimited coinage can be secured.

If it be claimed by our 16 to 1 free silver friends that such an international agreement can not be secured, which I do not admit, then I reply that full bimetallism, by which I mean, as is popularly understood, the concurrent circulation of both gold and silver full legal-tender coins under unlimited coinage, is possible under existing conditions in no other way; and I can only add that M. Meline, the French premier, recently stated in the French Chamber of Deputies that this is the view which France holds.

And I further reply that in such a contingency the only way that remains to secure the concurrent circulation of both gold and silver legal-tender coins is by limited coinage, which is precisely the method by which we have to-day four hundred and fifty-six millions of full legal-tender silver, all but seventeen millions of which are in circulation either in the form of coin or certificates of deposit, and precisely the method by which France has about four hundred millions of such silver in use as money—all in both countries kept as good as gold.

16 TO 1 MEANS SILVER MONOMETALLISM.

And I still further reply that the free and unlimited coinage of silver at the ratio of 16 to 1 by this country alone, which our silver friends dub "bimetallism," would simply result in silver monometallism by taking gold out of use as money in this country, just as it has resulted in Mexico and every other country which has tried it under the conditions that have existed since the great reduction in the cost of producing silver and the unexampled increase in the yield of that metal in the last quarter of a century.

It is because I believe, as does every scientific bimetallist in the world outside of politics, that 16 to 1 free and unlimited silver by this country alone would make the United States a silver monometallic country like Mexico and China, and would give us a silver basis that would obstruct our trade with gold-standard countries that now take 90 per cent. of our exports, and prove a serious menace to our progress, and because I believe that it would seriously injure our credit and standing as a nation, that I appeal to gentlemen on this side of the House to maintain the pledge which the Republican party made at St. Louis to keep all our currency, whether silver or paper, as good as gold and preserve inviolable the public faith and credit, and to gentlemen on the other side of the House to maintain the standard of value which Jackson's Administration gave the country sixty-four years ago and the honor and good faith of the nation so carefully preserved by the fathers of the Democratic party, and to take the opportunity offered by the resolution now before the House to show to the country and world that the good name of the nation is safe in our hands. (Loud applause on the Republican side.)

HOW THE TELLER RESOLUTION PASSED THE SENATE.
(From the remarks of Hon. Albert J. Hopkins, of Illinois.)

How does it happen that the Senate has become a free-silver legislative body? Mr. Speaker, it is easy of explanation. Under our constitutional form of government the Senators of the United States are elected, not by the people, as are the members of this House, but by States. Each State is entitled to two representatives in the Senate regardless of the population of the State. It so happens, therefore, that the State of Nevada has two representatives in the United States Senate who voted for this resolution now under consideration. The State of Illinois has only two Senators in that body, and they voted against it.

We thus see that Nevada in the Senate of the United States has the same legislative vote as the State of Illinois. In 1896 the whole number of votes cast in Nevada aggregated only 10,815, while in Illinois the whole number of votes cast was 1,089,888. Ten thousand voters in the little State of Nevada are thus enabled, in the Senate of the United States, under existing constitutional conditions, to have the same power and voting capacity that 1,089,888 voters have in the State of Illinois. Less than 40,000 inhabitants, who form the population of the State of Nevada, in the Senate of the United States, on a great question like the one now under consideration, can offset the power and authority of more than 4,000,000 people who form the present population of the great State of Illinois.

The vote in the Senate which adopted this resolution and sent it to the House for consideration, as announced, was ayes 47, nays 32, thus giving a majority of 15 votes in favor of the resolution. These 15 Senators who constitute the free-silver majority in the Senate of the United States come from the States of Colorado, Wyoming, Idaho, Montana, Washington, South Dakota, Nevada, and Utah. The entire population of these States aggregates only 1,621,311, which is 2,400,000 less than the population of the State of Illinois alone.

It is from these figures easy to determine the fact that the sparsely settled silver States have in the Senate of the United States an influence vastly greater than their population and importance warrant. The Senators who voted against the adoption of this resolution when it was considered in the Senate the other day represent in the aggregate 5,000,000 people more than those who favored the resolution. It is thus made clear that the action of the Senate cannot be taken as a fair expression of the sentiment of the people of this country on the great question embodied in the resolution.

INJURY TO NINETY-NINE TO STRIKE A BLOW AT ONE.
(From the Speech of Hon. Thomas H. Tongue, of Oregon.)

It is by law declared to be the established policy and duty of this Government "to maintain the two metals on a parity with each other" and "to maintain at all times the equal power of every dollar coined or issued by the United States in the markets and in the payment of debts."

The friends of the resolution under consideration in the Senate voted down an amendment substantially declaring the existence of this law. That vote has neither changed nor repealed nor weakened the binding provisions of the statute. But why vote down such an amendment? If deemed necessary or important to declare what the existing law is, why not declare it fully and truthfully? But this vote on the part of the friends of this resolution, and under the lead of the Senator who introduced it, was significant. It can have no other meaning than a declaration of the intention of the friends of this resolution that, if intrusted with executive and legislative power, they will destroy the parity now maintained between the two metals and refuse to "maintain the equal power of every dollar coined or issued by the United States in the markets and in the payment of debts." * * * * *

Why make the bonded indebtedness the occasion for a national financial policy? Why seek to bring disturbance into our business arrangements, to inflict severe injury upon 99 per cent. of the creditors of the United States in order to strike a vicious blow at 1 per cent.? You can not coin a dollar for the payment of bonds that will not be used to pay labor, to pay pensions, to pay insurance policies, to pay bank depositors, and to pay the farmer for every product he has to sell. There should be and can be no misunderstanding of the purpose and intent of the friends of this resolution. It is proposed to abandon the present monetary standard of the United States, the standard we have maintained for more than fifty years, the standard of every intelligent, civilized country, the standard by which all our property has been bought and sold, by which all our business transactions have been measured, and to commit us to the standard of semicivilization and barbarism.

It proposes to abandon bimetallism in practice and in business for silver monometallism. It proposes the most stupendous ex post facto law ever conceived in the brain of the wildest dreamer. It proposes that the standard by which business transactions and business contracts amounting to $40,000,-000,000 were measured at the time of the making shall be changed at the time of the settlement, and that the settlement of these business transactions shall be measured by a standard not contemplated by either party. It proposes such a stupendous revolution that it would stop business, paralyze industry, bind the hands of enterprise, take from labor both its employment and its reward, and precipitate national and industrial bankruptcy.

————— ◄◄►► —————

THE SHOP LABORER EQUALLY INTERESTED WITH THE BOND-HOLDER.
(Hon. D. B. Henderson, of Iowa.)

Severe reference has been made in this debate to the recent utterance of President McKinley when addressing, January 27 last, the great National Association of Manufacturers. What did he say? Listen to him:

The United States will discharge all of its obligations in the currency recognized as the best throughout the civilized world at the time of payment.

There is the language of a patriot and of an honest man. This resolution would cut in two every dollar to be paid by the Government upon its bonded obligations. Cut that in two and you will cut in two every dollar in the country, whether paid to bondholders or to contractors, laborers, pensioners, or Government employees. In brief, gold would be driven out and free coinage of silver, with silver monometallism and a 50-cent dollar, would follow.

Ruin to capital and labor would result, and suffering such as our people have never known would certainly follow. President McKinley, the Republican party, and hundreds of thousands of patriotic Democrats voted against this in 1896, and will again in 1900 with such an issue before them.

While the Republican party is in power such conditions will not be allowed to blight our land.

Mr. Speaker, in this battle I recognize a familiar monogram which I saw upon the Bryan banner in the last national campaign.

Mr. BAILEY. And you will see it there in the next one, too.

Mr. HENDERSON. All right; and we will tear it down as we did last time. (Applause on the Republican side.) That monogram is "R. R. R.."—Radical, rascally repudiation. That is your monogram.

Now, what does this declaration mean? It is nothing but a repetition of the howling recently heard in Demo-Popocratic national conventions. That is all. To pass resolutions, as you did at Chicago, to be trampled under foot by the Sound-Money Republicans and Democrats of this Republic. (Loud applause on the Republican side.) Do not do that, boys; do not interrupt, as my time is limited.

Howl at the bondholders, scold away, gentlemen, but you cannot pare down the money to be paid to the bondholders—and here I want the attention of my friend from Ohio (Mr. Norton)—without cutting in two the pension money paid to the old soldier and his widow. (Applause on the Republican side and jeers on the Democratic side.) You cannot cut in two the money to be paid to one citizen of the Republic without cutting in two the money to be paid to the laborer in the shops of my country.

Mr. SIMPSON, of Kansas. How about the old pensioner?

Mr. HENDERSON. A man is a very mean man who would try to steal a piece of five minutes (laughter), and none but a Popocrat would do it, too. (Renewed laughter.) What does this proposition mean? What is this declaration for? It is to put this country on a single silver standard, on silver monometallism, cutting in two the dollars paid to the hard-handed farmer in my State and in yours, to the toiler in the shop, the pensioner, and every man who wants to give honest work for honest pay.

Confound the party that will advocate such a doctrine! (Laughter on the Democratic side and loud applause on the Republican side.) You talk about the declaration of McKinley. God bless little Mac for what he said. (Loud applause on the Republican side.) "Every creditor shall be paid in the best money." That takes in the bondholder, the hodholder, the plowholder, the penholder, and the holder of pension vouchers. Face this music, as you have started it. You say you want to "meet the Republicans across the aisle." All right. Meet the boys across the aisle now, in November, and in 1900, and we will thrash you even worse than we thrashed you before. . (Loud cheers on the Republican side.)

———————— ◄◄ ◄◄►► ►◄ ————————

CONDITIONS UNDER WHICH THE 16 TO 1 RATIO WAS SAFE.
(From the speech of Hon. Charles H. Grosvenor, of Ohio.)

In the Ohio Legislature of 1876-77 a resolution was brought in which I will show you was in exact consonance with the Republican attitude of that day and not in any degree inconsistent with the attitude of the Republican party of this day. Let me call your attention to two conditions which then existed. First, the relative value of gold and silver, the ratio between the silver in a dollar and the gold in a dollar, was 17.22 to 1, varying by only this small fraction from the legal distinction between the gold and the silver dollar. The divergence had been fluctuating—sometimes a little higher, sometimes a little lower; but the divergence at that time was so small that there was a general impression in the Republican party, west of the mountains at least, that by restoring the coinage of the silver dollar and its restoration to the uses of the Government as money of redémption there might be a coming together of the two metals which would render unnecessary any further agitation of the question.

There was pending in the Congress of the United States a proposition—it may not have been drafted into a bill—which afterwards became known as the Bland-Allison Act. That act provided for the purchase of a certain amount of silver, to wit, two and one-half million ounces, and the coinage of it into silver dollars that should be lawful money for the redemption of the currency of the country. Under the fear, which no man could explain or answer, that the Government might be put to protest upon its legal-tender paper, on the 1st of January, 1879, the Legislatures of a number of Republican States of the country passed resolutions looking to the further-ance of the enactment of the Bland-Allison law.

A resolution of that character made its appearance in the Legislature of Ohio. I was a member of that Legislature. Both branches of the Legislature were strongly Republican. That resolution was introduced in the Senate by a Republican Senator; it was reported favorably by a Republican commit-tee; and it was passed, if my recollection is not at fault, without a dissent-ing voice. There was not more than one Senator, if any, who voted against it. It came to the Ohio House of Representatives. It was referred to a committee; it was reported back from the committee, as I recollect, by a unanimous vote, and passed in the House by a vote of every member of the House, both Democrat and Republican; and by an examination of the record I find that I went out of my usual way and voted for the measure, although I was Speaker of the House, and not ordinarily called upon to vote.

That was the unanimous voice of the Republicans and Democrats of the State of Ohio. In what did it culminate? It culminated in the passage of the Bland-Allison Act. These votes of members of Congress that have been spoken of here so fluently were cast in the approaching hours of the conflict that ended in the enactment of the Bland bill amended by the Allison amendment.

So the Republicans made their record. They were in favor of the two metals; strictly speaking, in favor of bimetallism in the coinage of the country so long as there would be no wider discrepancy than that which existed in 1877 and 1878.

Then came the Bland-Allison Act, and I shall not travel through the years that it was on the statute books of the country. It was repealed by what we called the Sherman Act, for which I voted, and which was in substance a Republican measure. Then came the repeal of the Sherman Act in its purchasing clause at the demand of a Democratic Administration. And now I want you to bear in mind that the attitude of Mr. Cleveland to this silver question was just as well known in 1885 as it ever became known. He had written his famous letter to General Warner before taking his seat as President of the United States, denouncing the whole plan and theory of bimetallism, and yet you Democrats not only supported his Administration through four years, but you renominated him for President in 1888. It was at his demand that Congress came together. It was at his demand that you marshaled the Democratic power on the floors of the two branches of Congress in extra session.

GENERAL GRANT SAID OUR BONDS WERE PAYABLE IN GOLD.
(From the speech of Hon. J. P. Dolliver, of Iowa.)

My friend from Missouri (Mr. Bland) says that nobody is in favor of the settlement of the public debt in gold except the bankers and brokers and the money power. And he inquires where we get the inspiration for such treatment of the bonded indebtedness of the United States. I do not know where he gets his inspiration, but I know where the Republican party get theirs. They get it from the history and record of the times when the debt was contracted, as interpreted in the first inaugural address of Ulysses S. Grant as President of the United States, who was elected upon a platform requiring the Government of the United States to make good its promise to pay its debts in dollars which every human being at that time understood to be the gold-coin dollars of the United States. What did General Grant say?

"To protect the national honor every dollar of Government indebtedness should be paid in gold, unless otherwise expressly stipulated in the contract."

(Applause on the Democratic side.).

Now, I ask these gentlemen, will any man rise and state what bond issue of the United States, made to provide money to carry on the war, contained the express stipulation that it was to be paid otherwise than in gold?

Mr. WILLIAMS, of Mississippi. Every bond which says "coin" says otherwise than gold. It says "either gold or silver."

Mr. DOLLIVER. When I was speaking a moment ago, the Democratic party on this floor, with its irrelevant applause, nearly ruined my speech (laughter) undertaking to interpret the meaning of General Grant when he used the words in his first inaugural—"unless otherwise expressly stipulated in the contract"—which I had the honor to read. It will take me less than a minute to read for the benefit of the House the interpretation of those words put upon them by General Grant himself. I read from a letter of his to Mr. Washburn, from Paris, in 1873, contained in the North American Review for August, 1897:

The whole Democratic party cried itself hoarse over the outrage upon the Constitution when the nation in its desperation adopted the "legal tender note." Now the whole party seems to be willing to issue an unlimited quantity of this money in spite of their previous declaration, in spite of the solemn promise that above a certain amount—four hundred million—should not be issued, in spite of the solemn obligation that those issued should be redeemed in coin, understood at the time to be gold coin.

(Applause on the Republican side.)

Yet it is to-day claimed on this floor that the contract to pay in paper was wickedly changed so as to make paper bonds payable in coin, and the word "coin" wickedly changed to mean "gold."

What are the facts?

The loan act which authorized the 5.20 bonds became a law February 25, 1862. Jay Cooke & Co. were the loan agents of the Government. By the authority of the Secretary of the Treasury these agents advertised a 6 per cent. loan, interest and principal payable in coin. There is not a loan bill on the statute books by which the kind of money in which coupon or principal is payable is mentioned, and yet the hard-money policy of the Government has been uniform.

The question was not raised during the finance debate of 1862. The evidence is overwhelming that these bonds were to be paid in coin. A sinking fund of coin was set apart to be used each year to liquidate the very debt that was being created. At that date nobody supposed the legal-tender currency would be issued beyond the $150,000,000 authorized, whereas the principal of these bonds was $500,000,000. Every member of Congress knew it. They were sold alongside of the coin-bearing bonds under the 10-40 act and met as ready a sale. Can any man believe that the buyers understood that they were getting paper bonds? I have examined the contemporaneous debates and I say to you that at the crisis in which these securities were issued no man, here or abroad, supposed they were to be paid otherwise than in coin.

No member of either House of Congress suggested such a thing. I have heard the old wheel horse of the Administration of Lincoln summoned from his grave to lend the weight of his influence to the schemes of the inflationists. I am prepared to show that Mr. Stevens never gave a syllable of countenance to paper-money payment until long after the contracts had been made. I find in his speech on the loan bill in the House on February 6, 1862, three direct admissions that in his view the bonds were redeemable after twenty years in gold. In the same debate Mr. Hooper, a member of the Committee on Ways and Means, of which Mr. Stevens was chairman, used this language (Globe, second session Thirty-seventh Congress, page 691):

The proposed issue of Government notes guards against this effect of inflating the currency by the provision to convert them into Government bonds, the principal and interest of which, as before stated are payable in specie.

This was after the committee had reported the bill almost unanimously. Mr. Stevens rose immediately afterwards and suggested that the debate close without intimating that Mr. Hooper was wrong. I am convinced, not as a partisan, but as an honest investigator, that the Government and the public understood this contract alike. In the debate of 1863 on the 10-40 loan act, the intimation was for the first time made that the paper of the Government could pay the 5-20 bonds.

At this point in the debate Mr. Thomas. of Massachusetts, moved the express provision for payment in coin, which was carried after this remark from Mr. Horton, an influential member of the Ways and Means Committee, from Ohio.

I wish to state here that the Committee on Ways and Means in framing this bill never dreamed that these twenty-year bonds would be payable in anything other than gold until the gentleman yesterday told it upon the floor of the House. I say to the gentleman and to this House that I never heard an expression that these bonds were to be paid in anything other than coin. The form here proposed is the form always used by the Government, and they have always been paid in coin up to this day.—*Globe, first session Fortieth Congress,* page 800.

To learn the truth of these contracts an intelligent man has only to turn to the reports of Secretary Fessenden and the official messages of the President and the concurrent and unanimous judgment of both Houses of Congress. The agreement interpreted by the history of the times was to pay them in money and not in depreciated promissory notes. And the only coined money known at the mints or in the business of the people was gold. Without that understanding not a bond would have been taken in any market. Bull Run was not a very good advertisement for United States bonds. The existence of the Government, not to speak of its solvency, was at stake when these bonds were put upon the doubtful markets of Europe and America.

www.ingramcontent.com/pod-product-compliance
Lightning Source LLC
Chambersburg PA
CBHW060558030726
47498CB00005B/1450